Louisa Heaton [...] a set of twins) [...] When not wrang[...] animals, she can [...] the beach mutte[...] points. In her spare time, she reads a lot, or crochets. Usually when she ought to be doing something else!

USA Today bestselling, *RITA*®-nominated, and critically-acclaimed author **Caitlin Crews** has written more than 130 books and counting. She has a Masters and Ph.D. in English Literature, thinks everyone should read more category romance, and is always available to discuss her beloved alpha heroes. Just ask. She lives in the Pacific Northwest with her comic book artist husband, is always planning her next trip, and will never, ever, read all the books in her to-be-read pile. Thank goodness.

Maisey Yates is a *New York Times* bestselling author of over one hundred romance novels. Whether she's writing strong, hardworking cowboys, dissolute princes or multigenerational family stories, she loves getting lost in fictional worlds. An avid knitter with a dangerous yarn addiction and an aversion to housework, Maisey lives with her husband and three kids in rural Oregon. Check out her website, maiseyyates.com or find her on Facebook.

Hidden Heirs

Hidden Heirs: A Double Secret

LOUISA HEATON

CAITLIN CREWS

MAISEY YATES

MILLS & BOON

First Published in Great Britain 2023
by Mills & Boon, an imprint of HarperCollins*Publishers* Ltd,
1 London Bridge Street, London, SE1 9GF

www.harpercollins.co.uk

HarperCollins*Publishers*
Macken House, 39/40 Mayor Street Upper,
Dublin 1, D01 C9W8, Ireland

HIDDEN HEIRS: A DOUBLE SECRET © 2023 Harlequin Enterprises ULC.

Pregnant with His Royal Twins © 2017 Louisa Heaton
His Two Royal Secrets © 2019 Caitlin Crews
The Queen's New Year Secret © 2016 Maisey Yates

ISBN: 978-0-263-31853-1

PREGNANT WITH HIS ROYAL TWINS

LOUISA HEATON

This book is for anyone who suffers from anxiety.

Who has to find the courage from deep within just to leave the house.

It's an endless battle, but this book is for you.

xxx

CHAPTER ONE

FREYA SURREPTITIOUSLY SLIPPED the packet from her locker and into her uniform pocket, hiding it under her notepad. The lack of her period and the increasing nausea she was experiencing each morning seemed obvious signs enough, but Freya wanted proof. Scientific proof.

Night shift it might be, but to her this was morning, and walking into the staff room and smelling the strong coffee that had been put on to brew had almost made her share with everyone the ginger biscuits she had forced down for breakfast. It had taken a gargantuan effort to control her stomach, and a sheen of sweat had prickled her brow and top lip as she'd fumbled with her locker. Her fingers had almost tripped over themselves in her haste.

Heading to the ladies' loo, she told Mona she'd just be five minutes and that she'd catch up to her at the staff briefing in a moment.

'Okay, hun, see you in five.' Mona smiled and headed off, her hand clutched around a mug of that nausea-inducing coffee.

The toilets were right next door to the hub, so Freya slipped in and locked the door behind her, leaning back against it, letting out a long, slow breath of relief. She took a moment to stand there and see if her stomach settled.

There didn't seem any doubt about what was happening

to her, but she needed to do this just the same. She pulled the pregnancy test from her pocket and stared hard at it, not quite believing that she was actually going to.

She'd always *hoped* that one day she would become a mother. But the actual chances of that ever happening to her had—she believed—become very slim the day she had been scarred for life. Because who would want her now?

'Come on, Freya…you're better than this,' she whispered to herself, trying to drum up the courage to get herself through the next few minutes.

Freya loved the nightshift, working on Maternity here at Queen's Hospital. There was something extra-special about working nights. The quiet. The solitude. The intimate joy of bringing a new life into the world and being with that family as they watched their first sunrise together. A new day. A new family. Life changing. Getting *better*. New hopes. New dreams. There weren't the distractions of daytime— telephones constantly ringing, visiting families all over the place. It was secluded. Fewer busybodies.

It was the perfect hiding place for her, the hospital at night time, and those nights afforded Freya the anonymity that she craved. Lights were kept low. There were shadows to stay in, no harsh fluorescent lighting to reveal to her patients the true extent of her scarring.

It was better now than it had been. She had some smooth skin now, over her cheeks and forehead, where just two years before she'd had angry red pits and lines, her face constantly set and immovable, like a horrific Halloween mask.

Not now. Not now she'd had her many, *many* reconstructive surgeries. Thirty-three times under the skilled scalpel of her plastic surgeon.

And yet she was still hiding—even more so—in a bathroom. Her hands sweating and fidgety as she kept glancing down at the testing kit.

'Only one thing to do, really,' she told herself aloud,

shaking her head at the absolute silliness of giving herself a pep talk.

She peed on the stick and laid it on the back of the sink as she washed her hands and then took a step back. She stared at her reflection in the mirror, refusing to look down and see the result. She saw the fear in her eyes, but she also recognised something she hadn't seen for years—*hope*.

'This is what you've always wanted,' she whispered.

But wanting something and actually *achieving* it, when you believed it to be impossible, was another thing altogether. If it *were* possible then she'd finally get her childhood dream. To hold her own child in her arms and not just other people's. To have her own baby and be a mum. Even if that meant she'd have to revert back to living in sunlight. With all those other people.

Even if they didn't stare at her, or do that second glance thing, she still felt that they were looking. It was human nature to look at someone different and pretend that you weren't. And your face was the hardest thing to hide.

Still…this wasn't exactly how she'd imagined it happening. As a little girl she'd dreamt of marrying a handsome man, having his babies and being in a settled relationship.

She had no one. Even 'the guy' had been a mad, terrific impulse, when her body had been thrumming with joy about the fact that she was out amongst people, having fun, enjoying a party behind the veil of her fancy dress costume.

It had been so long since she'd last been to a social event. Too long. Years since she'd stood in a room full of people, chatting, laughing at poor jokes, being *normal*.

Mike had taken that away from her. That joy and freedom. His jealous actions had imprisoned her in a world of night and pain, surgeries and hiding. Feeling unable to show her face to the world without fearing people's reactions. A frightened child turning away as if to clutch her mother's skirts when a stranger did a double-take and tried not to look appalled or disgusted or worse.

The veil she'd worn that night had hidden everything. The high-necked Victorian steam punk outfit had hidden the scars on her neck that had not yet been tackled, and the veil had added a note of mystery.

That night people had looked at her with intrigue and with delight. They'd smiled...they'd complimented her on how *wonderful* she looked. Their words had made her giddy with happiness. She'd been normal there. Like them.

And then *he'd* been there. The guy. The pirate. He'd seemed uncomfortable. Had appeared to be waiting for enough time to pass so he could make his escape.

She knew how that felt. She'd felt a kind of companionship with him, despite their not having exchanged a word.

It had helped, of course, that he had seductively dark eyes and a wickedly tempting mouth, and she'd almost stopped herself. She'd taken a moment to register the fact that she was *attracted* to a man when the very idea of that had been anathema to her for so many years.

But not that night. The costume, the veil, had given her a sense of bravery she hadn't felt for a long time.

'I'm Freya. Pleased to meet you.'

'Jamie.'

'I saw you eyeing up the exit. Getting ready to make a break for it?'

'I've been thinking about it.'

'Please don't. Stay for a little while longer. Let me get you a drink.'

It had been crazy how emboldened she'd felt. Her entire body had been thrumming with adrenaline and serotonin, her heart pounding like a revved-up engine. She'd felt alive, happy, normal again—having a conversation with an attractive man, feeling the thrill of first attraction.

Silly. Childish, maybe, when she really ought to have known better, but it had just felt so good!

He had made her feel that way. The way he'd looked at her, his eyes sparkling with inky delight, his full lips curved in a wicked smile. He'd laughed with joy at her anecdotes, had genuinely seemed happy to stay.

She'd felt warm and wanted again. Desire had filled her the second he'd let go of the stem of his glass and let his fingers trail delicately over the back of her hand. She'd focused on that movement, watched his fingertips on her skin—her very sensitive skin. She'd looked up and met his eyes, and the most extraordinary question had left her lips.

'Are you married?'

'No.'

'With someone?'

'No.'

'Do you want to be?'

She'd startled herself with the sheer audacity of her question. That wasn't *her*! Freya MacFadden did not proposition strange men!

She'd pulled her hand away then, retreating into the shell she was so accustomed to being inside. But then he'd reached for her hand again. Not to stop her from running away. Not to try and possess her or control her. But just to get her to make eye contact with him.

'I'm guessing you didn't mean to say that?'

'No.'

'Then we can both forget it. Don't worry.'

'I'm sorry.'

'Don't ever be.'

He'd been so kind. So understanding. So she hadn't bolted and neither had he.

They'd continued to sit with each other and talk about what the other guests were wearing and why the charity they were there to support was so important. They'd laughed and had a good time, enjoying each other's company.

He'd offered to walk her out at the end, and she'd let him, intending to say goodbye at the door. To fetch her coat and leave. For ever to remain an enigmatic stranger at a party that he would remember with fondness. Like Cinderella leaving the ball at midnight, only without the glass slipper.

Freya let out a deep breath. She couldn't stay here in the bathroom for too long. There was a hand-over from the day shift.

Freya loved her daytime colleagues, and they her, but she was happy when they went home. Because then she could begin to craft the intimacy that the night shift brought. Lowering the lights. Softening the voices.

It was time.

She couldn't wait any longer.

It was now or never.

She looked down.

And sucked in a breath.

'I'm pregnant.'

She looked back at her reflection, disbelieving.

'I'm *pregnant*?'

She didn't know whether to laugh hysterically or to cry, to gasp or anything else!

She was pregnant.

There was no question as to *how* it had happened. She remembered that night all too well. The father of her child was quite clear in her mind. How could he *not* be? Even if she didn't actually know *who* he was. Or where he came from.

Their meeting that night had been quite by chance—as sudden and exciting and as passionate as she'd imagined it could be. Scary and exhilarating, and one of the best nights of her life. She'd thrown caution to the wind and felt fully alive again for just a moment. For one desperate moment she had been someone else.

She had gone to the ball knowing she would be able to hide behind her veil and costume all night. It had been very gothic-looking, high-necked, with lots of black and dark purple, layers and petticoats. And there had been a top hat, embellished with a large swathe of plum ribbon, copper cogs and whatnots, and a veil of amethyst silk covering her nose and mouth like a Bedouin bride, leaving only her eyes visible.

Her best feature. The only part of her face not scarred or damaged by the acid. She'd been lucky in that respect. Most acid attack victims were blinded.

Her dashing admirer had tried to remove her veil when he'd leant in to kiss her, but she'd stopped him.

'Don't, please. It's better this way.'

He'd smiled and used his mouth in other ways...

Now everyone at the hand-over would be waiting for her, and they'd all look at her when she went back through. The longer she left it, the worse it would be.

She put the cap on the test stick and slipped it into her pocket, then unlocked the bathroom door. Shoulders back, trying to feel relaxed, she headed off to the briefing.

Okay. I can do this. I'm an expert at pretending everything is fine.

The staff were all gathered around the hub of the unit. Whenever a new patient was admitted, or whenever family came to visit, they would walk down this one corridor that led to the hub. From there they would be directed down different corridors—to the right for postnatal and discharges, straight ahead for medical assessment and long-stay patients, to the left for labour and delivery, and beyond that, Theatre.

From the hub, they could see who was trying to buzz through the main doors to gain access to the ward, with the help of a security camera. They could also see the admissions boards, listing who was in which bed and what stage they were at.

There were usually thank-you cards there, perched on the desk, or stuck to the wall behind them, along with a tin or a box of chocolates kindly donated by a grateful family, and on the walls were some very beautiful black and white photographs of babies, taken by their very skilled photographer Addison.

Senior midwife Jules was leaning up against the hub, and she smiled when she saw Freya coming. 'Here she is! Last but not least.'

Freya sidled in amongst the group, keeping her eyes down and trying desperately to blend in. She could feel all eyes upon her and folded herself down into a chair to make herself smaller. She had kept people waiting when they just wanted to go home.

She gratefully accepted a copy of the admissions sheet that Mona passed over to her.

'It's been a busy day today, and it looks like you girls aren't going to have it easy tonight either. In the labour suite, we've got two labouring mums. In Bed One is Andrea Simpson—she's a gravida one, para zero at term plus two days, currently at three centimetres dilated and comfortable, but she had a spontaneous rupture of membranes at home. She's currently on the trace machine and will need to come off in about ten minutes. In Bed Two we have Lisa Chambers, she's a gravida three, para four. Two lots of twins and currently about to deliver her first singleton baby. She's had two previous elective Caesareans and is trying for a VBAC on this one.'

Freya nodded, scribbling notes. A VBAC was a vaginal birth after Caesarean—a 'trial of scar', as some people put it, to see if the mother could deliver vaginally.

'She's labouring fast. At six-thirty she was at six centimetres and she's currently making do on gas and air.'

Freya sat and listened to the rest of Jules's assessment. They had in total twenty-one patients: two on the labour ward, seven on Antenatal and twelve on Postnatal, five of whom were post-surgery.

And the phones would continue to ring. There would also be unexpected walk-ins, and no doubt A&E would send up one or two.

But she didn't mind. Her job was her life. Her passion. The only thing that brought her real joy. It was all she'd ever wanted to be, growing up. A midwife and a mum. And, as of ten startling minutes ago, it looked as if she was going to achieve being both of those.

Freya was excellent at her job, and she truly believed she was only so good at it because it was something she adored doing. Every new baby born was a minor miracle. Every witnessed birth a joy and a privilege. Every moment she sat and held a mother's hand through a contraction was another courageous moment.

It was a weird place, Maternity. A place where staff and patients met often for the first time, total strangers, and then just hours later Freya would know so much about a person—about their family, their hopes and dreams, their sense of humour, what their favourite foods were, what they craved, what they wanted to be, what they wanted to name their children...

She saw them at their worst, but more often at their best and bravest, and when her patients left Freya knew she would always be remembered as being a part of that family's life. Someone who had shared in their most special and cherished moments. Never to be forgotten.

It was an immense responsibility.

Jules put down her papers. 'Now, ladies, I want you to calm yourselves, but we have in our midst a new midwife!

His name's Jamie and he's hiding at the back. Give us all a wave, Jamie!'

Jamie? No. Relax. It's a common name.

Freya didn't want to turn and look. She knew how that would make the poor guy feel, having all those women turning and staring at him, eyeing him up. But she knew that it would look odd if hers was the only head that didn't turn. It would single her out. So she gave him a quick glance.

Lovely. No...wait a minute...

She whipped her head back round, her mind whirling, and pretended to scribble some more notes about what Jules had just reported on her sheet. But her pen remained still above the paper.

It's him. It's him! Oh, God, oh, God, oh...

Her trembling fingers touched her lips and her nausea returned in a torrent so powerful she thought she might be sick with nerves right there and then—all over Mona's shoes. She wanted to get up and bolt. Run as fast as she could. But it was impossible.

She frantically eyed the spaces between the rows of staff and wondered how quickly she could make a break for it at the end of the briefing.

It couldn't be possible. How *could* it be him? Her one-night stand.

'Jamie is with us for a couple of months, filling in for Sandra who's away on maternity leave, so I'd like to say welcome to the team, Jamie, it's good to have you here. For the rest of you—Jamie has been working all over the country in various midwifery posts, so he's got a lot of experience, and I hope you'll all take the time to welcome him here, to Queen's.'

Jules smiled.

'Right, then. We're all off. Have a good shift, ladies. And Jamie!'

She smiled, waved, and the majority of staff disappeared off to the locker room, to grab their things and go.

Freya, frozen to the spot, wished she could do the same. *Okay, so the simplest thing to do is to stay out of his way.* So far she'd done a sterling job of that.

Mona was showing him around, pointing out where everything was, getting him acquainted with the temperamental computer and how to admit people to the ward—that kind of thing. Freya, on the other hand, had just been given the task to introduce herself to the two labouring mothers and work on the labour ward—which she was very happy about because that gave her the opportunity to stay in her patients' rooms and not see or have to engage with *him*.

The irony of the situation was not lost on her. The first time they had met she had been brimming with temporary confidence, an urge to experience life again as a normal woman meeting a handsome guy at a party. But now she was back to reality. Hiding and skulking around corners, trying her best to avoid him. The man she'd propositioned.

And what the hell were the odds of him turning up on the very same day that she took a pregnancy test? It had to be millions to one, didn't it? Or at the very least a few hundred thousand to one?

Jules had said he'd been working in various posts around the country. Why hadn't he got a job at one of those? Why did he keep moving?

What's wrong with him?

The weight of the pregnancy test in her left pocket seemed to increase, its weight like a millstone.

She entered Andrea Simpson's room quietly.

'Hello, it's Andrea, isn't it? I'm Freya and I'm going to be your midwife tonight.'

She smiled at her new charge and then glanced over at her partner, who was putting his phone in his back pocket and standing up to say hello.

He reached over to shake her hand and she saw him do that thing with his eyes that everyone did when they noticed her face—noticed that she'd been burned, somehow, despite her corrective surgery and skin grafts. Noticed that she'd had *work done*.

His gaze flittered across her features and then there was *that* pause.

'Hi, I'm George,' he introduced himself. 'I'm just here to do what I'm told.'

Freya smiled. 'Mum's the boss in this room.'

She glanced over at the belt placement on Andrea's abdomen and checked the trace on the machine. The trace looked good. No decelerations and the occasional contraction, currently seven or eight minutes apart. Still a way to go for Andrea.

'I want you to stay on this for ten more minutes, then I'll take it off—is that all right?'

Andrea nodded, reaching for a bottle of water and taking a short drink.

'Do you have a birth plan?'

'Just to have as much pain relief as I can get.'

'Okay. And what sort of pain relief are you thinking of?'

'I want to start with gas and air, see how I go with that, and then maybe get pethidine. But I'm open to whatever you suggest at the time.'

Freya smiled. 'So am I. This is *your* birth, *your* body. I'll be guided by you as long as it's safe. Okay?'

'Yes…'

Freya could see that Andrea had questions. 'Nervous?'

Andrea giggled. 'A bit. This is all so *new*!'

Tell me about it.

Freya had seen hundreds of babies come into the world. She never tired of it. Each birth was different and special, and now she knew that if all went well and she didn't miscarry she'd be doing this herself in a few months. Lying on a bed…labouring. It was actually going to happen.

'You'll do fine.'

She laid a reassuring hand on her patient's and wondered who'd be there to hold *her* hand during labour? Her mum?

Her mind treacherously placed Jamie beside her bed and she felt goosebumps shiver down her skin.

No. It can't be him.

It can't be.

But isn't that what you always wanted? A cosy, happy family unit?

It had been. Once.

It was *her*. He'd have known those blue eyes anywhere. The eyes that had been haunting his dreams for weeks now.

He'd been invited to that charity ball after he'd attended a small event in Brighton that was meant to have been low-key. But word must have reached the ears of the hospital that the heir to the throne of Majidar, Prince Jameel Al Bakhari, was around and an invitation had got through to his people.

It had been for such a good cause he hadn't been able to refuse it. A children's burns unit. He'd seen the damage burns could cause, from a simple firework accident right through to injuries sustained in a war zone, and it was shocking for anyone. A painful, arduous road to recovery. But for it to happen to a child was doubly devastating.

So he'd attended, dressed as a pirate, complete with a large hoop earring and a curved plastic scimitar that had hung from his waist by a sash.

He'd not intended to stay for very long. He'd made them keep his presence there quiet, as he didn't enjoy people bowing and scraping around him. He hated that whole sycophantic thing that happened around members of his royal family. It was part of why he'd left Majidar. To be a normal person.

It was why he tried to live his life following his passion. And his passion was to deliver babies. Something that was not considered 'suitable' for a prince back in his own country.

But what could you do when it was your calling? Delivering babies was what he had always yearned to do, and he'd never been destined for the throne. His elder brother had been the heir and was now ruler. So surely, he'd reasoned, it was better to spend his life doing something worthwhile and selfless instead of parading around crowds of people, smiling and waving, a spare heir that no one needed?

He'd faced some considerable opposition. Mostly from his father, who'd been appalled that his second son wanted to do what he viewed as 'women's work'. His father had forbidden him ever to speak of it again and, respecting his father, he had kept that promise. Until his father had passed away. Then his brother Ilias had taken the throne, and Jamie had approached his new King and told him of his vocation.

Ilias had proudly granted his younger brother the freedom to pursue it.

So he'd gone to the ball, telling the organisers that he didn't want to draw attention to himself, and asking that they did not make any special announcement that he was there, just let him join in as any other person would.

Jamie had mingled, smiled, shaken people's hands—and found himself losing the will to live and wondering when would be a polite time to leave... And then he'd spotted *her* in a corner of the room.

Almost as tall as he, she'd been dressed from top to toe in black, accented in dark purple, with some weird cogs and a strange pair of pilot goggles attached to her hat. Her face had been covered by a Bedouin-style gauze veil that had reminded him of home.

Her honey-blonde hair had tumbled down her back, almost to her waist, and above that veil had sparkled the most gorgeous blue eyes he had ever seen. Blue like the ocean and the sky, and just as wild and free.

'I'm Freya. Pleased to meet you.'

'Jamie.'

'I saw you eyeing up the exit. Getting ready to make a break for it?'

He had been. But not any more.

So he'd stayed. And they'd talked. And laughed.

Freya had been delightful, charming and intelligent, and so easy to be with. She'd told him a story about the last time she'd attempted to flee a party. She'd been eleven years old and it had been the first time her parents hadn't stayed with her. She'd been frightened by all the noise and all the people and had scurried away when no one was looking and run home to hide in her dad's garden shed.

She'd grimaced as she'd recalled how she'd stayed there, terrified out of her wits not only about being found out, but also because there had been a massive spider in the corner, watching her. He'd laughed when she'd told him she'd almost peed her pants because her bladder had been killing her from drinking too much pop. But she hadn't been able to go home too early, or her parents would have known that she'd run away.

'No spiders here,' he'd said.

'No.'

'Nothing to be afraid of. I'll protect you.'

'Now, why would you do that? You hardly know me. I might be dangerous.'

'I think I can handle you.'

His pulse had thrummed against his skin, his temperature rising, his whole body aware. Of *her*. She hadn't re-

moved the veil, but she'd kept on peering at him over it with
devilment in her gaze, and he'd felt drawn to her excitement
and bravado. She hadn't been drunk on alcohol. Her eyes
had been clear, pupils not pinpointed, so no drugs. But she'd
definitely been intoxicated by *something*, and he'd begun
to suspect that he was feeling the same way, too.

There'd been something about her. So different from everyone else at the party. But what had it been? What had
made her unique? Had it been the veil? The air of mystery?
Or just those eyes? Eyes that had looked so young, but had
also spoken of a wisdom beyond her years. As if she knew
something that no one else did. As if she'd experienced life
and the gamut of emotions that came with it. And yet that
night she'd been drawn to him, and he to her. She a purple
and black veiled moth and he the flame.

'Do you trust me?'

She'd smiled. *'Can any woman trust a pirate?'*

'I'm not just a pirate.'

The corners of her mouth had twitched and she'd glanced
at his mouth, then back to his eyes, and he'd been hit with
such a blow of lust he hadn't been able to help himself. He'd
tried to look away, to take a deep breath, to regain control
over his senses.

'I need to go,' she'd said.

'Let me walk you home.'

'No need. I have transport.'

'Then let me walk you to it.'

He'd offered her his arm and she'd taken it, smiling
through the gauze and looking up at him, her eyes gleaming.

He'd been overcome by a bolt of desire.

But what to do about it? He considered himself a gentleman. He had principles…he'd only just met her…but there
was *something*…

They'd stood there staring at each other, each of them

trying to force the words to say goodbye, but neither of them ready to leave just yet. Her eyes had glinted at him in the darkness, with a look that said she wanted more than this...

The first door they'd tried had been unlocked, and they'd found themselves inside a supply closet, filled with clean linen and pressed staff uniforms.

He'd stood in front of her, just looking at her, noticing the small flecks of green and gold in her eyes. They'd shone like jewels, and her pupils had been large and black as she'd reached for his shirt and pulled him close.

He'd lost himself in her. Completely forgotten who he was, where he was. All that had mattered had been the feel of her, the taste of her, as he'd hitched up her skirts, her million and one petticoats, slid his hands up those long, slim legs...

Freya...

Like two lost souls that had found each other, they had clutched and grasped, gasped and groaned. He'd reached to remove the veil, so that he could kiss her, so that he could seek out her lips and claim her for his very own, but she'd stopped him, stilled his hand.

'Leave it. Please.'

'But, Freya...'

'No kissing...please.'

He'd respected her wishes. That veil had made her seem like forbidden fruit. An enigma. Her hat had fallen to the floor and her long blonde locks had tumbled around her shoulders like golden waves. And the dark stockings on her ever so creamy thighs had aroused a feeling in him that he'd never quite experienced before.

They'd given each other everything.

And when they were spent they had slumped against each other and just stood there, wrapped in each other. Just breathing. Just existing. It was all that they'd needed.

A sound by the door had made them break apart and rearrange their clothing.

She'd glanced at him, guiltily. *'I must go.'*

He'd stared at her, not knowing what to say. He'd felt as if there was so much he *wanted* to say to her, but it had all got stuck in his throat and he'd remained silent. He'd wanted to tell her to stay. To come back to the hotel with him. He'd wanted to ask her if he could see her again and that had both shocked and scared him—because he *never* made commitments.

But she'd slipped from the closet, and by the time he'd adjusted his clothes and made himself presentable again she'd been gone.

He'd scanned the ballroom, looking for her fall of blonde hair, looking for those all-seeing eyes, but she'd gone.

Jamie had signalled his security people and told them to look out for her, to check the car park, but like an enigmatic spy she had simply disappeared. Disappointed, he had got into his own car and been driven home.

But now she was here.

She'd turned to look at him after Jules had asked everyone to welcome him. She was *here*. Of all the places in the world he could have looked. In this hospital. On this ward. With him. Those eyes of hers had pierced his soul once again, reawakening his dormant desire and making every cell of his body cry out for her.

But there'd been something else. Something that had rocked him. Something he hadn't noticed before. And now he understood about the veil.

Freya was scarred. Something had happened to her. To her face. She'd had work done. Skin grafts, no doubt. Painful surgeries and recovery. How many? What had happened to her? A house fire? Was that why she'd been at the charity event for the burns unit?

And he'd sensed her fear. Her shock. Had seen the horror in her eyes as she'd realised who he was. Then he'd seen her shame, because she'd noticed how he'd reacted when he saw her properly.

Angry with himself, he'd wanted to reach out, touch her, tell her that she should not be ashamed—but she'd bolted.

Jamie sensed a soul like his own. Someone who preferred the everyday to the limelight. Someone who avoided crowds and adulation. Someone who preferred to hide behind a mask.

He felt her magnetism. Her draw.

And helplessly he allowed himself to be pulled in.

'It is you, isn't it?'

Freya had quickly run to the kitchenette to make her patient's husband a cup of tea. She'd slid into the small room, breathing a sigh of relief, wondering just how the hell she was going to get through work for the next few weeks if *he* was going to be here, covering for Sandra.

She'd just been kneeling down to put the milk back in the fridge when she'd heard the door open behind her and then his voice.

Freya closed her eyes and looked down, hoping the loose tendrils of her hair would cover her face. She didn't want this. Didn't *need* this. Tonight had already been overwhelming—finding out she was pregnant—but to have him here too? To have to have *this* conversation? Now? At work?

'I'm sorry, I need to take this drink to my patient.'

She held the mug of tea in her hand, not turning to face him, but so very aware of his presence behind her in this small, suddenly claustrophobic room.

This man had made her body sing. Nerve-endings that she'd thought were dead had come alive that night and she had felt every single part of her body as he'd played her like a delicate harp. Knowing what to touch and how to touch, how to make her gasp, sigh and groan. She'd experienced things with this man that she had never felt before. He'd made her reveal a side to herself that she'd never known.

But he'd been with a woman who didn't exist in reality, and she didn't need to see his disappointment when he realised.

Just being this close to him now was doing crazy things to her insides and turning her legs to jelly. And was it hot? Her armpits were tingling with sweat.

They'd had an amazing night. And it would stay that way as long as he didn't ruin the illusion by seeing her for who she really was. He'd probably thought that she was some rare beauty, but if he saw her properly he would soon be surprised. No doubt about that.

She didn't want to have to watch it happen right in front of her. That *look*. She'd already noticed his shock when they were at the hub, and work was meant to be her happy place. He was ruining everything.

Holding the mug of tea before her, she kept her head down to pass him so she could get to the door.

He stepped back, keeping a respectful distance, which she appreciated, but as she reached for the handle he spoke again.

'It *is* you.'

Keeping her eyes downcast, she stared at the floor, not wanting to see him take in her scars, her wounds. To see that she was damaged goods. This man had *wanted* her! Wanted her so badly! And it had been wondrous—a memory she'd cherished since that night. A moment of freedom from the poor existence with which Mike had left her. And she had revelled in that.

Did she want to see him realise that the woman he had given himself to was not the one of his dreams? No. Just for once she wanted to be a good memory for someone. For them to believe her beautiful.

'I'm sorry, I have to go.'

'Look at me.'

'Jamie, please…' She glanced upwards for just a moment and painfully met his gaze, her eyes blurry with unshed tears, waiting to see him realise his mistake…

Only it didn't happen. He simply looked directly at her. Showed no shock this time. No horror.

'If only you knew how much I've wanted to see you again.'

Confused, she stared back. Felt the tears finally escape her eyes and trickle down her cheeks.

'What…?'

What was he saying? What did he mean? Why wasn't he reacting to her face like everyone else did?

'You're unforgettable—do you know that?'

She swallowed hard, looking away, down at the steaming mug. 'For all the wrong reasons.'

She got out of the kitchenette as quickly as she could. What *was* it with them and small rooms? Kitchenettes. Supply cupboards. Was Jamie set to startle her in anything less than six by six? Should she stay away from bathroom cubicles, too?

As she hurried back to her patient's room she madly wiped her eyes and sniffed a few times, to try and look presentable for Andrea and her husband.

What had just happened? How had he managed to turn her understanding of the world completely on its head?

She slipped her hand into her pocket, to reassure herself that the pregnancy test was still there. Only it wasn't. Her pocket was empty except for her notebook and pen.

She looked back to the kitchenette and saw Jamie come out, his face a mass of confused emotions as his eyes met hers.

Over the small white stick in his hand.

CHAPTER TWO

IT MUST HAVE fallen from her pocket. But when? And how?

And then she remembered crouching down to get the milk from the fridge. Something similar had happened before, due to the design of the pocket on her uniform. It was below the waist, low down. She'd lost her mobile phone once that way, hearing it clatter onto the floor. She'd not heard the test stick fall. Probably because she'd heard his voice instead. Felt his presence.

'It is you. Isn't it?'

His words had cut through everything.

Her mind had been on other things. Other concerns. She'd closed that fridge fast. Stood up quickly and made that tea, trying not to look at him, trying to get away as quickly as she could.

She was saved from going over to him and taking the test from his hands. The call light above Bed Two flashed and she went in to see how Lisa Chambers, her labouring mother there, was doing.

Lisa was pacing the room, her abdomen swollen before her, her hands pressed into her back.

'I felt the need to push with that last one, Freya.'

She handed the mug of tea over to Lisa's husband and then guided Lisa back to the bed. 'I'll need to check you before you can push.'

She didn't need Lisa pushing too early. It might cause a swelling of the cervix and make delivery more difficult.

Regaining control of her own body, she checked her patient's. 'You're right, Lisa. You're ten centimetres. You can push with the next contraction.'

Lisa got up off the bed. 'I can't lie down, though.'

'That's fine. Let your body lead you and I'll help. Just tell me when you're ready.'

Lisa beckoned to her husband to stand on the other side of the bed and take her hands. Then she squatted on the other side.

'When the contraction comes, take a big, deep breath, Lisa—chin to your chest and *push*, right into your bottom.'

Lisa nodded, waiting, then closed her eyes and sucked in that breath.

Freya quickly washed her hands, dried them and gloved up. Lisa might be five times a mother, but this was her first vaginal delivery. It might take some time and, with the best will in the world and not wanting to prolong her patient's suffering, she hoped that it would.

Because she herself needed some time before she could leave this room. Needed to think of what she would say. What she would do. How she could escape this situation she'd found herself in.

Lisa was an excellent patient, though, and obviously keen to see her fifth child. Because within forty-five minutes of her first needing to push, her son slithered into Freya's waiting hands.

She passed the baby to his sobbing mother, clamped and cut the cord, then helped Lisa into bed and wrapped a towel around her son to help keep him warm.

The baby cried—bursts of pure sound, a completely new person announcing his arrival. Freya smiled at the newly created family of seven and quietly gave Lisa the injection of syntocinon that would hasten delivery of the placenta, as per her patient's request.

It seemed to take no time at all to deliver it, check it, assess the baby's APGAR score, then Lisa's, and realise that Lisa hadn't torn at all. Her five-pound, twelve-ounce son had arrived perfectly.

There was no reason for Freya to stay at all. She prided herself on leaving her families to have some private time as soon as she could after the birth. So they could welcome and get to know their new baby on their own. But tonight she hesitated by the door.

'Congratulations, you two.'

'Thanks, Freya. I couldn't have done it without you.'

'Nonsense. You were a model patient.' She smiled, trying to pluck up the courage to go out there and face him. *That* conversation.

She could only hope and pray that he was busy with a patient of his own.

But she had no such luck.

Jamie was just walking back to the hub desk, sliding his pen into his top pocket. His dark eyes instantly met hers. Challenged her. Demanded an explanation.

She almost faltered. But she had Lisa's notes to finish writing up, and when that was done she needed to check on Andrea. She'd taken her off the trace a while ago and she'd been steadily contracting every five minutes the last time she'd seen her.

Jamie stood still as she walked past him, and she hoped he wouldn't see that her nerves were making her hands tremble and shake as she sat down at the desk.

'It's not what you think.' She glanced up at him, then away again. *Dammit.* He was just as handsome as she remembered. Even more so, this close. He was hauntingly beautiful.

Jamie sat down in the chair next to her. 'What *do* I think?'

She paused, her pen over Lisa's notes. 'It belongs to a patient.'

'A patient?'

'Yes. I must have put it in my pocket without realising and—'

'We don't do pregnancy testing here. Mona was quite clear when she showed me around that the fertility clinic is in a whole other ward next to this one.'

She tried her hardest not to look at him. Not to meet the searing gaze that she knew would instantly divine the truth. If her cheeks could have flamed red, then they would.

She looked at him, guilt filling her eyes.

He gazed at her for a moment, his face deadly serious. 'Tell me the truth. It's yours?'

Her eyes closed, almost as if the admission would cause her pain. 'Yes…' A whisper.

'Am I…?'

The words choked in his throat and she opened her eyes again in anguish. She hardly knew this man. He was a temp. A locum. A drifter. How could she tell this stranger that the baby in her womb was most definitely his? Because she didn't sleep around. She never met anyone—never gave herself the chance to.

She didn't need to get that kind of close to any man, to develop feelings for any man, because look at what had happened to her when she did. She'd suffered more than she'd ever believed it was possible for one body to suffer after getting involved with Mike. The pain she'd gone through, both emotionally and physically, had almost destroyed her.

She never wanted that again. Never wanted to risk it. Having that one night with Jamie—a stranger—had been a moment in which she'd thrown caution to the wind, feeling herself so physically attracted to the pirate she'd met at the

ball that she'd decided she would risk it. Keeping her anonymity, she would never have to deal with him afterwards.

Because why *shouldn't* she have slept with him? It was
allowed, and it had felt *so good* to let all that other stuff go.

But they'd both been stupid. Believing that one night
wouldn't have consequences. Believing that they could
walk away.

They should have known the risks.

They'd been wrong! And no one could be angrier with
her than she was with herself.

She'd once sat on a hospital bed, with a plastic compres-
sion mask over her burnt features, and promised her mother
that she would never get involved with another man ever
again. Would never cause her family anguish ever again.
Because what Mike had done—throwing that acid at her
face—hadn't just affected her. The tragedy had affected
her family and even Mike's family, who were distraught
that their son was in prison.

And all because she'd got involved with him.

And now she was pregnant. With Jamie's baby.

'Yes. You're the father.'

She saw him look down at the ground. Could almost
hear the cogs going around in his skull, almost sense his
thoughts as he tried to distance himself from her. Maybe
even planned to leave this place. Get a temporary post
somewhere else less complicated.

'Right.' A pause. 'It's very early on. Four…maybe five
weeks?'

She nodded.

'You need to start taking folic acid.'

'I know.'

'You need to look after yourself.'

She knew he was just trying to say the sensible thing,
trying to help and maybe trying to make sense of it in his
own head. This had to be a huge shock to him too. But to

Freya it sounded as if he was telling her what to do, and no man would ever tell her what to do again.

Her control was slipping. 'You don't need to tell me how to do anything. You don't own me.'

'I'm not. I'm just trying—'

'You're just trying to take over! So back off, Jamie, I don't need this in my life!'

She tried her hardest not to shout, but it was difficult. All she wanted to do was run away, but it was as if the walls were closing in and she would soon be trapped with him. A man. A stranger. Tied to him for eternity when she knew nothing about him. He could be anybody.

He sat forward in his chair. 'You're pregnant with *my child*. I don't think you realise what this means.'

She leaned forward too, anger and rage fuelling her bravado, matching his stance. 'I'm a midwife. Of course I know what it means.'

She stood, grabbing her notes and pen, deciding she would check on Andrea. She would finish her notes in there—give Jamie a chance to think about what she'd said.

He was *not* going to tell what to do.

He was going to be a father.

Of course if nothing went wrong they would have to marry. If the people of Majidar ever found out that he'd got a woman pregnant and then abandoned her to have the child alone they'd be appalled. And so would he. He wasn't just a prince, he was a man, and as such he had a responsibility to do the right thing. No child of his would grow up to be illegitimate—he just wouldn't accept it. The baby was his and he would be its father.

Honour in this country was different from honour in his. He saw it on the television every day—men getting women pregnant and then leaving them to raise the child alone. There were single parents everywhere, and that was fine for them—but not for him. Not at all. He could never knowingly sire a child and then abandon it to God only knew what kind of future.

This was *his* child. And, whether Freya liked it or not, he had a duty to it.

And to her.

But what had happened to her? What was making her so frightened and on edge? Why couldn't she look him directly in the eye? Was it her scars? Her face? Did her shame stem from that? Or was it the unexpected pregnancy?

Clearly she was in shock. All he'd tried to do was make this easier for her. Try and shoulder some of the responsibility.

Because it was his and his alone. And because of who he was it was imperative that he do the right thing.

He would need to speak to his advisor.

At just after six in the morning Andrea delivered a healthy baby girl.

Freya was reluctant to leave her patient's room and go back out there and face Jamie again, but she knew that she had to.

She could only hope that as there was less than one hour until the end of her shift he might be busy elsewhere and she would be able to get through it without having to see him.

She'd had her fill of pushy men. To be fair, she'd only been with one, but that one—Mike—had been enough for two lifetimes.

It had started innocently enough. Mike had asked her not to go out with her friends from college one evening.

'Why not?'

'I just can't bear to imagine you out on the town like that. I've seen gaggles of girls dressed to impress and off their heads on tequila shots. I know what guys think of girls

like that, and I don't want them looking at you like you're a piece of meat.'

She'd thought he was being sweet! That he cared so much about her.

He'd begged her not to go, and to make him feel better she'd cancelled. The next week, when the girls had wanted to go out again, rather than just accept the invitation straight away she'd said she needed to check with Mike first.

Slowly she had stopped having any contact with her friends. Then he'd started making comments about how her family looked down their noses at him and how family meet-ups made him uncomfortable—could they stay home?

Bit by bit he had isolated her, until her entire life had been his to control and manipulate. She'd felt as if she couldn't breathe and she'd tried to break away. He'd found her, begged her to stay, promised he would change.

Only he hadn't. If anything he had got worse—his insecurities, his paranoia.

She'd bolted one day when he was at work and run home to live with her mum again. She'd thought she was free, that her life was hers again, until that terrible day on the high street…

Freya was grateful to see that the hub looked clear and she headed over, her back aching slightly, and slumped into a chair to complete Andrea's notes. The open tin of chocolates called her name and she unwrapped one and popped a caramel barrel into her mouth.

Mmm…just what I need.

The chocolate began to soften in her mouth, and as she chewed she realised just how hungry she was. She'd not really taken a proper break whilst Andrea laboured, and suddenly she was starving—craving a full English breakfast, washed down with a mug of strong tea.

A banana was placed right in front of her. She frowned and looked up to see who had given it to her.

'Jamie…'

'Eat this. You haven't had anything all night.'

She moved the banana away from her. 'Thank you, but I have other plans.'

'So you say—but you're not the only one who gets to make decisions about yourself any more. This is my baby too and you need to eat. *Healthily*, preferably.'

He grabbed hold of the tin of sweets and moved it away from her.

Angrily, Freya grabbed the tin back. 'Keep your voice down. I don't need the whole ward hearing about it.'

'Are you going to eat the banana?'

She glanced at the fruit, lying harmlessly on the desk, and felt repulsed by it. The idea of taking a bite of it turned her stomach. She craved hot food. Preferably dripping in grease.

'Not right now.' She felt a little hypocritical. She'd often lectured pregnant women about eating well for a healthy pregnancy and here she was craving fat. And maybe another chocolate from that tin.

'So when are you going to eat?'

'When I get out of here. At home, where I can cook myself something.'

She didn't want to tell him that she didn't like to go out during the day. Didn't like to sit by herself in cafés filled with staring people.

'Where do you live?'

She looked at him incredulously. 'Why would I tell you that?'

'Because, like it or not, we're involved now and I want to look after you.'

'I don't know you!'

'You knew me enough to make a child with me.'

He stared hard at her, his eyes dark and dangerous, as if daring her to try and wriggle out of that one.

'Well, I didn't know I was doing that at the time.'

It was enough to make her remember their assignation—her back against the wall as he hoisted her legs around his waist and thrust into her, her hands frantically grasping at him. Both of them made courageous by darkness and anonymity.

No. She would not tell him her address. He might be anyone and her home was her safe space. Her haven. A place where she could relax and just *be*. It was her bolt-hole, and there was no way she was going to give him that information.

'You're not going to do this, you know.'

'Do what?'

'Go all alpha on me. Order me about.' She could hear her own voice quaking as she stood up for herself.

'I care about you.'

'No, you don't. You got me pregnant and now you think that you've got to be seen to be doing the right thing. Well, I'm giving you an out. You're off the hook—you can walk away.'

It would be easier, wouldn't it? To do it alone? Without a man? Because men were frightening. They didn't know what it felt like to be a woman. To know that half the population was bigger and physically stronger than you. That they could overpower you if they cared to try. Not to be able to walk down a street without fearing the footsteps you could hear behind you. Always having to be aware of your surroundings. Of who might be looking at you strangely. Were they just curious, or were they about to pounce?

He leaned forward and stared at her. 'I don't know what experiences previous men have given you, but let me tell you something. *I am not that kind of man.* When I do something I take full responsibility for it. And that means taking care of you and taking care of that baby.'

'But you don't have to. I can do it alone.'

'I do have to. It's my child. It has to be honourable.'

'Why does it have to be *honourable*?'

Even as she said the words she realised how childish she sounded. Why wouldn't she want her baby to be honourable? Was she cheapening it already? By saying it didn't matter if it was 'honourable'?

But this was *her* baby! She had dreamt of this for years!

He recoiled as if she'd slapped him, as if he was appalled that she could think anything else.

'Because it has to be. I won't have it any other way.'

She moved the banana. She could smell it and it was beginning to turn her stomach.

'If everything you do is "honourable", then how come you had a quickie with a stranger in a closet? Surely being *honourable* would make you at least a hotel-room-with-satin-sheets kind of man?'

'Maybe I am?' he challenged, pushing the banana back towards her. 'There is plenty that you don't know about me, Freya MacFadden.'

The use of her name made her narrow her eyes as she looked at him. God, he was beautiful. Almond-shaped eyes, dark as ink, cheekbones a model would die for, and his lips...

Oh, goodness, I remember those...

Freya cleared her throat and tried to sound as if she was in control of this conversation. 'Well, perhaps you'd care to enlighten me?'

Jamie checked around them, as if keen to make sure they were alone and no one was listening in.

'I can't tell you right now. You wouldn't believe me. Perhaps if you agreed to meet me here?'

He pulled a card from his uniform pocket and slid it across to her. It was a glossy black card with the name of a hotel in silver.

Why did he want to meet her in a hotel? What kind of

movie did Jamie think he was living in? He was deluded.
This was normal life. People didn't do that. There was no
way she was going to meet a total stranger in a *hotel*!

'Can't you just tell me?'

'You wouldn't believe it. Please meet me there.'

It would be a public place. Safe. But it would be in daylight. When there were other people about. Not in his room.
Nowhere they could be alone. But she would have to face
other people's stares.

'When?'

'Tomorrow? Before your shift? We do need to talk about
this and we can't do it here.'

She could maybe put on some sunglasses and wrap a
thick scarf around her neck, then no one would stare at her.
She could get there before everyone else was up and mill-
ing around for breakfast. She could listen to what he had
to say, give him his five minutes, then slink out quietly.

'Fine. About six? That gives us an hour before work.'

'Thank you.'

She nodded, then picked up the banana, gave it back to
him and said, 'Now, take that away, please, before I throw
up all over this desk.'

His mouth curled slightly at the corners. 'Tomorrow I'll
bring you grapes.'

The Franklin Hotel sat atop a hill, so that as Freya drove
towards it she had a sense of awe and magnificence as she
approached the beautiful Georgian manor. Looking at it
from a distance, she wondered how Jamie could afford to
stay in such an opulent place.

*I don't have to go in. I don't have to hear what he has
to say.*

But she knew she would. Because, no matter how terrified she felt, she knew that she owed her baby the chance
to know something about its father. So she could look her

child in the eye and tell him, or her, that she'd tried everything.

It looked welcoming and warm, with yellow lights gleaming out in the darkness of the early morning, the sky above a blue which was fading from inky navy to palest azure.

Parking her little hatchback next to rows of expensive cars with chauffeurs sitting in them made her feel a little uneasy. Why had Jamie asked her to meet him here? What was it that she was about to learn from him?

He was a midwife. A damned sexy one, if she was honest, with an accent to die for and eyes that looked right into her soul and grasped her by the heart. She'd never met anyone like him. The mystery was what could he tell her here that she would never have believed if he'd just told her at work?

Whether she liked it or not, whilst this baby nestled in her womb they would be tied to one another—and Jamie seemed determined to be in her life.

Adjusting her scarf and lowering her sunglasses, she strolled across the gravel driveway, her nerves jittery, her legs weak. In the hotel, gentle music playing from a piano met her ears. To her right was a reception desk, where exquisite and perfectly presented staff waited to attend to every guest's needs.

'May I help you, madam?' asked a young man in a navy suit with enough gel in his hair to sink a ship.

No, it's fine. I'm just leaving.

'I'm supposed to be meeting a Mr Jamie Baker?'

'Miss MacFadden? We've been expecting you.' He smiled, revealing perfectly white teeth. 'Please take the lift to my right and go up to the third floor.'

Take the lift? Go to the third floor? That wasn't meeting in a public space. That meant going to his room. Where there was a bed.

'Oh…um… What room number?'

'Mr Baker has the entire third floor.'

Freya blinked. What? Who went to a hotel and took up an entire floor? That was the sort of thing celebrities did with their entourages, or royalty, or…

'You wouldn't believe me if I told you.'

What was going on? It was all so confusing. He was just a guy, right? A normal guy.

Was he rich?

The night they'd met at the gala she'd known there was a member of royalty there. She'd heard the rumour but she'd never been introduced to anyone. There'd been no announcement. Everyone had hidden behind their masks and it had been exciting. You could talk to *anyone* and not know it!

Including royalty.

Have sex in a closet with them, if you so chose…

Freya swallowed hard, trying to control her rapidly weakening legs as she hesitantly went over to the lifts and pressed the button.

I could still go. I could run. Just get the hell out of here!

She stood there, fidgeting with the tassels on her scarf, as she waited for the lift to come down to the ground floor.

I owe it to our baby.

Was Jamie a member of some royal family? How could that be?

She thought about turning tail and running—changing her mind and hiding somewhere. Her parents' beach house on Hayling Island, perhaps. It was the place she went when she needed to hide and think. She'd gone there when she'd first been released from hospital, months after the acid attack, and she'd had to wear that damned orthotic burns mask every day, marking her out as different.

She'd felt like a leper. As if there was a bright neon arrow over her head screaming that here was someone *not normal.*

The house on Hayling Island would soon be filling up with summer rentals, but hopefully no one was there right now. Jamie wouldn't know where to find her. It would be good for her to take a break while the morning sickness was in full swing.

The lift pinged, signalling its arrival, and the doors slid open. On the back wall of the lift was an ornate mirror and she gazed at her reflection, wondering what the woman in the mirror should do. Run like hell? It was like staring into a prison.

All ye who enter here...

But Freya had seen more than enough women arrive on her ward to give birth alone, without a father involved, and she had felt sorry for all those children who would grow up without an interested father.

Jamie *wanted* to be involved. He'd said he would not shirk his responsibility. All she'd ever wanted was to be loved and to have a baby—something she'd thought would never happen after her acid attack—and here she was, pregnant and with a guy who said he wanted to be involved. She owed him a chance, the opportunity to show her what he could provide for their child.

With hesitation Freya stepped into the lift and pressed the button for the third floor, eyeing the reception area with longing as the lift doors closed her in.

As the lift ascended she gripped the strap of her bag as if it was a lifeline. An anchor to real life. The sensation that her world was about to change for ever was drowning her in anticipation, and she wished she'd eaten more of those ginger biscuits before coming, because her stomach felt as if it was about to explode.

The lift stopped rising. *Ping!* The doors slid open to reveal two men in dark suits.

Her stomach flipped and she looked from one to the other.

Guards? Why does Jamie need guards?

They were wearing those earpieces that secret service men had on television. They asked her to put her bag through a scanner, and then she had to walk through a metal detector shaped like a doorway before they escorted her down the corridor towards a pair of ornate doors.

What on earth have I got myself into?

Silently she followed, feeling like a little girl between giants. Were they wearing guns beneath their jackets? Her mouth went dry at the thought of it and she gripped her bag tighter, as if that small item would somehow protect her from what was to come.

At ornate double doors the men stopped and grabbed a handle each, stepping back to open the doors wide.

Freya sucked in a steadying breath as her eyes hungrily took in the details of the room. A four-poster bed set with golden drapes in an opulent room adorned with fine art and floor-to-ceiling windows. Gilt-edged tables, fresh flowers in vases that were almost as tall as she was. And standing in the middle, in a long white tunic and trousers, was Jamie. As if he'd been waiting for her.

She stared at him, not sure what to do. Or say.

Now she could understand why he hadn't just told her all this.

'You're right,' she said, clearing her throat and looking straight at him. 'I would never have believed you.'

Jamie poured her some tea, adding two cubes of sugar to the drink. He frowned slightly when he saw how her hands were shaking when she went to take it from him, then set it down on the table instead and took her hands in his to calm them.

'It's all right, Freya.'

'Is it?' She looked at him askance. 'Who *are* you, Jamie?'

'My name is Jameel Al Bakhari and I am heir to the

throne of Majidar. My older brother Ilias is King, ruling with his wife Queen Jasmeen, but they have been unable to sire any children so I am next in line. I also have a younger sister, Zahra, who has just married.'

It all sounded as if it was from a film. 'Heir to the throne…?'

'Yes.'

'Royalty?'

'Yes.'

It was a struggle to process. 'But…but you work as a midwife.'

'Yes.'

'Why? Why do that, when you're a…a prince?'

He smiled. 'I did not ask to be born a prince. Ruling a kingdom and waving at crowds from a distance is not what I felt I was meant to do. I want to *know* people. Help them personally. When my father sat upon the throne he took us with him to a hospital, where he was opening a new neonatal unit. I was very young—maybe eight or nine. We toured the labour ward, saw the new state-of-the-art theatre and the incubators that held tiny newborns. I was fascinated by the babies, and when we returned to the palace an idea took hold. The more I thought about it, the more I realised I wanted to deliver babies. To hold the miracle of life in my own two hands and experience the joy of bringing a new life into the world.'

Freya nodded. 'But why be a midwife? You could have been a doctor. An obstetrician. A surgeon!'

'I could. But those paths didn't interest me. I wanted to deliver the babies. An obstetrician gets called in only if there's a problem. A surgeon just takes care of Caesareans. I wanted to be there through the whole labour—to monitor progress, develop that close relationship a midwife creates with each patient. My mother spoke fondly of all her midwives. I would beg her to tell me, over and over again, the stories of our births—mine, my brother's and my sister's. Even after all those years she could remember every detail, and it was the midwives of whom she spoke the most highly. I wanted to be that person. To have that impact on people's lives. To be remembered in such a way. Selfish, perhaps, but true.'

'I don't think it's selfish.'

He inclined his head in thanks. 'I asked my father if I could study towards midwifery. Focus on the sciences so that midwifery could be my calling. But he would not allow it. He said it was not appropriate for a prince of my standing to attend to such work usually reserved for women.'

Freya couldn't imagine what she might have felt if her mother had forbidden her from becoming a midwife. 'What happened?'

'I had to put my wishes to one side until my father died and my brother Ilias took the throne. I assumed then, like they did, that they would soon overwhelm the palace with little babies and that I would no longer be next in line to sit upon the throne and rule. So I begged Ilias to let me come to England to follow my education and have the life that I wanted. Ilias is much more modern in his thinking and he agreed that I should have the life of my own choosing.'

'You said your brother doesn't have any children?'

'No. Ilias and Jasmeen have never been blessed. Therefore I am still next in line to sit on the throne—something I have no desire to do, but must endure when the time comes. And it *will* come. Eventually. My brother, as considerate as he is, has begun asking me when I will return. He tells me that I must be seen to be upholding some of my royal duties, so that when my time comes the people will know me better and accept my succession.'

'So you have to go back?'

'Not immediately. Ilias is still young—just a few years older than me—but his health is not the best.'

Freya looked down at her tea. The nausea and shock had subsided somewhat now, and she felt more comfortable about taking a sip. 'So what you're trying to say, in a roundabout way, is that I'm carrying the heir to your throne?'

Jamie inhaled a deep breath as he looked at her. She seemed tiny suddenly. He hadn't wanted to scare her, or overwhelm her, but he'd known if he'd tried to explain this on the hospital ward she would never have believed it. She needed to see it. Experience this.

'Yes.'

His acknowledgement was too much. Too overwhelming. She suddenly felt as if she was being suffocated as her mind whirled with all the possibilities that would entail. She got up and began to pace. Walking back and forth, back and forth as she thought hard about how she could get out of this situation.

A royal baby? Heir to a throne? It would mean her life changing. Never to be hers again. All her choices taken from her. All her control gone and given over to someone else.

'Tradition dictates that if everything remains well we should marry before the child is born.'

What? Marriage? No, no, no, no...

She shook her head frantically. 'I'm sorry, but no. I can't. I can't do that, Jamie. I *won't*!'

He stood up too, and reached for her arm, but she swiped his hand away.

'Marrying you would make me...what? A princess? A *queen*? I can't be that! Stared at... With people judging me on a global scale... Why do you think I do night shifts? I love my little world. I'm happy there. I'm accepted. Do you think I want *any* of what you're offering?'

'But, Freya, we need to—'

It was all spiralling away. Her control—everything. Disappearing into a black hole that was vast and powerful. It couldn't happen. She wouldn't let it! She had the right to say no!

She didn't know this man. Even though she'd been intimate with him, conceived a child with him, worked with him. She didn't know him.

Didn't know how he would react if she backed away...

Would he be like Mike? Refuse to let her go?

I need to get away.

Her hand reached into her bag and grasped her mobile phone. She pulled it out and activated the phone keypad, pressed the numbers nine-nine-nine and hesitated. Ready to press 'Call' if anything went wrong.

'No, Jamie. *We* don't need to do anything. *You* don't need to do anything. You can forget about me—you can walk away and pretend that I never existed. You can go back to your kingdom, when the time arrives, and marry a proper princess—someone beautiful, someone the people will expect.'

'You *are* beautiful.'

She laughed at his response. 'You're just saying that. Do you really think you would have asked a girl like me to marry you if I wasn't pregnant? With *this* face? I don't think so.'

He stood in front of her. 'Your face doesn't matter. You are a strong, beautiful woman.'

'Of course it matters. It's what people see! It's what they judge you on. I know this better than anyone. I appreciate that you're trying to say and do the right thing, but it's not the right thing for Majidar. It's not the right thing for *me*. Your people don't need me by the side of their King. A one-night stand who got pregnant? A commoner from another country? *No.* I absolve you of all responsibility. Send me money each month, if that will make you feel better about it, but please, Jamie, I beg of you, walk away. It will be better for you if you just let me go.'

She was trying to sound reasonable. Trying to sound calm and steady so that he would remain so, too. Her thumb hovered over the 'Call' button. He hadn't seen the number she had keyed in and she appreciated that he was keeping his distance physically. But she would press it if she had to.

'I cannot. I *will* not.'

Freya sighed, her eyes filling with sorrow. 'I can't be who you need me to be. I can't live that sort of life. That's not who I am.'

'Neither am I. But it is my destiny. And now, because of the child, it is also yours.'

Freya closed her eyes as if she were in pain, and then she opened them again, looking at him with tears in her eyes, as if she were sorry to be causing such distress. Sorry to have to deny him.

She was afraid to say the next words, but knew she had to, so that he was clear on where she stood. 'No, Jamie. Never.'

And then she backed away. She yanked open the large doors to his suite and hurried down the corridor, expecting at any moment that the guards would drag her back, her finger still hovering over the button on her phone.

But the guards simply followed her at a respectful distance.

The lift was waiting for her and she got in and punched the button for the ground floor. Only when the doors slid closed and she was safe inside did she clear the numbers and slip her phone back into her bag.

It had taken every ounce of her strength to refuse him. To say no and walk away, not knowing how he might react. The likelihood of him being like Mike was slim, but then she'd thought Mike was okay, too. And look at what had happened there.

As she ran across Reception and out into the cool morning air she hoped this meant it was all over. That he would not bother her again.

She had given him her answer.

He would do much better if he were to accept it.

CHAPTER THREE

SHE TRIED TO stay away from Jamie at work. She sensed he was giving her space, and she appreciated that, but she could tell by the way he looked at her from across the room that as far as *he* was concerned this was far from over.

There was no way she could accept his terms. *Marry* him? Become a princess, or whatever she would be? Have her child schooled to become a king or queen themselves? Living a life of privilege, no doubt, but one that would be like a prison. Never to pop to the shops when she wanted, go for a walk when she liked, without fearing that someone might get too close to the royal person...

It was ridiculous.

Her child wouldn't live like that. She wanted a normal life for her baby—a normal education, real friends, a real life and choices. She wanted to sit on the South Downs and have a picnic with her child. Fly a kite and take a dog for a walk. She wanted to walk barefoot on the beach and jump waves with him or her, laugh out loud and eat ice cream and fish and chips.

Normality.

It was the only thing she craved for her child. For herself. To live a normal life. Not the life that she had had since the attack, hiding from people and crowds. Not the childhood that Jamie had had, raised behind the walls of a palace. Something else. The childhood she'd had when she'd been growing up. When her face had been unspoilt by sulphuric acid—when her future had looked bright and the whole world had been a possibility.

Mike had limited her. Told her what she should wear, what she should eat, who she could talk to. And when he hadn't been able to control her, hadn't been able to keep her, he had tried to make sure that no one else would want her.

Saying no to Jamie had taken every ounce of bravery she had. But she wouldn't allow another man to control her, and Jamie's request demanded something of her that she couldn't give. Basically, it seemed to her that he wanted her whole life—her dedication, her child—to be given to him and his country. A country she had never even heard of just one week ago.

Jamie had a duty to his throne, but she didn't. Nor did their child. And she refused to tie either of them down to it.

A person's skin is made up of proteins. Protein makes up the structure of cells and the enzymes within them. Acid, when it comes into contact with protein, changes its innate structure and causes it to break down immediately upon contact. It's excruciating, the pain—difficult to relieve. The strongest medications often have no effect...

Freya sat in the hospital staffroom, waiting for her shift to start. Her mind was torturing her with the memory of that day so long ago, when her world had been turned upside down.

She'd tried to hold up her hands to protect her face, but it had been too late, and then suddenly—instantly—the terrifying scorching of her skin had begun.

She'd thought those screams were from other people, but they'd been her own. Freya had collapsed onto the pavement, her eyes squeezed tightly shut, afraid to open them in case she couldn't see, screaming at people to help her.

Some guy had tried pouring water over her face to dilute the acid, but it had simply run down her neck and begun burning her there, too.

It had seemed an age before the paramedics had arrived. Before the morphine had hit her veins, before they'd tried to irrigate her skin and whisked her to hospital.

Despite the burning she'd begun to feel cold. Shock, they said. Apparently, burns could cause hypothermia. Who knew?

It was a day she would never forget. And all because a man had refused to let her go.

She'd told Jamie no. She'd turned down his marriage proposal, refused to let him take her and the baby back to his country. How would he react now?

As if her worries had summoned him, Jamie entered the staffroom. His gaze met hers, briefly, and then he looked away.

What did that mean? Was he upset? Angry? Was he the type to seek revenge?

So far he seemed reasonable. Normal. A little sad, maybe, but nothing like Mike. But for how long? What about when he got called back to his country and the time came for him to leave? Would he put pressure on her then? Would he try to blackmail her? Threaten her?

She didn't want to tar him with the same brush as Mike, but her history with men so far had not been good. She couldn't read him yet. Didn't understand him. Perhaps if she remained polite and respectful he would remain that way too? Perhaps if she got to know him a little more she might understand him better?

But she was afraid to do that.

Getting to know him meant spending time with him…

Caroline Müller was well into her labour—contracting every two minutes, alternating between taking amusing selfies with her husband Stefan when she was between contractions, and breathing and retreating into herself when she was having pain, going all Zen, peaceful and in control.

It was a marvel to behold.

Freya was happy she could distract herself at work—the place where she could absorb herself in her patient's labour and just for a few hours forget about her own life.

'How are you doing, Caroline? Still coping?'

Caroline had requested no pain relief. She wanted to try and give birth naturally to her first child. Freya wanted to support her in that, but also to let her know that she could change her mind whenever she needed to.

'I'm good, I think.' Her patient nodded, as if she were reassuring herself that she could do this. 'Do you think I'm doing okay?'

Freya smiled. 'You're coping wonderfully. Eight centimetres dilated and still no pain relief! You're a marvel.'

Freya was very keen on honouring a woman's choice. Of all the things in the world a woman could do, going through labour and childbirth was an extremely personal thing. No one else could do it for her. She was on her own. Pulling on the resources and reserves that only she had within her own body.

It was an eye-opening and eye-watering experience. No one could know how they would cope with those levels of pain. And if a mother wanted to give birth without pain relief or with every medication going then Freya would support her either way. Childbirth wasn't a competition, and the mother alone was the one who must decide her course of treatment. It was important to empower a woman with the knowledge that any choice over her body was her own.

Caroline blew out a breath and nodded. 'Thanks. Did you know Stefan's mother wanted to be here at the birth?'

Freya looked at Stefan. 'I didn't.'

'I told her she wasn't welcome—which didn't go down

very well. I didn't want my own mother here, so there was no way I was having my in-laws loitering around my nether regions.'

Freya and Stefan smiled at each other.

'My mother can be quite controlling,' he said. 'This is her first grandchild and we've had to be quite firm with her about not booking things in advance.'

'What sort of things?'

'Enrolling him or her in a private nursery, hiring a nanny, booking her personal swimming instructor to give our newborn swimming lessons, *and* pre-book a German teacher so that our child will grow up to be bilingual. German is my mother's natural tongue,' he explained, smiling with amusement.

'Wow!' Freya mused. 'She sounds wonderfully keen to provide your little one with the very best.'

'She has to be reined in or she doesn't know when to stop!' Caroline said, and grimaced as another contraction began to build.

She closed her eyes, relaxed her brow and began to breathe steadily in through her nose and then slowly and smoothly out through her mouth. She stood to one side of the bed, leaning on the mattress, swaying her hips from side to side as the contraction intensified.

'That's it, Caroline, you're doing really well. Keep breathing.'

Freya rubbed the small of her patient's back, wondering how royal families raised their babies.

Weren't they all surrounded by nannies? Whisked off to nurseries and only brought to their parents to hold when they were clean and fed and presentable?

Actually, she had no idea how royals looked after a new baby. Nor did she have any idea about a desert kingdom's culture.

But what she *did* know was that she didn't want her

child to be taken away from her. This was *her* baby and she wanted to raise it. With Jamie's help, if he wanted, but she would have the final say in everything.

There would be no taking the baby away to a nursery at night time. She wanted to deal with midnight feeds and nappy explosions. She wanted to soothe her baby when it started to teethe. She wanted to be the one who took her child to the doctor for vaccinations and check-ups, to comfort it when it cried because some stranger had poked at it with a needle or a stethoscope.

Was it too much to ask? This might be Jamie's baby too, and he might come from a royal line of kings, but it was also *her* baby and she *wasn't* royal. She was normal—girl-next-door. And she wanted her child to have a normal life.

Caroline began to groan out loud—thick guttural noises coming from deep within her. 'Oh, I think I want to push!'

'Try not to. Not just yet. I need to check you again… make sure you're fully dilated.'

She was. With a wide smile she informed Caroline that with the next contraction she could start pushing, and that hopefully, within the next hour, they would have their longed-for baby.

'Will I really?' Caroline began to cry. Happy tears springing from her eyes as she reached for her husband's hand, clutching it tightly.

He squeezed back. 'We will.'

Caroline wanted to remain standing between contractions, and then lowered herself into a crouch beside by the bed each time she pushed. She pushed long and hard, her face reddening, sweat pouring down with her efforts, until after about forty minutes she began to crown.

'You're nearly there now!' Freya watched intently and quietly as Caroline gave birth to the baby's head. It had thick black hair and Caroline reached down to touch.

'My baby!' she cried.

'One final push, Caroline! You can do this!'

Freya supported the baby with her gloved hands as it was delivered, and then passed the crying baby over to its mother, who lifted her up from between her legs to cradle her against her chest.

'Oh, my God! It's a girl! We have a little girl, Stefan!'

Freya clamped the cord and Stefan cut it, and then she helped guide the new mum onto the bed, so she could rest whilst Freya took care of all the little things that needed doing. The syntocinon. Checking to see if mum needed stitches. For any sign of haemorrhage.

She draped a couple of towels around the baby to help keep it warm as Caroline placed her daughter against her skin beneath her hospital gown. Then Freya checked the placenta to make sure it was complete and healthy.

After she'd written the pertinent times and details into her patient's file, she took the baby to weigh it and check its APGAR score—the scale against which all newborn babies were measured to ensure they were coping with life outside of the womb.

Handing the baby back for more skin-to-skin, she asked if Caroline and Stefan had chosen a name yet?

'Hannah Rose.'

'That's beautiful,' she said.

'Thank you. Thank you for everything, Freya—we really mean it. We couldn't have done it without you.'

She smiled her thanks. 'I couldn't have done it, without you! I'll leave you on your own for a little while. Press the buzzer if you need me, but I'll be back to take you down to the postnatal ward.'

She left the new parents to it—Stefan already taking pictures with his phone—and quietly closed the door behind her. Then, carrying her patient's notes, she headed over to the desk and sat down.

Freya was hungry…thirsty. She hadn't had anything for

hours, having stayed with her patient for most of the night, popping out only once to use the toilet because her bladder had threatened to explode if she didn't.

Mona came out of the small kitchenette, carrying a tray filled with mugs of tea. 'Ah! Perfect timing. Want one?'

'Ooh, yes, please!' Freya grabbed a hot mug and gratefully took a sip. 'My patient just delivered a baby girl—Hannah Rose. Isn't that a beautiful name?'

'Gorgeous! How did she get through it?'

'Not a single scrap of pain medication!' Freya stated proudly.

'Good for her! I have no pain threshold whatsoever. I practically needed an epidural for a tiny blister I got on my heel. What about you?' Then Mona's face darkened as she realised what she'd said. 'Sorry...'

But Freya wasn't offended. Mona was her closest friend here, and she knew she hadn't meant anything nasty by it.

Freya thought back to her days spent in hospital after the acid attack. The pain she'd been in. The pain she'd had to live through for months as her face recovered. The nightmares. The flashbacks. The searing, agonising torture of debridement. She'd had enough pain for one lifetime.

She smiled. 'I want everything they can give me.'

Jamie had been watching her carefully over the last few weeks. As much as he could, anyway. Clearly she was trying to avoid being with him. He kept catching her noticing him arrive in the staffroom or at the reception desk and suddenly getting that *I'm busy* look before she got up to go and do something.

He was finding it terribly frustrating when all he wanted to do was talk to her. Find out how she was. Whether she was feeling okay. She had to be due for the first scan of the baby any day now, but she'd made no mention of it to him and he didn't want to miss it. Nor did he like this distance she was creating between them, as if she didn't want him involved, because that was not how he planned to have his first child. Being cast aside as if he was just a sperm donor.

Having a baby was one of the most wonderful things a woman could do. To become a parent one of the most rewarding privileges. He really hoped that Freya would thaw towards him, but he could understand why she hadn't yet.

Mona had told him what had happened to her years ago. Some possessive ex had thrown acid in her face. The very idea of that made him feel sick. It caused a rage to build in him towards a man he knew was already in prison.

Mona hadn't said much else, clearly reluctant to gossip about her friend, but he'd had to ask. He'd spent so many nights wondering why she was keeping him at such a distance. Why she seemed so edgy and uncomfortable. Why she kept looking at him as if he was some firework that might go off at any minute. It had made him wonder what had happened to her. And now he knew.

Freya MacFadden was having a strange effect on him. She was so petite, so dainty, and he loved seeing her walk in with her long blonde hair hanging loose down her back, watching her scoop it up, twist it and pin it into place each shift. It was an action so casually done, without looking in a mirror, and she always managed a tousled look which, with those big blue eyes of hers, was a winning combination.

The scars didn't bother him at all. Not like that. What bothered him about them was that someone had done that to her. Intentionally. That she had suffered, and that her life had been changed for evermore. He'd visited clinics that cared for women attacked like this, and he'd never seen such suffering before or since. It was a memory that haunted him, but he'd learnt something from those women—that they had tremendous courage. That they bore a bravery within them that he could never hope to emulate.

Freya was the same.

He was worried that she didn't seem to be letting him in, but he understood why and knew that he would have to bide his time if she were to trust him.

He leaned against her locker, straightening when he heard her coming down the corridor, chatting to Mona. He hoped to end this stalemate between them—to get them talking again. Ask her how she was…if she needed anything.

He saw her notice him. Watched as she debated whether to avoid using her locker after all. But then she seemed to overcome that hesitation and came over to him.

'Excuse me, I need to get inside.'

He stepped back, giving her space. 'Could we talk for a moment?'

She looked up at him hesitantly. 'About what?'

'About us.'

'There is no "us".' She glanced over at their colleagues, afraid of being overheard. But no one appeared to be listening.

She shoved her bag into her locker and hung up her coat. Then she did the hair thing that he loved and clipped her ID badge to her uniform.

'Can you tell me if you're feeling okay? If there's anything I can do?'

'I'm feeling fine. A bit sick, but eating often seems to help.'

He could see in her face that she was still closed off from him. Unwilling to share. He understood that, and he was willing to wait.

'Well, if there's anything I can do for you then please let me know.'

She nodded and bit her lip.

'Can I get you a tea? A coffee?'

She glanced over at their friends by the kettle and the sink. 'No, but thank you.'

'Have you told anyone?'

Her eyes darkened. 'No. Not yet. Have you?'

He shook his head. 'No.'

'Right. What will happen when you do?'

He imagined the reaction of his family. They would be insistent upon marriage. They would be insistent about him coming home and building his life as a father and future King of Majidar.

'They'll be delighted.'

Her eyes narrowed, as if she were trying to assess him for the truth. *'Right.'*

'Oh, I brought you these.' From behind his back he drew out a brown paper bag filled with grapes. 'As promised.'

A small smile *almost* broke out across her face, but she checked it and instead frowned. 'I'm not sick.'

'No, I know.'

'You don't have to do this…' she whispered.

He nodded and whispered back, 'I do. So if you need anything—*anything*—I hope you will ask me.'

And he left her at her locker to go and grab himself a drink.

Little inroads…small kindnesses. That was what she needed. He needed to build her trust. He needed to show her that he could be relied upon to look out for her and keep her safe. She needed to see that he was everything that the man who'd attacked her was not. That he believed in kindness and respect and love. That he believed in honour and duty and that he would shirk neither.

Baby steps.

The next shift they had together Freya nodded her head towards him, as if to say *good morning.* The one after that she actually said hello.

Jamie gave her more space and time.

One night shift she came in and straight away headed

for the staff toilet, emerging fifteen minutes later looking a little green. He presented her with ginger tea—something that his mother had sworn by. Another time when she looked queasy and was meant to check on a patient in Postnatal, he offered to answer the call bell instead.

Where he could, he took the time to try and lighten her load. To make it easier for her whilst she was going through this difficult time.

Their colleagues had begun to suspect that something was up, and Mona had been the one to ask Freya during a night shift.

'Are you *pregnant*?'

Clearly Freya had realised it was pointless to try and deny it. Not when the signs were so obvious and she was surrounded by people who specialised in pregnancy and babies.

The team had been delighted! Hugging her and congratulating her.

'Who's the father?'

Freya had baulked at answering, but she had looked at him, as if to give him permission to answer.

He'd stepped forward. 'I am.'

Well, that had sent the gossip mill into high speed!

He had seen that Freya wasn't overly happy about being the centre of attention, but she'd seemed to cope with it— probably because these were her friends and people she trusted.

After that everyone had tried their best to help Freya out whilst the morning sickness was so devastating. She really was suffering, poor thing.

'Are you guys, like, together?' Mona had asked him.

Jamie had longed to say *Not yet*, but had felt that would be pushing too far, before Freya was ready. This was not a world in which two people could be forced into marriage. It was not something that had been arranged since they were children. It was not a unification of two countries solidifying a pact by marrying off a prince and princess.

This was real life. Freya was a commoner. A woman from the west. She had different expectations from life and a whole lot of baggage that she needed to sift through before she realised he was a good guy.

'Your first scan should be soon,' he said as he brought her another cup of ginger tea one day.

'It is.'

'I was wondering…only if you feel right about it…if I might come with you?'

She looked at him carefully, almost as if she were appraising him. She'd been giving him this look a lot just lately.

'Okay.'

His heart almost burst with joy. *'Okay?'*

'Sure. It's your baby too.'

'Thank you, Freya!'

He almost imploded with excitement, but managed to contain himself. Strong emotions, sudden reactions, were not the kind of thing that would make Freya feel safe. She needed to see that he was stable, even if his insides were fizzing with glee and he wanted to jump about and yell for all the world to hear.

They sat together, waiting for the ultrasound technician to call Freya's name.

She felt uncomfortable. Not just because she'd had to drink a huge amount of water beforehand, and hold it in, but also because she was back in what she considered the 'normal' world. Daylight hours. Where there were too many people about. People who, she noticed, kept glancing at her, trying to work out what was different about her. Noticing her face…

Part of her wanted to stare back at them. Challenge them

with a single raised eyebrow as if to ask, *What are you looking at?* But she wasn't brave enough or rude enough.

Freya had been raised to show respect to people. To be polite and to treat others the way she wished to be treated herself. She couldn't do that to strangers. They didn't deserve it. They were just being curious. It was human nature to take a second look at something that didn't quite fit.

She wondered how many of them were wondering how on earth she could be sitting there with this gorgeous man next to her.

Jamie clearly had no idea of his allure. Ink-dark hair, midnight eyes that penetrated the soul, and a bearing that screamed royalty—due, no doubt, to a childhood that had consisted of years of being told to sit up straight, shoulders back. Not to slouch. To meet people's eyes. Assess the situation. Listen. Look commanding.

She felt tiny next to him. Inconsequential. He was so tall, proud and strong, and she was small, scarred and nauseous.

How much of her feeling sick was due to the pregnancy, though? Her stress levels were high. She dreaded to think what her blood pressure was. But she had to admit she wouldn't have got through these last few weeks of her first trimester without Jamie's help.

He had been instrumental in getting her through it, and she'd quickly come to realise that she had begun to rely on him being close. Always there with a hot, steaming mug of ginger tea, or some peppermints, or one of the strawberry milkshakes which she had begun craving. Whatever she'd needed—a rest, a moment to herself, someone to take care of her patients whilst she clutched the toilet bowl—he'd provided it. Her friends, too, yes. But Jamie had been the most considerate and for that she was grateful.

And scared.

He was getting under her skin. She was beginning to like him. Once she'd come on shift and, when she'd realised that he wasn't rostered on with her, a huge sense of disappointment and loss had hit her like a brick.

How had that happened?

She never wanted to rely on a man again.

And yet here she was. Not only was she tied to this man but he was also a prince, he had a duty, and she was refusing to accept that. She knew she must somehow be tearing him in two. He had a duty to his country. To his people.

I'm hurting him and yet he doesn't complain.

They didn't look right together—no wonder people were staring. She was just a girl. A scarred, damaged girl. And he... Well, Jamie was something else entirely, and he deserved a beautiful princess to stand by his side and make pretty babies with him.

'Freya MacFadden?'

She straightened, rising to her feet. Behind her, she felt Jamie stand and follow her into the darkened room.

They went through the preliminaries with the technician. Date of last period, how many weeks pregnant she was, whether she felt well.

Frightened, she lay down, not sure what was scaring her more—the prospect of seeing her baby on screen, at last, or the fact that she wanted Jamie at her side. She'd anticipated doing this alone. Not telling him. Sneaking in to the appointment after everyone on the night shift had gone and having this moment all to herself. Knowing she would cry. Knowing she would get emotional because finally, *finally* this day had come. The day she would see irrefutable proof that she was pregnant. With a baby she'd thought she would never have.

The technician squirted the gel and applied the probe to Freya's abdomen.

Freya bit her lip. She might have got this all wrong. Perhaps she wasn't even pregnant at all? A false positive? A molar pregnancy? Then everyone could go back to their normal lives. Jamie could leave and go on to another post, or back to his country, and she could remain unchanged on the night shift, revelling in the joy of other people's babies and just imagining what it might feel like to hold her own baby...

The technician was smiling. 'Everything looks wonderful here.'

Freya let out a breath she hadn't realised she'd been holding. 'Really?'

'Any history of multiples in either family?'

What?

The technician turned the screen so that Freya and Jamie could see. There, in black and white, was her womb. Filled with not one but *two* babies, separated by a very fine line which meant...

'Twins? Non-identical twins?' Jamie stared at the screen, laughing with shock and delight.

Freya had to remind herself to breathe. She couldn't quite believe it! Twins? Her grandmother had been one of a pair of twins, but she'd never imagined that this would happen to her. 'Oh, my God...'

'Freya, can you believe it?' Jamie scooped up her hand in his and kissed it, his dark eyes sparkling with unshed tears in the shadows of the room.

She stared at him, seeing his joy, his beaming face, his eyes twinkling in the semi-darkness of the room.

She felt her body flooding with adrenaline. *Twins.* Non-identical twins.

This was crazy. Unbelievable! It was...

She stared at the screen once again. Counted again. Two babies. Growing inside her.

Two.

'I don't believe it.'

The technician continued to make her checks. Measuring the babies, the length of their femurs, checking the Nuchal fold at the backs of their necks.

'Your babies look beautiful. Perfectly healthy and a good size. It probably accounts for all that morning sickness you've been having. You'll get more scans and check-ups due to this being a twin pregnancy, so if you have any problems don't hesitate to shout.' She smiled at them both. 'You ought to go and celebrate.'

Perhaps. But Freya didn't foresee having a party. She liked the idea of keeping it quiet. Just telling family and the people at work. They were the only people she knew anyway.

Jamie probably had loads of people he needed to tell. His family. His staff. His advisors. What would they all tell him to do? He couldn't walk away now, could he? She was carrying *two* royal children.

If she hadn't felt trapped before, she most definitely felt it now.

She began to hyperventilate and felt Jamie's fingers wrap around her own.

'It's okay, Freya. Just breathe slowly. In and out. That's it, slow your breathing.'

She focused on his face. On his voice. On him, her only connection to this world. She felt spaced out, as if she was adrift in a vast universe and he was the umbilical cord connecting her to reality.

He had intensely dark eyes. Eyes she could lose herself in. She had once before and now she needed to again.

Was she about to get swept up into a load of royal political intrigue? Be married and whisked away to live in a desert? Something like that?

How could she continue to live the private life that she loved? Was she about to lose all control over her every decision? Because she wasn't sure she could do that.

This life, her *babies'* lives, were too important. Jamie's demands were not more important than her own.

She'd lost all control once. Had all decisions taken from her. She had lived a life trapped in a hospital, in pain and afraid, with staff all around her, checking on her every hour of the day, waiting on her hand and foot. It had been unbearable. Living a half-life, staring out of windows, watching the world go by and wishing she could be in it. Wishing that the pain would go away, so she could escape...

I won't have that happen again.

Slowly her breathing came back under her control. Jamie was smiling at her, with relief on his face that she was calming down. Sitting up, she pulled her hand from his. She had relied on him enough.

'I'm okay. I'm all right.'

The sonographer passed her a couple of scan pictures. 'Twins can be a bit of a shock. It might take some time to get used to.'

Jamie was watching her, assessing her. He offered her his hand, so she could get up off the bed, but she did it without his help.

She couldn't keep relying on him. He had other commitments. Other duties. No matter what he said their lives were incompatible, and no matter how much she might want something else she couldn't have him and he couldn't have her.

I just need to keep telling myself that.

The rush hour traffic was building around the hospital. The car park was filling with vehicles. Staff were arriving, visitors...

Freya pulled up the collar of her jacket and adjusted her scarf. Aware of too many pairs of eyes all around her.

Jamie stood beside her, gazing down at the scan pictures the technician had given them.

'This doesn't change anything,' she said, hoisting her bag strap firmly into place on her shoulder.

'No?'

'No.'

He stared back at her, frowning, a small divot forming between his dark brows. 'There must be something I can do. To make this easier for you.'

Why did he have to have such a beautiful voice? Deep, slightly accented, smooth and delightful. He was already handsome and charming. Helpful and kind. Did he have to be sexy, too? Couldn't the man have one single fault?

He does. He's royal.

She was struggling not to cry again. Her hormones washed through her with renewed force now that she knew she was carrying twins.

'You could leave. Get a contract someplace else.'

'That's never going to happen. You think I'm going to walk away from you? All three of you?'

With eyes blurred from unshed tears, she glanced up at him and then away as she headed for her car to go home.

'You're under no obligation to be with me, Jamie. I told you that. Why can't you just go? Pretend this never happened? I'll never ask anything of you.'

She heard his footsteps as he hurried to catch up with her. Felt his hand upon her arm, turning her.

'I'm *never* walking away from you. You need to stop asking me to do that.'

She wasn't sure she could do this. How had she got herself into another situation where a man was refusing to let her go? Demanding to stay in her life? It was scary. She didn't want it. *Any* of it! She just wanted to be left in peace. To deal with this alone. Why couldn't she be living her happy dream? The one where she was married and was about to have a family with the man she loved and who loved her and where everything was normal and light and easy? And not terrifying.

'Jamie, I can't be who you need me to be.'

'Who do you think I need?'

'A princess. A queen. A *wife*. Someone who can stand by your side proudly. Someone who can wave to cheering crowds. Someone who can be loved by your people.'

'They'd love any woman I chose to have by my side.'

'Because of their duty?'

'Yes.'

'I don't want love out of *duty*, Jamie. And I could never stand beside you like that. I could never live away from my family. My job. My life. My life and my babies' lives will be *here*. Not in Majidar. You need to accept that.'

She pointed her key fob at her car to unlock it and opened the door.

'You *will* be called at some point to take your brother's throne and be King, so leave me now, leave *us* now and then no one will have to get hurt.' She got in, closed the car door shut after her and gave him one last look.

Did he not understand how much this was hurting *her*? She'd dreamed of this day! She'd never imagined she would ever be blessed by one baby, never mind two, but in that dream of having babies she'd hoped to have a wonderful man by her side too. In her imagination he'd always been a tall, dark and handsome figure, his face blurred. She'd never been sure who he might be. She'd dreamt of a family. Her children, her husband.

Mike had taken that dream away from her the second he'd thrown that acid, but now it was within her grasp again. And it was all wrong.

She wished she could develop something with Jamie, but he had another calling, apart from midwifery.

He was going to be King.

And she could not leave everything and everyone she

knew to live her life beside him. A life of publicity, of always having her photograph taken, with her every choice of clothing or hairstyle criticised and appraised. Her face discussed and talked about in newspapers and on television channels, her relationship with Mike dredged up from history, where she'd consigned it. They'd no doubt track him down in prison, interview him, get the inside scoop on their relationship and publish that too.

A life with Jamie would mean a lifetime of judgement.

All she'd ever wanted was to be loved.

And love did not come from duty.

Jamie pressed his hands against her window and begged her to lower it so he could speak.

She dropped the window slightly and the coolness of the outside air filtered into the car's interior.

Jamie stared at her. 'People are already hurting, Freya. You are. I am. We need to work together to sort this—not just for us, but for our children.'

Her hands went to her belly, protectively wrapping around them. 'They're who I'm thinking of.'

His eyes had narrowed slightly and frustration crept into his voice. '*Are* you, Freya? Or are you just thinking of the man who did that to you? Letting his actions dictate how you think your life must be?'

She bit her lip. Because he was right. Mike—his actions years ago, his attack, her fear—was being allowed to run every decision she made.

But who was Jamie to think he could tell her this? Say it? Confront her with it? As if he had the right?

'I'm their father, Freya. Let me be with my children!'

CHAPTER FOUR

WALK AWAY AND no one would get hurt? Did she think he was made of stone? He already had feelings about this. About the babies. About *her*.

Freya didn't seem to understand that.

He was *already* involved. Already in too deep and he always would be—until the day he took his last breath. These were his *children*!

And she...she was *scared*.

He understood that. What she'd been through... He couldn't even begin to imagine *half* the pain she must have experienced. She must have thought her life was over. Her face ruined. Her life destroyed by what had happened. Had she believed she didn't have a future?

All he wanted to do was help her feel safe. Make sure she was all right. But she seemed determined to keep pushing him away. It was very frustrating and he was trying his hardest not to make demands.

She truly was remarkable. He had nothing but admiration for her. Her spirit, her bravery made her shine from within. She didn't understand that. She didn't realise just how much people cared for her because of who she was. She believed they judged her purely on what she looked like.

She was still beautiful. Imperfections on her face meant nothing. It was who someone was that made them attractive.

Clearly Freya was still bothered by her face and he understood that. Women today were bombarded with messages about what constituted beauty, and it was all focused on outward appearances—being model-thin, having long, luscious hair, drop-dead gorgeous features. Beauty was never seen in acts of charity, or kindness, or caring. No one was ever told that having a good, loving heart was beautiful.

So he would protect her. Care for her as much as she would let him. And hopefully she would begin to let down her walls. To trust him.

He tried to make sure she always had a drink or a snack, as she kept staying in her patients' rooms and not coming out for a break, and he couldn't allow that. She needed to keep her strength up. But when he did these things for her she would give him a look that was almost like fear. As if she was worried about what he might do next. A look that said *You really don't have to do this.*

But he did. Whether she liked it or not they were joined now. For evermore. With or without rings on their fingers.

He brought her mugs of tea. He'd even offered to massage her aching feet once, when she'd complained about them, but all she'd done in response was look at him as if he was mad and then she'd got up to go and do something else. When she should have been resting!

She wouldn't let him in. Wouldn't let him get close.

His security people had told him that after she left the hospital and went home she stayed in. Never went anywhere. Didn't seem to have a life. There had been one visit, where she'd gone to someone's house, but a quick background check had discovered that it was her mother's home. He'd debated about calling in, hoping to meet her mother, but had refrained, not knowing how she'd react to that. If she thought his making her a cup of tea at work was bad, he felt sure she wouldn't want him pushing into her life before he was invited.

The security detail he'd assigned to her reported in every day. It broke his heart that she lived such an isolated life. Was there some way in which he could help her to open up her world? Or perhaps she was happy? Perhaps she was an introvert who enjoyed her own company? He wasn't in any position to judge.

'Would you like to meet me for coffee one day?' he asked her during a break on the ward.

She looked at him askance. 'Why? I see you every day at work.'

He smiled. 'It's different at work. We don't really get a chance to talk. We should be getting to know one another a bit more. We could meet in the open somewhere. In a public place, if that will make you feel better.'

He thought he was suggesting a *good* thing. Neutrality. Safety and security in numbers.

'I was attacked in a public place, Jamie. Surrounded by people. Numbers don't always make you safer.'

No. Of course not. He should have considered that. Freya liked privacy and quietness. She liked being alone.

'Chichester Cathedral.'

She frowned. 'What?'

'Let's meet at Chichester Cathedral. It's quiet, not too many people. There's a place to get coffee. Some grounds to wander in where we could find a private nook.'

'Because you want to talk?'

'Because we *need* to talk. Please, Freya, I beg of you.'

She seemed to consider his proposal. A divot formed in her brow. 'It's still too public for me.'

'Then where? Name it and I will arrange it.'

She thought of her bolthole on Hayling Island. The place she'd gone to after the attack. Her sanctuary.

'There's a path called the Billy Trail on Hayling Island. It starts just after the bridge to the mainland, on your right. We could meet there. I'll bring Rebel.'

Now it was his turn to frown. 'Who's Rebel?'

'My mother's dog.'

He wasn't the biggest fan of dogs, but he could get past that if she could get past her fears. 'Okay. When?'

It was Sunday afternoon, and the sun was burning down through a pure blue sky. He'd had to have the air-conditioning put on full when he'd got into the car because it was so hot. But he was glad the weather was good. He thought that if it had been raining, or bad weather in some way, Freya would have cancelled and they *needed* this. This time together. They needed to know more about one another. More beyond work and pregnancy and past horrors.

He and Freya were from vastly different backgrounds. It was no wonder they were clashing. But they both had the same desire and that was to do the best thing for their babies.

His driver located the small car park just past the bridge. He'd never been this way before, and he'd been positively delighted at the beautiful harbours the bridge had driven them through. The soft stillness of the calm water, the white boats sitting on the surface, the stretch of coastline and beyond, across the water, the views to Portsmouth and the spire of the Spinnaker Tower.

He stood waiting for her to arrive and pretty soon saw her small car turn into the car park. He gave her a smile and a wave. He had butterflies in his stomach! He so wanted this meeting to go well between them. It was imperative that it did so.

His nerves grew worse when he saw her let a large German Shepherd dog out of the boot of her car. For some reason he'd expected something smaller, but Rebel was massive! He was dark with intense eyes, his ears up and alert, ready to protect his mistress.

His mouth dry, he began to walk towards them.

'Hi.'

He stopped, looking down at the dog. Rebel was pant-
ing from the heat, but all Jamie could see were rows of
sharp white teeth.

Freya had him on a short leash. 'Rebel, sit.'

Instantly the dog sat and looked up to her, waiting for
the next order.

He was impressed, but also trying to control the feeling that he needed to bolt. He desperately wanted to run
away from this dog, but he had no doubt that it would run
after him and pull him to the ground with a well-placed
jaw around his arm or leg. Or somewhere worse!

'Are you okay?' she asked.

'Bit nervous of dogs, to be honest.'

She smiled, amused. 'Rebel's all right. You can trust
him.'

'Does he know he can trust *me*?'

Her smile broadened. 'We're both still trying to work
that out. So, shall we get going?' She slung a backpack over
her shoulder and locked her car.

'Sure. How…um…how close should I get to you?'

'Beside me is fine. Don't worry, he won't rip your throat
out unless I tell him to.'

'Oh, good. That makes me feel a lot better.'

She laughed. 'Come on!'

Clearly Freya felt at ease with the dog at her side, and
he had to admit he really rather liked this relaxed Freya.
The dog? Not so much.

Freya looked relaxed in her white tee shirt and blue
shorts, sunglasses over her eyes and her hair swept back
in a ponytail. She looked fresh and happy, and already he
could see a slight swelling to her abdomen. Only three
months pregnant, maybe, but this was twins so she was
slightly bigger than normal.

Three or four people on mountain bikes went cycling past as they headed onto the path.

'You found the place all right, then?' she asked.

'My driver did.'

'Of course. You have servants. I forget that when I see you at work.'

'Just a driver. Some security. A valet at the hotel. Not much.'

'Not much, huh? You have the entire third floor. I think you have plenty.'

'Just a security issue, that's all.'

'Where are your guards today? Are they lurking behind bushes on the trail? Are they going to walk behind us at twenty paces?' She looked behind them, as if to check.

'Nothing like that.'

He didn't tell her that his security team had already swept the entire five-mile length of the trail. That he had one or two undercover men posing as walkers and another pretending to be a wildlife photographer. The trail passed a nature reserve, so it was the perfect place to hide men in plain sight.

'It must be hard to live a life that's watched over like that.'

'You tell *me*.'

She frowned. 'What do you mean?'

'Don't you think that everyone is constantly looking at *you*? Watching your every move?'

She looked away. 'That's different. That's a perception. Your life is a reality. One you can't escape from.'

'Is that why you don't want to be a part of it? Because people are always watching? Observing? Making judgements?'

'Partly.'

At least she was being honest.

'You don't notice it after a while,' he said.

'I would. I notice everything. Every little glance. Every raise of an eyebrow. Every frown. Every reaction—shock, fear, disgust. That last one I get more than you'd realise. Have you ever thought what that might feel like? To observe someone looking at your face and see that they're disgusted? Of course you haven't. Not looking the way you do. The world is open to those who are good-looking. It's a proven scientific fact. Beautiful and handsome people get better jobs, better pay, more opportunities. Disabled and disfigured people always seem to be at the bottom of the pile.'

'Life must have been hard for you.'

'Must have been? It still is.'

He didn't know how to answer that. He would never know exactly what she had been through. What she still went through, looking in the mirror and seeing a different face.

'But a new phase of our lives is opening up to both of us now.'

She nodded, stopping as Rebel bent his head to sniff at a small post in the ground. 'We have two separate, completely incompatible lives, Jamie. How are we going to manage this?'

The truth? He didn't know. He wanted to be a father to these babies, and to be in their lives, but he would be called upon to rule Majidar at some point and would have to leave this country. He didn't want to leave them behind and she refused to go with him.

He *loved* Majidar. Even though he had left it to come to England and make his life there. It was still his home. It was still the place where his family was. Where his heart was. His people were gracious and kind and understanding, but would they understand when they learned that he had left his children behind? Because he wouldn't. He couldn't get his head around it.

He loved these babies. Already. He'd seen their little hearts beating, had seen them in her womb, two gorgeous little beans that were *his*. He felt he would die for them. Lay down his life for them. Already he dreamed of holding them in his arms, teaching them, playing with them, laughing at their chuckles and watching them grow.

Be a king. Or be a father.

It seemed to be one or the other, and it was an impossible decision to make.

'We *must* manage it. We must find a way.'

'But how?'

He smiled at her. 'Today is a good step forward. We can't afford to shut each other out; we don't have that luxury. I know it's hard for you—hard for you to trust me and let me in.' He paused over his next words, but knew he had to let her know that he *knew*. 'I know what happened to you.'

Freya stopped walking. So did Rebel, who turned back to look at her. 'Who told you?'

'No one was gossiping. I asked. I brought it up. I needed to know why you were shutting me out.'

She started walking again, Rebel loping by her side. 'I see.'

'I don't want you to be frightened of me, Freya. I'm not that kind of man.'

'I can't tell any more. My perspective on men is skewed.'

'Hence the big dog?' He smiled.

She glanced at him. 'Tell me why you're afraid of dogs.'

He thought about why he was afraid, glancing at Rebel's teeth. 'My brother and I were once playing out on the sand dunes. We'd gone out with our father, who was hunting with his falcons and his dogs. We had these big boards—like surfboards—and if we threw them right down the sloping side of a dune we could jump on and surf to the bottom. We were doing that…laughing and joking…having a brilliant time. I'd jumped onto my board and was sitting on it, surfing down the dune, when one of the dogs must have had his hunting instincts activated by our movement and high-pitched cries. This dog—this hound that was almost as tall as I was—raced over to me, and when the board stopped moving it grabbed onto my head, sinking its teeth into my scalp.'

Freya looked fascinated. Interested.

'My father got the dog to stop. It let go and I was rushed to the hospital with four puncture wounds to my skull. After that I couldn't go near any dogs. They made me too nervous.'

She nodded. 'So you know how it feels.'

He looked at her. 'I do. I know you don't know me well enough to be sure I'm not going to pounce, not going to sink my teeth in, but all I can say is I'm not like the man that did this to you. Just like Rebel, there, is probably nothing like the dog that attacked me.'

'You have to trust that.'

'As do you.'

He touched her on the arm, making her stop. Then he sucked in a breath as he contemplated what he had to do. Show her that if he was willing to work past his fear, then so should she. With some hesitation he held his hand out towards Rebel, hoping the dog wouldn't sense his fear. Hoping he wasn't about to lose a chunk of his hand. His heart racing, he watching in horrid fascination as Rebel licked his fingers, then began sniffing the cuff of his shirt.

Jamie knelt down in front of the dog and reached out to stroke it. His arms were trembling, but he was determined to do this. Rebel's fur was soft and thick and, most surprisingly, the dog didn't seem to mind him at all. Slowly he stood up and breathed a sigh of relief, a smile breaking across his face.

'Well, that went better than I'd imagined.'

A small smile broke across her face. 'That must have taken a lot of courage. Were you really that scared?'

'Terrified. But I trusted that I'd be okay. I hope you can do the same with me. Because only then can we get through this. As equals.'

They began walking again, side by side, enjoying the views over the harbour and its old oyster beds, where masses of birds were nesting.

'I'll try. That's all I can do.'

Jamie nodded. 'It's all I ask.'

Freya looked about her, then sucked in a breath and began talking. 'I guess I ought to tell you about him. About Mike—the guy that did this.'

'Only if you want to.'

'I do.'

Freya stooped to undo the clip on Rebel's lead and set him free.

Jamie felt a surge of anxiety, but decided he had to stay calm. She still had control of the dog. And the way the dog kept looking at her, waiting for instruction, showed that she did.

'Mike made me think we were equals. At the beginning. He seemed to adore me. Wanted to be with me all the time. I thought that was just so wonderful, you know? But over time it became insidious, the way he manipulated that. He made me feel bad about going out to see other people. He questioned my clothing. He wanted to know why I needed to wear make-up. Was it for someone else? Was I flirting? I tried to prove him wrong by not wearing make-up, but then he wanted me to cut my hair short. Said it made me look flirty, being so long, that men looked at women with long hair in the wrong way.'

She paused.

'It sounds crazy now, but at the time I was just so afraid of upsetting him. His moods were terrible. We were so good together when he was happy, and I wanted to do what I could to keep him that way. But I refused to cut my hair, so he told me to wear it up, so that it looked a bit less feminine. Less pretty. He began questioning me if I was ever late coming home from work. Who had I been talking to? Was it a man? Didn't I know how scared it made him feel when I didn't come home on time? It was just a part time job at a bar, to help with college fees, but he figured the place was filled with nothing but lecherous guys.'

She paused again.

'I began to realise I had no life outside of college and work. I hadn't seen my family in ages. My friends no longer asked me out. All I did was spend time in the flat with Mike. I was just eighteen. It seemed like no life at all, and I didn't want it to stay that way. It had seemed like a compliment at first, the way he seemed to need me. But I began to see that my life had become a prison. A prison I needed to escape.'

'And he let you go?'

'I waited until he went to work, then packed what few possessions I had and took a bus home to Mum. He went crazy when he came home and found out I wasn't there. Called me on my phone. When I told him we were over there was the longest silence, and then he called me all these vile names, said my life wouldn't be worth living without him, and that if I didn't come back to him by the morning I would regret it.'

'Freya...'

'I thought it was just him letting off steam. I thought he was saying stuff like that because his pride had been hurt. But he really was that crazy. I was shopping when it happened. Out on the high street and suddenly he was there, throwing acid into my face.'

'My God! I'm so sorry.'

'I should have seen it coming. I knew he couldn't let go—knew he was a little unstable. I should have expected it.'

'You can't blame yourself.'

'I do, though. For getting involved with a man like that in the first place.'

'You were just *eighteen*, Freya.'

'I know, but…but I feel I should have had more sense.'

Rebel had been up ahead, but now he came loping back, his large paws pounding the ground. He came running up to Jamie, sniffing around his jacket.

Jamie tried not to freeze. Tried to keep walking. To act normal.

'Rebel, heel!'

The dog left him instantly and went back to its mistress. Jamie breathed a sigh of relief. He understood how hard it was for Freya. She couldn't know. Even if she suspected the worst, she couldn't know if or when it would happen. It was impossible. His own hesitation and fear around dogs was similar, but Freya's fear had to be tenfold. He would do whatever he could to make things easier for her.

'You did what you thought was right at the time, with the knowledge you had. You couldn't have asked any more of yourself back then. Or now, come to think of it.'

'What are we going to do, Jamie? I can't marry you. I can't be your wife and leave everything to go and be Queen in some foreign country. That's not me. That's not what I want from my life. And I can't have my children raised behind walls with security guards for protection. I want them to be free.'

'I know. I understand. I *do*. But I can't leave you behind. A king has to be, above all, a good role model for his citizens. I can't leave my children here and go back to rule as an absent father. But I can't let my people down, either. They'll need me. At some point they'll need me on that throne.'

'We have a stalemate, then.' She pulled a small treat from her pocket and fed it to the dog.

'In the future, yes, but right now we can try and work something out.'

'How do you mean?'

'I might not have to be King for many years. In the meantime let me be with you—and them. Let me be who I need to be. I *have* to be in their lives.'

Could she hear the desperation in his voice?

She looked up at him, considering him, judging him. He knew she was still scared. There was no way that was just going to disappear. But he could see that she was thinking about acquiescing to his request.

'I want my children to know their father,' she said.

'That's good.'

'But I don't want their father running out on them. I won't have their hearts broken, Jamie. I won't.'

'I would never want to hurt them in any way.'

'But it will happen. Eventually. Wouldn't it be easier if—?'

'No.'

He knew what she was going to say. *Wouldn't it be easier for them if they just didn't know about you at all?*

'I can't forget about them. They're here. They're a part of me. They are my sons or my daughters. I can't walk away from that. Could you?'

She let out a heavy sigh. 'No, I couldn't.'

They walked on a little more. An older couple were walking towards them, holding hands, chatting. They looked so comfortable with each other. So safe in their little bubble.

He envied them. Envied them their easy lives.

'I have a responsibility to do the right thing. A father stands by his children *and* the mother of those children. As a man, I have to show them that's what I should do. Take re-

sponsibility for my actions. As King, I need to think about
my people and how they need a good, strong leader they
can respect. But most of all I have to respect myself, and
that means doing the best by all of you. That doesn't mean,
and nor would it ever mean, walking away.'

Freya nodded. 'Okay. We'll work something out.'

He nodded too, sure they would find a way.

'We will.'

'I've brought you something.' Back at work, Freya stood
awkwardly in front of Jamie, holding two mugs of tea.

Jamie put down the magazine he'd been reading and
looked up at her in surprise.

'It's tea.' She thrust the mug towards him.

He took it. 'Thank you. That's very kind.'

'It's just tea.'

But they both knew it was more than that. It was an olive
branch. A step forward. A slight lowering of the barricades.
The walls were still there. Freya didn't know if she would
ever be able to trust another man. But she was willing to
give him a chance to show her that she was wrong after
the way he had approached Rebel. Willing to trust. Being
scared, but doing it anyway.

'May I sit with you for a moment?'

'Please do.' He sat up, straightening, and watched her as
she lowered herself into the chair opposite him.

'We…er…ought to get to know one another a bit more.'

He smiled, pleased. 'That's a very good idea.'

'Thank you.'

'How do you suppose we do that?'

She wasn't sure. She hadn't thought that far ahead. To
be honest, she hadn't thought she'd get past offering him
the tea before chickening out and walking away again, but
she had done it. And now here she was.

'We should meet outside of work. What sort of things do you like to do?' he asked. 'That don't involve big dogs?'

She smiled. 'I like to read.' Then she realised that they were hardly going to sit and *read* together, were they? 'I don't really have any other hobbies.'

'What did you do when you were little? There must have been something.'

She thought for a moment. 'I loved to swim. But I haven't done that for years.'

'Swimming's very good for pregnant women. We should do that.'

'Oh, I couldn't possibly—'

'I'll arrange for us to have the pool area at my hotel all to ourselves. What day do you fancy?'

Oh. She hadn't thought he would be able to do that. But what did she know? He was a prince—he could probably do anything he wanted. He was right. There was so much they didn't know about each other. But swimming? Wearing just a swimsuit? Was it too late to back out?

'Saturday evening?' she said.

'Perfect. Thank you, Freya.'

'For what?'

'The olive branch.' He sipped at his tea and smiled. 'It tastes lovely.'

She'd had to get herself a new swimsuit, and had bought one online. She'd had to go for one especially for pregnant women, that allowed for a burgeoning belly, and had found a nice dark navy one with a crimson and cream pleat around her boobs.

Trying it on at home, she stood in front of the mirror to see what Jamie would see. She needed to shave her legs, that was for sure. Maybe paint her toenails?

The swimsuit covered her nicely, though, and even coped with her growing breasts without making her look as if she was hanging out of it. So all in all she was quite pleased with her purchase.

It revealed the scars on her neck, though.

She reached to touch the roughened skin where a graft had failed to take and was reminded of the first time she had looked in a mirror after the attack. The doctors had given her a small hand mirror and then left her to look by herself. Even her mum had left the room, giving her privacy for such a moment.

She'd almost not looked. Why had they all left like that? she'd wondered. Was it because the damage was so bad that they didn't want to see her distress?

Lifting up the mirror, turning to see, had been the most heartbreaking moment of her life. Her face had been ravaged by the acid, her nose almost gone. Angry, red, livid skin...

She'd wanted to die. Right at that moment she had thought that life was no longer worth living. That she would never look better than she did there and then. That her life was over at eighteen years of age and that she would now be one of those relatives kept hidden away in a house, never to be seen again.

But time was a great healer. And the body had an amazing ability to repair itself. It had been a long, hard, painful road, but after each surgery, after each debriding, after each skin graft, she had looked into the mirror and seen progress. Incremental progress. The skin had become less angry. Smoother. Flatter. Her nose had been rebuilt, new eyebrows tattooed into place.

Slowly but surely, normality had seemed to be within reach. She knew she would never be perfect again. Never have the face she used to have. But she would no longer look like some kind of monster.

She'd grown used to the scars, but to everyone she met they were brand-new and she still feared their judgement.

Swimming, though… She hadn't done it in years, because she'd been too afraid to go to a public pool. All those people? Not likely. But she had missed it. So much so, she actually felt a small frisson of excitement at the idea of having a pool to herself and just being allowed to float in the water, quiet and serene, without the worry of people watching her.

She knew she shouldn't be so sensitive to that, but she couldn't help it. A person's face was what they presented to the world, and *her* face was different. Not different in that she had too big a nose, or a massive spot on her chin. Her face just had *that look* after all the skin grafts. The hint of something that was awful underneath in the way her top lip was slightly pulled to one side, her nostrils not quite normal.

The thought of returning to the Franklin Hotel caused butterflies in her stomach. The last time she'd been there it had been made clear to her just exactly who Jamie was. This time she already knew. But he would find out who *she* was. And she wasn't used to people probing around inside her life like that.

Suck it up. You're doing this for your babies.

She parked the car and crunched across the stones on the driveway into the entrance hall. Jamie was already there, waiting to meet her, and he surprised her by kissing her on both cheeks.

'I'm glad you came.'

She nodded, trying to make sense—quickly—of how it had felt when his lips had pressed against her face. She'd stopped breathing. Felt hot. Uncertain.

It's nothing. Just get on with it.

But she hadn't been ready for him to touch her face like that. And with his lips. His perfect lips…

'Shall we go through to the pool? I can show you where the changing rooms are.'

Freya nodded hurriedly, glad that she didn't blush any

more the way she'd used to. Following him through the reception area, down a small corridor, through a set of double doors, she was suddenly hit by the smell of chlorine.

It was like going back through time. She'd both forgotten
that smell and remembered it intently at the same time. It
was so strong! And there was that slight echo in the room,
the reflection of the blue water, bouncing off the walls...

'The ladies' changing rooms are off to the right.'

'Thank you.'

Freya headed off to get changed, letting out a strained
breath as she got to the changing area.

What was she doing—coming here? Doing this? Was
she really about to strip down to a swimming costume in
front of Jamie? It was practically like being naked. Naked
meant vulnerable, and she didn't like feeling that way.

She sat down on a wooden bench for a moment, to
breathe and gather herself.

*I'm not doing this for me. I'm doing this for my chil-
dren, so that when they're grown up I can tell them that I
tried my best.*

Suitably emboldened, she got up and began to undress.
She put on her swimsuit and wrapped herself in a large
towel before heading out to the pool.

Jamie was waiting for her. Wearing just a pair of trunks
that emphasised his physique. She tried not to stare as she
took in his beautiful body. His slightly hairy chest, his
toned muscles, his flat stomach and long, strong, powerful thighs...

He was a thing of beauty, with his dark toned skin,
whereas *she* hadn't been out in the sun for ages and was
milky white, pale, swollen and...

She almost chickened out. Almost turned around to go
back inside the changing room saying *I'm not doing this*, but
then he smiled at her, padding towards her to take her hand.

'Are you all right?'

She nodded, not trusting herself to speak, fighting the urge to flee, but also wanting to get into that water so very much! She'd missed it. Swimming. Relaxing. Floating in the water with the weight of the world off her body.

'Let's get you in, then.'

He walked ahead of her down the steps, her hand in his, allowing her to slip off the towel and get chest-deep in the water before he turned back to look at her.

She appreciated him being a gentleman like that.

'How does the water feel?' he asked.

It felt wonderful. She felt instantly lighter—her bump supported, the strain off her back—and the temperature was perfect.

'Amazing!' She smiled, treading water and moving her arms.

'How many years has it been?'

'Erm… About twenty years. Maybe more.'

He swam alongside her, dipping his head to get his hair wet.

She glanced at him when he came up for air, and then looked away again. God, the man was sexy, all wet like that! Flustered, she allowed the weight of her legs to drop to the bottom of the pool and stood up. She was feeling strange things happening in her body. Tingling anticipation.

'When did *you* last swim?' she asked, to try and think of anything else but her body's primal reaction to this man beside her.

'Yesterday.' He smiled. 'I always do a few lengths after a shift.'

'*After?* How do you have the energy?'

'I just do. But, then again, I'm not growing babies inside me. How are you feeling?'

'Better now the morning sickness has disappeared. It wasn't too bad. I was never actually sick. But I'm feeling much better, thank you.'

'I'm glad.'

She stared at him for a moment. They were facing each other, about a metre apart, treading water. He looked so relaxed, and she wondered how he could be that way with so many worries upon his broad shoulders.

'How do you do it?'

He frowned. 'Do what?'

'Have those men following you around all the time? Your security? I've noticed I've got some of my own now. They're discreet, but they're there. It scared the hell out of me when I realised I was being followed.'

'I should have mentioned them to you. I'm sorry, I should have thought.'

'You should.'

'You get used to it. After a while you hardly notice.'

'Really?'

'Really.'

'I wonder what they think of all this? Having to follow *me* around?'

'I don't know. They do it because I order them to.'

'To protect me?'

He nodded.

'I don't need protection.'

'Maybe not, but those babies of mine do.' *Duty*. Would it always come back to that? He had a duty to his children, not to her. He *had* to do it, not because he wanted to.

She felt some similarity in her own life. She'd survived because she'd had to. She was trying to let him in because she had to. She owed it to her babies. But was it what she wanted? Yes—in a way. Her desire to be a mother was incredibly strong, and the need for her children to know their father was equally so. Even if she did suspect that at some point he would have to leave them behind.

She thought of women who were married to soldiers. Didn't they do the same thing? Knowing that at some point they might lose their husbands? That one day they just wouldn't come home?

But Jamie wouldn't be dying, would he? He would be choosing his duty, his country, over them.

She turned and began to swim breaststroke across the pool. Jamie swam alongside her. And now that the olive branch had been accepted, now that she wasn't having that knee-jerk reaction to keeping him at arm's length, she was curious about the man whose babies she was carrying. His life. His past.

'Tell me about your childhood. What was it like, growing up as a prince?'

He gave a wry smile. 'It was privileged life—no surprise there. But it was also very difficult.'

'In what way?'

'I was a young boy who wanted to run off and explore. Beyond the palace was a thriving town, and beyond that an oasis. I wanted to go there all on my own, but that was never allowed. I felt my freedom was restricted, and along with my schooling I was given many hours of instruction on politics and court etiquette and council procedures, which was all very dry and uninteresting to a boy who only wanted to be able to go to the falconry or the stables or have friends round after school.'

She tried to imagine him. Tried to imagine her own children having such a life. It didn't sound the best.

'Sounds lonely.'

'I was never lonely—which was half the trouble. There was always someone there, standing in the background, waiting, watching. Once my father had forbidden me to learn midwifery I was very angry for a while, and I would often try my best to evade my guards so I could sneak out of the palace grounds and be free for a little while.'

'Did you manage to do that often?'

He smiled. 'I did—much to their disappointment and anger. But I really felt like I didn't belong there.'

Neither did she belong there. Or her babies. It was part of their heritage, but did they deserve to spend their lives like that? Yearning for freedom and escape? She knew how that felt. She'd been there. Wanting to escape from four walls and having family and doctors constantly watching over her. It had been stifling.

'But you have a wonderful brother?'

'I do. He's only a few years older than me, so hopefully he'll be on the throne for a long time. Who knows? Maybe our children will be fully grown and living lives of their own before I have to return to Majidar.'

She stopped swimming as she came to the edge of the pool and leaned back against it. Wouldn't it be wonderful if it happened that way?

'I hope so, Jamie. I do.'

He smiled, before sinking under the surface and swimming towards her, rising from the depths like a merman, his face right in front of hers. It was unnerving, having him this close. She could see him looking at her, taking in every feature of her face.

'Tell me about *your* childhood, Freya.'

His dark eyes were looking into her own with such concentration. Nervous, she began to talk.

'I've lived my whole life here in Chichester. I was very much a girly girl, playing with dolls and babies. I would line them all up like they were in a hospital nursery, covered with little blankets I'd made myself on my mother's sewing machine.'

'You can sew?'

She shrugged. 'Moderately. Simple things—cushions, blankets, curtains.'

'Go on.'

'I loved to play mum. I wanted a brother or sister desperately, but I never got one.'

It had been lonely, growing up without siblings. At least her twins would have each other. Didn't twins usually have a strong bond?

'I loved to swim. I wanted to have horse-riding lessons, but Mum could never afford it.'

'I have horses.'

She lifted her eyebrows in surprise, smiling. 'You do?'

'In Majidar, yes.'

'Oh.'

'Beautiful stallions. Racehorses.'

'Do you miss them?'

'I'm kept up to date on their progress.'

'But only from afar. It must be hard to be kept from something you love?'

Jamie stared at her. 'It can be.'

She could see him having a proper look now. Seeing the edges of her scars around her hairline. Tracking the damage that must have been done and had been repaired. Realising how many operations she must have gone through to look as she did today.

The intense scrutiny made her uncomfortable.

'Love does strange things to people. Makes them act out of character. Makes them crazy. Makes them not think straight.'

Jamie's hand reached up out of the water and she sucked in a breath as his fingers traced the edges of her face, down her cheek, along her jaw. Such a tender touch—respectful and gentle.

'You're beautiful, you know?'

What?

She hadn't expected him to say that. Never in a million years had she expected to hear *anyone* say that to her. Not the way he had. As if he meant it. He'd not been patronising her. His voice had spoken the truth as he saw it.

Moved to strong emotion, Freya blinked back tears at his words.

'Have I upset you?'

'No.' She wiped her eyes hurriedly and tried to smile bravely, to show him that she was okay. Her mum would tell her she was beautiful, but she'd always dismissed that—mums were duty-bound to say that.

'You're crying.' He reached out and pulled her gently towards him.

At first she resisted. Just slightly. But then she gave in, allowing herself that moment. She rested her head against his shoulder, put her arms around his back, completely in shock that this was even happening. This, she had *not* expected. To be held like this…

'I'm okay,' she said, her face against his wet shoulder.

His hand smoothed down her hair. 'No, you're not. But I'll hold you until you are.'

And he did. They both stood there, in the warmth of the pool, in each other's arms, until the tears dried in her eyes, she stopped sniffing and the water was still, like a pond.

When everything was calm again, and her breathing had settled into a steady in and out motion, she felt him release her.

'We should have a change of scene. Let's go to dinner,' he said. 'Before you get cold.'

And she suddenly couldn't think of anything she wanted more than to sit with him. Talk. This man had been nothing but gentlemanly and kind to her. He'd never shown her pity. Never reacted the way everyone else had.

'I'd love to have dinner with you.' She meant it. Smiled her thanks. And, though she tried her hardest not to look down at his mouth, at those lips that had once brushed her skin in the most intimate way, she couldn't help herself.

She wondered what it would be like to let down her guard completely and kiss him all over again?

The hotel's restaurant was dimly lit, and they were seated in a small alcove near the back, away from prying eyes, where they could pretend it was just the two of them.

From the reception area she could hear the piano being played—gentle, soothing music.

She'd got out of the pool and gone back to the changing room to get dressed on very shaky legs, unsure as to what was happening between the two of them. She wanted to let him in—but just a little bit. To let him know that they could talk about things, discuss the future. But something else seemed to have happened. An anticipation of so much more.

Hope.

Never in her wildest dreams had she ever thought she would be in this position—pregnant, about to become a mother, but also having a man tell her that she was *beautiful.*

It was a word she'd never thought would be used to describe her again. *Brave* got used an awful lot. *Courageous. Stubborn*, maybe.

But beautiful?

She'd stared at the mirror as she blow-dried her hair, focusing intently on her own face, gazing at the façade that it had taken her years to get used to. Inside, she still felt that she looked the way she had before the accident, so every time she looked in the mirror it was a stark reminder that she was different.

She'd tried to embrace that and look forward. Never allowing the melancholy and disappointment to overwhelm her. Never letting what Mike had done beat her down, because then he would have done what he'd set out to do. Never allowing the depression to set in, as it had with so many others affected in a similar way.

She was living the best way that she could. Under *her* rules. *Her* control. And now she was handing some of that control over to him.

She was different now. Not just in looks, but in character. She cared more for the underdogs in society; she listened, empathised, and she worked damned hard to make sure her patients felt empowered and brave and strong. She was their cheerleader. Their support. She knew she could coach women through the scariest moments of their lives, even as they felt they were being split in two, and she knew they *all* had the strength within them to get through it. She gave them everything they needed and asked for nothing in return.

But now Jamie was here and he wanted to pay her attention. He wasn't family, but he was trying to give her everything she needed and a whole lot more besides. He was able, it seemed, to see past the prickly exterior that she had first presented to him. He had pushed it to one side, had powered through, because he was invested in *her* well-being. *Her* thoughts and feelings. *Her* health. *Her* happiness.

And that felt odd. Disconcerting.

Good, but strange.

It had happened at university, too. During her training. Her teachers and lecturers had seen past her face and made sure she qualified, made sure she became the midwife she'd always wanted to be.

Perhaps she needed to give more people the benefit of the doubt?

'I'll have the Caesar salad to start, please, and I think I'll have the pan-seared chicken for my main, thank you,' she said to the waiter from behind her menu card.

'Smoked salmon and the pheasant for me, thanks.'

The waiter disappeared, having removed the menu cards with him.

Freya took a sip of her water. 'You must be used to English food now. Is there anything you miss from back home that you can't get here?'

'You don't serve as much goat as there was back home.' He smiled. 'Or *luqmat al-qadi*.'

She frowned, having never heard of that before. 'What is that?'

'They're like your pastries. A leavened dough that has been deep-fried, then soaked in a very sweet syrup.'

'Like a doughnut?'

'Not quite. My mother made them. Sometimes she would add cinnamon or sweet spices to them. They were out of this world.'

'Your mother cooked?'

'Occasionally. Not as often as she would have liked.'

'My mum likes to cook. She likes to feed people. There's always something on at her house.'

'It was the same at mine.'

She smiled. 'But, to be fair, your house was a palace, so…'

He laughed, good-naturedly. 'True.'

She took another sip of water. 'Is your mother still alive?'

His eyes darkened. 'No. She passed away a few months after my father did. It was a huge shock to lose them both so quickly like that. But I believe she died of a broken heart, after losing my father so suddenly.'

'She must have loved him very much.'

He nodded. 'Al Bakharis love deeply.'

Her breath caught in her throat as she imagined that sort of passion. The depth of love that one person could have for another. It was the type of love she had once imagined for herself. The type of love she had thought she had found with Mike, in the way he had so quickly and deeply fallen for her.

That kind of love was scary. Terrifying. It could totally

condemn you to a future filled with pain, misery and grief. Case in point: Jamie's mother dying of a broken heart. Perhaps love was more dangerous than people realised and they were fools to seek it out? It was best to keep things light. Casual. Even if it did leave you wanting...

'Have you ever felt that way about someone?' she asked.

'Not yet. That kind of love is the kind that stays for eternity. You will always be together, until the end of your days. If I had already found that, then you and I would not be in the situation we now find ourselves in.'

It was a stark reminder of exactly what this was between them.

A *situation*.

That was all. There was no point in reading anything else into it—even if he *had* told her she was beautiful. Even though he had cradled her in his arms until she'd stopped crying. Even if they had shared that one magical night together.

They'd been caught out by Mother Nature and now they were having to deal with the consequences.

That was all this was. Nothing more, nothing less.

So, despite the fact that they were sitting together in a restaurant, having only just a few minutes before shared a most intimate connection as she was wrapped in his embrace, Freya had to remind herself not to get carried away with *hope*. With *possibility*.

But she'd always been a dreamer and it was hard to switch that part of her brain off.

If the accident hadn't happened she would never have been at that charity ball. She would never have had that night with Jamie. She wouldn't be pregnant with twins. But they still would have met at work, and she would still have been attracted to him. The way she was now.

It was hard to tell herself that he probably didn't feel the same way. No matter what he'd said.

Reality hurt when she thought about that. She might have defied the odds and got pregnant, but Jamie was *not* going to be her knight in shining armour and she would do well to remember that.

'Please excuse me a moment.'

She stood, needing to escape to the bathroom for a minute alone—because she could feel tears threatening to fall down her face, and if she cried again he would comfort her again. He would touch her. Hold her. Try to make her feel better. And, despite her best instincts, she realised she *wanted* that.

Even though she shouldn't.

And she couldn't have that.

She stared at her tear-stained reflection in the bathroom mirror.

Why was life testing her so harshly?

CHAPTER FIVE

JAMIE WAS VERY pleased with the way their relationship was progressing. Freya's walls were starting to come down, and now she was letting him sit and talk to her at work. They socialised together sometimes, getting to know one another, and when they went to her check-ups and other appointments with her consultant they asked questions as if they were a real couple.

He'd sat by her side when she'd had her twenty-one-week scan, gripping her hand tightly in his, and they'd both been over the moon when the scan had confirmed that they were going to have non-identical twin boys.

Sons!

That was a big deal for Jamie. He'd always dreamed of having sons and raising them to be good, strong men. Sons to be proud of…sons he would support in their desire to do anything. He would not restrict their lives the way his had been, and if they wanted to become pilots or nurses, whatever their dreams could possibly be, he vowed to himself that he would help them achieve them in any way that he could.

His sons would be his heirs. Heirs to the throne. It was their destiny, but what would they know of it? What would they know of Majidar? With its rolling dunes, its intense heat and its beautiful people. He himself had yearned to leave and live a life he couldn't get there. Should he be the one to tell them that they must follow that path when he didn't want it for himself? Who was he to decide what they should do? He was their father, so shouldn't he want them to be happy more than anything else?

He'd sent news of the babies to his brother Ilias and younger sister Zahra. Both had responded with joy and delight, but both had asked him when he was coming home. With Freya at his side.

It was an awkward question to which he had no answer.

Zahra was already gushing about their wedding and all the things they'd need to organise. How could he tell her that it was probably never going to happen?

So he'd kept silent, swearing them to secrecy in his last email, until he knew what the next few months would bring. He'd used work as his main excuse. Said he was still under contract for another six months, with the possibility of a permanent post, and that he would not let people down when they were depending upon him.

Zahra had emailed back.

Six months? But the babies will be born by then!

It was all so difficult. So confusing. If he'd had his way then he and Freya would already be married. No need for a big ceremony in Majidar...no need to be driven down the streets in an open-topped car, waving to adoring crowds. He would present his marriage as a *fait accompli*. Everyone would just have to accept it.

If only Freya would accept it!

That would be easier, wouldn't it?

He hadn't mentioned it to her for a while, not wanting to raise such a difficult subject again when things between them seemed to be going so well.

When he'd first mentioned marriage he'd done it out of

duty. Done it because of the moral code that told him it was the right thing to do. Not for him, or for her, but for their children. Whether Freya liked it or not, her babies carried royal blood and he would not have them being illegitimate. He hadn't thought too much about whether a marriage between them would work out or not. It just had to be. Details, emotions, feelings—all those could be worked out later, as time allowed them to know each other more.

But now...?

Life was even more complicated.

He liked Freya a lot. He cared for her. And the more he got to know her, the more he realised that if they were to get married then he would have a happy life with her, a happy marriage. He felt it in his bones. She was strong and loving and kind, the bravest woman he had ever known, and he felt proud that a woman like that was carrying his children. What a role model she would be! How much she would love them!

His feelings for her were deepening every day. Each time she laughed or smiled his heart expanded a little bit more. Each time she trusted him with a hint of intimacy— a confession, a secret, a story from her past—his feelings for her grew.

It was confusing. The line between emotion and duty was blending, merging. How could he get her to understand how he felt if he didn't even understand it, himself?

It was the end of November, and at seven months pregnant Freya felt huge. It had been many weeks since she had last been able to reach her own feet, and she thanked the Lord that Jamie, at least, seemed quite happy to lift her feet up onto his lap and massage them for her when they had a break at work.

Her body was protesting. She was knocking back strawberry milkshakes as if they were going out of fashion, and she dreaded to think about how much extra weight she was putting on. But it was all for a good cause, so she was trying to be relaxed about it.

There wasn't long left, and this probably wouldn't happen again, so she was trying to enjoy her pregnancy for as long as she could.

The babies were good movers, kicking and stretching at all hours of the day and night, and she would often sit at work with one hand on her swollen baby, feeling their movements. It was very reassuring.

They were good sizes, too. She and Jamie had attended many scans which had not only marked the growth of the babies, but also the growth of their ever-changing relationship.

She'd started to get the nursery ready at home. Jamie had even come over one evening to help paint the walls and put up some stencils. He'd even climbed a ladder to hang up the new curtains she'd made.

It was almost as if they were a real couple getting ready for their future.

Only without the living together and the sex.

And sex had been high on her mind lately, despite her burgeoning size. It had to be the hormones! She was blaming them entirely as her mind filled with X-rated images of her and Jamie doing really naughty things together.

It didn't help that he was so easy on the eye. Or that he was kind and thoughtful and gentlemanly. Seeing him smile delighted her, and she often found herself reaching out to touch him—a hand on his arm, his shoulder. Touching the small of his back as she passed behind him at work. Just a small contact. But enough to make her desires surge and make her brain remind her of what that one night had been like and how wonderful it would feel to experience that again. To touch him in other places. To have him touch her...

Enough, Freya!

It would never be like that between them again.

Would it?

She blinked, trying to dismiss the thrilling images she'd created, and instead focused on the patient notes she was filling out. Her patient, Rosie Clay, had been progressing through labour quite well until suddenly the baby had started showing decelerations. The infant had gone into distress and Rosie had been rushed to theatre for an emergency Caesarean section. Rosie was now fine, but her baby girl was in the NICU, having aspirated meconium, which meant she had passed her first stool whilst still in the womb.

She dropped the pen to stretch out her shoulders, thrusting them back and trying to roll them. She suddenly felt hands slide down over them.

'Tense?' Jamie asked.

You betcha.

'Yeah, a little. It got a bit frantic in Theatre just now.'

'I heard. The baby's in NICU?'

'A little girl.'

'Little girls are strong.'

She thought of her own babies. Of the struggles they might have in the future together. Alone, without a father.

'So are little boys.'

Jamie's hands felt great, massaging away the tenseness of her muscles, releasing the knots and strain that she'd been carrying all night. She could groan because he was making her feel so good!

'You can stop now.'

She pulled away, not wanting to embarrass herself. Jamie was just doing it out of duty, anyway. She'd accepted that ages ago, and reminded herself daily not to get too carried away with what was happening between them. It was the babies he was interested in. And she was dreaming again. Allowing herself to get carried away with fantasy.

It was her ability to dream and fantasise that had got her through the long, painful days after her attack; it had been the only way she could escape the pain and the four walls that had bound her so tightly.

He settled into a seat beside her. 'Do you need anything to drink? Eat?'

'No, I'm fine, thank you,' she answered, and heard a harshness coming out in her voice that she hadn't intended. But this was so frustrating! Having something so close she could almost touch it. Wanting something—*someone*—so badly, but knowing it could never happen.

'You're sure?'

She nodded, fighting the urge to yell at him, to tell him to leave her alone because that was what he was going to do anyway. At some point. And the idea of it was breaking her heart.

She'd grown to love his friendship, his kindness, his support—even his attentiveness. But sometimes she got angry—mostly with herself—knowing it wouldn't be for ever.

Freya had tried to keep herself distanced from it, but lately it had become nigh on impossible and her hormones were probably to blame for that too! It was as if her body had become conditioned to let him in. To allow him to care for her as the natural father of her children. But she had other feelings developing too, and they were dangerous and stupid!

Beside them, the buzzer rang. Someone required admission.

In the evening, the doors were locked for security, so anyone turning up in the middle of the night, in labour or otherwise, had to buzz to be let in. There was a security camera so the staff could see who was there.

Freya looked at the monitor and its grainy black and

white image. A man stood there, desperately looking up at the camera, wrapped in a coat and scarf.

She picked up the phone to speak through the intercom. 'Hello?'

'My wife! My wife's having the baby!'

'Okay, sir, I'm going to buzz you through.' She went to press the button.

'No, you don't understand! She's having it *now*. In the car! I can see the head!'

Freya glanced at Jamie, who got up at a run and raced down the corridor, grabbing a mobile pack from the supply room as he did so.

'Someone will be with you in a moment. Hang on!'

She knew she wouldn't be able to run like Jamie, but he would need back-up. It was freezing out. And there was a frost.

She got to her feet and moved down the corridor as fast as she could, her feet protesting, the babies kicking at the sudden rush of adrenaline in her system. She grabbed extra blankets and slapped the button release to open the doors, then took the stairs.

It would be quicker than waiting for the lift. It was just two flights.

She held her belly with one hand as she hurried down the stairs, her other hand on the rail, and by the time she got to the bottom she was out of breath and the twins were kicking madly. She burst through another set of double doors, hurried across the lobby and pressed the buzzer for the outer doors, feeling a wall of cold air hit her as she raced outside.

There was a car parked in the dropping-off bay, its doors open on one side—the guy from the monitor was in the front and Jamie was crouching by the back. She could see there was already a little bit of ice forming on the path. She hoped the gritters would be along soon...

'That's it, Catherine, push as hard as you can!' she heard Jamie say.

'What have we got?' She pulled her penlight torch from her top pocket and shone it into the interior of the car.

A woman was lying in the back, her dress up around her waist and her baby's head already born. There was no point in trying to get this patient into a wheelchair and whizzed upstairs now. She was going to have this baby in the car.

'Catherine—thirty-nine, forty weeks' gestation.'

'Okay, anything we need to be worried about?'

'Just the cold.'

'I've brought extra blankets.'

Jamie turned to grab them and laid them over the head-rest, so they'd be ready when he needed them. He already had his gloves on, had the kit open, and was ready to clip off the cord.

'Catherine, one more push with the next contraction. I want you to push as hard as you can, okay? Let's get this baby out and safe into your arms.'

Catherine nodded furiously, sucked in a huge breath and began to push.

At first nothing happened, and for a brief second Freya worried about there being a possible shoulder dystocia, but then slowly the baby began to emerge. Catherine sucked in another breath and began to push again, and this time the baby slithered out, crying immediately in protest.

'Well done, Catherine!' Jamie had caught the baby and immediately put it into its mother's arms, grabbing the blankets to drape over them both before he clipped and cut the cord.

'Oh, my God!' Catherine cried, looking down at her baby with love and joy.

'You did it! You gave birth in the car!' cried the new dad. 'The upholstery's probably ruined, but I don't care!'

Behind her, Freya heard the doors open and Mona appeared, pushing a wheelchair. They needed to get the new mum and baby inside so they could do the proper checks and get the placenta delivered.

Jamie took the baby and passed it to Freya, so that he could help get Catherine out of the car, lowering her gently into the wheelchair. She was shivering and shaking, so he wrapped the last blanket around her shoulders.

'Let's get her inside.'

They all hurried into the lobby, and Freya pressed the button for the lift before passing the baby back to its mother.

Catherine gazed into the loving eyes of her husband. 'We have a *son*!'

The man laid his forehead against his wife's and kissed her. 'We do. Well done! I'm so proud of you.'

He turned to look at Freya and Jamie.

'I'm Martin—pleased to meet you.' He shook their hands. 'This little one is so precious to us. He's an IVF baby.'

'Congratulations.'

'We thought we'd left it too late, but now we have him. A son. Thank you all so much!'

'Catherine did all the hard work,' said Freya, and smiled.

The lift doors pinged open and they wheeled Catherine through to an empty room and helped her onto the bed. They injected the syntocinon and the placenta was delivered almost without Catherine noticing as she cradled her little boy.

'Have you thought of a name yet?' asked Freya, who'd donned gloves and was beginning to check it.

Catherine smiled wanly, looking tired. 'Jackson.'

'That's a beautiful name.'

But something was wrong. The placenta was not as it should be. Freya felt the hairs go up on the back of her neck and instinctively knew. Catherine had gone incredibly pale, and now she rested her head back against the pillow.

She caught the baby before Catherine could drop him.
'Martin, take the baby!'

'What's going on?'

Jamie lifted up the sheet and grimaced. 'Haemorrhage.'

He smacked the red button behind Catherine's head and
an alarm sounded. Before they knew it the room was filling
with people and Catherine was being whisked out on her
bed, headed for Theatre. Jamie went with them.

Freya was left with Martin and the baby, in a room with
blood all over the floor.

'What just happened?' asked Martin.

'It looks like Catherine is losing too much blood.' She
examined the placenta more and realised there was a piece
missing. 'Retained placenta. That's why she began to bleed
so heavily.' She laid a hand upon his arm. 'They'll look
after her.'

'I *can't* lose her. I can't lose my wife!'

'Come and take a seat, Martin.'

She guided him safely to a chair and helped him sit. She
needed to examine the baby, but she was very conscious of
the fact that Martin would probably be reluctant to hand
his son over right now.

'Emergencies can be frightening, but she was in the
right place when it happened. If she'd given birth earlier
and you hadn't made it here… You did, though. She's in
good hands.'

'She'll be okay?'

'Everyone will do their best.'

She couldn't promise him anything. She couldn't tell
him everything would be all right because she didn't know.
Haemorrhages happened, and sometimes they went badly.
The medical team would do everything they could for her.

'I need to check Jackson. I'll just take him over to this
cot—is that okay? You can come with me. Watch what
I'm doing.'

He nodded and handed her the baby.

Freya took him gently and with the utmost respect. This man had just watched his wife collapse and be taken from him. He felt lost and bereft, and the only thing he had to cling on to with any certainty was his son.

She decided to talk him through it, so he would understand all that she was doing. If he understood what she was doing perhaps he would feel he had a bit of control over *something*.

'First I'll check his breathing.' She looked to Martin to make sure he was listening.

He nodded.

'He cried immediately after birth, and his respiratory rate is good, so he scores two points on the APGAR scale. The scale is out of ten points overall, and the higher the score, the better.'

'Okay...'

'Now I'm going to use my stethoscope to check his heart rate, and this is the most important.'

She put the earbuds in her ears and laid the stethoscope on Jackson's chest. Over a hundred beats per minute.

'He scores two for this as well. His heart rate is *good*, Martin.'

'Good.'

'Next I need to check his muscle tone, and I can see here that he has good active motion, so again he scores two.'

She talked Martin through checking for a grimace response or reflex irritability, and because Jackson began to cry she again scored him two.

'And now skin colour. His entire body is nicely pink, except his hands and feet, but that's normal. His circulation is good, so that's another point. A score of nine. You have a healthy little baby boy, Martin.' She wrapped Jackson up again and handed him back to his father. 'Do you have clothes and a nappy for him?'

Martin thought for a moment. 'Oh, it's all in the car.'

It was important to get Jackson dressed and wrapped up warmly. 'I can go and fetch them for you, if you want?'

'Would you mind?'

'Of course not.'

He reached into his back pocket and pulled out some keys. 'It's all in the boot. The lock release is on the key fob.'

'Okay. I'll do that, and then I'll get you a cup of tea. I think you've earned it.'

'You too, I would imagine.' He looked at her belly. 'How far along are you?'

'Seven months. With twins.'

'Life's about to get crazy for us all, then?'

She nodded. He had no idea how crazy her life already was.

'I'll be back in a few minutes. Any problems, just hit the orange call button on the side of the bed. Someone will come and check on you.'

She closed the door behind her and began to waddle down the corridor once again.

Boy, were her ankles killing her! And what a night shift this was turning out to be! The last time she'd helped deliver a baby in a car parked outside it had been in the middle of summer, when the nights were a lot warmer and they didn't have to worry about tiny babies freezing in the night air.

And this had been her first delivery working with Jamie. Usually they got to work alone, sometimes with another midwife, but she'd not yet had the chance to watch him in action like that. She'd been with him in Theatre before, but that had been different—their patient had been unconscious under a general anaesthetic, because it had been an emergency delivery.

Tonight she'd seen how good he was with a patient. How calm and encouraging. How he'd coached his patient to breathe and push. She could see why he loved midwifery so much, because he'd simply been alive with all that had been going on around him, and even though it had been an unusual delivery, out of the hospital, he had remained cool and in control. Even when the haemorrhage had begun he had worked quickly and calmly.

The lift doors pinged open. She didn't feel like taking the stairs again so soon. She waddled her way across the lobby and opened the double doors to go outside. The cold air hit her again and she glanced down at the keys in her hand to see which side of the fob she needed to open the boot of the car.

She walked straight out, without thinking, onto the pathway, and it happened almost instantly.

Her feet began to slide on the black ice, she lost her footing and slipped and, not having any control over her centre of gravity, she went up into the air backwards, her arms flailing, and landed heavily on the ground, the back of her head smacking hard onto the concrete.

Pain shot through her skull and her back and her belly. She reached up to rub at her head, but felt the world begin to fade and grow dark.

The last thing she saw was the clear dark sky, inky black with shining stars twinkling way beyond her, and then there was the sight of two men in dark suits appearing over her, one reaching into his jacket for a walkie-talkie and saying something in a language she didn't understand.

She closed her eyes and drifted away.

Jamie was relieved. They'd managed to save their patient. Catherine's haemorrhage had been contained, the retained piece of placenta removed and checked. The bleeding had slowed and Catherine's womb had contracted fully. Her pressure was slowly coming back up and her heart rate was getting better.

The surgeons had done it.

He let out a huge sigh of relief and removed his mask and gown, disposing of them in the trash and going to wash his hands, whilst a porter took his patient to a side room for recovery and to be monitored.

It had been touch and go there for a while, he thought as he stood washing his hands. But they had prevailed. *All* of them. Working together to save their patient and give her a chance at life. There was nothing like this feeling in the whole wide world. This miracle they called life. He watched new life coming into the world every day, and it was a privilege to be amongst those who helped women achieve it.

Days like today reiterated for him the rightness of his choice. It had been *right* to leave Majidar, and it had been *right* to pursue this dream of his. Look at what he had done this night. Earlier he'd delivered one baby, safely in a hospital bed, and now he'd safely delivered not only a baby in a car, but a mother too. Everyone in the team had done that.

Outside, he could hear a bit of a commotion. Loud voices. Men. His guards, by the sound of it. What on earth was going on?

He dried his hands on paper towels and disposed of them in the bin. He wanted to see whatever this noise was about, sort it out, and then go check on the new baby. He'd delivered the little boy—it was up to him to write up the notes.

When he pushed through the doors he froze as he saw his security men were on the ward, arguing with Jules. Whatever were they doing in here? Why did they seem so upset? They had strict instructions not to come onto the ward unless there was a just cause.

The only thing he could think of was Freya, but she'd been safe in that delivery room when he'd left with his patient for Theatre, so that left something to do with his brother the King.

Ilias? No, it can't be. He's sick, sometimes, but it can't be now!

Jules threw her hands into the air as the two guards barged past her towards Jamie.

'Jamie, these men—'

'Sadiq? Mujab? What's going on?'

But before they could say anything Jules barged through them and laid a hand upon his arm. 'It's Freya. She's had an accident.'

CHAPTER SIX

IT WAS THE pain she felt first, as she began to become aware of the world once more. Everything felt sore, but the worst thing was her headache. It was as if she had a crown of intense burning fire around her skull. Her mouth felt dry too, and she tried to lick her lips.

'Freya? Open your eyes.'

Jamie.

Jamie was here. Why was he in her bedroom? What had happened?

As she struggled to implement his instruction to open her eyes she began to remember some weird, hazy things.

A woman in a car.

A baby wrapped in blankets in her arms.

The cold.

A set of car keys.

The twinkling stars above.

Two stern-looking men crouching over her, babbling in a language she didn't understand.

And then she remembered.

The black ice.

Slipping on the pavement and falling.

She opened her eyes, struggling to focus, but she could only just make out a face. A man's face. Dark hair and midnight eyes.

'Jamie…'

She saw a relieved smile break across his face and she tried to reach up to touch him, to make sure he was real, but it was as if she was uncoordinated, or didn't have the strength.

'You've had a nasty fall. Knocked yourself out. The babies are okay. You've had a little bleeding, but they're okay. We're keeping you in for monitoring and bed rest.'

Freya blinked as she processed this huge amount of information. 'What? Keeping me in? No.'

She panicked, tried to get up, tried to get out of bed, but dizziness assailed her and she felt his firm hands holding her arms, pressing her down.

'You need to stay in bed.'

'No, I'm—'

'Freya, for once you are going to have to do as you are told!'

And then she heard it in his voice. *Fear*.

He *cared*.

She blinked again and tried to focus on his face, but she just felt so tired. Slowly, inexorably, her eyes closed once again and she drifted off to sleep.

'Concussion?' She stared at Jamie.

'Yes. You're also still bleeding and you have high blood pressure, so you're staying in on bed rest.'

Staying in. In hospital.

Adrenaline was pulsing through her, making her legs twitch. She wanted to run. Wanted to get out of there.

'But the babies are fine, you said.'

'I did.'

'But I need to stay on bed rest? Are you kidding me?'

'What would *you* say to a patient seven months pregnant with twins, who's had a nasty fall, hit her head, has high BP and is bleeding? Would you tell her to carry on, or would you tell her to stay in bed?'

She bit her bottom lip, eyeing the door. He was right, but she didn't want to admit it. She *would* tell a patient in that situation that she needed to stay in. But this was different.

She'd been trapped in a hospital bed before. Lying there, gripping onto the bedrails, whilst a doctor and a nurse debrided the dead tissue from her face. It had felt as if the acid was being splashed onto her all over again. The pain interminable.

Being back in a hospital bed, being told she had to stay there, was making her feel trapped. Claustrophobic. As if she couldn't breathe.

She turned away, upset but not wanting to let him see her cry, her gaze falling on the fruit baskets and the balloons filling her room and all the cards on the windowsill that sent best wishes from her work colleagues and her family.

It was all terribly familiar. She was unable to move, feeling terrified and afraid. Her own life was out of her control. In the hands of doctors.

How had she forgotten what that felt like?

'I'm not sure I can do this,' she whispered.

'You have to.'

'You can't make me. I can discharge myself.'

'You'd have to get past the guards I'll put on your door first.' He raised an eyebrow. Daring her to challenge his authority.

She stared at him. He'd never ordered her about like this before. Never challenged her.

She baulked at his attempt. 'You wouldn't…?'

He leaned forward over the end of the bed. 'Try me. I've let you do this your way ever since day one. I have acquiesced to your wishes and tried my best not to upset you. But, damn you, Freya, if you get out of that bed and endanger yourself and those babies then, so help me, I will not be held responsible for my actions!'

He meant it. Every word.

She crossed her arms and looked away.

Again her life was being taken out of her control by other people. She had vowed never to let that happen to her again. This was *her* life and she wanted to be the one in charge, making all the decisions.

However, she had no doubt that he would post guards on her door, and then everyone would know who Jamie was. And as soon as that little nugget got out her life would most definitely not be her own. There would be reporters and gossip and her happy, quiet little life, hidden away on the night shift, would be destroyed.

'Fine.'

It wasn't fine. Far from it. But this wasn't just about her any more. She wasn't in this bed alone. She had two babies to think of.

He stared hard at her, his hands on his hips. 'Fine?'

'I'll stay in bed.'

'Good.'

'But on one condition.'

There was that eyebrow again. Wary. 'Yes?'

'Someone brings me a goddamned strawberry milkshake!'

There was the ghost of a smile and then he bowed, almost to the floor. 'Yes, Your Majesty.'

Freya was a cranky patient. Short on temper, irritable, bad of mood. Nervous.

But didn't they say that medics made the worst patients?

'I know it's difficult, but you need to try and relax,' he'd told her.

She'd glared at him. 'How can I? When being here reminds me of what it was like before?'

He'd placed his hand on hers. 'I know. But this is different. No one is going to hurt you now. I won't let them.'

She'd had another scan, and the babies looked fine. The consultant believed the bleeding was coming from a small lesion on her cervix, but it was nothing sinister. They'd tested it and believed the lesion had occurred as a result of her fall. The pressure of two babies on her cervix as well as the severity of the impact of her hitting the concrete had caused a small tear.

He'd given her books to read, had brought delicious yet healthy treats, and he would often sit with her, slowly massaging her feet or her shoulders as she tried to relax.

His favourite moments were spent watching her as she read. The small divot that formed between her brows, the cute way she sometimes bit her bottom lip, the way she would hurriedly turn the page, as if she just couldn't wait to find out what would happen next. Those were the moments when she forgot where she was.

She looked up at him and caught him staring. 'What are you doing?'

He smiled. 'Looking at you.'

Freya frowned and smiled at the same time. 'Well, don't.'

'Why not?'

'It's weird. I don't like people looking at me.'

'No, and you don't like people making assumptions about what happened to you. You don't like people showing sympathy. Was I doing *any* of those things?'

She looked as if she was thinking about that. 'I guess not.'

'Well, then, I'll continue to look at you.'

'But why?'

'Because I like doing it.'

It was true. He did. She was such a complicated person, prickly when scared, but fascinating. And she really was beautiful. Outwardly and inside. Her scars—shocking because of how she'd got them—were totally a part of her character. Who she was.

'But why?' She really sounded confused.

He sighed. 'Does it ever occur to you that you might be worth looking at?'

Her eyes clouded over. 'No.'

'Well, then, you're wrong.'

'Are you sure *you* didn't get the bump on the head? Perhaps you should be lying here instead of me?'

'Perhaps I should be lying *next* to you? Beside you?'

That stopped her from speaking. She immediately looked down at her book, tried to read on, but he could see that she wasn't taking anything in.

Eventually she looked up at him, exasperated, and said, 'You can't say things like that, Jamie. It's not fair.'

'Even if it's true?'

'Even if it's true. Even if you did want to be lying here next to me you shouldn't say it—because then I start to get the feelings, and I don't want to get the feelings, because some day you're going to leave. You'll leave us, Jamie, you *will*. You can't deny that.'

No. He couldn't. She was right. One day he would get called back and then what? If he tried to start a relationship with this woman it would always be there, hanging over them like a swinging blade, ready to fall down and sever them in two. Was that fair? On either of them? On the babies?

'I'll go and make us some tea.'

He got up and slipped from the room, his mind dark with thoughts of ascension to the throne and responsibility and living a life behind walls. Never to enjoy himself again. Never to deliver another baby.

Away from Freya and his sons.

He fought the urge to punch a wall. It was all just so maddening! He'd fought to get access into her life, which she had finally given, and they were becoming used to one another, liked one another—but for what?

Either way, he was going to lose someone or something. Majidar, or Freya and the babies.

Or maybe he'd just lose himself?

'Mona, please stop fussing.' Freya laid a hand on her friend's as she continued to fiddle about with Freya's sheets.

If she was going to visit, she'd prefer it if her friend just kept her up to date with what was happening on the ward, had a cup of tea with her and chatted. Not fussed about like an old mother hen.

'I can't help it.'

Freya smiled. 'Sit. Eat one of these.' She passed over a box of chocolates that her mum had brought on her last visit. 'They're truffles.'

'Oh! Okay.' Mona took the box.

'The praline one is nice.'

Mona checked to see which one that was, and then popped it into her mouth and began to make appreciative sounds.

'Told you.'

Freya lay back against the pillows and turned away from the bright light pouring in through the window. It made a pleasant change from the dark, grey wintry days they had been having recently. Life was passing her by and she was still stuck here.

'I got the Christmas decorations out just now. I'm going to pop them up later.'

Freya frowned. 'It's still November.'

'It's never too early.'

'I beg to differ.'

'Well, *you* would. You've always been a Grumpus around Christmas.'

Mona was wrong. Freya loved Christmas. But these last

few years she'd begun to resent it. Everyone she knew was married or in a relationship, or had kids, or both, so they had a reason to enjoy Christmas. They were with their loved ones. They were making memories. For Freya every Christmas was spent with her mum, and though she loved her mum it wasn't what Freya wanted.

She had big dreams of what Christmas should be. Of a Christmas morning on which she could sit and watch her children open their presents with squeals of delight. Of a festive season during which she could go out and build snowmen and have snowball fights, visit Santa in his grotto, go to see a pantomime.

Her mum was great company, but she didn't want to do any of those things. She liked a quiet, understated Christmas, where her only concern was whether the turkey would be cooked and whether they'd finish eating in time to watch the Queen's Speech. Then she'd fall asleep in her chair, until Freya woke her later in the evening to see if she wanted a mince pie.

'Wait 'til next Christmas. You'll have twins!' exclaimed Mona.

Freya nodded. But would she be alone with them? Or would Jamie be there? How was she going to cope with raising two babies? She would have to brave *everything*. Living during the day time. Seeing all those people. Changing her shifts at work because the hospital nursery only took children during daylight hours.

Her whole life was going to change.

It wasn't meant to have happened like this! She was meant to have been *happy*! Thrilled that she was having children. She *was* thrilled, but it wasn't turning out to be the fairy tale she'd imagined it would be.

'Are you and Jamie spending Christmas together?'

'I think he's working.'

'But he'll have *some* time at home. Are you going to do anything special?'

'I don't think so. I'll be at Mum's, as usual, I guess.'

'You aren't spending *any* time together?'

This line of questioning was making her feel very uncomfortable. 'He hasn't said anything.'

Mona handed her back the box of chocolates, looking sceptical. 'Is there something you're not telling me, Freya?'

'Like what?'

'About Jamie? Who were those men in suits? They looked like bodyguards.'

She hurried to try and put Mona off the scent. 'Oh, I don't know. Just some guys who were passing, I think.'

'Well, for guys who were *just passing* they hang around a lot. And they talk to Jamie a lot.'

'He's probably just thanking them.'

'He's not some secret undercover boss, or anything?' Mona grinned. 'Because if he's secretly the CEO of the NHS then I think we need to enlighten him about a few things.'

Freya laughed. 'Jamie? No!'

'I just think it's strange, that's all. They even wear those earpiece things...like Secret Service guys.'

Thank goodness she didn't blush as she'd used to. 'Really? That's weird. But, no, Jamie is just a midwife. Honestly.'

Mona nodded, watching her. 'Okay.' She got up and went to the door, put her hand on the handle. 'You know, I still don't understand why you two aren't together. You obviously slept together, and you seem to get on. So what's keeping you apart?'

Freya shrugged. 'He's a temp. He'll be leaving soon— there's no point.'

'But Sarah from HR told me that they've offered him a permanent post, which he's accepted.'

That was news to Freya. Why hadn't Jamie told her? That he was planning on sticking around for her and the babies?

'I didn't know.'

'It's clear he has feelings for you.'

Her smile was tinged with sadness. 'For the babies, not me.'

'You really think that? I've seen the way his eyes shine when he talks about you. The way his face lights up.'

'He talks about me?'

Mona nodded. 'Frequently. He *cares* about you. You must see it.'

She cared about him, too. Probably more than she should. But she'd been holding back. Afraid of showing any of it. Alone in the day, she dreamed about what it would be like to be with him, and at night her dreams were filled with his smiling face and his steaming hot kisses.

No wonder she woke up cranky. She couldn't have what she wanted the most. Was afraid to let herself have him in case she lost him.

'It's complicated.'

Mona laughed. 'When isn't it? Look, I've got to go, but he'll be in later. Do me a favour and be nice to him. He's doing his best, but you're a bloody expert at keeping people at a distance. Let him care for you, Freya. He's not Mike.'

No. She knew that.

'It's difficult.'

'"*Tis better to have loved and lost, than never to have loved at all.*" Who was it who said that? Was it Shakespeare?'

'I never was any good at English.'

'Me neither.' Mona opened the door. 'But we're very good at chemistry!'

And she gave Freya a tiny wave before she headed off to do her shift.

Freya lay there on the bed, thinking over all the things her friend had said. Jamie was staying on permanently. He had feelings for her. She had feelings for him. The babies would be here soon.

We could be a family.

If she were only brave enough to let it happen.

Was it better to love someone and then lose them than not to love at all?

It sounded to her like devastation. And Jamie's mother had died of it.

Could she let her babies grow to love their father in the knowledge that he would desert them at some point? And would her babies one day leave her too?

But the temptation to give in, to try it, to accept the love and care that Jamie clearly wanted to give her, was extremely potent. The proximity of all that imagined happiness was intoxicating.

If she gave herself the chance to explore that happiness, to cast all her concerns to one side and just live in the moment with him, what would that be like?

Her heart soared at the idea. At the hope. At the possibility of such happiness.

Didn't she deserve it?

No matter how short-lived?

Jamie opened the door to Freya's room and stopped, frozen in place, when he saw how she looked.

Out of bed. Getting dressed.

Smiling. No. *Beaming.*

'What's happened?'

'I've been told I can go home and start my maternity leave. As long as I rest.'

He frowned and went to the end of her bed, picked up her chart and began to read it. 'The bleeding's stopped?'

'For almost a day now.'

'And your blood pressure is down?'

'Almost to normal levels. I can get out of here. You've no idea how much I've longed to hear that.'

'Well, I know how much you've been bugging your consultant about it, so I have a fair idea.'

He smiled. These last few days had been hard for her.

'All this bed rest... I could have done it at home in the first place. There was no need for me to have taken up a bed.'

'There was *every* need. Here, I've brought you a milk-shake.' He passed her the drink he'd bought from the café downstairs. 'Why don't you sit down? I'll do your packing for you.'

She held up her hand. 'No, thank you! I don't need you seeing all my knickers and things.'

He smiled, picking up a pair of unflattering maternity pants. 'Why ever not? I've seen—no, *tasted*—what's underneath.'

And then he grinned, because he saw how flustered that comment made her.

She snatched them from him. 'I haven't been allowed to do anything for myself for days now. At least let me do this.'

'Okay.' He sank onto her bed and watched her busily pack her holdall, the excitement in her eyes at finally being able to leave the hospital almost palpable. 'I hope when you get home you do actually rest.'

'I'm fine. I've been discharged. There are things I have to get done. The nursery isn't ready and—'

'Then I'll help you. Tell me what needs doing and I'll get it sorted.'

She stopped to look at him. 'How will you have the time? Now that you're a *permanent* member of staff? Yes, I know about that. Why didn't you tell me?'

'I was waiting until I'd actually signed the contract.

Which I did about twenty minutes ago. So here I am. Telling you. Don't change the subject.'

'I'm not.'

'You did. Now, what do you need help with in the nursery?'

'I've ordered two cribs, which are going to be delivered, and some furniture—all of which will need building.'

He nodded. 'I'll do it.'

'I can do it. I'm not helpless.'

'I know you're not, Freya, but you are still meant to be resting.'

'Don't I get *any* say in this?'

He thought for a moment, then smiled. 'No.'

She smiled back. 'You're infuriating, you know?'

Jamie nodded, happy to be so if it meant she was taking it easy. He had no doubt that if he let her go home without supervision she'd be up ladders and cleaning and painting and building wardrobes and putting herself straight back into a hospital bed. He couldn't allow that to happen.

'How are you getting home?'

'Mum's coming over on the bus, then we're using my car to drive back. It's been in the staff car park ever since my fall on the ice.'

'Okay.' He knew her mum would take good care of her. 'I'm on shift now until seven, but I'll pop round straight after—see what needs doing and formulate a plan.'

'You don't need to babysit me.'

'I know.' He stood up and dropped a kiss onto her cheek.

She looked a little startled. 'I'm a grown woman.'

He smiled again, as his mind handily provided him with flashbacks to that steamy night many moons ago. 'I *know*.'

'Stop it.'

'What?'

'Remembering what we did.'

'I'm not allowed to remember?'

'Not that, no.'

'Why?'

'Because of the way it makes you smile. The way you look like you hope it will happen again.'

He stood up and stepped between her and the holdall. 'Would that be a bad thing?'

She was breathing heavily, and licked her lips. She tried her hardest not to look at his lips, but failed.

'Yes.'

'We wouldn't know unless we tried.'

She licked her lips again, bit the lower one and then looked away. Then back again.

'I'm on bed rest.'

'We could be in bed.' He smiled.

She swallowed. 'Please don't, Jamie.'

'Why?'

'Because we *can't*!'

'Who says?'

'The consultant. He said no sex.'

Well, wasn't *that* interesting? Freya herself wasn't saying no. She wasn't turning him down because *she* didn't want to, but because it was a strict order from her consultant.

He smiled, feeling a swell of joy not only in his heart, but elsewhere too.

'I can wait.' He paused to stare at her, then laid his hand on her arm, stilling her, drawing her close. 'Won't you give us a chance to be together?' he whispered.

Her eyes looked up at him, full of conflict, yearning and desire.

Until he bent his head and kissed her.

CHAPTER SEVEN

HIS LIPS WERE SOFT, gentle. It was the most tender kiss. As his lips met hers it was as if the world slowed. Everything around her faded into nothingness, and all that mattered, all she could feel, was his lips pressed against her own. She forgot her scars, forgot her fears.

Tenderness. Heat. Her heart racing inside her chest... pounding away within the cage that contained it.

He's kissing me!

She'd thought about what it would be like to kiss him again, without hiding behind masks and anonymity.

She knew him now. Knew who Jamie was. *What* he was. He'd become her friend as well as her colleague, and somehow, without her realising how, he had wormed his way into her affections. She cared for him. Worried about him. Feared for their future.

And she had wondered what it might be like for them both if their lives were different. If he weren't heir to the throne of some faraway kingdom, and if she weren't the woman who hid behind the scars on her face.

And now he's kissing me.

She felt herself sink further into his embrace. Felt her body press up against his. God, she needed this! Needed *him*.

Freya had never imagined losing herself to something so wonderful as this.

But it felt so right. It felt so *good*.

She was almost dizzy with all the sensations running rampant through her system, with all the emotions she was experiencing. What was it doing to her blood pressure?

I need to breathe.

She pulled back, looked at him, her eyes dazed with confusion.

'You kissed me.'

'Yes.' His eyes shone darkly, with a heat in them she had never noticed before.

'Why?' It was a whisper.

'Because I needed to.'

'Needed?'

A smile. 'Wanted.'

'Me?'

Another smile. Broader this time. 'Of *course* you. When will you start to believe that?'

Her words caught in her throat for a moment, a painful lump of disbelief that she had to swallow down, blinking rapidly to stop the tears from falling.

'I see you, Freya. Who you are. I see the woman who stands before me today and she's the bravest, strongest, most wonderful woman I know.'

'I don't...'

'You keep comparing yourself to who you used to be. I don't know who you used to be, or what you looked like before, and I don't need to know. That was the past. What matters is the present, the *now*, and the woman before me is beautiful. She is caring and loving, fragile yet strong and courageous. As beautiful on the inside as she is on the outside. That's who I see.'

He tucked a strand of her hair behind her ear.

'But...'

'No buts. No whys or maybes. Just accept it. Can you

accept the fact that I have feelings for you and that I'd like us to be more than just friends?'

It was everything she could possibly want to hear. Everything she's thought she'd never hear. And here he was. This man. This drop-dead gorgeous, handsome *prince* was saying it to her!

And suddenly she felt afraid. Afraid of what it all meant. If she accepted it—if she let him in—then wouldn't she be making herself vulnerable all over again?

But she was teetering on the edge of a giant abyss and she wanted to fall for him. Wanted to believe so much!

Her heartbeat pounded in her ears. She felt hot and dizzy with it all. But she wasn't ill. Just lovesick. And she wanted that happiness, even if it was just for a short while. She'd accept it and have him for as long as she could have him.

'I can.'

Hesitantly she smiled at him, watching as his face lit up.

He let out a heavy breath and beamed at her, before pulling her back into his embrace. 'Then let's get you safely home and we'll take it from there.'

It was strange to be back home. Her mum put on a pot of decaffeinated coffee to brew. Freya sat on the couch, her feet up, cradling her mug.

'I think Jamie and I are going to give things a go.'

It felt odd to say it. *Jamie and I.*

Her mum smiled at her over her own mug. 'Really? Oh, I'm so pleased to hear that. I really am.'

'We don't know what's going to happen, but we're going to take it a day at a time. It's all we *can* do, really.'

'Stop downplaying it, Freya. You're already making it sound like it's doomed before it starts.'

'I'm just being realistic.'

'No, you're trying to protect yourself before you get hurt and it won't work that way. If you are going to give it a try with Jamie then you've got to be in it wholeheartedly. One hundred per cent. Not with one foot already out of the door.'

'You think that's what I'm doing?'

Her mum put her mug down and came over to sit beside her. Took her hand in her own. 'I know that's what you're doing. But Jamie's different. He's honourable and kind and I think he cares deeply about you. You can't play with his feelings because you're scared. Be in it totally, give everything of your heart, one hundred per cent, or don't give anything at all.'

Tears began to sting her eyes. 'I want to be with him.'

'Then do it.'

'But what if—?'

'No what ifs, Freya. No fear. You are having two babies with this man, and whether it works or not he will be in your life until your last day on this earth. So make it work. Give him your whole heart, not half of it.'

The tears began to fall. 'I think I might love him.'

Her mum was tearing up too.

'Then you both have my blessing.'

She leaned forward and kissed Freya on the cheek, then pulled her into a hug.

Casey Benson looked calm. She was sitting in her hospital bed, serenely tapping a message into her mobile phone. But then again, Jamie mused, Casey had been through this three times before. She was an experienced mother.

'Hi, Casey. I'm Jamie, and I'm going to be your midwife today.'

She turned and smiled, her smile freezing slightly when she saw him. 'I get *you*?'

He nodded. 'You do.'

'For when I give birth?'

'That's the plan!'

'Oh.'

She looked a little perturbed, and he wondered if she was feeling uncomfortable at having a man deliver her child.

'Is that all right?'

'Yes! Course it is, it's just...'

'Yes?'

She blushed. 'You're very attractive.'

Well, that was very flattering, but he didn't understand why that should be a problem.

'An attractive man down at my—' She stopped and blushed again. Her face going very red.

He tried to change the subject, feeling amused. 'Are you here alone today?'

'I always do this alone.'

He saw on her file that she was married. 'Is your husband at work?'

'You could say that. He's in the Antarctic.'

'Oh, really? Doing what?'

'He's part of a research team studying the biodiversity of a special organism, or some such thing. He hopes to be back when this one is about two months old.'

'No other family who can be with you?'

'There is, but I'm happy to do this myself. It never takes long—they usually pop out after an hour or two. I'll be home in a few hours.'

'Who's babysitting the others?'

'Mum is. She's not very good with blood and gore, but she's an absolute whizz with spilt milk and baby dribble, so she's keeping an eye on the troops.'

'Glad to hear it. So it's just you and me, then. Unless you'd like a chaperone?'

She smiled at him over her mobile. 'Just you and me is fine.'

Casey had been right. She did labour easily. Though her contractions were showing up good and strong on the trace she remained calm, breathing easily through each of them as she leaned over the back of her bed, her knees on the mattress.

'You're doing brilliantly, Casey.'

Casey beckoned him over. 'Come and join me for a selfie. Otherwise no one is going to believe I had *you* deliver my baby.'

He capitulated, and put his head close to hers for a photo, smiling as the camera on her phone clicked the two of them together.

'You still all right with just the gas and air?'

'Absolutely!' She settled back on her haunches whilst she waited for the next contraction. 'Still all systems go here. Though, if I'm honest with you, I can't believe I'm back here, doing this again. I swore the last time that Benji was going to be my last baby, yet here I am.'

'Does your husband get to come home often?'

'Every six months. He gets home for about four weeks and then he goes off again. And obviously, because we haven't seen each other in all that time, we're very keen to see each other as much as we can, if you get my drift, and that usually results in me peeing on another of those ruddy sticks. Mind you, I love being a mum. I love all my kids—we have such a great time.'

'Do they miss their dad? What with him not being around?'

'Of course they do! They play up every now and again, but don't all children? They know their dad loves them, and that he's off doing some very special scientific work, and it's good for them to see that their dad is dedicated and works hard for a cause he believes in. It's good moral grounding for them.'

'It must be hard for him, too. Being away from his children?'

She nodded. 'It is. But he absolutely adores what he does,

and I don't think he could be away from them unless he did. Why would he lose all that time he could have with them if he was stuck somewhere hating what he did? No, it's good he has that passion. Do you have kids?'

He smiled. 'I have two on the way.'

'Twins, huh? Wow. But I imagine you'll be the same. You must love what you do? Because when they're born... when they're finally here and you hold them in your own arms...you can't imagine spending any time away from them. Missing any of it. Not unless you love what you do.'

He nodded. She was right. He wanted to spend as much time as he possibly could with his babies when they came. And if at some point he got called away to be King of Majidar that would be his crisis point.

Because he could *never* imagine himself wanting to do that. Could not imagine himself being stuck inside a glittering palace, getting bogged down in politics and laws, stuff he didn't care for, when instead he could be with his children. Doing a job he adored.

Majidar was never meant to be his. Ilias should have had his own heirs. He was a midwife. It had always been his calling. His vocation. He'd never wanted to rule, but it was the family he had been born into. And he felt a responsibility there, too.

The people of Majidar expected him to be their next King. And he knew, because it had been reported to him, that his people were *proud* of him for following his passion, for working far away from them in another country, bringing life into the world. But they knew he would come back. They *expected* him to come back.

But he wanted to be with his children. And Freya.

Unexpectedly, he had built a life here. Was putting down roots for the first time ever. And it was exciting and thrilling and the most terrifying thing he had ever done.

But it also felt like the *right* thing.

Knowing he would have to leave at some point, knowing he would have to walk away from them, was killing him inside.

Casey pulled herself back up over the bed railing and began to breathe heavily. 'Okay, let's do this.'

'I'm ready when you are.'

Casey gave birth to a healthy seven-pound, four-ounce baby girl that she called Francesca.

Jamie escorted her through to Postnatal for a little while and, as she'd predicted, waved her on her way home a few hours after that.

She'd given him a lot to think about, and he wondered if she'd made light of her situation at home. It had to be hard for her, living as a single parent, with her husband away for long periods of time.

Would that be Freya's life too? Stuck here in England alone? Knowing that he was away, and knowing that he'd put his *duty* to his country before his duty to his own children?

Casey was able to do it because she knew her husband was passionate about what he did, and she valued the life lessons she could show her children—that their dad was working hard at something he believed in. That he was doing it for *them*.

Would Freya be able to say the same to their two boys? Jamie *did* believe in the honour and privilege that it would be to sit on his country's throne, but would he be able to like himself for doing something he didn't actually want to do? Forcing himself out of duty?

He arrived at Freya's flat bright and early, knocking on her door and waiting for her to answer.

She opened it and he held up his box. 'I've brought tools.'

She smiled at him. 'Milkshakes or chocolates are my preferred gifts.'

'Maybe, but milkshakes and chocolates can't build bedroom furniture, can they?' He stepped past her, then stopped, turned, smiled and lowered his head to kiss her. 'Almost forgot this part,' he whispered, his lips closing over hers.

He'd missed her. Even more so since spending time with Casey. He felt the need to be with her. Her and the babies. Whilst he could. Her lips were full, soft and warm. She was comforting to him. It made him feel good just to be with her, and already he could feel his cares and worries being soothed away.

He wanted more. Could feel his body awakening to her touch, her presence. But more was forbidden. Which made the idea of it all the more desirable, and he had to pull back, bite his lip and just look at her with adoration and maddening frustration.

'Has everything arrived?'

'It's all in the nursery, awaiting your attention.'

'Good.'

She stared back at him, licked her lips, and he tracked every motion. The way her tongue swept over her lips, wetting them, leaving them glistening, before slipping back into her mouth.

'Can I make you a drink?'

He let out a sigh, imagining what that tongue could do to his body. 'Tea, please.'

He watched her head off to the kitchen and forcibly pushed aside his very sinful thoughts of all the things he wanted to do to her. That would have to wait. They had time. Time, at least, was on their side.

'I thought it might snow.' He followed her and watched her make the tea. 'They've forecast it in the paper.'

Freya laughed cynically. 'Let me tell you something about England, Jamie. They *always* forecast snow. They give us dire warnings every year, but we never get it. We can barely manage a frost down here, near the coast. It's very disappointing, actually.'

He smiled. 'This time last year I was working in Edinburgh, and we had snow. First time I'd ever experienced a heavy snowfall and it was wonderful.'

'Well, you'd better keep a hold of that memory, because you probably won't get it again.' She handed him his tea, smiling. 'Shall we get to it?'

'I'd love to. But apparently there's furniture that needs building.' He smiled.

She smiled back. 'That's what I meant.'

'You can supervise. And pass me things.' He pointed at her. 'No heavy lifting.'

Freya saluted him. 'Yes, sir.'

'Orders from your consultant.'

'I get it—don't worry. Are you sure you don't want something to eat before we start?'

He turned to look at her, devilment in his eyes. 'Freya, what I want to eat is, unfortunately, not on the menu at this moment in time.'

The instructions for the two cots seemed to be written in gibberish, and the pictures showing where to place the locking nuts didn't seem all that clear either. It took over an hour to do the first cot, through a process of elimination, but by the time he'd started the second he actually felt he knew what he was doing.

Freya sat beside him in a rocking chair, reading a book about what to expect in the first year of their child's life. She looked so cute, rocking away, one hand resting on her ample stomach, intensely concentrating on the words. He sat and watched her for a moment, quite unable to believe that this was his family now.

'Good book?'

She closed it and wiggled her eyebrows. 'Scary book. There seems so much to watch out for and worry about.'

'Like what?'

'Like colic, whooping cough, vaccinations and sterilising everything to within an inch of its life! What if they choke on something? What if I wean them too early and it does them more harm than good?' She let out a sigh. 'Being a mum seemed so much easier when it was just hypothetical.'

He could see that she was feeling nervous and needed reassurance. 'We'll be absolutely fine. We can do this. Thousands do.'

'And thousands of parents end up in A&E with their babies—we both know that. They get gastroenteritis and need rehydration drips and monitoring, or they swallow some coin or a marble or a little toy gun—I don't know, *something*—and they need an operation.'

He went to kneel beside her and took her hands in his. 'We can't protect them from everything.'

'But we're their parents. We're meant to protect them from things that will cause them harm!'

'You can't protect them from illness. Germs will get in no matter what you do. And, yes, they might swallow something they shouldn't. I believe I swallowed a small plastic camel when I was two years old, but here I am, absolutely fine and without trauma to my system. It's okay to worry, Freya. It's part of being a parent.'

'But I never thought I'd get the chance at this and now I am! And it's getting closer now, and I'm just worried that I'll get it all wrong!'

'Every mother worries. This is natural. Let's focus our energies on things we can control—like baby names, for instance. Have you had any thoughts on what you might want to call them?'

She let out a sigh and he saw a small smile begin to

emerge as she focused on happier things. 'I quite like the name Samuel.'

He mused on it. 'Samuel MacFadden. That sounds like a good strong name.'

She smiled. 'Samuel Al Bakhari. I'm going to give them your surname.'

He sat back on his heels, pleasantly surprised. And honoured. 'You are?'

'And I figured if you let me pick their first names, then you could pick their middle names. Something Arabic? So they get a name from both our cultures?'

'Wow… I don't quite know what to say.' The gesture meant a lot to him.

'Just suggest some good names!'

He smiled back at her, stroking her beautiful face and staring into her eyes.

They decided upon Samuel Dawoud and James Kadin. 'Good, strong names.'

'For good, strong boys.' She rubbed her tummy. 'They'll be here soon.'

He squeezed her hands. 'And we'll be ready for them.'

Once the cots were up, and Jamie had powered through constructing a wardrobe, a baby-changing station and a set of drawers, Freya cooked them both something to eat.

It was wonderful to have Jamie there with her, now that she was determined to step forward into the future with him at her side, instead of fighting him every inch of the way. Watching him work on the bedroom furniture, seeing how careful he was, how focused, making sure everything was put together correctly and securely, made her feel warm inside.

'I can't wait to see them in those cots.'

She smiled. 'Me too.'

'Can't wait to see their little faces. Hold them. Love them.'

She knew exactly what he meant. She felt it too.

Passing him a bowl of pasta, she sat down on the couch opposite. 'Thanks for today, Jamie. It feels good to see the nursery taking shape. Makes me feel like I'm a bit more prepared.'

'I'm glad. I'd do anything to make this easier for you.'

'It must be difficult for you too. Not knowing what's ahead?'

He nodded. 'I don't want to screw this up. Us… The twins… Majidar…'

'I never wanted to come between you and your country, Jamie. You have to know that.'

'Of course I do.'

'I just feel like…'

'Like what?'

'Like I'm making you choose. And I know I won't win.'

He put the pasta down. Sat beside her. Kissed her on the forehead. 'This isn't your fault. You're not making me do anything I don't want to.'

'But you have a responsibility to your people. A million of them. I'm just one. Soon to be three. I can't compete with that. I don't want to think of the day when you'll have to make that decision.'

His eyes darkened as he felt her pain. 'I don't want to leave you. You know that?'

She nodded.

Jamie let out a heavy sigh. 'We can't worry about that yet. It could be decades away. Let's consider brighter, better things.' He thought for a moment. 'What do you want to do over Christmas?'

Christmas? She hadn't really thought about it. She'd figured she'd be spending it in the normal way. 'I'll be at my mum's house.'

'I'm scheduled to work over Christmas. The afternoon shift from two p.m. But I wondered…well, I *hoped* that maybe we could spend the morning together?'

'Oh… Okay… Well, why don't you come to Mum's? It'll give you both an opportunity to get to know each other a bit more and we'll get to share the day together. We eat at midday, so you'll get lunch.'

He smiled and nodded. 'Sounds good. I'd love that— thank you.'

'I'll let Mum know there'll be an extra mouth to feed!'

Freya felt good about that. This would be her last Christmas without children. Maybe next year she and Jamie would be living together? Inviting her mum over to their place? Cooking for her instead? And there would be the joy of watching the babies rip open their presents. Would they be toddling by then? Crawling? Making mischief between the pair of them? Babbling away in their own little twins' language?

The idea of it made her smile. Made her feel warm and happy. Her future with Jamie might be uncertain, but whilst he was here they would make good memories together. Memories they would both cherish. Every moment would be precious.

Life was changing—and for the better. She couldn't quite believe she'd resisted this so much! Look at how well she and Jamie got along! All she'd needed to do was give him a chance. Give *them* a chance. And, even though she still felt apprehensive about the future, everything was looking much brighter now.

Maybe they *could* do this?

Together.

'We're going out.'

Freya frowned at Jamie. She'd just opened the door to him, expecting to invite him in for them to spend the evening together the way they usually did—watching a movie, eating popcorn, that kind of thing. She hadn't been expecting to go out, and she was wearing jogging bottoms and a maternity tee shirt that was having difficulty stretching over her twins-filled abdomen.

'What?'

'I've arranged something special. Just for you. So get dressed—we're heading into town.'

'Into town? Oh, no, I really don't think that I could—'

He pressed a finger to her lips, silencing her with a smile. 'Trust me.'

Freya stared back at him. Going into town was not her favourite thing. She'd done it a few times after the attack. It had been part of her therapy—heading out with her counsellor to show that she was okay being around crowds of people.

She'd been in a crowd of people when Mike had thrown the acid at her. It had happened in town. On the main street. He'd been lucky it hadn't hit anyone else and scarred them too. For a long time she'd been afraid to go out. Had almost become agoraphobic. Her counsellor had worked on exposing her gradually, getting her back out into the world.

It had been a long, difficult road, but one she had accomplished with much pride, even standing in the very spot on which the attack had happened, her eyes closed, breathing everything in—the familiar sounds of people all around her, the faint music from a clothing store playing far away, a busker a little further along, the aroma of freshly brewed coffee, the ringing of the church bells, the hustle and bustle of life all around her.

She'd done it. It had been fine. Until she'd opened her eyes.

Then she'd seen it. The stares of people passing her by. Had watched them notice her scarred face, seen the looks of repulsion, the pity, the sympathy, the recognition of who she was—that girl from the news who was attacked.

Her counsellor had told her not to worry about other people's reactions, but that had been easy for her to say—she hadn't been the one with a ruined face. It had been horrible to be looked at so differently.

Freya had always been pretty. Had always been aware that people looked at her with appreciation. That they'd wanted to know her, be her friend. She'd never had to try too hard with her looks, hadn't needed loads of make-up or anything like that. A natural beauty—wasn't that what everyone had said?

It had been torture to see that change. To look in the mirror and see what everyone else saw. Her face told her story. Her past relationship, her pain, her journey to recovery. Every operation, every painful skin graft—all there on her face for the world to judge. She would always be 'the acid girl'.

It was easier not to expose herself to people like that. To work nights, to order online, to keep to her small group of family and friends and the patients she saw on shift.

She had to admit that her patients had all been fine with her. No one had reacted with shock or pity. One or two had asked her what had happened, but the majority had decided it wasn't any of their business and hadn't asked at all.

Perhaps she needed to let the rest of the world have that chance?

'What have you got planned?' she asked nervously.

'It's a surprise.'

'I don't like surprises. Besides, I'm meant to be resting,' she added, trying to use her pregnancy as one last grip on the door.

'I've taken all that into consideration.' He stepped into her flat and closed the door behind him. 'Now, go and get dressed.'

'Jamie, the town…for me, it's—'

He pulled her towards him and held her tightly. 'I know. I *do*. But we won't be going anywhere near that part of it and I'll be with you every step of the way.'

What had he got planned? She didn't like surprises. Surprises were bad news.

Reluctantly she rummaged in her wardrobe for anything that might fit her and found a pair of maternity jeans and a pink hoodie that said *I'm Doing Nine Months Inside*.

Then she brushed her hair, put it up into a ponytail, added a bit of mascara to her lashes and some lip gloss, a quick spritz of perfume and stood in front of the mirror. Psyching herself up for this 'surprise'.

When she was ready she headed out, grabbing her handbag. 'Will I do?'

His face lit up in a smile. 'You look perfect.'

'Where are you taking me?'

'I told you—it's a surprise.' He got her coat and helped her put it on, slipping her arms into the sleeves, and then grabbed her long, woolly scarf and wrapped it gently around her neck, before dropping a soft kiss on her nose.

She followed him down to his car and he opened the door for her, closing it again once she was safely inside.

Butterflies gathered in her belly as he drove her towards town. They could be going *anywhere*. To do *anything*! She was meant to be resting—which was why Jamie had been spending every spare moment with her when he wasn't on shift. How he got any sleep and managed to function, she had no idea, but he must be power-napping or something, because he always seemed wide awake when he was with her.

And she liked it that he was spending this time with her. It was good for them. Snuggling on the sofa, holding hands, each kiss he gave her heartfelt and meaningful, warming her, making her feel safe and secure and loved.

Oh, there'd been times when she'd wanted a whole lot more! But they were both on strict instructions. No sex until the babies were born! And, as they were determined to keep the twins inside her for as long as they could, they were both being extremely diligent about that rule.

Jamie drove them through the streets towards town, and Freya had to admit it looked really pretty at night. The Christmas lights were up, adorning most of the streets in the city centre, Christmas music was being played, and everyone seemed to be in a happy, relaxed mood. Perhaps everyone was feeling goodwill to all men?

Jamie parked in a small service road to the rear of one of the big shopping centres.

Where on earth were they?

Jamie got out, walked around the outside of the car and then opened her door. 'Madam?'

She smiled nervously. 'Where are we? What are we doing?'

'I need my guys to watch the car, so I've parked here; it means my security looks a little less conspicuous. And I think you'll find that we'll be met in just a moment.'

He pressed a buzzer beside a set of double doors and instantly they were opened by a woman wearing a pretty blue dress and a name tag that read *'Michelle'*.

'Mr Bakhari? Miss MacFadden? Good evening and welcome to The Nesting Site.'

The Nesting Site? She'd read about that store in the local paper when it had opened up a few years ago. It was a stylish baby store, selling everything from plain muslin squares right through to the most hi-tech buggy anyone could possibly hope to purchase. It was exclusive—and a bit pricey, too. She'd heard some of her patients, when they'd come in to give birth, talking about browsing there, just to look at the beautiful things.

'I have a lift on hold, waiting for us.'

Michelle stood back to let them in and Freya breathed in the woman's perfume as she passed her by, feeling completely underdressed in her jeans and hoodie. She leant in towards Jamie for security and comfort, and felt better when he took her hand in his and give it a squeeze.

Michelle was looking at her with a polite smile. 'How many months are you?'

'Seven and a half, but it's twins, so...'

Michelle nodded, as if she understood perfectly. 'I had twins. One of each. Do you know what flavours you're expecting?'

'Two boys.'

Michelle smiled. 'Two princes. How wonderful!'

Freya looked at Jamie in shock. Did this woman know *who* and *what* Jamie was? She'd thought he didn't tell anyone that. But Jamie just smiled enigmatically at her and said nothing.

The lift doors pinged open and Michelle invited them in to the amazing store.

Freya sucked in a breath at all the beautiful things she could see—cribs with white lace curtains, the most beautiful rocking chairs, baby clothes in all manner of colours and designs, from plain white with gold embroidery through to brightly patterned Babygros in pinks and blues and the palest of palettes.

Michelle indicated a large reclining chair, stuffed with cushions, for Freya to sit down upon—which she did, wondering just what was about to happen here.

'I've arranged for us to have the store to ourselves, and for personal shoppers to bring us anything we wish to see. We don't have any clothes yet for the little ones, and I'd like us to get a few things.' Jamie smiled and squeezed her hand once more.

'Jamie, you didn't have to do this. I could have ordered online, like I always do.'

'I thought it would be better to see the items in person, before we buy. And I know you don't like crowds, so we have the place to ourselves. Now, what sort of thing should we look at first?'

'How about their going-home outfits?' Michelle suggested, snapping her fingers at some staff who must be were hidden away beyond Freya's eyeline. 'Would you like some tea? I can have a tray brought in.'

She almost felt dizzy with the possibility of it all.

Was this what it felt like to be a princess?

A princess in a hoodie and jeans…

CHAPTER EIGHT

'JAMIE, THIS FEELS WEIRD.' She leant over to whisper to him.

He smiled at her. 'Why?'

'All these people running around after me. Fetching and carrying. It's not right.'

'It's what *you* do when you're at work. Don't you look after your pregnant mothers? Fetching them cups of tea? Getting them epidurals or pethidine or gas and air? Don't you rub their backs and mop their heads with cool flannels when they need it? Hold their hands?'

She could understand his point. But that was different, surely? That was her *job*. Her patients needed her to do that because that was what she was trained to do. It was what she was there for.

'It's what they're here for, Freya,' Jamie said, echoing her thought process. 'It's what they're paid to do.'

'It just doesn't feel right to be on the receiving end of it, that's all.'

'Enjoy it whilst you can. When Samuel and James get here you'll look back on this moment and wonder why you didn't take full advantage of getting to put your feet up for a short while.'

She smiled as she imagined her babies in her arms. Who would they look like? Would they be dark-haired, like Jamie? Or blonde, like her? Would they have his intense midnight-dark eyes or her blue ones? Would they be happy, giggly babies? Or cry all the time with colic?

It was getting so close now, and she couldn't wait to hold them in her arms. To feel their little bodies snuggled up close to hers. She was looking forward to breastfeeding, if she could, although she worried about producing enough milk for both of them. She knew her body was designed to produce as much milk as the babies needed, but she couldn't stop worrying. Fretting about this and that. All the *what ifs* and all the horrors that might befall them.

She knew it was a normal part of being a new parent. She and Jamie were about to take on a huge responsibility and that they, more than anyone else, had uncertain futures.

I can't think about that now. I told myself I wouldn't.

The personal shoppers arrived, pushing a small clothes rail from which hung a plethora of baby clothes on tiny hangers. She went through them one by one, holding them, touching them. Laughing and smiling with Jamie as they imagined their sons dressed in each item and cooing over the small size of each piece.

She picked out baby vests and Babygros, tee shirts and tiny pairs of trousers. There were the most gorgeous pairs of baby shoes and trainers, pure white scratch mitts and the cutest knitted hats that looked like raccoons and foxes. She chose them both a winter snow suit, and picked out towels with white stripes that were adorned with tiny white sheep, and a gorgeous set of soft cherrywood brushes for their hair.

Michelle suggested a range of handmade bibs that were more like neckerchiefs, and then they moved on to car seats, and a double buggy that they both practised putting up and collapsing down. Freya chose a V-shaped pillow to assist with breastfeeding support, and a cute bedroom thermometer that looked like an owl. Plain and patterned fitted sheets and cellular blankets went onto the purchase pile. Then there were all the toys—teddy bears and rattles and soothers.

As each item was scanned Freya began to feel a little queasy. She saw the total totting up but, glancing at Jamie, she saw he was totally unfazed and realised that cost was not a concern for him. How nice it must be, she thought, not to have to worry about the pennies.

'And where shall we deliver this?' Michelle asked.

Jamie gave them her address and arranged a time for delivery tomorrow, promising Freya that the men would bring everything up to her flat and pack it away for her, so that she didn't have to do a thing.

'Oh, no—I'd like to do it, if that's okay.' She very much wanted to go through everything by herself. Sorting out where to put the clothes and how to organise everything in the wardrobes that Jamie had put up the other day.

'Just the clothes,' Jamie agreed. 'You're meant to be resting.'

Michelle escorted them back through the store, down into the lift and back to their car, waving at them as they drove off, with a big smile on her face.

'Well, if she works on commission I think we've just bought enough to give her the rest of the year off,' Freya joked.

Jamie laid his hand on hers. 'Did you enjoy it?'

She smiled. 'I did. You were right—it was lovely to actually see the items in person, rather than online. Some of those clothes were just so *dinky*!'

He laughed. 'They were, weren't they?'

Freya out a long sigh. 'So, are we going back home now?'

'I thought we could go and get something to eat, if that's okay?'

She thought of the crowds, and her mood dipped slightly. 'What did you have in mind?'

'How about pizza?'

Oh, yes! 'You read my mind.'

Jamie parked the car by the marina and left the engine on, keeping them warm as they ate their pizza. The boats were lit with security lights and bobbed about on the gently rocking waves as the wind whipped across the bay, biting at any exposed flesh on passers-by.

'Thanks for tonight, Jamie. It was amazing—it really was.'

'Once you got over what it felt like to be looked after for a change?'

She laughed. 'I guess.'

He peered out of the window. 'Still no snow.'

'I told you.'

'Yes, you did.' He wiped at his mouth and fingers with a napkin, before closing the lid on his pizza. 'That was delicious.'

'The pizza? Or me being right?'

He smiled at her. 'Both. And I wouldn't have it any other way.'

Wouldn't he? She knew this situation wasn't ideal for either of them. They both wanted the same things for the years ahead. They wanted to stay here in England. But he knew he would have to leave at some point. To be King. It was a dark thought that cast a long shadow over both of them.

'I'm sorry, Jamie.'

He turned to her and frowned. 'For what?'

'For not being able to leave here. For not agreeing to be your wife. I know it's me that's making this difficult for you and that if I just changed my mind then everything would be okay.'

Jamie shook his head. 'I would never force you to do anything. *Never.* I love the fact that you have been honest with me.' He took one of her hands in his and kissed the back of it. 'You were true to yourself. You told me the truth and I appreciate that. It makes what we have all the more special.'

She squeezed his fingers. 'What *do* we have, Jamie? Sometimes I'm not sure of anything.'

'We have a promise to be there for our children together, as much as we can be. To love them, and each other, until we can no longer do so.'

And each other? What did he mean by that? That he loved her? Or that the babies would love each other? That they would have a loving family? What he'd said was ambiguous. It could mean anything. And, although she was desperate to know whether he loved her, she felt at that moment that she couldn't ask him. The words were stuck in her throat.

She nodded. 'I don't want them to miss out on anything.'

'They won't.'

'I don't mean we should spoil them. I mean...' She looked away, out across the bay, past the boats and out to sea, where God only knew what was waiting. 'I mean that they should know just how much they are loved, by *both* of us. Even if one of us isn't there.'

'They will.' Jamie's voice was deep and full of emotion.

She loved it that he cared about this as much as she did. That his love for their babies ran as deeply as hers. Desperately she wanted to grab his hands and beg him never to go. Never to leave them. But she knew she couldn't ask him that. He had a duty. Over a million people would need him one day.

She couldn't make him choose between Majidar and her! He would always resent her for making him do it. So she knew that one day he would have to leave, and the idea of that, as her babies' birth grew closer, was beginning to break her heart.

Her feelings for Jamie had changed and grown. Especially over these last few weeks. Why did they have to be in this situation? Why did he have to be born to such a duty? Why couldn't he just be a midwife? Some random guy whom she'd met one day?

Why did he have to be a prince? Heir to a throne?

Why would she have to break her own heart one day and let go of him?

It wasn't fair.

Christmas morning arrived in the middle of a downpour.

Freya would not let the rain sully her day. It didn't matter. What mattered was that today was a day for family, and that for the first time in for ever she wouldn't be spending it alone with her mum. Jamie would be with them, arriving mid-morning, having lunch with them, before he had to leave for his shift at the hospital.

She hoped he'd like the present she'd got him. It had taken her ages to find something she thought he might like. What did you buy a *prince*—a man who could buy anything?

In the end she'd been rather sneaky, asking the security guys who followed her to get her a picture of Jamie's most successful racehorse so that she could have a painting done. One of her patients was an artist, and she'd commissioned her to do it.

Freya had to admit the painting looked amazing. Jamie's horse, Pride of Jameel, was a magnificent-looking animal, and Susie had painted the stallion standing tall and proud on a sand dune, his black coat gleaming.

As a little something extra—something silly—she'd got him a pair of teddy bears that played a recording of their twins' heartbeats when their bellies were squeezed.

'Merry Christmas, Mum!'

'Merry Christmas, Freya!' Her mum turned and blew her a kiss before turning her attention back to the frying pan. 'Full English for you?'

'Erm…just bacon and eggs, please.'

'What time are we expecting your young man?'

'Around ten, I think.'

'You've told him we don't open our gifts until after lunch?'

Freya nodded.

'And he's okay with turkey?'

'Yes, Mum.'

'What about the sausages? They're pork.'

'If there's anything he doesn't want he'll just leave it.'

'I don't want to offend him.'

'You won't, Mum. Honestly.'

'It's such an important day. I wouldn't want to ruin it.'

She helped her mum prepare all the vegetables, peel the potatoes and baste the turkey, which was already in the oven. The kitchen was filled with succulent aromas as they made the bread sauce, the cranberry sauce, and her mum's special stuffing. In the background Christmas carols played from the radio, and Freya realised as she sliced and chopped that she had never felt happier. It was Christmas, she was going to be a mother, and she had a man in her life whom she loved.

She'd fought it. Oh, how she'd tried to fight it! But she had to be honest with herself and admit the truth. She loved Jamie. He'd made it impossible for her not to.

Part of her still couldn't quite believe she had made herself that vulnerable again, but the other part—her love for Jamie—kept telling her it didn't matter, because she felt sure he loved her too and that he would never try to hurt her the way that Mike had, that by opening her heart and allowing him in she was not going to get burned this time.

There was only one way Jamie could hurt her, and that was by leaving, but she was being optimistic and trusting in what Jamie had said. They might have *years* together yet. Samuel and James might be grown men before he got called back to Majidar, so why waste all that time being lonely and miserable when they could be together, happy and loved?

The doorbell rang, breaking her thoughts, and instantly a smile lit her face. Wiping her hands on a tea towel, she went to answer the door.

Jamie stood on the doorstep beneath the shadow of a large black umbrella, holding a small sack of Christmas presents in his other hand.

'Merry Christmas!'

He smiled and stepped forward, planting a kiss upon her lips that made her hungry for more. She could have stood there all day, kissing him in the doorway, if it hadn't been for her mum coming to the door.

'Well, let the poor man in, Freya—it's bucketing down out there!'

'Something smells good.'

'It's your lunch. I hope you're hungry?'

He met her gaze. 'Starving.'

Freya could have melted there and then. The heat between them had been growing uncontrollably, and it was a terrible struggle not to let things advance between them physically when it was what they both wanted.

'Come on through. I'll make you a cup of tea.'

'Nope.' He took the bag of presents back from her. 'I'll make the tea. You put your feet up. Just show me where to put these and I'll get right on it.'

Freya showed him where to put the presents and then allowed him to settle her down on the couch, lifting her feet onto a foot rest.

He leaned over her, his hands either side of her, his face close to her own. 'I've missed you.'

'You saw me just yesterday.' She smiled, glancing down at his soft, sultry lips.

'And I missed you the second I left. I'm so happy to be here with you today. You have no idea.'

How was everything going so right for her? How was she so lucky? To have this—Jamie, the babies, Christmas, the *future*. Just a year or so ago her future had seemed quite lonely, but now...now she had everything she could possibly want. Perhaps it *was* her turn to be happy. She'd had what felt like a lifetime of pain, disappointment and grief. Her luck was turning at last.

Jamie slid onto the couch next to her and she rested her head against his strong, broad shoulder. She sat there feeling content. *Happy*.

CHAPTER NINE

'YOU'VE NOT GOT long now. Just a few more weeks before those babies arrive. What are you planning on doing once they get here?'

Freya frowned at her mum. 'How do you mean?'

'Well I know you're getting the flat ready, and the nursery is all decked out, but do you have any plans to move in together?'

Freya looked at Jamie, unsure. They hadn't talked about this.

'I'd be lying if I said I hadn't thought about the future, but I don't want to push Freya unless she's ready,' Jamie answered diplomatically.

It was scary. Terrifying. But she said it anyway. 'I might be ready.'

He raised an eyebrow, smiling. 'Really?'

'I'll need all the help I can get when the twins are born, and it would make sense, wouldn't it?'

Freya's mum was looking between them. 'What a romantic you are, Freya! You could sound a little more enthusiastic if you're asking him to move in!'

If she'd been able to blush properly she would have. Instead she looked at Jamie uncertainly. 'I'd love you to move in. If *you're* ready?'

Did he know how much it was taking for her to say this?

Jamie put down his knife and fork, dabbed at his mouth with a napkin and then got to his feet, walking around the table to kneel by her side. He took her hand in his and kissed it. 'I'd love to move in.'

Freya's mum clapped her hands together in excitement. 'Oh, yes! What a merry Christmas it is, indeed!'

Jamie embraced Freya in a quick hug, kissed her on the lips and then went back to his seat. 'Let's have a toast.' He raised his glass of juice and waited for Freya and her mum to do the same. 'To moving in and to bright futures.'

'To moving in and to bright futures!'

Their glasses clinked.

Freya had got her mum a scarf, hat and mittens set, along with a couple of books she wanted and some Belgian chocolates to satisfy her sweet tooth.

In return she'd received a gift voucher, some perfume, a new pair of pyjamas and a book in which to record all the twins' milestones as they grew.

'Thanks, Mum.'

'You're welcome, love.'

'Your turn, Jamie.'

Her mum had bought him a bottle of aftershave and a jumper, which he immediately tried on and declared that it fitted perfectly.

'Thank you, Mrs MacFadden.'

He handed Freya's mum an envelope, and when she opened it she realised, to her immense delight, that she'd been given a pass for a spa day at the Franklin Hotel.

'Jamie, that's brilliant—thank you!'

'After all your hard work in the kitchen today, you deserve it.'

'Open this next.'

Freya passed Jamie her present. The painting of his favourite horse, wrapped in bubble wrap and Christmas paper and tied with a huge, sparkly silver bow.

Curious, he began to unwrap it, struggling a little with all the tape Freya had used, until eventually he turned it around to see what it was.

'Freya, that's just *gorgeous*! It looks like Pride of Jameel.'

'It *is*!'

She laughed at the pure delight and amazement on his face, pleased that she could make him so happy—the same way he made *her* feel. This was what it was all about. Moments like these. When you could make the person you loved feel joy.

'How did you manage it?'

'Well, seeing as you've insisted I have bodyguards follow me around, I put them to actual work and told them to get me a photo of your most beloved horse.'

'It's amazing!' He kept admiring it, turning it this way and that to catch the light and admire new aspects of the painting. Then he put it down and kissed her. 'Thank you.'

'There's this, too.' She handed him the wrapped teddy bears.

He opened the gift, smiling when he saw it was two honey-coloured bears.

'Squeeze their tummies.'

He did, and his face broke into a huge smile when he heard the babies' heartbeats, which she'd had recorded at one of her antenatal visits.

'Samuel and James. I'll treasure them. Always.'

Freya felt she could burst with happiness! She hadn't been sure how he'd feel about the gifts, but she was thrilled with how much he liked the painting of his horse. It meant so much to her that he did.

'There's only two gifts left. Both for you, Freya.' Her mum smiled, passing over the gifts.

They were both small boxes. Jewellery-sized boxes. The type that rings came in...

Feeling nervous, Freya accepted the first one and began to unwrap it.

She'd been right. It was a small, red velvet box, shaped like a heart.

What if he was going to ask her to marry him again? Here and now? What would she say?

Sucking in a deep breath, she pushed open the lid.

There, nestled on a cushion of dark blue silk, was a pair of beautiful earrings. Silver, each encircling a beautiful jewel.

'They're platinum, and the jewels are black diamonds. The largest I could find.'

'They're beautiful!'

'Put them in, Freya,' urged her mum.

Part of her felt relief that his gift wasn't a ring. But there was still that second box. There could be a ring in there. It wasn't over yet.

She smiled nervously and put in the earrings, which both her mum and Jamie admired.

'They look beautiful on you, love.'

'Diamonds for my diamond.' Jamie smiled.

She leant over as much as she was able to and kissed him, meeting his gaze and holding it, trying to tell him without words just how much he meant to her and how frightened she was by his next gift.

It had to be the ring in that box, didn't it? And she wanted to say yes, but how could she? When the worst happened and Jamie got called back to Majidar she would have to go with him if she were his wife. It would be expected. But if she said no then she'd be ruining this beautiful day and breaking both their hearts, when right now they were both so happy.

Why had he done this? *Why?*

She felt a small surge of anger inside, irritation flooding her that it was all about to go wrong. She was about to feign a headache, or something, when the front doorbell rang.

Her mum frowned. 'Who on earth could that be? It's Christmas!'

'I'll go,' Jamie said, getting to his feet.

But Freya, feeling the need to escape the anticipation of what was in that tiny box, laid her hand upon his arm, stopping him. 'No. I'll go. You two have been looking after me all day—I need to stretch my legs for a moment.'

It was an excuse, but a welcome one, whoever it was. She just needed time to try and think. To try and decide what to do.

More than anything she would love to be Jamie's wife. To stand by his side with their babies as part of a loving family. But she knew she couldn't put herself under that much scrutiny. The world's press would have a field-day.

'Just coming!' She waddled down the hallway, exhaling loudly as she approached the door. She had no idea who it could be.

Standing before her was a man wearing a long white robe and a traditional *keffiyeh* on his head. He looked sombre, and bowed slightly at her appearance. 'Madam Mac-Fadden. My name is Faiz and I am the personal emissary of His Majesty King Ilias Al Bakhari. It is imperative that I speak with his brother, Prince Jameel.'

Freya froze for a moment as she took in his appearance and his message. Personal emissary? Why would Jamie's brother send a message on Christmas Day? It could hardly be a festive greeting. She was sure that they didn't celebrate Christmas over there in Majidar.

'An emissary?'

Faiz bowed again. 'Time is of the essence. If I may be allowed entry to speak with My Prince?'

Freya blinked rapidly as her brain raced through a thousand and one possibilities. Numb, she moved back and said nothing as Faiz stepped inside and past her.

'Who is it, Freya?' she heard her mum call from the room where moments ago everything had been perfect.

A chill crept over her as she began to suspect the reason for Faiz's visit. No. It *couldn't* be that. Could it?

Fighting back tears, she followed Faiz to the living room, where he stood just inside the doorway.

Jamie had got to his feet, his face stoic and ashen. 'Faiz?'

'My Prince. I must speak with you privately.'

Jamie glanced at her. The briefest eye contact. He must have seen the horror on her face before he looked away again.

'Anything you have to say, Faiz, can be said in front of everyone here.'

Faiz gave her a considered look, then nodded. 'Your brother has been taken ill. He is in hospital and it is imperative that you return to the kingdom.'

'Ill?'

'It is believed that His Majesty has suffered a stroke.'

Jamie stared at the floor, his body tense, his fists clenched at his side. 'Is Jasmeen with him?'

'The Queen has not left his side.'

'So you need me to return?'

His voice was thick with emotion, and more than anything Freya wanted to go to him and put her arms around him and comfort him, but her own grief kept her glued to the spot.

Jamie was leaving.

Now.

She wasn't ready. She wasn't ready to let him go! They'd only just started to be happy. They'd only just decided to be together. This wasn't fair! What about the babies? It was so close to her due date...he'd miss seeing them born!

'Jamie?' Her voice croaked in a painful whisper of grief.

He couldn't look at her. He just kept staring at the floor.

'Faiz? Are you absolutely sure that I must return?'

'I am not to return without you.'

Her mum hurried over to her and draped an arm around her shoulders. She turned into her mum's body and began to cry.

Behind them, she heard Jamie dismiss Faiz. 'Give me a moment.'

'Yes, My Prince.'

'Freya?'

She couldn't look at him. It hurt too much. She just clutched her mother harder.

Freya? Please...'

Her mother released her and stepped away. 'I'll be in the kitchen.'

Freya folded her arms around herself and stared at Jamie through her tears. 'You can't go!'

'I must.'

He stepped forward and reached for her, intending to hold her, but she couldn't bear the idea of him touching her. If she let him hold her then she would never let him go.

She stepped back. 'Don't.'

'I never expected this. We were meant to have years...'

'But we both knew that it would happen one day,' she threw back.

'I'm so sorry. I never wanted this.'

She couldn't say anything. Words were not enough to express how she felt right now.

He looked remorseful. 'I could be back in time for the birth. Ilias may recover.'

'He might. But I can't compete with a million people who need you. And that's how it should be. The needs of a million people outweigh my own. You have to go. I understand.'

'I want to stay.'

'But you *can't*!' Her voice broke. 'We knew this day would come. We were fools to think we could cheat it.'

'There must be a way?'

She nodded. 'There is. Accept your fate. It's always been there for you. Coming to England, meeting me...it could never stop that wheel from turning.'

He looked hurt. 'You know that I would stay if I could?'

She nodded, fresh tears running down her cheeks.

'You'll keep me informed?'

She frowned. 'How?'

'I'll leave my men. They can get messages to me.'

'No, Jamie. Take them all with you. Leave nothing behind.'

'I'm leaving *you* behind.'

She stared directly at him, through her tears and her pain. 'Exactly.'

He shook his head. 'I can't believe this is happening. Do we have to end this? Now?'

'We do. Because I can't live a half-life, Jamie. I've already done that for far too long...hiding from the world, living in the shadows. I've got to live for me now. For my children. And I deserve—*we* deserve—a happy, full life.'

'I can't walk away from my children.'

She winced. So he *could* walk away from her?

'But you will, Jamie. You've already made your choice. You've been called and you're going and you *should* go. Your brother is sick—has had a stroke. You need to see him, just in case his condition does not improve. You will be called upon to rule the country in his stead, and if he does not recover you will rule permanently. By going now you're choosing Majidar over us—as it should be. It's your duty.'

'You truly are the bravest woman I have ever known.'

She swallowed down her pain. 'You need to go now. Just *go*, Jamie.'

He looked away, his gaze taking in the twinkling Christ-

mas tree, the wrapping paper discarded on the floor, the
presents, the painting of his horse. And the small gift that
she still had to open.

Jamie picked it up and held it in his hands. Staring at
it for a moment, twisting it this way and that. Then he put
it in his pocket, bent to pick up the teddy bears and gave
her one last look.

'I love you, Freya MacFadden.'

She stared back, her heart breaking at this one last message, more tears falling freely down her face. 'And I love
you, Jameel.'

And he went.

He turned his back and disappeared through the doorway.

Grief and pain tore sobs from her as she sank to her
knees on the floor.

And on the television was the Queen, in her annual
speech, talking to the nation. She focused on the Queen's
face. A monarch addressing her people. Her whole life com-
mitted to her country.

How had she ever believed she could come between a
man and such a love?

The house on Hayling Island had been closed up for a while.

Freya went through it, opening windows, letting in the
aroma of the sea air despite the winter cold.

She turned up the thermostat on the central heating,
made herself a mug of tea, and then stood outside on the
small balcony and looked out to sea.

It was very still, calm, as if it was waiting for something.
Grey-green, dully reflecting the grey sky above.

Down by the water she could see a dog walker, wrapped
up in a thick jacket, throwing a tennis ball for three small
dogs that chased after it happily.

This was what she needed—calm. The relaxed, unhurried way of life here, where no demands could be made of her and where she wouldn't have to find a brave face when inside she could feel herself crumbling.

She and Jamie had had their time cut short. Much too short. Both of them had believed—hoped—that they would have years...decades, perhaps. She'd begun to believe that her two sons would have a father. A great father. One who would adore them, teach them, raise them to be good boys. Good men.

Only now she would have that task alone.

What would she tell them about him? And when? As they got older they would begin to understand what a prince was, what a king was. Would they want to go to him?

She toyed with the idea of going with them one day. But she could only foresee agony in doing so. Meeting Jamie after many years... What if he had moved on? Married, as a king would be expected to do? What if he had a new family? Would she be welcomed in Majidar? Or spurned? Would Samuel and James always be known in Majidar as the King's illegitimate children?

And if they did visit there would always have to be another goodbye, and it wouldn't just be Freya who would be distraught afterwards it would be the boys, too, and *she* would be the one who would have to deal with the fallout. She would be the one to pick up the pieces of her children and slowly put them back together again.

Perhaps it might be best not to tell the boys who their father was? But the idea of lying to them, of manipulating the truth, made her feel sick.

What to do?

This was why she had come here to Hayling Island. To get some space. To think clearly. Not to see the nursery every day and be reminded of the ticking of the clock. She had mere weeks left of her pregnancy, and as if in reminder of that she felt her first Braxton Hicks contraction.

A tightening of her belly. Her body preparing itself for the battle to come.

She rubbed her hand underneath her bump and breathed through it. There wasn't any pain, just a tightness, her belly going hard and rigid before slowly softening and relaxing again.

'I'll always be here for you,' she said to them, before going to close all the windows she'd opened. so she'd feel the benefit of the central heating.

She wanted to go down to the water, to walk along the beach and feel that sea air invigorate her lungs.

She grabbed her coat, hat and scarf and wrapped up well, then opened the door and stepped out, locking up behind her.

As she turned to begin her walk she felt something touch her cheek. Then her nose.

She looked up and saw that snow was finally beginning to fall, and it pained her to know that he was missing it.

'Oh, Jamie…'

Security guards lined the floor of the private hospital in which his brother the King lay. Escorted by Faiz and his own personal assistant, Rafiq, Jamie strode down the corridor towards his brother's room.

He had been kept informed throughout his seven-hour flight back home on the Bakhari private jet. And the briefcase of documents awaiting his attention on the plane had reminded him of the life he had left behind when he'd first come to England.

He was trying his hardest to remain stoic, but his mind was a mess. He'd left her behind.

I left her behind!

Freya and his two babies. His sons. His heirs.

My heart.

But duty had called him and he felt helpless to try and

fight it. He would never be the same again now that he'd been ripped in two.

Part of him hoped that when he walked into that hospital room and saw his brother lying in a hospital bed Ilias would open his mouth to speak and smile, maybe hold his brother in greeting, give him a hug, pat him on the back and say, *Welcome home, brother.*

That would be the best solution for them all.

His duty, his future, hung over him like a guillotine. He hated to refer to his noble duty in such a way, but it was how it had always felt to him. He'd never asked to be royal, never asked to be born into such a family, and being King had *never* interested him. Not once.

Leaving his country, his family, and flying thousands of miles away as a young man had taken a lot of courage, but he had followed his heart and done what he'd thought was right.

He came to his brother's room and placed his hand upon the door. The doctors had informed him that Ilias appeared to have a blood disorder. They weren't sure of it yet, but they were running tests.

He hoped they would learn what it was soon. So his brother could be treated and recover as quickly as possible.

He opened the door.

CHAPTER TEN

THERE WERE MONITORS sounding out the beats of his brother's heart.

He is alive.

But then he saw him—pale and wan against the hospital pillows, with his wife Jasmeen dutifully by his bedside, clutching his hand.

The shock of seeing him looking so ill stopped Jamie in his tracks.

'Jameel? You're here!' Jasmeen let go of her husband's hand and came over to embrace her brother-in-law.

'How is he?'

'The doctors say he is stable...but I have never seen him like this before.'

'Nor I.'

Jamie took a seat by his brother's bed and took hold of Ilias's hand.

'Ilias? It's Jameel. I'm here. I've come home.'

'He sleeps deeply since the stroke. It's like he has a tiredness that cannot be quenched.'

'Can he speak yet?'

'Sounds, but not words. It distresses him greatly. He tries to write, but he is right-handed, so it takes a while to read his words.'

Jamie squeezed his brother's fingers and felt tears sting

the backs of his eyes. But he refused to cry here. Crying would be an admission of just how out of control he was, when he was desperately clinging to the one bit of hope that he still had.

'Ilias?'

His brother moaned and then began to blink, looking about him to find the source of his brother's voice.

'Nurgh...'

Tears appeared in Ilias's eyes when he saw his brother, and Jamie leant forward to kiss his brother's cheeks.

'I am here, brother. I am here.' He held his brother's face in his hands, touching his forehead to Ilias's.

His brother signalled for his writing pad and Jasmeen presented it to him.

I'm sorry you had to come home.

Jamie read the tight scrawl and smiled. 'Don't be sorry. You couldn't have known this was going to happen.'

You're about to become a father.

He nodded, thinking of Freya and her huge belly, of his hand resting on her abdomen, feeling the boys kick and stretch inside. He'd left them. Left them behind. Maybe never to see them again.

The ache in his chest was palpable. 'Yes.'

I did not want to do this to you.

'It's not your fault, brother. None of this is. I am just so grateful that you are still alive. You must fight hard, Ilias. Fight hard to get better.'

He turned to look at Jasmeen.

'Has he seen any physiotherapists yet?'

'They come three times a day.'

Ilias began to scribble again.

I don't think I can remain King like this.

Jamie's stomach dropped like a stone. 'You don't know what the future holds.'

Jasmeen gave a weak smile. 'The doctors hoped that his speech would be back by now, and though the weakness on his right side has yet to improve they hope with time that it will get a little better. But they are unsure of a full recovery.'

Jamie thought about what that meant for a moment. 'I see.'

'I have been talking to Ilias, Jameel. We have talked long and hard and taken everything into consideration. Ilias loves Majidar and its people so much—he believes it needs a strong leader. Right now he does not feel that that is him.'

Jamie shook his head and tried to implore his brother. 'It *is* you.'

'He wants to abdicate.'

Jasmeen's words dropped into the room like a grenade.

Abdicate? *Abdicate?* But if Ilias abdicated that would mean that he...

Jamie stood up and began to pace the room, coming to a stop by the window to stare out, far and wide over the desert in the distance, on the outskirts of the city. Freya was so far away.

'Nurgh...'

Jamie's eyes closed at the sound of his brother's voice. He felt awful. Pathetic. Thinking only of himself when his brother was in such distress and pain! What sort of man did that make him?

He turned to see that Ilias was holding up his writing pad. He read the words.

It doesn't have to be you.

It was New Year's Eve and the snow had been falling for a few days now. Thick, heavy flakes, tumbling silently, covering the world in a white blanket of softness.

It made everything look beautiful, but it had certainly put paid to Freya's ideas of getting some walks in. All the heavy rain there had been before the snow meant that there was a thick layer of ice beneath it, so the pavements and roads were treacherous.

The weather forecasters predicted more heavy snow and informed people that they should not travel unless they had to. Gritters were out, trying to line the roads, but they were fighting an endless battle.

Freya stayed in the small house, drinking lots of tea and eating plenty of warm, buttery toast in front of the log fire, flicking from channel to channel on the television to try and find something interesting to watch.

Today she'd found a few films and had settled in to watch those, aware that her Braxton Hicks contractions had been coming a lot more frequently just recently. This morning they had begun to start hurting, and every now and then she'd find herself having to stop and breathe, clutching onto the back of the sofa or a kitchen unit.

She dutifully called her mum and told her she was fine.

'I'm so worried about you, stuck out there with all this snow. What if you go into labour?'

'Then I'll call an ambulance, Mum. Stop worrying, I'm fine. I've got a few weeks left.'

'Two weeks left, Freya. *Two weeks.* Those babies could come any time.'

'Well, I *am* a midwife, Mum, so I'll know what to do.'

She managed to get her mum off the phone eventually, sighing heavily, and decided to run herself a bath.

A soak in warm water helped soothe her troubled nerves, and she was soon settled back on the couch with a nice cup of tea.

A sudden pain, low in her belly, had her gasping, and she had to reach under her bump to rub at her abdomen. Slowly the pain eased and she lay back again, wondering if she'd sat down awkwardly and maybe pulled a muscle?

But the pain was gone now, and she felt confident that she'd know if she was really in labour.

On the screen, a newsflash came up on the local news to say that most roads in the area were becoming inaccessible and it was recommended that people did not drive anywhere unless it was absolutely necessary.

She glanced out of the window. The snow was still falling and there were drifts right up to the ledge.

She'd never known it to snow like this before. Not down here. Not by the coast, where you'd imagine there'd be enough salt around to prevent it. But there it all was. A thick white blanket. Would it snow like this next year? Would she be able to let the twins out in it? See the wonder on their faces?

The thought made her smile—a smile that soon faded when she got another pain.

Oh, God. Is this it? Is this labour?

All her bravery, all her bravado because she was a midwife, went out of the window. She suddenly realised just how *alone* she was here, how isolated. And if she needed to call an ambulance would it be able to get here?

There was only a single road on and off the island, connected to the mainland by a bridge. What if that was blocked? Impassable?

She hauled herself up and began to breathe through the panic, pacing back and forth.

Okay...okay. This could just be early labour, and I'm a first-time mother so my labour could be hours yet. Plus, it could still die down. There's nothing to say that these pains will continue.

But they did. Every eight minutes she got a pain, and as the hours passed they increased to every five minutes.

She picked up the phone, but the line was dead. She scrabbled in her handbag for her mobile and dialled 999.

'Ambulance, please.'

She was put through to Control and gave her address and situation. The guy on the phone told her that someone would be with her as quickly as they could, but because of the snowfall their ambulances were busy elsewhere. She was to try and find someone to be with her, so they could call again later if she needed to deliver at home.

Panicking, she put down her phone and began to think. Who could she get to help her? These properties were mostly summer holiday lets, and it was New Year's Eve!

A knock at the door had her struggling to walk over to it. Whoever it was, she would tell them what was happening. See if they could help her or if they knew someone else who could help. There were first responders on the island, surely? Perhaps they could get to her? She knew they didn't usually attend labouring women, but when needs must...

She grabbed hold of the door handle, turned the key and yanked the door open.

And there—shivering, wet, and very, very cold-looking—was Jamie. His face was red and glistening, his hair flattened by snowflakes.

Hesitantly, he smiled. 'I told you it would snow.'

'Jamie?'

'The one and only. Can I come in? Only I've been trudging through snow for the last couple of hours.'

'How did you know where to find me?'

But before he could answer another contraction ripped

through her, and she gasped and let go of the door to bend
over and put both hands on her knees to breathe through it.

'Freya? Are you in *labour*?'

She couldn't answer him for a moment. The contraction had completely obliterated her ability to talk whilst it
was going on. The most she could do—the *only* thing she
could do—was remain upright and breathe.

When it receded, and when normal thought and the real
world returned, she stood straight again and looked at him
with tears in her eyes. Her heart felt overwhelmed with relief and love for this man before her.

'For about four hours now.'

'*Four hours?* Why didn't you call for an ambulance?
Stranded out here like this!'

'I did. They don't know when they can get to me. Apparently they're busy.'

He rummaged in his pocket for his mobile. 'I'll get
someone here.'

He tapped at the screen and then held the phone to his
ear, shouting instructions in Arabic before snapping it shut
again.

'I've got a paramedic being choppered in.'

'A helicopter? In this? How did you know where to find
me?'

'There's a GPS tracker on your phone.'

'What?'

'They all have them. Don't worry—I didn't place some
secret bug in it, or anything. I'm not that kind of guy.'

Another contraction began to build. 'Oh, God!'

She turned to lean against the stairs and felt Jamie's
hands hold her steady and rub the small of her back. When
it was done, he guided her back to the lounge so she could
sit down.

'That last contraction was about a minute and they're
coming fast.'

'You don't need to tell *me* that. I'm the one having them.'

'We need to prepare. Where are your towels? I'll put on some hot water, and we'll need scissors I can sterilise for cutting the cord—just in case.'

'Wait a minute. You can't come sweeping in here like a white knight. You need to tell me what's happening. How's your brother? Are you King?'

'Ilias has Von Willebrand's disease. He's being treated for it. The stroke has caused deficits, which hopefully will improve over time, but he has decided to abdicate, feeling that it's in the best interests of our country to have a ruler in full health.'

'He's *abdicated*? Can he do that?'

Her abdomen tightened with another vice-like contraction.

'*Ohhhhh...*'

She leaned forward and gripped the sofa, her eyes tightly shut as the feelings within her body overwhelmed her. Pain. Intensity. Breathing was the only thing she could manage for sure.

She felt Jamie take her hand and she gripped his fingers tightly, squeezing the blood from his digits. 'Oh, I think I need to push.'

'I'll need to check you first. Can I do that?'

She nodded quickly and removed her pyjama bottoms and underwear, wincing at the dying pain in her belly.

'I'll wash my hands. Do you have any gloves?'

Freya pointed into the kitchen. 'Beneath the kitchen sink are some latex gloves. Mum uses them for when she has to touch raw meat.' She tried to laugh, recalling her mother's squeamish nature.

'I'll be back in a moment.'

She lay back on the couch and wiped the sweat from her forehead.

Jamie was back. But how? If Ilias had abdicated, didn't

that mean that Jamie was now King? *Why* had he returned? Had they allowed him some kind of compassionate leave to be with her for when the babies arrived? So he could see them and *then* leave? She hoped not. Because even if that was good for him, it would be doubly difficult for *her*.

Having him here, holding her hand, mopping her brow, seeing the joy and love on his face as he looked at his sons and then having to wave him goodbye again... *No.* She couldn't allow that. She wouldn't survive it. The birth would be hard enough without being deserted right afterwards.

Jamie came back into the living room wearing a pair of latex gloves. 'Right, let's take a look. Has the contraction gone?'

'Yes. But maybe you should leave, Jamie?'

He looked up at her, confused. 'Leave? I just got here—and I don't think there's anyone more suitably qualified to help than me right now. I don't think I'll be fetching your elderly neighbour from next door, who needs a magnifying glass to read the evening paper.'

Now it was her turn to frown. 'Does he? How do you even *know* that?'

'I have *people*, remember? I'm going to examine you now. Try to relax.'

She lay back, opening her legs. 'Why does every man say that when he has to do an internal? Perhaps if men had a vagina they'd realise exactly how hard it is to *relax*!'

'Good point.' He smiled up at her. 'And good news. You're fully dilated. You can start to push with the next contraction.'

Freya's eyes finally began to leak tears of relief and happiness. 'I can?'

'You can.'

Jamie removed the gloves, pulling them inside out before discarding them in a small wastepaper bin. Then he pulled another pair from his pocket.

'Now—quickly—where are the towels kept?'

I can push. They'll be here soon. Samuel and James.

'Upstairs. Second door to the left is a small airing cupboard.'

'Don't do anything exciting without me.'

He kissed her on the cheek and raced upstairs and she watched him go, shocked by the feel of his kiss still upon her skin.

He seemed okay. He seemed as if he was in control. Was he really? Or was this all a front?

She still didn't know what was happening. Still didn't know whether he was staying. The hope that he might stay was building much too quickly, and she was struggling to fight it down, because she really wanted him to stay with her.

But reality told her that if Ilias had abdicated then Jamie was soon to be King, and he was only here on loan. His country had claimed him. And the knowledge of that was destroying her.

She began to cry.

Why was he doing this to her? Why had he come back and made her think there was hope? Made her think there was a chance for them still? It wasn't fair. Did he not know how hard it had been for her after he'd left the first time? If he did know then he wouldn't have done this.

She heard him come running back down the stairs and he appeared at her side with a huge pile of towels.

'You need to go.'

He frowned. 'Don't be ridiculous. I'm not going anywhere. What kind of man would I be to leave you in this state in the middle of a white-out?'

'A man with principles. I can't have you here, Jamie. Not like this! Not knowing you're going to leave me again!'

Another contraction hit and she heard nothing as his words faded beyond the pain she could feel surround her whole body. She sucked in a breath and, remembering all the advice she gave to labouring mothers, tucked her chin into her chest, curled around her baby and pushed down into her bottom.

It felt *good* to push! Excellent, in fact. There was almost relief there, because now she wasn't a passive observer of her pain, letting it roll over her in waves. Now she could do something about it!

She pushed against it, shoved back, using the pain of the contraction to start moving and birthing her babies.

'That's it, Freya! You're doing really well! Keep pushing right there. That's *it*!'

She let out a breath, then immediately sucked in another and began again. She managed two more huge breaths and two more pushes before the contraction died down and she could breathe properly again.

'Freya...' He took her hand and made her look him in the eyes. 'I'm not going to leave you. Not tonight. Not tomorrow. Not ever.'

Not ever?

'But—'

Another contraction began. *God, they're coming thick and fast now!* But she knew that was good. This was what was *meant* to happen.

'I can see a head, Freya! You're *doing* this! You're really doing this!'

When it was over, she reached down to touch the head of her first son and gasped when she felt it. 'Oh, my God!'

'With the next contraction his head will be born. Okay?'

She nodded, sucked in a breath, and began pushing again as the next contraction built.

'Keep pushing! Keep pushing! That's it—just like that. Now, stop! Pant it out!'

She panted, huffing away like an old-fashioned steam train, and then Jamie was telling her to give one last push.

She felt her son slither from her body and into Jamie's safe, waiting hands. He lifted Samuel up onto her belly. 'Here he is!'

'Oh, Jamie!' She grasped her son, her darling Samuel, ignoring all the stuff he was covered in—the white vernix, the smears of blood—and cried again out loud when her son opened up his lungs for the first time, letting out a long, strangled cry. 'Oh, he's so beautiful!'

He was. He was a good size—between six and seven pounds, she estimated—and with a thick, full head of dark hair like his father.

Jamie draped a couple of towels over his son, so he wouldn't get cold, then tied off the cord with string and cut it with the scissors he'd sterilised in a bowl of steaming hot water.

Then he looked at them. With *such* pride. 'I'm so proud of you.'

Freya beamed at him as she cradled her son. 'I can't believe he's here.'

'Safe and sound.'

'Thanks to you.'

'Thanks to *you*.'

She smiled and reached for him, so that he would lean forward and place a kiss upon her lips. A soft, gentle, reaffirming kiss. And then he stooped over his son's head and laid a kiss on his son's head, too.

'Oh, my! I can't believe this has happened so quickly!' She looked at him. 'And you're here! And you can *stay*?'

He nodded, smiling. 'I can stay.'

'How?'

'Ilias told me that I didn't have to take the throne. That my sister Zahra wants to do it. She's a good, strong woman. She's always wanted to get more involved with the running of things and she's a good choice. The people will look up to her.'

'But I thought you *had* to do it?'

'So did I. But what kind of King would I be? With my people knowing that I had deserted my own two sons to sit on the throne? Knowing that I had left behind the woman I loved? Above all, my people would want me to be happy— as my brother Ilias wanted me to be happy by letting me come to England in the first place. He knows my life is here now, as do my people. They will understand. And Zahra is much loved. She will make a fine monarch. A brilliant one.'

He could stay? For good? With her and Samuel and James and without any possibility of his desertion hanging over them?

Another contraction began to make itself known. 'It's starting again...'

'Do you want me to take Samuel?'

'Please. I don't want to squash him.'

She passed her firstborn safely over to Jamie and began to breathe through the contraction. Jamie would need to check her first, before she began pushing again. To make sure James was in a good position.

He checked her and smiled. 'He's head down. He's right there, Freya.'

'Okay. I can do this again, right?'

He smiled back at her. 'You can do *anything*!'

She had to believe him. Had to believe that she could give birth again even though she felt exhausted after delivering Samuel.

Hunkering down, she began to push.

It felt a little easier this time. She pushed and pushed, and before she knew what was happening the head was delivered.

'One more push and it will all be over.'

'I hope so!'

She gave a quick glance to Samuel, lying on the floor beside Jamie, wrapped up in towels, resting from the trauma of being pushed through the birth canal.

She'd often wondered if babies cried because of the pain in their skull bones, overlapping to fit through, or whether it was just the shock of all the tiny alveoli in their lungs suddenly inflating for the first time. Maybe it was both?

But Samuel was here and he was safe, and he had a mother *and* a father, and of course she could do it again.

She sucked in a breath.

'That's it, Freya! Push! Harder!'

From somewhere she found a reserve she hadn't known she had. Whether it came from the knowledge that if she just did this one last push, as hard as she could, it would all be over, or whether she really did have that endless supply of energy distinctly found in women giving birth she didn't know. But she found it, and she used it, and she pushed with all of her might.

James was born. Into his father's hands and then up onto her stomach, the same as Samuel had been.

Crying with relief, she held him weakly, glad the pain was over, overjoyed that her babies were finally here, safe and well.

And Jamie...? Jamie was here to stay, it seemed. They could have the future that both of them wanted.

With the cord cut and the placentas delivered, Jamie sat himself next to her. They held a baby each. From above they could hear a helicopter, looking for a suitable place to land.

She smiled at her babies' little faces, gasping with delight at each tiny noise, each little snuffle, each beautiful yawn.

'Look at them, Jamie. They're so beautiful.'

'How could they not be with a mother like you?'

She smiled and leant her forehead against his. 'You're truly here to stay?'

'I'm here to stay. If you'll have me, of course.'

She turned to look at him. Looked deeply into those midnight-black eyes of his. Of course she wanted him! It was what she had always wanted but had been too afraid to admit, because she'd always thought he would have to desert her.

But that threat was gone now.

'Can I ask you something?'

She waited for him to look at her. He was still gazing at his sons with such love.

'Of course you can. You can ask me anything.'

'Will you marry me, Jamie?'

His gaze locked with hers and a delighted smile appeared upon his face. 'Yes. A thousand times, yes!' He leant forward until their lips touched.

Closing her eyes in exhausted delight, she kissed him back, pouring every ounce of her love for him into it. Oh, how she needed this man! She'd never known what was missing from her life. She'd convinced herself that her life was fine, hiding herself away on the night shift, pretending she was doing herself a favour.

That hadn't been any way to live. And Jamie had seen that. Known that. He'd looked beyond the mask she was wearing and called her on it. Not allowing her to get away with it.

He'd made her into the woman she'd been *before*. The woman she'd thought she would never be again.

'I love you, Jameel.'

He stroked her face. 'And I love *you*.'

MAJIDAR WAS MORE beautiful than she could ever have imagined. A vast desert kingdom, filled with a thriving populace that had roared and cheered their delight at Jamie's return for a two-week visit.

She'd been nervous. All those people! And she had taken Jamie from them. She had stopped him from being their king.

But the people were thrilled to have her there. They waved and smiled, and small children brought her bouquet after bouquet, which she passed back to the bodyguards who escorted them on their tour wherever they went. Everyone had treated her with deference, and she did not doubt their love for her as Jamie's wife.

Now, as she stood on the palace balcony, looking out across the oasis beyond, she felt Jamie's arms come around her from behind.

'How do you feel?'

She smiled and laid her head against his shoulder. 'Loved.'

'I told you they would all love you.'

She turned to face him, to look deeply into his eyes. 'But to be loved *this much*... I never would have thought it was possible.'

Jamie smiled back and lowered one of his hands to her slightly rounded abdomen. 'When should we tell them?'

She was pregnant again. This time carrying only one baby. She hoped it might be a girl, but she didn't really mind.

'Let's do it tomorrow. Let's tell the whole world.'

She knew it would be all right.

He smiled and pulled her towards him.

* * * * *

HIS TWO ROYAL SECRETS

CAITLIN CREWS

For Flo, my favorite twin.

CHAPTER ONE

"THE ONLY THING that matters is the line," Crown Prince Ares's dark and intimidating father told him when he was little more than five.

At that age, Ares had no idea what his father meant. He didn't know what line his father was referring to or what bearing it could possibly have on him anyway. At five, Ares had been primarily concerned with how many hours a day he could spend roaring about the palace grounds, out of sight of his nanny, who was forever trying to make him "act like a gentleman."

But he had learned, already and painfully, never to question his father.

The king was always right. If the king was wrong, you were mistaken.

By the time he was ten, Prince Ares knew exactly what line his father was referring to, and was already sick to death of hearing about his own blood.

It was only blood. No one cared if he skinned his knee, but it was clearly very important that he listen to lectures about *the purpose* of that blood. Its dignity. Its import.

When it was still the same blood that welled up

in any scrape Ares might get while doing things he shouldn't around the palace. Things his old nanny liked to tell him were responsible for her gray hair.

"You do not matter," his father would rant during Ares's scheduled appointments with him. "You are merely a link in a noble chain, nothing more!"

The king was forever flinging brandy and various decanters this way and that in his private compartments as he worked his temper into a lather. Ares did not enjoy these appointments, not that anyone had asked him.

And Ares had been schooled repeatedly not to move when his father raged. To sit straight, keep his eyes averted, and refrain from any fidgeting or reacting. At ten, he found this to be a kind of torture.

"He likes a moving target, child," his mother would tell him, her voice cracking as she sat with him, her hands cool against his face and her eyes kind. "You must work on keeping your posture perfect, and never betray your emotions by so much as a flick of an eyelash."

"What would happen if *I* threw something at the wall?"

The queen's smile was always so sad. "Don't do that, Ares. Please."

Ares came to think of it as something of a game. He pretended to be a statue, like the ones that would be made of him someday to grace the King's Gallery that had stood in the Grand Hall of the Northern Palace since—or so the story went—the islands that made up the kingdom of Atilia rose up from the sea. Marble and gold, with a fancy plaque listing his accomplishments.

"Our line has held the crown of Atilia for centuries,"

his father would thunder, while Ares would think, *I am stone*. "And now it rests entirely in your hands. You, a weakling, who I can hardly credit sprung from my own loins."

Stone straight through, Ares would tell himself, his eyes on the windows and the sea outside.

By the time Ares was a teenager, he had perfected the art of sitting deathly still in his father's presence. Perfected it and also complicated it, because he was an adolescent and more certain by the day that he had not one drop of the old king's blood in him—because he hated him too much to be related to him.

"You must never, ever say such things out loud," his mother told him, her voice as exhausted as her gaze was serious. "You must never give anyone in your father's court leave to doubt your parentage, Ares. Promise me."

He had promised, of course. Ares would have promised his mother anything.

Still, sometimes the crown prince was not in a mood to play statues. Sometimes he preferred to stare back at his father with as much insolence as he could muster, wordlessly daring the increasingly old and stooped king to throw something at him. Instead of at the stone walls of the palace, as he usually did.

"You are nothing but a disappointment to me," the king thundered at every appointment—which, thankfully, occurred only a handful of times a year now that Ares was dispatched to boarding schools all over Europe. "Why should I be cursed with such a weak and insolent heir?"

Which, naturally, only encouraged Ares to live down to the worst expectations his father had of him.

Ares accordingly…enjoyed himself. Recklessly, heedlessly, and thoroughly.

Europe was an ample playground, and he made friends in all the desperately pedigreed boarding schools he was eventually kicked out of. Together he and his bored, wealthy friends would traipse about the Continent, from the Alps to the beaches, and back again. From underground clubs in Berlin to parties on superyachts somewhere out there in all that Mediterranean splendor.

"You are a man now," his father told him bitterly when he turned twenty-one. "Chronologically."

By the law of their island kingdom, twenty-one was the age at which the heir to the throne was formally acknowledged as the Crown Prince and Heir Apparent to the Kingdom. Ares's investiture cemented his place in the line of succession, and further, that of his own heirs.

It was more of the same bloodline nonsense. Ares cared even less about it now than he had when he was five. These days, Ares was far more interested in his social life. And what antics he could engage in now he had access to his own vast fortune.

"Never fear, Father," he replied after the ceremony. "I have no plans to appall you any less now I am officially and for all time your heir apparent."

"You've sown enough wild oats to blanket the planet twice over," the king growled at him.

Ares did not bother to contradict him. First, because it would be a lie. He had indeed. And second, because the hypocrisy might choke him. King Damascus was well-known for his own years of sowing, such as it were.

And unlike Ares, his father had been betrothed to his mother since the day of her birth.

It was yet one more reason to hate the man.

"You say that as if it is a bad thing," he said instead, no longer playing games of statues in his father's private rooms.

He was a man grown now, or so everybody told him. He was heir to the kingdom and now would be expected to carry out duties in the name of the crown he would wear one day. He stood by the windows in his father's compartments and looked out over the sloping hills and crystal blue sea.

This would always be Atilia to him. The murmur of the ocean waves. The soft, sweet scent of flowers on the breeze. The Ionian Sea spread out before him.

Not the king and his penchant for smashing things and causing as much distress as he could at the slightest provocation.

"It is time for you to marry," his father intoned.

Ares turned, laughing, and then laughed harder when he saw his father was serious. "You cannot imagine I will be amenable to such a thing. Can you?"

"I have no interest in suffering through the sort of twenties you will inflict upon me. And upon this kingdom."

"And yet suffer you must," Ares replied with a soft menace that was as close as he'd ever come to taking a swing at his father or his king. "I have no intention of marrying."

His father broke a decanter that day that had been in the family since the 1700s. It burst to pieces slightly to the left of Ares, though he hadn't moved a muscle. He'd only stared back at the old man.

But it had broken something in Ares nonetheless.

It wasn't the shards of priceless crystal raining down on his traditional regalia. It wasn't his father's temper, which Ares found little more than tedious at this point.

It was the whole...show. The titles, the land, the bloodline. It all meant more to his father than he ever had. He hadn't been raised by his parents, he'd been monitored by a succession of servants and paraded in front of his father only every now and again. And only when everyone could be certain his behavior was perfect.

Or tolerable, at any rate.

He couldn't help thinking that really, he would prefer not to be a prince at all. And if he had no choice in that, well, there was no need to participate in passing the mantle of blood and nonsense on to the next generation. Ares had no intention of marrying. No interest in it.

But he was adamantly opposed to having children.

He couldn't help but think it was the bloodline itself that had made his father a monster, coupled with the crown. And he was a monster primarily to his son. He was cold to Ares's mother, but it was Ares who got splintered decanters and rage.

Ares had no intention of passing that rage along to his own children. Ever.

"You should not rile your father so," his mother said years later, after Ares had indulged in yet another conversation with the king about his marital prospects. He was twenty-six. "We shall have to start importing decanters from the Southern Palace."

Atilia was an ancient island kingdom in the Ionian Sea. The Northern Island was the most geographically north of the islands that made up the kingdom and was where the business of the country took place. The Northern Palace was accordingly the more stately residence of the royal family. The Southern Palace, on the most southern edge of the most southern island in the kingdom, was about relaxation, not matters of state. Beaches and ease and what breathing room a man could have when the weight of the kingdom sat on his shoulders.

Not that Ares intended to hoist up that weight himself, but still, he preferred the south. It was where he'd been enjoying a few weeks of recuperation after a long goodwill tour before his father had issued his summons. Because clearly too much time had passed between unpleasant conversations about Ares and the bloodline.

"I can't control what riles the man," Ares replied, dryly. "If I could, the last twenty-six years would have been markedly different. And there would be a great many more breakable objects left unattended about the palace, I imagine."

His mother had smiled at him the way she did, soft and sad. Ares always assumed it was because she couldn't save him from his father. She couldn't make the king treat the prince the way he treated her—with icy disinterest. "It is not the worst thing in the world to start turning your thoughts toward the next generation."

"I don't have it in me," Ares told her then. The conviction had been growing in him for years, by then. He studied his mother, and her drawn, dear face. "If you are an advertisement for the institution of marriage, or what one must bear to become queen of these islands, I cannot say that I am greatly inspired to foist this dubious pleasure on anyone."

That was true, but what was more true was that Ares enjoyed his life. He kept a home of sorts in Saracen House, a separate, palatial estate that was part of the palace complex on the Northern Island. But he was never there. He preferred the energy of Berlin. The hustle and rush of London. The mad, thrumming energy of New York City.

Or, really, any place his father was not.

And besides, Ares had yet to meet a woman he wanted for more than a night or two. Much less a lifetime of bloodlines and pomp, tradition and circumstance. He very much doubted the woman who could make him reconsider existed.

Nor was he particularly upset about this lack.

"I see how you are looking at me," his mother chided him. She sat as she always did, upright and elegant, on the chaise in her favorite room of the palace where the sunlight stood in for happiness. Or so it had always seemed to Ares. "And I'm not so old, thank you, that I cannot remember the excitement of youth and the certainty that I could predict the twists and turns of my own life."

"I hope you're not planning to give me any details of the excitement of your youth," Ares said. "Particularly as I was under the impression you spent most of it in a convent."

The queen's smile hinted at secrets, and made Ares glad. He liked to think his mother had more to reflect on in her life than his father and the glacial coldness he knew their marriage contained.

"You must find a wife of similar background," his mother told him quietly. "You are to be the king, Ares. Whatever your marriage is like, whatever bargains you and your spouse make with each other, she must be a queen without stain. So, too, must your issue be without blemish. Do you understand what I'm saying to you?"

He did. But understanding did not equal obedience.

"That I should put off marrying as long as possible," Ares said, and grinned at her. "I am more than happy to oblige."

Ares was halfway through his thirties when his mother died suddenly, lost to a quick-moving cancer she'd thought was a bout of the flu. And Ares was still reeling, still mourning when his father called him back to the Northern Palace some months after the funeral.

"You must know that it was your mother's dearest wish that you married," the king growled, his hand clenched around a crystal glass like it was a weapon. "The bloodline is your most sacred duty, Ares. The time for games is past."

But as it happened, Ares was even less a fan of his bloodline than he had been before. Something he would have thought impossible.

His mother had left him all her papers, which included the journals she had kept since she was a girl. Ares, missing her in the bleak months after her passing, had lost himself in those journals. He wanted to hoard every memory he had of her. He wanted to feel close to her again.

Instead, he learned the truth about his parents. Or about his father, rather, and the royal marriage. Once Ares had been born, they had tried for a spare until the doctors had made it clear that the queen could likely not have any more children. The king hadn't missed a beat. He'd openly flaunted his mistresses.

All those ladies of the court who had cooed at Ares when he was young. All those noblewomen he'd been instructed never to speak with in private. How had he missed their true role?

His father had broken his mother's heart.

Over and over again, every time he took a new woman to his bed.

And Ares had never been overly fond of the king. But this made it worse. This made him hate his father, deeply and irrevocably.

"You betrayed my mother casually and constantly," he said now, his own hands in fists because he did not require a weapon. And wanted only an excuse. "Yet you imagine you can speak to her dearest wishes now she has passed? Do you dare?"

The king rolled his eyes. "I grow weary of coddling you and your refusal to do what is required of you."

"If you're so interested in your bloodline," Ares told him now, "I suggest you expand it on your own, as you seem so predisposed to do. You do not need me to do your dirty work for you. And let me be perfectly clear on this. I will not do it."

His father sneered. "Why am I not surprised? Once a weakling, always a weakling. You would even give away your throne."

But Ares didn't think of it as giving away a throne—

and one he'd never wanted anyway. He was ensuring not only his freedom, but the freedom of any potential children he might have had. He was making certain no child of his would be raised in that cold palace of lies.

And he refused to treat a woman the way his father had treated his mother.

Ever.

His father married again, quickly, to a woman younger than Ares. Ares caused a scandal by refusing to attend the wedding.

The kingdom was in turmoil. The royal advisors were beside themselves.

"The throne has a stain upon it," cried the most senior advisor, Sir Bartholomew. He'd come all the way to New York City to plead his case before Ares, who had refused to grace a room that also contained the king since that last, dark conversation with his father. "The kingdom is reeling. Your father has installed his mistress and dares to call her his queen. And he has claimed that any issue he gets upon her will supersede you to the throne. You cannot allow this, Highness!"

"How can I prevent it?" Ares asked.

He lived halfway across the planet. He spent his time carrying out his royal duties and running the charity he'd started in his mother's name and still enjoying his life as best he could. The tabloids loved him. The more they hated his father, the more they adored what they'd called his flaws as a younger man.

Ares had no intention of submitting himself to his father's court. He had no interest whatsoever in playing the royal game.

"You must return to Atilia," Sir Bartholomew cried,

there in the penthouse suite of the hotel Ares called home in Manhattan. "You must marry and begin your own family at once. It is only because your father continues to refer to you as the Playboy Prince that the people feel stuck with his terrible choices. If only you would return and show the people a better way forward—"

"I'm not the king you seek," Ares told him quietly. Distinctly. And the older man paled. "I will never be that king. I have no intention of carrying on this twisted, polluted bloodline beyond my own lifetime. If my father would like to inflict it on more unwary children, I can do nothing but offer them my condolences as they come of age."

Ares thought of his mother after his advisors left, as he often did. What he would not give for another moment or two of her counsel. That sad smile of hers, her gentle touch.

Her quiet humor that he knew, now, only he had ever witnessed.

You must marry, he could hear her voice say, as if she still sat before him, elegant and kind.

And he missed his mother. Ares understood he always would.

But he had no intention of following the same path his parents had.

He would die first.

His phone was buzzing in his pocket, and he knew it was more invitations to more of the parties he liked to attend and act as if he was a normal man, not the heir to all this pain and hurt and poison. He eyed the face in his mirror that he hated to admit resembled the King's, not hers.

Ares straightened his shoulders until his posture was as perfect as she would have liked it, on the off chance she could still see him, somehow. He liked to imagine she could still see him.

And then he strode off to lose himself in the Manhattan night.

CHAPTER TWO

Five months later

"PREGNANT?"

Pia Alexandrina San Giacomo Combe gazed back at her older brother, Matteo, with as much equanimity as she could muster.

She'd practiced this look in the mirror. For a good month or two already, and she still wasn't sure she'd gotten it right.

"That's what I said, Matteo," she forced herself to say, in a very calm, composed, matter-of-fact sort of way.

She'd practiced that, too.

"You cannot be serious," her brother blustered, a look of sheer horror on his face.

But Pia was standing before the wide desk in the library of the ancient manor house that had been in her father's side of the family since that early, hardy Combe ancestor had clawed his way out of the textile mills and built it. Or she thought that was how the story went, having always preferred to tune out most of the lectures about the grand history of both sides of her family. Because her parents had so dearly loved to lecture *at* each other, as if their histories were engaged in a twisted battle for supremacy.

And because she was standing there before her brother, wearing a dress that fit her more tightly than she might have liked—in all that unrelenting funereal black that Pia had been draped in for the past six weeks since their mother had died—she could feel it when Matteo's disbelieving stare landed on her belly.

Her belly, which, despite Pia's best attempt to pretend none of this was happening, was protruding. Sticking right out, whether she liked it or not.

There was no way around it.

Her mother, of course, had noticed that Pia was getting "chunky" in the week or so before she'd died. And Pia had learned a long, long time ago exactly what weight she needed to maintain to avoid the acid side of her mother's tongue. Her mother had seen the instant Pia had exceeded that weight, the way she had when Pia had been a rather moonfaced and shy young girl. To the ounce.

Puppy fat is for poor girls with no prospects, the legendary Alexandrina San Giacomo had said to her woebegone twelve-year-old daughter, her magnificent face calm—which made it worse. *You are a San Giacomo. San Giacomos do not have chipmunk cheeks. I suggest you step away from the sweets.*

After that Pia had been so determined to, if not live up to her mother's impossible standard of effortless grace and beauty, at least escape her scathing put-downs. She'd dieted religiously throughout her teens, yet her cheeks had steadfastly refused to slim down, until one morning she'd woken up, aged twenty-two, and they'd gone.

Sadly, she'd taken her fateful trip to New York City shortly thereafter.

And Pia couldn't say why her mother had done what she had done. She couldn't definitively state that it was because she'd discovered her unmarried daughter was pregnant, and on the verge of causing the kind of scandal that was usually her mother's province. Hadn't Alexandrina spent the bulk of Pia's childhood beating it into her—not literally, thankfully, though Alexandrina's tongue was its own mallet—that Pia was to walk the straight and narrow? That Pia was to make certain she remained peerless and without blemish? That Pia needed to be, above all things, Snow White—pure as the driven snow or Alexandrina would know the reason why.

The truth was, Alexandrina hadn't much liked the reason why.

Pia couldn't say that the news that she was not only not at all innocent any longer, but pregnant by a stranger whose name she didn't know, had made her mother decide to overindulge more than usual, as she had. And with such tragic results.

But she couldn't say that wasn't the reason, either.

And now it was six weeks later. Alexandrina had died and left their little family—and her planetful of admirers—in a state of despair. And then her father—brash and larger-than-life Eddie Combe, who Pia had thought was surely immortal—had collapsed with a heart attack three days ago and died that same night. And Pia was certain, now.

This was all her fault.

"You are serious," Matteo said, darkly.

She tried to keep her face calm and expressionless, as her mother always had, particularly when she was at her most awful. "I'm afraid so."

Matteo looked as if he had glass in his mouth. "You are aware, I feel certain, that we are moments away from our father's funeral?"

Pia decided that wasn't a real question. She waited instead of answering it, her hands folded in front of her as if she could stand there all day. She gazed past her brother and out at the Yorkshire countryside arrayed outside the windows, green hills beneath the gunmetal sky. Matteo, his gray eyes more dark and brooding than the stormy sky behind him, glared at her.

But when he spoke again, she had the impression he was trying his best to be kind.

"You look pregnant, Pia."

As if she might have missed that. "I do."

"There will be press at this funeral service. Paparazzi everywhere we turn. There was no avoiding them six weeks ago and it will be even more intense today. You must know what kind of commotion a visible pregnancy will cause."

To his credit, he sounded as if he was *trying* to talk without clenching his jaw like that.

"What do you suggest I do?" Pia asked the question quietly, as if it hadn't kept her up since the night her father had died. If she didn't attend the funeral, would that be worse than if she did?

"How the hell did this happen?" Matteo growled.

Pia had always considered herself close to her

brother. It was only the two of them, after all, caught up some ten years apart in the middle of their parents' famously tempestuous, always dramatic love story. Eddie Combe had been known as much for his tendency to take a swing at his business competitors as for his business itself, Combe Industries, that was the direct result of those tough Combes who'd climbed out of the mills.

Meanwhile, Alexandrina San Giacomo had been the most beautiful woman in the world. That was what they'd called her since she'd been all of eighteen. At her funeral, pop stars had sung elegies, the world had watched the televised version to weep along and post pictures of their black armbands, and rarely a day had passed since without Pia encountering some or other remembrance of Alexandrina that called her *La Bellissima, the angel of our time.*

And that was the more restrained lot.

Their parents' love story had transfixed a generation. Pia had always been transported by it herself, especially as her experience of their love came with the shouting matches, the broken crockery followed by Those Noises behind locked doors, and their utter and complete fixation on each other at all times. No matter who else was in the room.

Matteo, darkly handsome, broodingly intense, and excruciatingly dedicated to his role as the last San Giacomo heir as well as his father's successor in the family business, was precisely the sort of child one might expect to come from such a union.

Pia, by contrast, had been hidden away for most of her life, which she had always assumed was a direct consequence of her chipmunk cheeks. She'd been packed off to a convent, then a finishing school, while everyone in the family had gone to extreme and excessive links to keep her out of the public eye.

They all claimed it was to protect her, but she knew better. She was too awkward. Too chunky. The most beautiful woman in the world could not have an embarrassing, tragic daughter, could she? Alexandrina had been a swan by any measure. Pia was, sadly, still very much the ugly duckling in comparison, and she'd resigned herself to that.

Or she'd tried, very hard, to resign herself to that.

"Did you...ask me how it happened?" She stared at her brother now, feeling the wholly inappropriate urge to let out a laugh. Only her brother's likely reaction to such a thing kept her from it. "Not that you fling it about, or anything, but I was fairly certain you...already knew."

"Thank you for making light of the situation, Pia," Matteo snapped, that glass in his mouth getting the better of him. "I'm glad this is all a joke to you. Our father's funeral starts within the hour. You don't think you could have given me some advance warning about—" his gaze raked over her, and made her cheeks heat with shame "—this?"

"I thought I should do it in person," Pia said. That was true. What was also true was that she really hadn't wanted to do it at all. "And you've been down in London since—" But she didn't want to discuss their mother's death. "And I knew you would be coming up here for the funeral anyway, so I thought, why not wait until I saw you."

And Pia was nearly twenty-three years old. She

might have been protected to the point of smothering her whole life, but she was still a woman grown. So why did she find herself acting like a stammering child when her older brother glared at her?

"This is a disaster," he growled, as if she'd missed that. "This is not a game."

"You're not the one who can't wear most of the clothes in your wardrobe, Matteo," she replied. Airily, because what else could she do? "I don't think you need to tell me how real this is."

He stared at her, shaking his head. And Pia had tried so hard to put a brave face on all this. But the truth was, she was ashamed. She could feel that heat in her cheeks, and everywhere else, too.

And the way Matteo looked at her then, as if he was so disappointed in her it hurt, Pia was very much afraid that she would stay ashamed forever more.

"I'm sorry," she said quietly.

"Who is the father?"

But that only made that sickening shame inside her worse.

"Dad asked me that, too," she said, instead of answering the question.

Because the answer was so…squalid. Humiliating, really. Oh, she'd thought it was so delightful before. She finally had a secret! She was a modern woman at last, like everyone else she knew! She'd stepped smartly into her own future, seized the day—or the night, to be more precise—and had stopped keeping herself like some kind of vestal virgin, forever on the shelf, because for some reason her scandal-ridden family seemed united in their desire to keep her from making the mistakes they had.

Everything was fun and games until the morning sickness hit, she had discovered.

Matteo's glare darkened, which should have been impossible. "Dad knew about this?"

"Both Mum and Dad knew about it," Pia said, her voice small.

Of all the things she couldn't believe, what newly lived inside of her was really the least of it. She didn't understand how the world could continue turning without her parents in it. Her mother had been like the sky above, even in the quiet of her own sitting room. That vast and given to sudden storms. Her father had been like a volcano. Big and imposing, and always *this close* to eruption.

How could they both be gone?

And how could she live with the sure knowledge that she was what had killed them, one way or another?

Her hand crept over her belly, then froze when she saw Matteo's dark gaze follow the movement. A new wave of shame swept over her.

"What…" Matteo shook his head as if he couldn't take all the information in. As if he could make it go away by scowling at it. Or her. "What on earth did they say?"

"About what you'd expect." Pia tried to straighten her shoulders and stand taller, because Alexandrina had always told her it made a girl look a size smaller. "Mum wanted to make sure I knew that it was better to have a boy, as girls will steal your beauty." She opted not to mention the awkward moment that had followed that pronouncement, as Pia and her mother had stared at each other, neither one of them pointing out the obvious. That Pia had clearly done nothing of the kind. Her brother blinked, and she pushed on. "While Dad said, and I quote, 'I should have known you'd turn out to be nothing more than a common tart.'"

She even approximated their father's growl of a voice, with that broad hint of Yorkshire he'd played up, the better to discomfit those who thought they were his betters.

For a moment, Pia and Matteo stared at each other.

Pia felt her stomach turn over, and not with leftover morning sickness. But with disloyalty. Her parents had always had it in them to be awful. Temper tantrums were one of their primary forms of communication. They had always been capable of saying terrible things, usually did, and then went to great lengths to make up for it—usually not by saying anything directly, but with whirlwind trips to far-flung places. Or sudden bouts of affection and sweetness.

They had been disappointed in her. Pia knew that. But if they'd lived, the temper would have given way to something kinder, no matter what they'd said to her in the heat of their initial reactions. She should have said that, too. She should have made it clear she knew they would both have softened.

But it felt too late. For them, certainly.

And for her, the child who had always disappointed them.

Pia could hear the sound of movement in the house outside the library. The staff was getting ready for the gathering that would happen after the service and burial. When all their father's captain-of-industry contemporaries and associates—as Eddie Combe hadn't trafficked in friends—would clutter up the house, pretending they missed him. And all of Europe's heads of state would send their emissaries, because Eddie Combe might have come from the dark mills of Yorkshire, but he had married a San Giacomo. San Giacomos had been Venetian royalty in their time. At least one of their ancestors had been a prince. And that meant that the crème de la crème of Europe was bound to pay their respects today, no matter how little they had cared for Eddie personally.

Pia wanted no part of any of this. And not only because she was terribly afraid that she would cause a commotion simply by appearing in her…state. But because she still couldn't believe her parents were gone. Not when she hadn't had enough time to watch them come round. Not when she'd never know if this time, she'd disappointed them *too much* or if they'd soften the way they usually did. It seemed premature to mourn them.

And deeply unfair that she was expected to do it in public, as if she was part of a show for others to watch and judge.

"Do you not know who was responsible for getting you in this condition?" Matteo asked. Icily. "Or are you simply choosing not to name him?"

And maybe Pia was a little more emotionally fragile than she realized. Because that rubbed her the wrong way.

"I think you'll find that I'm responsible for getting myself into this condition," she replied. "I wasn't attacked, if that's what you mean. Nothing was done to me that I didn't enthusiastically participate in. I'm not a damsel in distress, Matteo."

There was a part of her that might have liked the fact she was pregnant—had it not horrified everyone who knew her. Pia had always wanted a family. Not the one she had, but a real family. The sort that she imagined everyone else had.

Matteo was studying her, and she could almost see the machinery working in his head. "That trip you took to New York. That was it, wasn't it?"

"If you mean the graduation trip I took to celebrate finally completing college, then yes." And oh, how she'd fought for that. It had been Matteo who had finally stepped forward and bluntly told their parents that Pia deserved as much of a chance as anyone to live her own adult life. Her cheeks burned all the brighter. Because she was imagining what he must be thinking of her now. "We had a lovely week in New York. It turns out, I happened to come back home with a little bit extra—"

"I don't understand. You…?"

There was the sound of footsteps beyond the door, and darker clouds began to pull together over the hills in the distance. And Pia stared back at her brother, her cheeks so hot they hurt.

"You don't understand?" she asked him. "Really? I've certainly seen your face and photographs with different women in the tabloids, yet you remain unmarried. How can this be?"

"Pia."

"If you're going to act like we're Victorian, Matteo,

I should have every right to ask about the state of your virtue. Shouldn't I?"

"I beg your pardon. *I* am not in the habit of having intimate relations with women that I do not know."

"Well. Okay, then." She drew herself up even straighter. "I guess I'm just a whore."

"I doubt that very much," Matteo growled.

But the word stayed in her head, pounding like a drum, because the doors to the library were tossed open then. The staff that Matteo had kept at bay came flooding in, his erstwhile assistant was there to whisper in his ear, and it was time to do their sad duty.

And she knew their father had thought exactly that of her, at least for that moment. He'd looked at her—really looked at her, for a change, because Eddie Combe had usually preferred to keep his attention on himself—only three days before his heart attack. And called her a common tart to her face.

She kept telling herself that wasn't cause and effect. That the heart attack hadn't had anything to do with her condition. And that, if he'd had more time, he would have found her in the next days or weeks and gruffly offer some sort of olive branch.

Yet as she rode down in her brother's car, tucked there in the back with him while he tended to the business of running the family company and his assistant Lauren handled calls for him, she accepted that she couldn't know for sure. How could she?

The last thing Pia knew Eddie had thought about her was that she was a whore. He'd said so. And then in a matter of days, he was dead.

Her mother had called her fat, which wasn't anything new. Then again, that was the worst thing Alexandrina could think to call another woman, and she hadn't yet cycled through to the usual affection before she'd passed.

Either way, Matteo and Pia were orphans now.

And Pia was still terribly afraid it was her fault.

But she snuck her hand over her belly because whether it was or wasn't her fault, that didn't extend to the next generation. She wouldn't allow it.

The funeral service was simple and surprisingly touching. It made Eddie seem far more approachable than he had in life, and Pia wondered if she would understand the man more as time went on. If her memories would mellow him into more of a father figure, lingering on his gruff affection. Or if he would always be that volcanic presence in her mind. The one that had thought his only daughter was a trollop right before he'd died.

The ride back up the hill toward the Combe estate was somber, and Pia was glad, in a fierce sort of way, that it was a moody day. The dark clouds threatened, though the rain held off, and they stood in a bit of a brisk, unpleasant wind as Eddie's casket was lowered into the ground in the family plot.

The vicar, who Eddie had hated in life, though had requested in his will in some attempt to torture the holy man from beyond, murmured a prayer. Pia kept her eyes on the casket that was all that remained of her father—of her childhood—until she could no longer see it.

And somehow kept her tears at bay. Because there were too many cameras. And how many times had Alexandrina lectured her about red eyes and a puffy face?

It hit her again. That Alexandrina was gone. That Eddie was gone. That nothing was ever going to be the same.

Then Matteo's hand was on her back and they moved away from the grave site to form the necessary receiving line for those who might or might not make it back to the small reception at the house. It was times like these that her years in finishing school came in handy. Pia was infinitely capable of shaking hands and making meaningful eye contact with every royal in Europe without noticing them at all.

"May I offer my condolences on the part of the Kingdom of Atilia and His Majesty King Damascus, my father?"

Something about that voice kicked at her.

Pia's hand was already extended. And even as she focused on the man standing before her, his hand enveloped hers.

And she knew that sudden burst of flame. She knew the shiver that worked its way from the nape of her neck down to pool at the base of her spine.

Her eyes jerked up and met his.

As expected, his gaze was green, shot through with gold. And as shocked as hers.

Pia panicked. How could this be happening? The last time she'd seen this man, he had been sprawled out, asleep, in a penthouse suite high above Manhattan. She had gathered her things, feeling powerful and shaken at once by her daring and all the things he'd taught her, and had tiptoed away.

She'd never imagined she would see him again.

"You," he said, almost wonderingly. "New York."

And part of her was warming, in instant response to the way his mouth curved in one corner. As if Pia was a good memory, as he had been for her. At least at first.

Before the morning sickness had sent her to the doctor to discuss the flu she couldn't kick.

But Pia couldn't indulge in memories, good or bad, because she was standing next to her brother. And he was focusing that dark scowl of his on the man still holding Pia's hand.

"New York?" Matteo asked. Demanded, more like. "Did you say you know my sister from New York?"

"Matteo. Stop."

But the man, still smiling slightly, seemed unaware of the danger he was in. "I met your sister in Manhattan some months ago," he said, amiably enough. He smiled at Pia. "Do you go there often?"

"*Miss Combe*, my *younger* sister, has been there once," Matteo growled. "And guess what? She picked up a souvenir."

"I beg your pardon?"

The man frowned. But in that way very important men did, as if inviting everyone around them to apologize for opportuning them.

"My sister is six months pregnant," Matteo bit out.

Pia had the sense that she was in some kind of slow-motion car accident. The sort she'd seen in movies a thousand times. She could almost hear the scraping of the metal, the screech of the tires. Yet everything before her seemed to move in tiny, sticky increments. She watched her brother ball up his fists and step closer to the man. The man—who had told her his name was Eric, though she doubted that was real—did not back up.

And they both turned and stared at Pia as if she was some kind of roadside curiosity.

"If your sister is or isn't pregnant, that is no concern of mine," the man said.

Far less amiably.

Just in case Pia had wondered if it was possible to feel worse about all of this. Look at that! It was. She rubbed at her chest as if that could make her heart stop pounding the way it was. Or at least, ache less.

"Pia," Matteo said, dark and furious. "Is this the man?"

"Have you forgotten where we are?" she managed to ask, though she was barely able to breathe.

"It's a simple question," her brother bit off.

"Once again, the state of your sister's womb has nothing to do with me," the man said.

And he wasn't just *a man*.

If Pia had been going to throw away a lifetime of doing the right thing and making the correct choice over any old man, she would have done it years ago. *This* man was beautiful. Those gorgeous eyes and silky dark hair, a jawline to inspire the unwary into song and poetry, and shoulders to make a girl cry. *This* man had walked into the party where Pia had already been feeling awkward and out of place, and it was as if a light shone upon him. It was as if his bones were like other people's, but sat in him differently. Making him languid. Easy.

His smile had been all of that, plus heat, when he'd aimed it at her, there beneath some modern art installation that looked to Pia's eye like an exclamation point. In bronze.

But best of all, this man hadn't had any idea who she was.

She could always tell. It was the way they said her name. It was a certain gleam in their eyes. But he'd had none of it.

He'd liked her. Just her.

Just Pia.

She'd planned to hold on to that. She'd *wanted* to hold on to that. But it seemed that would be one more thing she didn't get to have.

"Thank you so much for asking about my private life, Matteo," she said to her brother now. In a decent impression of her mother's iciest tone, which came more naturally than she'd expected. "But as a matter of fact, I have only ever had sex with one person."

Then she looked at the man before her, and her memories wouldn't do her any good, so she cast them aside. No matter how beautiful he was. "And I regret to inform you, but that one person was you."

But that didn't have the effect she expected it to have.

Because all the beautiful man before her did was laugh.

At her, if she wasn't mistaken.

"Like hell," he said.

And that was when Matteo punched him.

Right in the face.

CHAPTER THREE

ONE MOMENT ARES was standing straight up, looking one of his past indulgences in the face.

He'd laughed, of course. What could he do but laugh?

Because the truth was, Ares hadn't forgotten her. He hadn't forgotten the way her gray eyes had lit up when she'd looked at him. He hadn't forgotten her smile, shy and delighted in turn. And he certainly hadn't forgotten her taste.

He might even have toyed with the notion of what it would be like to seek her out for another taste, now and again over the past few months—

The next moment he was on the ground, and it took him a moment to understand that the Combe heir had punched him.

Hard.

Not only that, he'd chosen to do so in full view of the paparazzi, all of whom swooped in closer like the locusts they were at the sight. They took picture after picture and held up cameras to record every last detail of the Crown Prince of Atilia's inelegant sprawl across the wet grass in the middle of a funeral.

Ares glared up at the man who had laid him out.

He wanted—badly—to respond in kind, but restrained himself. Because he might not want to be king, but he was still a prince, whether he liked it or not. And princes did not swing on bereaved commoners, no matter the provocation. Moreover, he preferred to control the stories that appeared about him, especially when the press on his father was so dire these days.

He couldn't change the fact this man had hit him. But he could opt not to react in a manner that would only make it all worse.

He climbed back to his feet far more gracefully than he'd gone down. He brushed himself off, his gaze on the man scowling at him in case he started swinging again, then put his hand to his lip. When he drew it away, he noted darkly that there was blood.

Because of course there was blood.

Because everything was about his damned blood. Hadn't his father told him so a thousand times before Ares had turned seven?

Ares noticed movement in his periphery and held up his hand before his security detail handled the situation in a manner that would only make it worse. He glared at the Combe heir, whose name he hadn't bothered to learn as he'd run over his notes on his way here today.

That seemed like a significant oversight, in retrospect.

"You understand that I am the Crown Prince of Atilia, do you not?" he asked coolly instead. "Attacking me is considered an act of war."

"That doesn't frighten me," the other man retorted.

"What should frighten both of you is that this entire conversation is being recorded," Pia hissed at the pair of them.

And that was the thing. He could remember *her* name. Pia.

Such a little name when she had hit him with a good deal more force than her brother had just now.

And the hits kept coming today.

A closer look showed Ares what he should have noticed from the start. That she'd thickened around the middle. And she was a tiny thing—easy enough, if a man had a decent imagination and the necessary strength, to pick up and move around as he liked, and Ares certainly had liked—and her bump was clearly noticeable. Huge, in fact.

It was very clearly…exactly what it was.

But what it could not be was his.

"I have never in my life had unprotected sex," Ares said with as much regal hauteur as he could manage.

The Combe heir looked enraged. Pia only shook her head, her gaze darting around to their audience before returning to her brother.

"If you two want to roll about in the dirt, flinging your toxic masculinity about like bad cologne, I cannot stop you," she said, half under her breath. "But I refuse to become fodder for the tabloids for the first time in my life because of your bad decisions."

And she turned around and marched off, as if it wasn't already too late.

When Ares looked around he could see the speculation on every face within view. Because there had been a punch, and now Pia was leaving, and it didn't take a mathematician to put her belly and him together.

But it was impossible.

"I suggest you follow my sister up to the house," her brother growled at him.

"Or you will do what?" Ares asked, every inch of him the product of at least a millennia of royal breeding. "Punch something again? You do not tell me where I go or do not, Mr. Combe."

"Watch me."

Ares laughed again, more for the benefit of their audience than because he found any of this funny. Or even tolerable.

And then, because he couldn't see another option, he turned and made his way up the long drive that led from the family plot toward the big, hulking house that sat there at the top of the hill. But he took his time, chatting merrily with other guests, as if he was at a party instead of a funeral. As if he didn't have what he suspected was the beginnings of a fat lip.

And as if he hadn't been accused of impregnating a woman by her overprotective older brother, in full view of too many cameras.

He could leave, he knew. No one would keep him here, no matter what Pia's brother imagined. His security detail would whisk him away at a moment's notice.

But Pia's condition was not his doing—could not be his doing—and he felt compelled to make that clear.

He walked inside the manor house, wondering, not for the first time, how it was these northern Europeans could tolerate their stuffy, dark houses. The palaces of Atilia were built to celebrate the islands they graced. The sea was all around, and invited in, so it murmured through every archway. It was there, shimmering, just around every corner.

He asked after Pia in the grand entryway and was shown into the sort of library that made him think of all the headmasters' offices he'd found himself in during his school days. Usually en route to his latest expulsion.

She was standing at the window, staring out at the miserable British countryside, wet and cold. But what he noticed was her back was too straight.

And he didn't know why she would claim that he was the one who'd impregnated her, but it was hard to remember that as he looked at her from behind.

Because he remembered that night.

It had been their second round, or perhaps their third. He had woken to find her standing by the window, wrapped in a sheet from the thoroughly destroyed bed, her fingers against the glass. Manhattan had gleamed and glittered all around. Ares had gone to her as if drawn there by some kind of magnet. He'd brushed aside the weight of her dark, silken hair and put his mouth to the nape of her neck.

He could still remember the heated, broken sound she'd made. Just as he could remember the chill of the glass beneath his palm when he'd braced himself there and taken her from behind—

He shook himself out of that now. Especially when his body responded with as much enthusiasm as he remembered from that night.

"I'm not the father of your baby," he said, his voice grittier than it should have been when he knew he hadn't done this.

"When I realized I was pregnant, I tried to find you,

of course." Pia didn't turn around. She stayed where she was, her back to him and her arms crossed above her swollen belly. He couldn't stop staring at it, as if he'd never seen a pregnant woman before. "It's a decent thing to do, after all. But no matter who I asked, which was its own embarrassment, no one could remember any 'Eric' at that party."

"And because I lied about my name, you think it appropriate to lie yourself? About something far more serious?"

She let out a small sound, like a sigh, but she still didn't turn to face him.

"When I couldn't find anyone by the name of Eric, I thought that was fair enough. Not ideal, but *fine*. I would do it by myself. As women have been doing since the dawn of time. But that's easier to make yourself believe when no one knows. When you haven't yet told your whole family that yes, you had a one-night stand in New York City. And you don't know the name of the man you had that one-night stand with. But guess what? You're pregnant by him anyway."

"It is not my baby."

"But I withstood the shame," she said, her shoulders shifting. Straightening. "I'm figuring out how to withstand it, anyway. I never expected to see you again."

"Clearly not." Ares could hear the darkness in his voice. The fury. "Or you would not dare tell such a lie."

She turned then, and her face was calm. Serene, even. That was like a slap.

Until he noticed the way her gray eyes burned.

"And the funny thing about shame is that I keep thinking there must be a maximum amount any one person can bear," she told him. "I keep thinking I must be full up. But no. I never am."

Something twisted in him at that, but Ares ignored it.

"You cannot wander around telling people that you're having my child," he thundered at her. "This doesn't seem to be penetrating. It's morally questionable at best, no matter who the man is. But if you claim you carry *my* child, what you are announcing is that you are, in fact, carrying the heir to the Atilian throne. Do you realize what that means?"

Pia looked pale. "Why would I realize that—or anything about you? I didn't know who you were until fifteen minutes ago. Much less that you were a *prince*. *Are* a prince. A *prince*, for God's sake."

A man who had renounced his claim to a throne should not have found the way she said that so...confronting.

Ares pushed on. "Now you know. You need to retract your claim. Immediately."

"Are you denying that we slept together?" she asked, her voice shaky.

"We did very little sleeping, as I recall. But I don't see what that has to do with anything."

"I've only ever slept with one man," she threw out there. "You."

Or so it seemed to Ares as it sat there, bristling in the center of the library floor.

The implications of that statement roared in him.

But Pia was still talking. "If you are not the father, we have a far larger problem on our hands." She even smiled, which made the roaring in him worse. "Shall I contact the Vatican to notify them of the second immaculate conception? Or will you?"

Ares stared back at her as that scathing question hung in the air between them, too, joining in with all the rest of the noise. The roar of it. And it wasn't until that moment that he realized that for all he liked to think of himself as an independent creature, in no way beholden to crown or kingdom unless he wanted to be, he really was a prince straight through.

Because he was wholly unaccustomed to being addressed in such a manner.

It had never occurred to him before this moment how very few people in his life dared address him with anything but the utmost respect. Yet today he had been punched in the face. And was now being spoken to in a manner he could only call flippant.

Pia swallowed as he stared at her, and then wrung her hands in a manner that suggested she was not, perhaps, as sanguine as she appeared.

Ares didn't much like what it said about him that he found that…almost comforting.

"Happily," she said in a low voice, "it doesn't matter whether you believe me or not. There is a selection of tests to choose from to determine paternity, both before and after birth."

"It is not a question of whether or not I believe you."

"I'm not sure I blame you," she said, as if he hadn't spoken. Another new experience for Ares. Especially as she sounded as if she was attempting to be *generous*. "I can see how such a thing would be difficult to believe if I was…like you."

Ares's brow rose and he suspected he looked like all those pictures of his lofty, patrician, infinitely regal ancestors. "Like me?"

"I doubt you remember the particulars of our night. Or me. And why would you? You must have such adventures all the time."

He might have been caught on the back foot since he'd arrived in Yorkshire this afternoon, but he wasn't foolish enough to answer that question.

"Here is what I don't understand," he said instead, as a sort of low, heated pounding started up in his chest, then arrowed out into his limbs. His sex. "You claim you were innocent before that night. Why? You're not a child."

"Do children prize chastity? Or is it their natural state?"

"I could not say if they prize it or do not," he growled. "I know I never did. I shrugged it off at the first opportunity. I was under the impression that was the entire purpose of the boarding schools I attended." He prowled toward her, keeping his eyes fast on hers. "Were you locked away in a convent, Pia?"

Something like humor flashed across her face. "Yes."

That startled him. He came to a stop before her. "An actual convent? Complete with nuns?"

"Of course with nuns. It couldn't very well be a convent without nuns, could it?"

"What on earth were you doing in a convent?"

She looked wry. "Protecting and defending my honor and holding fast to my chastity, of course. What else?"

"And what? The moment you walked through the convent doors into the big, bad world, you decided the time was ripe to rid yourself of that pesky hymen? With the first man you laid eyes upon?"

He ignored the other thing in him, dark and male,

that didn't like that idea. Because Ares was not accustomed to being *any man*, indistinguishable from the rest. Notable only because he was male.

"First I went to finishing school," Pia said, and for all that her eyes were too big, and her face was pale, Ares noticed that she didn't back down. "There I learned excruciatingly important things. A bit of political science and economics to pepper my banquet conversation, and how best to talk about books to make myself seem important and intellectual, yet approachable. I learned how to dance graciously, as befits a hostess and guest at any gathering. I learned the various degrees of curtsies, and when to employ them. I was meant to be a kind of weapon, you understand."

"I do not understand." But he was too close to her now. He couldn't seem to pull his eyes away from her. There was not one part of him that wanted to, for that matter, and he remembered that magnetic pull, that night. How could it still affect him? "But I'm feeling the effects of your bombshell, nonetheless."

"I graduated six months ago," Pia said quietly, her chin lifting as she held his gaze. "My friends and I decided to take a trip to New York to celebrate. One of my friends knew the person who was throwing that particular party. And there you were. See? There's nothing nefarious."

"Save the fact that I have had what I could only term an epic amount of sex in my lifetime, *cara*," he said, almost drawling the words. "But no one has ever turned up claiming I left them pregnant."

"I didn't actually 'turn up.' You did. Here. At my father's funeral." Her gray eyes glittered. "But by all means, let's brush that aside and continue to talk about your feelings."

"It is not a question of feelings," he said, through his teeth. "It is a question of what is possible and what is not."

She lifted a shoulder, then dropped it. "There is only one possible way I could have gotten pregnant. Because there was only the one night. And only the one man."

"But I do not—"

"Please." Those big, gray eyes implored him, though the hand she held up was rather more of a demand. "There's no point arguing about this. Why don't you give me your details and I'll arrange a test. No point discussing it further until then, is there?"

"Pia. You cannot imagine that I will simply wander off into the ether, can you?" He didn't know what possessed him. One moment he merely stood there a foot or so away from her. And in the next, his hands were on her delicate shoulders, holding her there as if she'd tried to walk away. When he should have wanted that. "Or is that what you want me to do?"

A strange expression moved over her face, darkening her eyes. That wry twist to her lips was back, and deeper this time.

"That's a question you need to ask yourself, I think," she said softly. "In the absence of a test, who's to say who the father is? I certainly won't say a thing, no matter who asks."

That dropped through Ares like a stone. A heavy weight, sharp and cold and jagged, sinking deep inside him.

He could turn around and leave, right now. His lip would heal. The tabloids would speculate, but then, they always did. If he didn't feed them, surely the stories would die away.

And he could carry on as he'd always intended. As he'd planned.

But despite himself, he thought of his mother.

Of how disappointed she would be in him if she were here.

Nothing had been more important to the queen than her family. Him. All she had ever wanted for him was a wife. A child.

He could shrug off his father's obsession with bloodlines without a second thought, and had. He'd shrugged off his father as easily.

But never his mother.

Never.

He realized his hands were still wrapped around Pia's shoulders. Her head was tipped back, and that belly of hers was between them.

And he wanted nothing to do with this. He wanted to turn back time, refuse to come to this funeral, or go back further and make sure he was nowhere near that party in Manhattan that night.

Even if that would have meant missing out on that taste of her that haunted him still, loathe as he was to admit it.

"There are two things you must know about me," he told her gruffly, as if he was making vows. "First, I have no intention of marrying. My father, the king, would love nothing more than to knock me out of the line of succession entirely. And I have done my best to help him with that, as it is preferable to playing his little games. And second, but just as important, I had no intention of ever having children."

"Is this the royal version of congratulations?" she asked, but her voice quivered. He could feel it inside him, like shame. "It needs a little work."

"I want no part of this," he told her, dark and sure. "But I will do my duty. One way or another."

Ares wasn't sure what he meant by that. All he could seem to concentrate on was that he'd moved too close to her without meaning to. His mouth hovered worryingly close to hers. He could so easily tilt himself forward and help himself to those lips of hers, impossibly sweet and soft and *right there—*

But Pia twisted her shoulders and stepped back, out of his grip. He could have held her fast, and knew full well he shouldn't have felt a sense of heroism that he hadn't. And then he felt something far worse crawl through him as her hands went to cover her belly.

As if she was protecting her child from him.

His child, if what she said was true.

"I haven't asked you for anything," she said, very distinctly. Quiet, but sure. "Including your reluctant, begrudging sense of duty, thank you very much."

The door behind them opened, and Ares turned, astonished that anyone would dare interrupt him.

It was a day for astonishment, it seemed.

"Your Highness," the head of his security detail said, bowing his head apologetically. "I'm afraid there is a situation with the paparazzi. We must go."

CHAPTER FOUR

PIA FELT AS IF she had whiplash. Everything had been in hideous slow motion at her father's graveside, but now, it was as if events were tumbling of their own accord. A glance out the window showed the scrum of reporters, all shouting and shoving. Her gut felt much the same.

She felt as if she was a train on a broken track, careening out of control.

Though she knew better. There was no train. Events weren't carrying on of their own volition. And while she might feel out of control, that didn't make it so.

It was him.

Prince Ares.

His name was not Eric. It had never been Eric. And now that she knew who he was, she couldn't quite imagine how she'd believed he was just…some guy. That he was royal appeared stamped deep into him, today. How had she missed it in New York? It was the way he stood. It was the way he lifted that imperious brow of his. It was the way he assumed command, instantly.

He drew her back from the window. He barked out an order to his guard, then returned his considerable attention to her, green and gold and grave.

How had she convinced herself there was anything *regular* about this man at all?

"We cannot get to the bottom of this here," he told her in a tone that matched the expression on his face. And made everything in her careen about all the more. "You will have to come with me."

"Come with you?" she repeated, dazed. "What do you mean? Where?"

But Ares did not wait for her acquiescence. Perhaps he assumed it wasn't necessary. Perhaps, where he came from, agreement with his every whim and desire was the law of the land. He certainly acted as if it was. He strode off, his long legs eating up the floor of the library in only a few strides. And then he stopped at the door, turning back to her with that astonished, arrogant look of his.

"Pia. That is your name, is it not?"

In case she'd forgotten that every single part of this situation shamed her and humiliated her.

"It is, yes," she said, threading her fingers together and making herself smile the way she'd been taught. Serene and smooth. "And in all the confusion and violence, I believe I missed your formal introduction. You are...?"

She watched that hit him, like a slap. He blinked as if it had never occurred to him that any person alive might not know precisely who he was—suggesting that he'd thought she was only pretending not to know him in New York.

Pia should have been more sympathetic. After all, she knew what it was like to be known, often when she would have preferred to be anonymous. She knew what it was like to have an inescapable family identity that followed her around and often preceded her. And possibly, if she had been a better sort of person, she wouldn't have taken such enjoyment in watching Ares's struggle.

Alas.

"I am His Royal Highness, Crown Prince Ares of Atilia. Duke of this, Earl of that. But no need to address me by my full title. Ares will do."

He certainly didn't appear the least bit ashamed that he could have spent a night like that with someone and not know their name. Pia resolved she should feel no shame herself.

And while she couldn't quite get there, she could certainly fake it. She lifted her chin and tried to exude a sunniness she didn't quite feel.

"It's lovely to meet you, at last," she said. "But you should know that I have no intention of going off somewhere with you. I did just meet you, after all."

And she remembered every scandalous searingly hot detail of the night she'd spent with him. She had seen all kinds of expressions cross his face. She had seen him laugh, go tense and hot, shatter.

But she had never seen him look *dangerous* until now.

"You do not understand, so allow me to enlighten you." His voice was almost as striking as that expression on his face. Dark. Powerful. Nothing lazy or offhand about him, and his green eyes blazed. "You have made a claim to the throne of the kingdom of Atilia. If what you say is true, you are pregnant with my child."

"What does it matter?" she asked, with a brazen sort of calmness she did not feel. "You said you have no intention of marrying. And so what if you have illegitimate children? Don't all kings litter them about, here and there, down through the history books?"

His perfect, sculpted lips thinned and if possible, his gaze grew hotter. And more dangerous. "Atilia is an ancient kingdom, bound by ancient rules. I cannot imagine you truly want a lesson in our laws and customs regarding succession."

"I'm certain I didn't ask for a lesson in anything."

He ignored that. Or didn't care, more likely. "Legitimate issue takes precedence over illegitimate issue. But only if they are male."

"What a shock."

"I am next in line to the throne. Any legitimate child of mine would ascend that throne after me. In the absence of children, a line of succession would move on. Either to any children my father's second wife produces, or to my cousin. If any children I have are illegitimate, they would precede my father's second round of children only if my father had girls."

"That is a fascinating history lesson. Thank you." She smiled at him still, though it felt more...fixed, somehow. "An alternative would be for you to go away. And never tell anyone. I will do the same. And we will never again talk about *issue*."

Or anything else, she thought stoutly. And waited to feel relief rush in.

But instead, she felt something far more bittersweet flood her, though she couldn't quite name it.

"I'm afraid it is much too late for that, Pia," Ares said, with that quiet power of his that shook through her no matter how solid she told herself she was. "Because speculation already exists. Reporters clamor outside even now. What they cannot learn for certain, they will make up to suit themselves."

"You must know the folly of living your life by what the tabloids say," she chided him. Gently.

"I never have."

"Wonderful." She smiled. "Then no need to start now."

"You said yourself that you have never appeared in the tabloids before. There is no reason to throw yourself in the midst of a nasty little scrum of them, like a bone to pick."

If Pia didn't know better, she might have been tempted to think he was trying to protect her.

"More than that, there were reporters who heard you make your claim," Ares said. He shook his head. "Do you know nothing of the history of this planet? Wars have been fought for much less than a claim to a throne."

"You talk about war a lot," she said, and felt herself flush when his gaze turned considering. "In case you were unaware."

"I am a prince. One of my main roles in this life is preventing wars from ever taking place. One way to do that is to conduct my private affairs *in private*." He inclined his head, though Pia was aware it was a command and not a sign of obedience or surrender. "My car awaits."

"And if I refuse to get into it with you?"

"I have a security detail who will put you in the vehicle, no matter your protests. But you know this." Again, that dark, considering look that seemed to peel her open. "Is that what you want? Plausible deniability?"

For a moment, Pia didn't know what she wanted. She

felt the way she had when her doctor had come into the exam room and told her the news. Pia had been fairly certain she was dying of something. All those strange cramps. The fact that she kept getting sick. She was certain something was eating her away from the inside out.

It had never occurred to her that she could be pregnant. The word itself hadn't made sense.

She'd made the doctor repeat herself three times.

Looking at Ares, here in the library of Combe Manor where she had spent so much of her childhood, was much the same.

That train kept jumping the tracks and hurtling away into the messy night, no matter how still she stood or how gracefully she tried to hold herself together.

But she could hear her brother's clipped tone from the other side of the door, issuing his own orders. She'd seen that scrum of ravenous reporters out in front of the house, clamoring for a comment and ready to pounce.

"Let me tell you what sort of life you will lead," her mother had said in the days following her graduation from finishing school, right here in this very same manor house, stuffed full of pictures of all the battle-hardened Combes who had charged out of their circumstances and had *made something of themselves*, no matter what.

Pia knew she was meant to feel deeply proud of them all. When instead, all that desperate clawing for purchase made her feel…tired. And unequal to the task.

"Am I supposed to know what to do with my life?" Pia had asked. "I can't seem to make up my mind."

"It's not for you to decide, dear girl," said her mother, who only called Pia *dear* when she was in one of her less affectionate moods. Pia had sat straighter, waiting for the inevitable other shoe to fall. "Your father has gone to a tremendous amount of trouble to make you into the perfect heiress. Biddable and sweet enough. Reasonably accomplished in the classic sense of the term. And very, very wealthy, of course."

It had seemed wiser not to say anything. Pia had sat there at the breakfast table off the kitchen where her mother drank her hot water and lemon, murmured about how refreshed she felt with each sip, and raised her brows at Pia's slice of toast with a bit of creamery butter.

Which was to say, it was a normal breakfast at Combe Manor. Pia could have drunk the hot lemon water herself, but she'd long ago learned that it was better to disappoint her mother as early in the day as possible, so there could be no grand expectations over the course of the day she would then fail to meet.

Alexandrina had let her gaze sweep over her daughter as if she was sizing her up for market. "You will work in some or other worthy charity that we will vet, of course. You will dedicate yourself to your good works for a year, perhaps two. Then I imagine your father will suggest a suitor. He might even allow you to pick one. From a preselected group, of course."

"You make it sound as if he plans to marry me off."

Pia had spent much of her life despairing over the fact that while she had the same dark hair and gray eyes as her mother, Alexandrina's all…came together. She was simply beautiful, always, no matter what. It was a fact, not a to-do list. Pia had the raw material, but she was put together wrong. No matter how hard she tried to glide about, exuding effortless beauty.

"Dear girl, your brother will run the business," Alexandrina had replied, as if Pia had said something amusing. "He is already in line to do so. You are here to be decorative, or if not precisely decorative—" the look she'd slid at her daughter had been a knife, true, but Pia had been so used to the cut of it she hadn't reacted at all "—you can be *useful*. How will you accomplish this, do you think?"

Pia hadn't had an answer for her. Her accomplishments, such as they were, had always been a serene collection of tidy, unobjectionable nouns. She'd no idea how one launched off into a verb.

"What did you do?" she asked her mother instead.

She already knew the story, of course. Her father liked to belt it out at cocktail parties. Alexandrina had been set to marry some stuffy old title of her father's choosing, but then she'd met Eddie. First they'd made headlines. Then they'd made history, uniting the brash, upstart Combe fortune with the traditional gentility of the San Giacomos.

Pia rather doubted that an epic love story was in the cards for her. Epic love was the sort of thing that *just happened* to women like her mother, and led to decades of *true love*. Which in the San Giacomo/Combe family had always meant operatic battles, intense reunions, and a revolving door of scandals and sins. Pia had always thought that, really, she'd be quite happy to find herself *reasonably content*.

"You and I are not the same," Alexandrina had said softly that day, something making her gray eyes glitter. "And I can see that you think I'm being cruel to you. I am not."

"Of course not," Pia had agreed, staring at her plate and wishing she could truly rebel and order a stack of toast instead of her one, lonely slice. But she only dared antagonize her mother—who despaired over Pia's sturdy figure, inherited from the Combe side of the family and suitable for factory work, not fashion—so far. "I don't think that at all."

"We have wrapped you up in cotton wool as a gift, Pia," Alexandrina had intoned. "Always remember that."

Pia remembered it, all right. She'd decided she wanted no part of any cotton wool, so she'd charged right out and shed it in New York. Enough with *nouns*, she'd thought. She wanted to be about *verbs*, for a change.

And look what that had got her.

"You look as if you're mulling over a very important decision," Ares said, still watching her from the door. "But you must realize that you have no choice here."

"It's out of the frying pan, into the fire."

Pia hadn't meant to say that out loud. But there it was, dancing between them.

Ares didn't reply with words. He only inclined his head in that way of his, that she already knew was him at his most *royal*. Too royal to live, really.

And Pia thought of her father, blustering and brash Eddie Combe, who had called her names and then died. She would never see him smile at her again. She would never stand there while he blustered and bullied, then softened. He would never pat her on the head the way he had when she was small and tell her things like, *Buck up, girl. Combes don't cry.*

But another thing her father had said, so famously

that the vicar had quoted him in the service today, was
that if the worst was coming, you might as well walk
into it like a man rather than waiting for it to come at
you as it pleased.

Control the conversation, Eddie liked to say. And
had said, often.

And then did.

Pia told herself that was why she moved then, walking across library floor as if she was doing the bidding
of her unexpected prince. That was why she followed
after him, ignoring her brother and their guests as his
staff led them through the manor house, down and
around to the servants' entrance, far away from the
mess of reporters out front. That was why she got into
the car that waited for them there, meekly and obedi-
ently, and sat next to Prince Ares as he drove her away.

It wasn't capitulation, she assured herself. She was
controlling the conversation.

And it certainly had nothing at all to do with the
way looking at those green eyes of his made her heart
thump wildly in her chest.

Or that melting feeling everywhere else.

CHAPTER FIVE

PIA REGRETTED HER impulsiveness the moment the car started moving.

She regretted it as they left Combe Manor behind, taking the little-used back road off the hill and leaving the paparazzi—and her brother, and her entire life—behind them.

Pia told herself she was only getting a few tests. That she wasn't leaving anything, not for long. That this would all be perfectly fine once she and Ares were on the same page and plans were made for the future.

But she couldn't shake the sense of foreboding that squatted on her, there on the smooth leather seats of the royal town car.

The car swept them off to a private airfield, and Pia dutifully trooped up the stairs into the jet that waited there, assuming that the prince would take them off to London. Where there were doctors aplenty who could administer the necessary tests, and give him the answers she already had, but he needed to see on official letterhead of some sort or another.

She told herself that she didn't mind that he needed proof. After all, wasn't that at the crux of all this? He didn't know her. She didn't know him. That would perhaps suggest that they shouldn't have slept together, but they had, and it was only to be expected that he would require proof. Even if he really had been just some guy named Eric.

But the sound of the jet engines lulled her to sleep, and when Pia woke again because the air pressure was making her ears pop, she felt as if she'd been sleeping for a very long time.

"Where are we?" she asked sleepily, because a glance out the window into the dark didn't show the mess of lights she would expect above a city like London.

Ares sat across from her on one of the royal jet's low, gold-embossed leather couches.

"We will be landing shortly," he said, without looking up from his tablet.

Pia always forgot that her body had changed, and kept changing. She went to sit upright and struggled a bit, certain that she looked as ungainly and inelegant as she felt.

"Yes, but where?" she asked, hoping her business-like tone would divert attention away from what her mother would have called her *persistent ungainliness.* "That can't be London, can it?"

Down below the plane, there were great expanses of darkness, and a few lights. They were headed toward the light, but it was far too contained to be a city.

"It is not London," Ares said, something in his voice making her turn her head around to look at him directly. "It is the kingdom of Atilia. My home, after a fashion. I'm taking you to the Southern Palace."

"But... Why on earth would you take me...?"

"Where did you imagine I would take you?"

He considered her, and she became *aware*—in a hot rush that made her cheeks flare into red—that they were, for all intents and purposes, alone in this compartment of his plane. His security detail had stayed in the main bit, while Ares had escorted her here and closed the door. She had no idea how she had possibly slept so deeply when Ares was right here, taking up all the oxygen.

And that was all before she started thinking about the ways this man could *take* her.

Not to mention the ways he already had.

"I assumed, reasonably enough, that we would pop down to London."

"London is far too exposed. Here in the islands I can control who sees you and me together, what conclusions they might draw, and so on. And I can have my own doctors administer any tests."

"I didn't bring anything," Pia protested. And when that aristocratic brow of his rose, as if she wasn't making any sense, she felt her face get hotter. She cleared her throat. "Like a passport."

"I am the Crown Prince," Ares said dryly. "I do not suffer bureaucracy."

"Because you are the bureaucracy?"

She regretted that. Especially when all he did was fix that overtly calm green gaze on her, making her want to squirm about in her seat. She refrained. Barely.

"And after I take all the tests you need me to take?" She blinked a few times, trying to clear her head. And the sleep from her eyes. "My life is in England."

"If by some chance you are truly carrying my child

and the unexpected heir to the kingdom of Atilia," he said, with something far too complicated to be simple temper in his voice, "then you can be certain that life as you know it has changed irrevocably."

"Well, of course it has," Pia said. Crossly, she could admit. "But it has nothing to do with you. Impending motherhood generally changes a girl, I think you'll find. It's fairly universal."

The jet was dropping closer to those lights below, and Pia felt something like panic clawing at her. Maybe that was why she didn't wait for him to answer her.

"You can't spirit me away to an island and keep me there, Ares," she said instead. But if she was looking for some kind of softness on his face, there was none to be found. He could as easily have been carved from marble. "You know that, don't you? That's all well and good in the average fairy tale, but this is real life."

"I keep trying to explain to you who I am," Ares said quietly. Almost apologetically, which made every hair on her body feel as if it stood on its end. Because he was the least apologetic creature she had ever met. "I have never been a good prince, it is true, but I'm a prince nonetheless. And we have entered my kingdom, where my word is law. I am afraid that you will discover that I can do as I like."

"But—"

"Call it a fairy tale if you like, *cara mia*," he murmured. "If it helps."

It did not help.

That panic continued to claw at her as the jet landed. As Pia was marched off—escorted, she supposed, and politely, but it all felt rather more kidnap-ish than it had before—and bundled into yet another gleaming car. This time they were driven along a precipitous coastal road that hugged the looming hills on one side and dropped off toward the sea on the other. They skirted around the side of the island, until they came upon what looked to Pia like a perfect fairy-tale castle.

Just in case she didn't already feel as if she'd stumbled into the pages of a storybook already.

It rose as if from a pop-up children's book, blazing with light as it sat up over the sea on a jutting bit of hillside. It even had turrets.

"What is this place?" she managed to ask, half-convinced she was still dreaming.

"It is the Southern Palace, as I said," Ares said from beside her in the car's wide backseat. "If, as I suspect, you are merely pregnant yet not with any child of mine, you will stay here only as long as it takes you to sign the appropriate legal documentation that asserts you have no claim to the throne of my kingdom. And never will."

"I don't want your throne. Or your kingdom."

"Then it will all go very quickly." He turned then, the light from the palace as they approached the first wall beaming into the car and making him gleam. Making him even more beautiful, which was unhelpful. "But if, by some miracle, what you say is true? Then allow me to be the first to welcome you to your new home, Pia. You can expect to be here for some time."

"Once again," she said, working hard to keep her voice calm when she felt nothing but that panic inside her, shredding her, "you might be a prince and this might be your kingdom—"

"There is no *might*, Pia. I am who I say I am."

"Well, *Eric*," she replied, glaring at him, "you cannot actually kidnap women and hold them captive in your palace, no matter who you say you are. I think you'll find it's generally frowned upon."

Ares settled back in his seat as the car slipped into some kind of courtyard, then continued under a grand archway that led deeper beneath the palace. And if he was bothered by the name she'd used—the name he'd given her in New York—he didn't show it.

"You are welcome to register a complaint," he said after a moment, as if he'd taken some time to consider the matter. "In this case, your only recourse would be the king."

And he let out a laugh at that, which was not exactly encouraging.

Still, Pia kept glaring at him. "Is he more reasonable than you? He would have to be, I'd think. You could take me to him right now."

Ares laughed again. "My father is not a safe space," he assured her. "For you, or anyone else."

The car finally came to a stop. And Pia couldn't help the sense of doom that washed over her then. It was that same clawing panic, and something more. Something that made her heart ache.

Ares exited the vehicle with an athletic grace Pia would have preferred not to notice, nodding at the guards who waited there.

Her heart in her throat, Pia followed him, climbing out of the car to find herself in yet another courtyard. She was surrounded on all sides by thick castle walls. Far above was the night sky, riddled with stars. And it had never occurred to her before that there could only really be turrets where there were steep walls all around. That turrets belonged to fortresses, like this one.

But there were no walls steeper and more formidable than the man who stood there, watching her much too intensely as she looked around at her lovely, remote, fairy-tale prison.

Ares. Her prince.

Her jailer.

And whether he was prepared to accept it or not, the man who'd gotten her pregnant.

"I don't want to be here," she told him. But quietly.

"I do not want women wandering about the planet, telling people that I have left them pregnant when I have taken great care never to do such a thing," he replied, almost too easily. "Life does not often give us what we want, Pia."

"If you insist on keeping me here for the moment, I want an exit strategy. I want to know how and when and—"

"If I were you," Ares said, his voice low, "I would be very careful about making any demands."

He moved one finger, and a smartly dressed woman appeared before them as if by magic. "This is Marbella. She will be your chief aide. If you have any questions, you may address them to her."

And he didn't wait for her answer. He simply strode off, princely and remote, his footsteps echoing against the stone until they disappeared.

Pia watched him go, much longer than she should have, and then turned to face the woman who waited at her side.

If she expected a friendly chat, or even a smile, she was disappointed. The other woman bowed slightly, then beckoned Pia to follow her as she set off in a completely different direction into the palace. Each room they passed was more fanciful than the last. Everything was open, airy. Though it was dark, Pia could still sense the ocean all around them. The seething. The whispering. As if it was just there, around the next corner, out of reach—

Marbella led her down a very long corridor that opened up this way and that into galleries and salons, all of them lit up and done in bright, cheerful sort of colors that she imagined did nothing but encourage the sun to linger.

"Who lives here?" she asked after they'd walked a while.

"The Southern Palace has been the preferred retreat of the royal family for centuries, madam," Marbella replied with severe formality. "His Highness is the only member of the family who uses it with any regularity these days, though even he has not been here in some time."

"Does that mean no one else is here?" She thought about what he had said by the car. "Is the king here?"

She thought the other woman stiffened, but that seemed unlikely, given how straight she already stood. "His Majesty resides and remains in the Northern Palace, madam."

Pia nodded sagely, as if she knew the first thing about Atilia, its geography, or its palaces.

Marbella led her on until they reached a beautiful suite of rooms that was to be Pia's for the duration.

Pia did not ask how long that duration was expected to last.

Inside her suite, she found a selection of clothes laid out for her use, that she supposed had to have been flown in from somewhere. She flushed, trying to imagine how Ares had come by the measurements. Had he measured her while she slept? Or did he simply...remember her? And had only added a bit of pregnancy weight to his estimate?

It was amazing how red her face could get at the slightest provocation.

She was grateful when the other woman retreated, leaving her to a glorious set of rooms that she suspected overlooked the water, not that it mattered. A prison was a prison, surely, no matter the view.

Pia took out her phone, was delighted to find she had service, and quickly pulled up what she could find on the kingdom of Atilia. And better still, the Southern Palace.

The palace where she sat was on the southernmost island of the kingdom. What population there was here was spread out across the island in the small villages dotting it. The palace, on the other hand, had been carved out of the side of the mountain as a kind of folly for a long-ago queen. It looked like a fairy-tale castle, but it was, as Pia had felt when she'd looked around, a nearly inviable fortress. There was the Ionian Sea in front and a mountain in back, with only one road in and out.

If anything, she'd been underplaying what was happening here.

The man who had impregnated her was a prince. She

had hardly had time to take that on board. But in case she'd had any doubt, the castle put it to rest. Everything he'd said to her was true.

Ares was a prince. *The* prince. And he had every intention of holding her here.

Until and unless he felt like letting her go.

She was still in her funeral garb when the doctors came, an hour or so later. They'd set up their own makeshift exam room in the palace, and Pia thought about fighting it. Because she, after all, knew what the test was going to say. Surely there had to be a way to keep this from happening. She could refuse to submit herself to the examination...

But she knew without asking, or trying, that there was little point. Ares would keep her here either way until he had his answers. No matter what those answers were.

That runaway train barreled across uneven ground, far off the track, hurtling Pia right along with it.

And the funeral garb felt fitting, really, as she sat in one of the many brightly lit sitting rooms with Ares after the doctors were done with her, awaiting the results.

He stood by one of the open, arched windows that were really doors, looking out at the dark expanse of the ocean. The air this far south was thicker. It insinuated itself against her skin like a caress—but she told herself it was only the humidity. She sat, very primly, on the sofa and tried to keep herself calm.

She *tried*.

The door opened after what seemed like several eternities. Possibly more. All passed in the same tense silence.

Ares turned and the doctor bowed low. "Congratulations, Your Highness," the man said. "You are indeed
the father."

Pia couldn't seem to look away from Ares's face.
That arrested expression. Something cold and bleak
in his gaze.

It made her heart flip over, then sink.

But the doctor wasn't finished. Because of course he
wasn't finished. Pia braced herself.

"They are both male," the doctor said.

There was a short, electric pause.

"Both?" Ares asked, his voice a slap.

Neither the doctor nor Ares so much as glanced at
Pia, and still she felt as exposed and vulnerable as if
she'd been stripped naked and pinned to the wall.

"*Both?*" Ares asked again.

And the words Pia knew were coming sounded to her
like bullets when they came, as inevitable and terrible
as they'd been when she'd heard them for the first time.

"Yes, Your Highness." The doctor bowed lower. "It
is my great honor to inform you that you have been
blessed with twins."

CHAPTER SIX

THERE WAS NOTHING but white noise in Ares's head.

A long, sort of flat-line noise that he was fairly certain signaled his own end.

For what else could it be?

Twins.

Twin boys.

He couldn't make the words make any sense. The doctor retreated and Ares stared at Pia as if he could see through that black dress she wore. As if he could see inside of her, where there were *twins*. Boys.

Sons.

Ares's head pounded like a terrible hangover, when he couldn't recall the last time he'd drank to excess. His throat felt dry and scratchy, as if he'd caught a virus and was on the verge of tipping over into misery. He thought it was possible that he shook, too, though he couldn't tell whether that was in him or around him—and he couldn't seem to catch his breath long enough to truly make the determination.

What did it matter what shook? She was carrying twins.

His twins. His sons. *His.*

When he finally raised his gaze from her belly and

the impossibility—*two* impossibilities—she carried even now, Pia was still sitting there on the ancient settee that had stood precisely where it was now as long as anyone could remember. Her legs were demurely crossed at the ankles. Her hands were folded neatly in her lap. She gazed back at him, her eyes big and gray and solemn, and fixed on him in a manner that made him…restless.

"Some people might be offended by your reaction," she said quietly, into all that white noise and shake inside him. "But I'm not. My own reaction to the news was very much the same."

"Twins," he managed to say, though his tongue felt tied in knots. "*Twins.*"

She had the grace to look faintly abashed. "You claimed you couldn't have impregnated me with one baby. You were certain. I didn't see what throwing the reality that it was twins into the mix would accomplish."

Ares couldn't argue with that, which made him even more… Whatever he was. He ran a hand over his face, wincing when his palm hit his lip. He'd already forgotten that her older brother had punched him. Matteo, he'd learned on the flight, when he'd finally read the informational one-sheet his aides had prepared for him before the funeral. Matteo Combe, president and CEO of Combe Industries…though the tabloids were having a field day with the punch he'd thrown, even calling him unfit for his own office.

It seemed quaint, almost. A remnant of a former life.

A life where Ares could not possibly have been facing down the fact he'd gotten a woman pregnant. With *twins.*

"Well," Pia said, a bit too brightly. "Perhaps you had better explain to me how you think this imprisonment is going to work."

"How far along are you?" he heard himself ask.

She blinked, then tilted her head slightly to one side.

"I remember you, Pia," Ares retorted, his voice tight. "But I failed to mark that particular night down in my diary."

"Six months," she replied, the lack of inflection in her voice an indictment all its own.

But he was more focused on the span of time. Six months. It made his head swim. And it meant...

"So you will... That is to say, we will..."

He couldn't say the words out loud. Was he sweating?

"In a few months," she said. "But babies are tricky. They do what they like. And I'm told twins tend to come sooner rather than later."

"In the history of this kingdom, there have never been twins."

She dared to look amused. "Ever? Really? In the course of how many thousands of years?"

He thought his growl might have been audible, then. "In the royal family, I should say. There have only ever been single births."

"They say it skips a generation," she offered, helpfully. She studied him for a moment. "My father's aunts were twins."

"Twins," Ares said again.

As if, were he to say the word enough, it would change things, somehow.

Pia stood then, then smoothed out the front of her dress, though it required no smoothing.

"I don't think we're going to have a conversation with much sense in it tonight," she said quietly. Kindly, even, which made him want to...do things. "I suppose that even if you released me on the spot, there would be no leaving here before morning. Why don't we talk about this then. When you've slept on the news and let it settle a bit."

"What do you imagine there is to talk about?" Ares scarcely sounded like himself. "You have... This has..."

"Yes," she said, sounding faintly amused in a way he didn't care for. At all. "You've caught me. I schemed to get pregnant. And to get pregnant with twins, no less. I hunted you down, cold-bloodedly used you to do my evil will, and then, as a coup de grâce, I went away and never contacted you again. Because secretly I knew that my father would drop dead and you would show up at his funeral—"

"I am trying very hard not to blame you for this," Ares told her, and his voice, like the rest of him, was tight and taut and not him at all.

She gave the distinct impression of laughing at him without actually doing so. "That's very kind of you. Because as I recall, we were both there. Unless you'd like to pretend that you, in fact, are a twin and *Eric* is the real father?"

Ares wished that *Eric* was a real person, so he could knock him out.

"I don't understand how this is possible," he said. Possibly not for the first—or fifth—time. "I am a man who enjoys sex, I grant you. But I had no intention of procreating. Ever. I have never been anything less than scrupulous about protection."

She made a sympathetic noise, though she didn't look the least bit sympathetic. "Did you have a vasectomy, then?"

It seemed that Pia was the one delivering knockout blows tonight.

"I did not," Ares said. Stiffly.

"As it turns out, a vasectomy is only 99.9 percent effective. People do still get pregnant after them, though it's rare."

"I've just said I never had one." And he had stopped explaining himself decades ago, yet he felt the strangest urge to leap to his own defense now. "I suppose I might have gotten round to it, eventually."

The fact he'd been so adamantly opposed to procreating and yet hadn't taken steps to ensure he couldn't seemed, now, like the very height of foolishness. What had he been thinking? He had been so certain his blood was poisoned, given the example his father had always set of what happened when their long line of royals met the crown. He had been so clear about the fact he wouldn't risk poisoning any children himself, to end the misery with him. And yet...

"I've had a few months to research protection in a panic, as I, too, failed to understand how this happened," Pia told him in the same calmly informative way that made his teeth grind together. "And as it turns out, as they told us in the convent, the only version of protection that is one hundred percent effective is abstinence."

She even smiled faintly as she said that. And something in Ares turned over, bright with temper.

"Do you think this is entertaining?" he demanded,

his voice hardly more than a growl. "I understand that you didn't plan this. Yet it has happened anyway, apparently. And you have had months to come to terms with it. To make your little jokes about abstinence. But my world ended tonight, Pia."

And he watched, in that sickening mix of dismay and shame, and fury, too, as she slid her hands down over her belly as if she wanted to protect her children.

From him.

Ares shouldn't have cared about something like that.

But it turned out, he did.

"You're not the only person whose world ended today," she threw at him. "In case you've forgotten, you didn't discover this news at a garden party. That was my father's funeral. And thank you for asking, but both of my parents, in fact, were less than thrilled about this. I had the distinct pleasure of telling them that I got pregnant from a tawdry one-night stand with a total stranger. That went over very well. My father called me a tart."

"How can you possibly be a tart if the only man you've ever slept with is me?" Ares asked, and had no idea what that *thing* was that roared about in him. Almost as if he wanted to defend this woman against her own, dead father.

"I think it was the unmarried, pregnant, and no idea who the father was part that got to him," Pia replied. "But then he died a few days later, so I didn't get a chance to follow up on that."

But Ares was still stuck on the fact that she had never touched another man.

Something kicked in him. Something that wasn't

the fact he had *children* coming, like it or not. *Twins.* Something that wasn't all the ramifications of that he couldn't quite face. Not quite yet.

Something that felt a good deal more primitive.

He moved toward her, watching the way her eyes widened. But better still was that little kick of awareness he could see flicker in all that solemn gray.

"No man but me," he said.

"Yes," she said, her voice shakier and much less calm than it had been a moment before. "That is correct."

"You didn't tell me that night."

"Well. You know." Her face was red. Even the tips of her ears were red. "It didn't seem relevant."

He prowled even closer.

"You went to an actual convent. Then a finishing school. And straight after that, you found me in an otherwise forgettable party in Manhattan."

She looked as if she wanted to make a break for it, but stood fast. "That is the sum total of my life thus far, yes. Lucky me."

"I remember you, Pia," he said, his voice low and much too dark, and her eyes widened in response.

But he couldn't seem to help that. Just as he couldn't seem to help himself from reaching out and taking her chin in his hand.

As if she was his.

He expected her to jerk her face away from his hold, but she didn't. And he watched, mesmerized—fascinated— as her pulse went wild in her neck.

Her breathing grew labored. But what intrigued Ares was that he could feel her, inside him. He could feel the kick. The heat. Like touching her was sticking his fin-

gers into an electrical socket, sending sparks shower-
ing through him.

"I remember you," he said again, intent and sure, and
threaded through with all that electricity. "You flowed
over me like water. No hesitation, no concern."

"Perhaps I was significantly drunk," she said, her
voice tart, but he could see the softness in her gaze.
The melting heat.

"No," he said, remembering. "You were not."

"Perhaps that's what it's always like. I assumed it
was. All that..." Her cheeks pinkened even further.
"Flowing."

"No," Ares said again, though he sounded too hot,
too dark. "That is not what it's like. Not normally."

It had all seemed easy, to his recollection. As if they
had been meant to meet like that, then come together in
such a glorious, heedless rush. She had arched into his
hands as if she'd done it a thousand times before. He'd
found her mouth and the place where she was greediest,
then tasted both. Her cries had broken over him as if it
was a dance they'd practiced a hundred times. More.
She had felt explosive in his hands. A glorious, greedy
burst of light and sensation.

But more than that, he'd thought when he'd first
surged deep inside her and she'd shaken all around
him, familiar.

The word that had echoed in his head then was the
reason he'd made no effort to seek her out afterward,
no matter how often he'd thought of her since.

Home.

Ares, of course, had no home. He'd walked away
from his kingdom and had no intention of assuming

his throne. Any home he'd had, he'd buried with his mother.

Homes were for other men. Men who deserved them.

Men who were not poisoned with the blood of the Atilian royal family.

He ordered himself to drop his hand. To step back. To put more distance between him and this woman who had shaken him months ago, and here, now, might as well have been a full-scale tsunami.

But he didn't let go the way he knew he should. And instead of stepping back, he moved forward.

"Perhaps we should test it," he said.

"Test what?" She frowned at him. "The last time we tested something I ended up pregnant. With twins."

"Remind me how that happened," he dared her, low and dark.

And it didn't make any sense. He shouldn't want to be anywhere near her, not when his worst nightmare was playing out before him, inside her—

But he couldn't seem to help himself.

Ares bent and pressed his mouth to hers.

And the heat kicked through him, wild and hot. It lit him up, reminding him of that night in Manhattan while it stormed through him, new and mad.

He wasn't satisfied with the press of lips, so he angled his head, taking the kiss deeper. Making it dangerous. Making it clear how easy it had been to go from a conversation at a party to that very long night that had resulted in…this.

He pulled her to him, sliding his hands over her shoulders, then down her back.

And she kissed him back, meeting the thrust of his

tongue. She pressed against him as if she, too, wanted to get closer. Her hands came up and found his chest, and he could feel her belly between them, pushing into him, and that, surely, should have woken him up from the spell—

But instead, Ares kissed her deeper. Harder.

He slid his hands between them and felt the insistent mound of her belly himself.

Her belly. His babies.

And she was the one who wrenched her mouth from his then.

Everything was jumbled around inside of Ares. He had never put his hands on a pregnant woman's belly before. He'd certainly never done so with the knowledge that the babes within were *his*.

It should have disgusted him. He'd always been so revolted at the very idea of fathering a child.

Or maybe it was his own father who had revolted him, now he considered it.

And this was Pia, with her wide eyes, and that generous mouth that drove him crazy. Her taste was in his mouth again, making him wild. Making him hard. Making him feel like someone else entirely.

Someone who put his hands on a woman's belly, understood what he felt there were his own sons— *sons*—and felt a deep, possessive thrill at the notion—

What the hell was happening to him?

All of it was wrong. It was as if he'd been taken over by a different man. A stranger. And yet Ares didn't step away. He didn't even drop his hands. He felt that possessiveness in his chest. His sex.

"I don't think this is the answer to the situation we're

in," Pia said, though her voice wasn't any steadier than he felt. "I think sex has already caused enough trouble, don't you?"

"I don't know that there are any answers," Ares replied. "We might as well console ourselves with the one thing we appear to be so good at."

"I...don't know how to respond to that. I don't have any context."

"Then you'll have to take my word for it." He moved his hands over her bump, telling himself it meant nothing. That he was relearning her shape, that was all. That the fact his palms could not contain her belly, much less the lives within it, didn't matter to him at all. "We are very, very good at it."

And something shifted in him, turning over too fast. Ares found he could no longer tell what, precisely, he meant by that. He was talking about sex, surely. Wasn't he?

But Pia was clearly not inclined to parse the nuances. She stepped back further, almost running into the settee behind her in her haste. And he couldn't deny that there was something in him that took immense satisfaction in the fact that he affected her in this way.

Because no one else had ever touched her. Only him.

That primitive thing inside him, heretofore wholly unknown to him, stirred again.

Her lips were swollen from his kiss. Her body was swollen with not one, but two of his children.

And he might not want to accept what that meant. He might find all of this impossible and bewildering in turn, no matter what the doctor had said. But Ares couldn't deny that the sight of her, lushly fertile and entirely his, made him…

Deeply, darkly triumphant, on a level he hadn't known existed.

"No," she said, very distinctly.

"No?"

"Whatever that look on your face is. Whatever it is, no. I want no part of it."

"But all bets are off now, are they not?" He felt…ferocious. "I am a man who never planned to have children, yet you are carrying two, and they are mine. Who knows what else we think we cannot have, or do not want, that will happen here against our will?"

"I have no intention of spending the next few months trapped here," she told him, in that same sober, serious way. "You now know that you're the father of these babies. *My* babies. I'm glad. That wasn't a secret I meant to keep from you in the first place. But now that you know, there's no need for all these…" She looked around the room, and waved her hand as if to take it all in, and the whole of the palace besides. "All these royal shenanigans."

Ares had never felt the weight of the Atilian crown more than he did in the moment she dismissed it, and so easily.

"Here's the problem, Pia," he said, feeling as growly and uneven as he sounded. "I cannot decide what to do with you."

"I don't recall signing myself over into your care. You don't decide what happens to me. I do."

"You are a quandary," he told her, and the things that roared inside him were loud again. They competed with each other. They were made of furor and fang, and over and over again, they drew blood. That damned blood of his. "I have to decide how to proceed."

"Terrific. You go ahead and think on that to your heart's content. Meanwhile, I'll fly straight back to England and carry on with my life, shall I?"

"That's not going to happen." When she scowled at him, he laughed. Because what was there to do but laugh at the very notion that either one of them could wander back to their normal lives now? Or ever? "I think perhaps, *cara*, it is not I who am being unreasonable."

"Says the man who kidnapped me."

"You say you wish to go back to England. Where would you go?"

Pia's frown deepened. "Home. Obviously."

"The paparazzi already have their teeth in this story. Your brother is fielding calls for his resignation after his display of violence and I'm certain that the palace will already have received a thousand queries about whether or not his pregnant sister is the reason he belted me. Do you think they'll magically leave you alone?"

"They always have before," she said, and for the first time, he understood how very sheltered she'd been. It should have appalled him, surely. But instead, he had the strangest urge to shelter her.

"Convents and finishing schools do not capture the public's imagination the way a scandal does," he told her. "Or the world would be a very different place."

"We can still deny it." She sounded almost...desperate. "Matteo is a Combe. Combes are always punching people. What's a prince in the mix?"

"I think you know better."

"I don't see why anyone has to know about this if we don't tell them," she argued. "It's always seemed to me that the people the tabloids hound the most are the ones who court the attention. If we don't court it, surely they'll move on to something else."

"Pia. Remember, please, that I am not some debutante's gelded date, on hand to waltz on command at her coming-out ball. I am the Crown Prince of this kingdom, for my sins. The very hint that any woman's baby could be mine will send my people into a frenzy."

She shook her head, her face pale again. "What does that matter? You told me that you don't want children and don't want a wife. Frenzy or not."

"I don't."

"So there's no point to any of these conversations, is there?"

"What I want and what I plan to do with what has happened are two different things, I think," he said.

He wasn't sure why her reluctance made his temper kick at him. Only that it did.

And he stared her down until she lowered her eyes, there in the palace his ancestors had built while the blue blood he hated—and yet shared with all those who had stood here before him—stormed in his veins.

It made him feel alive, like it or not. It made him *want*.

It made him wonder how this was going to end.

"If I were you," Ares told her, all princely command, "I would resign myself to it."

CHAPTER SEVEN

PIA HAD NO INTENTION of resigning herself to anything, thank you, and especially not her own kidnapping.

Sure, she'd gotten into his car and onto his plane of her own free will. It had seemed vastly preferable to the baying press outside Combe Manor. But she hadn't expected to come here. That had to count against him. She was determined it did.

She broke away from that room where she'd felt as if Ares was holding her in his grip, where her mouth still throbbed from his kisses—God help her, that man could *kiss*—and hurtled herself out into the palace corridors. It took her longer than it should have to find her way back to her suite, and by the time she made it she was tired, emotional, and shaking.

Pia told herself she was peckish, that was all. Because once the morning sickness had stopped, she'd become ravenous. And hadn't stopped.

Her aide met her inside her rooms and quickly produced a lavish spread for Pia to choose from. And she wanted so desperately to be the sort of unwilling captive who could turn up her nose at anything she was offered. Not to mention, weren't there too many tales about un-

wary virgins who were lured into treacherous places
they could have left—if only they hadn't eaten there?

"Lucky that you're no virgin, then," she muttered
to herself as she helped herself to a heaping plate of
seconds.

But after the palace staff had swept all evidence of
her private feast away, Pia stayed where she was. She
sat up straight in the most uncomfortable chair in her
outermost sitting room. She channeled her many years
of being taught manners by unimpressed nuns, sat so
she wouldn't drift off to sleep, and waited.

The hours ticked past. The night wore on.

And when she decided it was late enough that even
infamous playboy princes—not that she'd worn down
her phone battery by Googling him exhaustively—had
taken themselves off to bed, if only because there was
precious little other entertainment to be had here on
the southern tip of the middle of nowhere, she stood.
She stretched her protesting limbs, let herself out of her
room again, and resolved that she would walk out of
this palace if necessary.

It took her a while to find her way through the maze
of halls and corridors again, and she got lost more than
once. But eventually she found herself on the ground
level, where she set about looking for a door that led
outside—instead of into yet another courtyard.

Unfortunately, there were courtyards everywhere, as
if every member of the royal family who'd ever spent
time here had built their own.

There were courtyards that opened up to the sky and
others that were really more like squares beneath the
floor above. There were courtyards that opened into the

sea itself, but Pia couldn't seem to find one that led to that road she knew they had taken in. She kept getting turned around. She thought she was retracing her steps when she turned a corner and yelped because someone was *right there*.

"Imagine my surprise," Ares said darkly, "to be roused from my slumber by my staff, and told that the palace was not under attack, but that one of my guests—my only guest—was creeping about the place like a criminal."

"I'm not creeping anywhere and I'm certainly not a criminal," Pia threw at him.

And only then did she take in what he was wearing.

Or more to the point, *not* wearing.

Because the Crown Prince of Atilia stood there before her wearing nothing but a pair of loose black trousers, slung low on his hips as if to suggest that he had been sleeping naked and had tossed them on when he came to find her.

And everything else was just...him.

Those wide, smoothly muscled shoulders. That broad chest that narrowed to lean hips. Ares kept himself in excellent physical condition—she hadn't built that up in her fantasies since New York, it turned out—all rangy muscles and that loose-limbed elegance he wore so easily.

He wasn't the only one who remembered that night in Manhattan. She did, too. How she had crawled over him in sheer, greedy delight. How she had tasted him, tempting them both nearly past endurance. How she had filled her mouth with salt and man and the dark heat that rose between them still.

Here. Now.

"Why aren't you dressed?"

She all but shrieked out the question, half in a gasp, and knew even as it escaped her lips that she'd revealed herself. That she'd given herself away.

Completely.

"Why, pray, would I be dressed?" he asked mildly, though his green eyes glittered there, in the deserted hall. "Perhaps you have not noticed, Pia, but it is the middle of the night. Why are you still dressed as you were hours before? And more to the point, why are you lurking about as if you are casing the place? Are you?"

Pia didn't know what came over her. One moment, she'd had a clear sense of purpose. Of direction. Or intention, anyway, no matter if she couldn't quite find her way.

And then in the next, Ares was standing before her half-dressed. And she was still trapped here in this fairy-tale fortress. And she was an orphan and a mother, both at the same time. And all of that seemed to crash into her.

As if that damned runaway train had looped around and plowed straight into her, flattening her.

Her face crumpled, no matter how hard she fought to keep it smooth. Unbothered. And as she fought off the huge sob that seemed to roll out of her, then on top of her like a great weight, she saw Ares's expression... change.

Pia kept thinking that she'd reached the absolute outer limit of the shame that any one person could feel. She kept thinking there could be no further depths to plumb.

And then something else happened.

She tried to cover her face, because she couldn't stand the fact that he was *right there*, watching her as she quite literally fell apart in front of him.

But his hands were on her, brushing her shoulders and then shifting. Before she knew what was happening he was lifting her up, hauling her high against his chest.

"Don't be foolish," she sobbed at him, her hands still over her face. "I'm hugely pregnant. You'll give yourself a hernia."

"Pia," Ares said in the most regal voice she'd heard from him yet. "Please be so good as to shut up."

She obeyed him. Or she tried, anyway, but she couldn't keep the sobs inside. And later she would find herself appalled and humiliated that she'd so easily surrendered. To her emotions, to him. To everything. But here, now, she tipped her head forward, rested against his shoulder, and let the tears come.

Later she would regret this, she was sure of it.

But for a while, there was only the width and strength of his shoulder, holding her steady as he moved. There was the scent of him, clean and male, with a hint of something else. Soap, perhaps. Cologne, maybe. She couldn't quite tell, but she knew that scent. She remembered it. And it soothed her.

She didn't understand why he should be capable of calming her when no one else ever had. When her life was filled, in fact, with people and places and things that did the exact opposite of calming her. But she didn't have it in her, just then, to fight him.

Not when he was so strong, and so warm, and when

his arms wrapped around her as if she was light and sweet and beautiful. As if he could carry her forever, and would.

And when he finally set her down again, she had to bite her own tongue to keep from protesting.

She wiped at her face, then looked around, and it took her longer than it should have to recognize that she was in a bathroom. A huge, suitably palatial bathroom, that was. If she wasn't mistaken, he had taken her back to her own rooms.

And she sat there, feeling limp and fragile with the force of her own feelings—none of which she could name—as the Crown Prince of Atilia filled her bath. She sat where he'd put her, there on the wide lip of the oversize tub. And she watched him, vaguely astonished that His Royal Highness knew how to go about such a mundane task.

The beauty of her convent education was that she and the rest of the girls from wealthy families who could afford to go there had been taught how to function like regular people. It was one of the convent's primary missions, in fact.

"You do realize I have servants to do this, don't you?" one of the girls in Pia's year had thrown at Mother Superior one morning as they'd all been scrubbing the floors of their dormitory.

"My dear child," Mother Superior had replied, in that mild voice that made them all wince, "you are being taught basic chores not for you, though you can certainly benefit from learning them, but for those servants. In the perhaps vain notion that a dose of empathy might allow you to inhabit your place in this world with more consideration for others."

That had stuck with Pia, along with the punishment Mother Superior had levied against their entire class for the rest of the semester—that was, scrubbing the whole of the great hall. On their hands and knees.

Now she sat in a palace with a man she barely knew but would have sworn didn't lift a single finger if someone else could do it for him. A prince who'd given her twins and spirited her away from her life—twice, now. And she wondered who'd taught him the same lesson.

And then wondered what was wrong with her that she wanted, so desperately, to believe that he was capable of something like empathy. Because that might make him into the father she knew he didn't want to become.

Why do you want him to be a father? she asked herself, harshly enough that she could have been one of her own parents. *You can raise these babies perfectly well on your own. You don't need him.*

That was true. She knew that was true. And still, Pia watched Ares sprinkle bath salts over the hot water as if this was church. Then she didn't know what to feel when he came back to her, there on the edge of the tub set in an alcove with the sea outside.

"I think it is time you took off this shroud you are wearing, *cara mia*," he said in a low voice.

Pia looked down. She knew she hadn't changed her clothes, but she hadn't really processed the fact that she was still wearing that same black dress, severe and solemn and not remotely comfortable, that she'd worn to her father's funeral. And then to his grave.

She raised her gaze to Ares. "I don't think I want to."

Something moved over his face. He crouched down before her so he was on eye level with her. His arms were on either side of her legs, caging her there against the tub, and she thought that on some level, she should hate her heart for the way it beat so hard when he was close. She really should.

Ares shifted, moving back on his heels, but he did not rise. And his eyes were green and gold and that, too, felt like betrayal.

"I understand," he said, astonishing her anew.

Pia wanted to believe that, too. With a fervor that boded ill for her.

A faint smile moved over his mouth as he saw her expression. "When my mother died she lay in state, as is the custom here. And then my father and I walked through the streets as we transported her to her final resting place. I wore the typical regalia of my station, a uniform I have never found comfortable in the least. And yet, when it was over, when I was out of the public eye and back in my private rooms, I found I couldn't bear to move. I couldn't bear to change out of that uniform." His gaze seemed particularly green then. "Because I knew that doing so would indicate that I was moving on in some way."

"You loved your mother very much."

"I did. Did you not love your father? Or your own mother?"

He moved a hand to rest it on her thigh, and Pia was…astounded. She could feel the heat of him, all that power and strength, and be aware of him as a man. But she could also find that grip of his comforting, apparently.

She felt too many things to choose one, much less name it.

"There is no right answer," Ares said. "I had an excellent relationship with my mother. I have no relationship with my father. Parents are complicated."

And Pia was sure she wasn't the only one of them who was painfully aware that they were soon to be parents themselves. That they could inflict God knew what on their own children.

It was an unbearable intimacy to share with a man who was as good as a stranger.

"My parents had children only as an afterthought," she heard herself blurt out.

Anything to stop thinking about herself and Ares as terrible parents. Or any kind of parents.

What she'd said was true, of course. She'd read articles that had said as much, and less nicely. But she had never said it out loud herself before. And in a way, it felt like grief to hear her own voice, speaking that truth.

But somehow, she wanted to keep going. "Or at least, *I* was an afterthought. I suppose they always planned to have my brother. The heir of my father's dynastic dreams, et cetera."

She stared down at Ares's hand, and wanted to slide her own on top of his more than she wanted to breathe. She would never know how she kept her hands to herself. Or how she pushed on when she wasn't sure how or why she was speaking in the first place.

"When they focused on me at all, I think they saw me as a project," she told Ares as the scent of the lavender bath salts filled the room. "I don't honestly know that they were capable of loving anything but one an-

other. I don't mean that in a bad way. I loved them both,
I think. But it was always bound up in the ways I disappointed them."

His green eyes were grave. "How could you possibly
be a disappointment?"

Pia didn't know how to answer him. And she knew
that the reason for that was ego, nothing more. Pride.
She didn't want to tell this man what he should have
been able to see with his own two eyes.

And would, now. Now that he knew who she was.
And therefore knew who her mother was. It was one
thing to be herself, Pia knew. She could do that. It was
when she was compared to Alexandrina that people felt
the most let down.

Her parents most of all.

But she couldn't bring herself to point that out to
Ares. She didn't have it in her.

"I'm glad I'm having boys," she said instead. "I think
that must be easier."

Whatever light she'd seen in his gaze shuttered then.
He moved his hand, which struck Pia as yet another
tragedy she was unprepared to face, and reached into
the water behind her.

He tested the temperature, then moved back, rising
to his feet in a lithe rush that was nothing short of daz-
zling, with all that muscle and grace.

"You should get in," he told her, sounding distant
and royal again. "Then I suggest you get some sleep. I
cannot promise you that grief goes anywhere, but the
sooner you start the process of moving on, the sooner
you'll get to the part that's easier. Eventually, you'll find
it hurts a lot less than it did."

"I think that must feel like losing them all over again," Pia said, without thinking.

Ares's gaze was too hot, too arrested as it snapped to hers.

"It does," he bit out.

And he left her there, sitting in her funeral dress on the side of a hot bath, wondering how and why he'd made drawing her bath feel like a gift. And why she wanted nothing more than to sink into it, fully clothed, and lie there until she stopped *feeling*.

When she stood, she felt unsteady on her feet. She found herself crying all over again as she pulled the dress off, then folded it neatly, placing it much too carefully on one of the nearby counters.

As if it was precious to her when really, she wanted to burn it. She had worn it twice in six weeks' time. She would never wear it again.

And when she sank down in the bath, and lost herself in the silken embrace of hot water, lavender, and steam, she let the tears fall until they stopped of their own volition. Pia didn't know who she cried for. The mother who had never loved her the way Pia had wished so desperately she would. The father who had viewed her as something to barter, or an amusement, but never a real person.

Or this new life she'd stumbled into, whether she wanted it or not. The babies she carried, the prince who had fathered them, and the terrifying, unknown future that loomed ahead of them all.

She cried herself dry, and only then did she rise up from the tub, towel herself off, and take herself into the vast, airy confection of a four-poster bed that waited in the bedroom. She crawled into the center of the bed, turned over onto her side to find the only position where she could be remotely comfortable, and wrapped one arm around her belly.

"I promise you this," she murmured out loud to the twin lives inside of her. "I will never barter you away. I will tell you I love you every single day of your lives. And you will never, ever find yourself wondering on the day of my death if you grieve because you miss me—or because you don't."

And still murmuring vows to the sons she would bear within a few short months, but treat better if it killed her, Pia finally fell asleep.

CHAPTER EIGHT

ARES HAD NO IDEA what was happening to him as each day bled into the next, then a week slipped by. Then another.

And he and Pia stayed suspended in the same waiting game.

It was easy enough to make the Southern Palace his base of operations. So easy, in fact, that he couldn't quite remember why it had been so important to him to live apart from Atilia in the first place.

He flew in and out, from one royal engagement to another. And despite the barrage of scandalmongering headlines about him and Matteo Combe—and the expectant state of the Combe heiress the world had ignored until the funeral—his actual life was the same as it had been before. Did it matter what he called his base when he flew everywhere anyway?

Ares assured himself that nothing had changed. Nothing but his location.

Except he noticed that he found himself almost eager to return to the palace at the end of each engagement.

Almost as if he couldn't truly be easy until he'd seen Pia again.

If she had cried again after that first night, she never showed it. Nor did she make further attempts to break out of the castle, which was a relief if only because it prevented Ares from sharing parts of himself when he never, ever did such things.

The reports Ares received about her in his absence were always glowing. She was unfailingly polite and kind to all members of the staff. She went on walks, around and around the many courtyards, and at low tide, down to the beach, where she was known to spend time on the rocks, staring out toward the horizon. She never tried to lose her security detail. She seemed perfectly happy to have regular checkups with the doctor.

Her only request had been a laptop computer, which Ares had been more than happy to provide, particularly as it gave him leave to monitor what she did.

After all, he had never promised her privacy.

And that was how he discovered that what Pia did with her time was write an online column for one of those internet magazines that Ares had always personally believed were the scourge of the earth. He found this discovery so astounding that he sat with it for nearly a full week before it occurred to him to do anything about it.

One night, after he'd flown back from some or other formal charity event in mainland Europe, he found her curled up in what the staff had informed him was her favorite room of the palace. It was known as the Queen's Sitting Room, in the ancient wing, and had been built to accommodate a queen who had loved the ocean, her books and needlework, and liked to sit where she could look out all day while the business of the court carried on elsewhere. During the day the light cascaded in through the arched windows. At night, light made to look like candles blazed from every surface while the waves surged against the rocks outside.

Ares moved soundlessly into the room, not sure what to do with the wall of sensation and something perilously close to longing that slammed into him the moment he saw her.

Every moment he saw her, if he was honest.

Pia sat cross-legged on the chaise pointed toward the windows, a pillow over her lap—or what lap she had, with her huge, pregnant belly in the way. She was frowning down as she typed, worrying her bottom lip between her teeth, and Ares was only a man.

And it had been a long time indeed since he had taken a woman, now that he thought about it. Too long. Months.

Ares found he didn't actually want to scour his memory, because he was terribly afraid that Pia really had haunted him. That he might not have touched another woman since that night in New York.

He didn't want to consider that possibility, so he considered her instead.

His gaze traced the elegant line of Pia's neck, and the little wisps of dark hair that had tumbled down from the knot at the top of her head. He leaned against the doorjamb, letting his gaze drift lower. Her breasts swelled against the loose top she wore and he remembered covering them with his hands in New York. Now he wondered if they would spill over from his palms, so generous had they become. His mouth watered.

And there was something about her lush, swollen

belly that got to him, no matter how he tried to pretend otherwise.

There was something about the fact that she carried his babies, that she was big and round by his doing, that made something dark and primitive wind around and around inside him until he was tight like a coil.

He didn't know how he felt about becoming a father, but that had nothing to do with his appreciation of what he had done to her body. Or how she seemed to take to it so easily, so naturally, like one of the ancient goddesses that the locals claimed had first lived here on the site where the palace stood.

He shook himself, bemused at the direction of his own thoughts.

"When did you become an advice columnist?" he asked her, unaware until he spoke that his voice had gone all...gravelly.

But he couldn't worry about that when he had the distinct pleasure of watching Pia jolt in surprise. She whipped her head around, and then Ares's pleasure turned to a deeper joy as her cheeks reddened.

The way they always did when she saw him.

As if she couldn't keep herself from flushing pink and deeper red, which made him wonder if she was pink and red all over.

The possibilities made him ache.

"How do you...?" she began.

But her voice trailed off. She looked down at the laptop before her, and Ares braced himself for her temper. For the outburst that was almost surely coming.

He had to wonder if he'd asked the question specifically to provoke her.

If he'd lowered himself to such games.

But when Pia looked at Ares again, her gray gaze was resigned. "You're monitoring this laptop. Of course you are. I don't know why I didn't assume you were from the start."

Ares inclined his head slightly. "For security purposes, naturally. This is a royal palace."

"And because you're nosy." Her gaze stayed steady. "You want to know things about me without having to ask."

He could see that moment shimmer between them, Pia in her funeral dress on the side of that tub and him too close and much too open, and he was sure she could, too. But she didn't say anything.

"You could be in league with the tabloid reporters who swarmed us in Yorkshire," Ares said mildly instead. "You could have been planted by my enemies."

"Do you actually have enemies?" Pia asked, her voice even more mild than his. It scraped at him. "Or is this a part of those many wars you appear to be waging, though no one is waging them back at you?"

Ares leaned one shoulder against the doorjamb, crossed his arms, and regarded her sternly. "I suppose you could say I am my own war."

He certainly hadn't meant to say that. He didn't even know where the words had come from. Only that once they were out there, he couldn't deny the stark truth of them.

Or the acrid taste they left behind in his mouth.

It was like the first night she'd been here and that bizarre urge he'd had to *tend to her*. Ares wasn't certain he had *tended to* another person in the whole of his life, save his own mother in her final days. He hardly knew her. He knew the urge even less. It felt as if he'd been hit on the head and had only come to—and back into himself—when she'd reminded him of the fact that she was having sons.

His sons.

Every time he thought less of the sweet ripeness of her body and more about what that ripeness would result in, it hit him in the same way. Hard. Debilitating.

A full-on body blow.

"If you are your own war, you are lucky, Ares. That means you can call it off at any time." She closed the laptop and set it aside, her gray gaze on him. "You can have an armistice whenever you like."

"It is not quite that easy."

But he sounded more uncertain of that than he should have.

"Why are you spying on me?" she asked him, direct and to the point, that gaze still firm on his.

And if her voice had been sharp, or accusing, Ares would have known what to do. He could have handled it with a dose of royal arrogance, or that edgy thing in him that was always too close to the surface when he was in Atilia. Or near her.

Instead, he felt something like...outgunned.

"I would not call it spying," he replied, after a moment, but the words didn't seem to fit right in his mouth. "I told you. There were security concerns."

"Yes," she said, lifting up that chin of hers again. "I write a column. It's silly, really. There are lots of people who go through life without having to suffer through a finishing school. After all, its only real purpose is to make a person—and let's not kid ourselves, it's always a female person—so scrupulously well mannered that she could be a queen, if necessary."

Something powerful seemed to roar between them at that.

But Ares refused to acknowledge it. And Pia's cheeks only got redder.

"Hypothetically speaking, of course," she hurried to say. She looked away then, and Ares wondered if he was reddening, too, deep inside. "There's that story of the Queen of England at some dinner party. They'd set out finger bowls and the guest of honor picked his up and drank from it, which ought to have humiliated him. And would have, if he'd known. Everyone froze, not sure what to do in the face of such a breach of etiquette. But what did the queen do? She reached over, picked up her own finger bowl, and downed it like a shot. I don't know if that's true, but I like to think it is."

"Because you like to advise your readers to drink the contents of the finger bowls they encounter?" Ares asked. Darkly.

He felt...not himself, already. But even more so when Pia only gazed at him so calmly that he felt as if he'd turned into some kind of beast where he stood, misshapen and overlarge.

"Figuratively speaking," she replied. "I pretend to talk about good manners in my column. But really what I'm talking about is how to be kind."

"Kindness is overrated," Ares heard himself growl.

But Pia only shook her head. "No. It's really not."

"I admire these lofty sentiments, I do," Ares said in that same dark tone, all beast and very little prince. "But if you know that I have been monitoring what you do on that laptop, you must also know that I'm aware you monetize those columns of yours."

If he expected that to get to her, he was disappointed when all she did was smile. Patiently. In a manner that made him want to...break things.

Or get his hands on all that round, tempting lushness.

"No one knows it's me, do they?" That smile of hers was so bland it bordered on offensive. "I can assure you, no one wants to hear from poor little rich girl Pia Combe about how to be a better person."

"You have been writing this column for years. Since your second year of university, if my math is correct." He knew that it was.

"Well, there's only so much finishing a girl can do," Pia said lightly. Airily. She didn't actually wave her hand through the air dismissively, but it felt as if she had. "I thought it was a more reasonable outlet than some of the other ones my friends took up. Unsuitable men, for example. Or tempting scandal and often fate itself in all sorts of disreputable nightclubs. Unfortunate substances. A little column I never expected anyone to read seemed rather tame in comparison, but then, I have always been the little brown sparrow in a family of nothing but brightly plumed parrots. It felt very me."

Ares scowled at her. "I have absolutely no idea why you are suddenly talking about birds. Much less *plumage*."

"I know who I am. That's all I'm saying."

"You certainly don't need the money," Ares said, as if he'd caught her involved in some kind of con.

"I don't keep the money," she said, making a face as

if he was the one drinking out of finger bowls at formal banquets. "It's not a lot, or not by the standards I imagine you're used to, but I give it away. There are always needy people trying to raise money for various causes, and I like to give where I can. Without any strings."

"You could do that with the interest off a single month of your trust fund, one assumes."

"I could. But I was raised by Eddie Combe, who liked to rant and rave about the value of an honest day's work. I'm not pretending to work in any mines, but there's something to be said about earning my own money and spending it how I like." Her gaze searched his. "In fairness, I suppose crown princes aren't generally encouraged to do such things."

"There are some kingdoms that exult in the sight of their royals getting dirty with the common folk, but Atilia is not one of them," Ares said. "My mother spent time in the Royal Hospital, but ministering to the ill was about as far as the country was willing to let her go."

Thinking of his mother didn't bring the stab of grief it normally did. Possibly because he kept thinking that his mother would have loved Pia unreservedly. Ares could almost see them together, sitting in this very room, passing that laptop back and forth and discussing who next to help.

He found he was clenching his jaw so hard he was surprised he didn't snap a tooth.

"If you can help, you should," Pia said quietly, so much an echo of his childhood that Ares had to blink to make certain he wasn't sitting with his mother again, letting her quiet goodness cancel out his father's latest tantrum.

"I had no idea when I met you in New York that you were such a saint," he heard himself growl then.

Pia blinked, then flushed a deeper shade of red, and he felt as if he'd slapped her. That made him feel monstrous again. A cartoon beast, all fur and fury.

But he couldn't seem to stop himself from making every one of these moments with her...worse.

"Did you not?" she asked, lightly enough, though her gaze had gone cool. Wary. "I felt certain I was wearing my halo."

"I don't recall you wearing anything at all."

And that electric thing was back, bright and hot between them. Ares could feel his pulse thick and hot in his temples. In his chest.

In his greedy, hungry sex.

"I sit here every day," she said, though her voice was scratchier than it had been a moment before and there was a light in her eyes that made his pulse...worse. He decided to take that as a kind of victory. "I read a lot of tabloid takedowns. Alternate reality versions of me. Versions where I cold-bloodedly trapped a prince with my uterus. Then pitted said prince against my own brother, using my unborn child as collateral. I spend a lot of time wondering how it's possible that a person who never appeared in a single scandalous story before, ever, could attract the hatred of so many so fast."

"Is this about to veer into sparrows and parrots again?"

"I already feel stripped naked, is what I'm trying to tell you." Pia swallowed, hard. "It's bad enough that every time I pick up my phone or open a search engine I'm treated to more side-by-side comparisons between me and my mother, who, you may have heard, is still widely held to be the most beautiful woman who ever lived. I don't need you to come in here and taunt me."

"Taunt you?"

Ares hadn't expected that. Just as he didn't see it coming when Pia rose to her feet, betraying a gracefulness he felt certain she didn't know she possessed—but he could feel. All over him like a caress. She picked up the laptop and clutched it to her chest, then looked at him as if he was still very much that cartoon monster.

"I don't know what you want from me," she said, so quietly that it felt like condemnation. As if she could see the poison in his blood from where she stood. "I don't think you know either, which is the only reason why I'm tolerating this."

"This palace, renowned the world over for its beauty and never made available to the public. A life of ease, waited upon hand and foot. This is what you feel you must 'tolerate.'"

"You didn't liberate me from a gutter," Pia said, in that same quiet, deliberate way. "I'm not dazzled by your material possessions. I can see quite clearly that this is a prison no matter how lovely the furnishings might be."

What Ares didn't understand was why he felt as if he was in prison, too, when he was the one who came and went as he pleased.

"Consider this a grace period," she told him, very much as if she was the one with the control here. "I had months to get used to the fact that I was pregnant with twins. It wouldn't be fair of me not to accord you the same span of time to come around to the notion. But the clock is ticking, Ares. You can't keep me here forever and even if you could, there will soon be three of us."

"I would not challenge me if I were you." And his voice was a dark ribbon of sound he hardly recognized.

"You will have to make a decision," Pia replied as if she couldn't see the threat in him. Or didn't care. "Or do you think that I will have these babies locked away here, and then raise them like this, isolated from the world? As if we don't exist? You may be ashamed of them. Of me. But I am not."

"I never said I was ashamed."

She drew herself up, which only made him more aware of her lushness.

"Your indecision might keep me here," she said, as if she hadn't heard him. "I might even like it, as it keeps me from having to have unpleasant conversations with my older brother and everyone else who is suddenly dying to know my personal business."

She moved toward him then, the laptop in one arm and the other one wrapped over her belly.

"Pia—" he began, as if her name in his mouth didn't remind him too much of her taste. As if he didn't *ache*.

"But you will not lock these babies away from the world, Ares. They will not be victims to your indecision. Do you understand me?" And he had never seen that expression on her face before. Fierce. Sure. *Maternal*, something in him whispered. "My children will walk in the sun. They will be loved. They will not be hidden away like someone's dirty secret, and I don't care if it is in a palace. I won't have it."

And he wanted to stop her. He wanted to somehow

talk his way through the great mess inside of him, but he found himself frozen solid.

Unable to do anything but stand there, more monster than man.

And Ares wasn't sure that ratio was moving in his favor as she swept past him and disappeared down the hall.

Leaving him to feel the true weight of this palace he'd made a prison, as surely as if he'd fitted it with bars.

Ares had learned a long time ago not to read tabloid interpretations of his life, but he still found himself flipping idly through the worst of them on his tablet the next day as he flew to the Northern Island for the grand dedication of something or other.

A bank, perhaps. A monument.

He didn't care about that. Because the tabloids were filled with base speculation and nasty insinuation. Nothing new, but Ares found it clawed at him in a whole new way when the subject was Pia instead of him.

His own face was everywhere, with shots of him laid out on the ground and the bloody lip Matteo Combe had given him.

Matteo had been taken to task by his own Board of Directors, who were muttering about a no-confidence vote. They'd even gone so far as to sic an anger management specialist on him for a time, which Ares couldn't help but find amusing.

But there was nothing amusing about the things they almost but not quite called Pia. Because instead of fading away with nothing new to add to the story, it seemed the tabloids had only gotten bolder in their coverage during the time he and Pia had been in the Southern Palace.

Playboy Prince's pregnancy scandal! the headlines screamed.

Ares supposed he should count himself lucky that no one had dared mention the tabloids to his face.

He was congratulating himself on that as he stood in the grand, marble lobby of the Royal Bank of Atilia that was being dedicated to the King, where he was meant to say a few words. But there was a change in the crowd, suddenly, as he prepared himself to speak. He could feel it in the air. The ripple effect. The whispering and the gasping, followed by deep bows and curtsies all around.

Ares swore beneath his breath.

But he knew that he betrayed not a single emotion on his face when his father came in all his considerable state to stand beside him. Ares turned, as was required, and performed his own bow to his monarch.

"Prince Ares," the King said by way of greeting, and only because people were watching and would likely expect him to greet his only son.

"I did not expect to see you here, Your Majesty," Ares said beneath his breath as they stood for a rousing go at the Atilian national anthem. And he should not have seen his father, because it was well-known amongst the palace staff that the crown prince and the king preferred never to be in each other's company. "My secretary must have made a mistake."

"There was a mistake, all right," King Damascus retorted, making no attempt to hide his glare and no matter that the crowd was on the *"long may our king in grace and wisdom preside*" part of the song. "It's about time you and I have a word."

Ares could think of very little he would like less.

But they were in public. There was the brief ceremony to get through, made ten times worse by the presence of his father and all the extra pomp and circumstance that went along with the presence of the King of Atilia at such a banal event. And when it was done, he had no choice but to exit several steps behind his father as custom dictated, then follow him as commanded.

Because a son could rebel against his father. But Ares's father was also his king, and what the king decreed was law.

The old man insisted that they return to the Northern Palace, where Ares had made it a point not to set foot since his mother had died.

He knew his father was well aware of this.

But King Damascus wanted to draw it out, because he was as sadistic now as he had ever been. He marched Ares straight back to that private sitting room of his, where he had been lecturing Ares in between bouts of temper for as long as Ares could remember.

This time, Ares took the seat his father indicated and lounged in it. Not insolent, necessarily, but not reverent, either.

"This feels nostalgic," he said after the silence had dragged on too long.

"I'm glad you think so," the king said. "I feel nauseated, myself."

Ares smiled. Thinly. "Shall I contact your staff, sir? Do you require medical attention?"

The king moved to his personal bar, and Ares watched with a certain sense of resignation as his father poured himself a drink from yet another crystal decanter that Ares imagined would soon be in broken shards all over the stone floor. He did not offer Ares a drink, because he was still as petty as ever.

"Do you want to explain to me why your pregnant little piece is all over every paper?" the king demanded.

Ares wasn't sure what, precisely, it was that surged in him then. But he knew it was violent. Dark and furious, and aimed at his father.

Which he knew was treason.

But he didn't care.

"I beg your pardon, Your Majesty," he said icily. "You must surely be referring to yourself. I have no 'piece,' as you put it."

"You told me this would never happen," his father snarled at him. "You *promised* me, or I would have married you off years ago."

"Nature will do what it will do, father," Ares said, with a great flippancy he in no way felt about Pia or the babies she carried. "I don't understand your concern. I am not married. There is no actual scandal, there are only tabloids making noise."

"Was it noise that knocked you flat?"

Ares made himself stay where he was, seated and unthreatening. "That was a misunderstanding, nothing more."

"Do not expect my permission to marry her," his father said, and though he grew smaller and more wizened every time Ares saw him, that glare of his was as baleful as ever. "Do not think that the fact she is a

San Giacomo in any way makes up for all that peasant blood in her."

"I will remind you, sire," Ares said, acidly, "that I do not require your permission to marry. You struck down that law yourself, the better to make way for your own mistress."

"You mean your queen," his father growled. "Her Majesty Queen Caprice to the likes of you, and I warn you, I will tolerate no disrespect."

Ares forced himself to lounge back in his chair, though he wanted to be the one to start breaking things, this time. "And what of our great and glorious Queen Caprice? My understanding was that her chief attraction was her supposed fertility. Yet I've seen no sign that she is expecting your heirs."

"Watch yourself, boy."

"One is tempted to conclude that the reason you sired but one disappointing child was your fault. Not my mother's, as has been commonly agreed."

He meant: *by you and your doctors.*

"Is that your goal? You think that if you start having illegitimate children it will make you the better man?" His father laughed, but in that angry way of his that allowed for no actual humor. "On the contrary, Ares, all it does is remind the kingdom what a waste of space you are. A profligate playboy, governed by his base appetites. I should thank you for doing me a favor."

Ares stared back at this man that he had feared and hated for most of his life. Here in this room, where he had been threatened, belittled, and shouted at more times than he could count. Here where he had made decisions based entirely on how not to be the man facing him.

And he could cite chapter and verse about the things he didn't want. The man he didn't wish to become. The blood in him he hated, that had run hot just now, so desperately did he want to respond to the sneering violence in his father's voice in kind.

But he had other weapons.

You are always in a war, Pia had said.

And Ares supposed that was true. He had always been in *this* war. He had been dropped in it at birth.

But all that meant was that he knew how best to aim, then take fire, at the man who had taught him how to fight—never realizing, apparently, that in so doing he betrayed his own weaknesses.

"Did I not tell you the good news?" he asked his father mildly. Almost kindly. "Pia has made me the happiest man alive. She has agreed to be my wife. I know you—and the kingdom—will extend us your deepest congratulations."

And the first wedding gift he received was the splintering sound of his father's decanter against the castle wall. It was such a touch of nostalgia he very nearly came over all emotional as he took his leave.

And it was not until he was on his plane, heading back toward the Southern Palace, that it dawned on Ares that he would have to figure out how best to share these glad tidings with the woman he had yet to ask to be the wife he'd never wanted.

CHAPTER NINE

ONE THING PIA'S childhood had taught her, like it or not, was that a person could get used to anything.

No matter how outrageous or absurd things seemed, and no matter how certain she was that they might, in fact, kill her—they never did.

She had gotten used to her parents' excesses. The further removed she got from the operatic marriage of Eddie Combe and Alexandrina San Giacomo, the more she started to think of them as eccentrics, somehow unable to behave in any way other than the way they had. In a decade or so, she was sure, she would find herself nostalgic for her parents, their tempestuous relationship, and all those endless, theatrical fights she'd found so difficult to live through while growing up with them.

So, too, was Pia becoming used to her life in her very own prison of a palace.

She felt like Rapunzel, locked away in her little tower, visited by nothing and no one—save the man who came to her, mostly at night, and made her head spin around and around without laying so much as a finger on her.

Pia spent her days writing columns about fussy manners as stand-ins for deeper emotions, reading revolting things about herself in the tabloids—then vowing to stop reading revolting things about herself in the tabloids—and repeating the same thing over and over.

Her nights were punctuated by unpredictable glimpses of Ares.

Would he appear in the doorway as the shadows grew long, not there one moment and then a great, brooding presence in her peripheral vision the next? Would he ask her to join him for a drink with a guarded look in his green eyes and the suggestion of a banked fire in the way he held his big body? Would she agree, then sip at fizzy water as he swirled stronger spirits in a tumbler, the silence thick and layered between them? Or would they go a few rounds of conversation that always seemed so...fraught?

Pia never knew. She only knew that she looked forward to Ares's appearances with an unseemly amount of anticipation. And missed him when his duties kept him away.

She could admit to herself, when she wasn't making arch remarks about her prison tower, that she had always been a person better suited to life outside the glare of media attention and tabloid speculation. That night in New York had been the one and only time she'd tried to...be someone else.

Maybe, she told herself dourly in a voice that sounded a bit too much like one of Alexandrina's mild rebukes, *the reason Ares cannot bear to spend more than a few moments in your company, and no matter that you are carrying his children, is because he sees only that terrible lie when he looks at you.*

She didn't like to think about that. But how could she not? Pia was not beautiful. She was nothing like her mother. A man like Ares could have anyone, and had. Why would he want to be tethered for the rest of his life to *her*?

Pia had thought she'd come to terms with her looks—or lack thereof—a long time ago. It was a natural consequence of being Alexandrina San Giacomo's only daughter. She had been destined to be a disappointment from the day she was born.

But she hadn't marinated on that sad fact in a long time. Apparently, being hugely pregnant and mostly alone, locked up in a castle like an embarrassment that needed to be hidden away from the light, got into a girl's head. And stayed there, hunkering down and breathing fire, whether she liked it or not.

"I will make sure that *our* branch of the family is better," she promised her babies every day, shifting around on her favorite chaise as the boys kicked at her. With more and more vigor as the days rolled by and they grew inside her. "I promise."

Pia was well into her seventh month of pregnancy when she discovered that her family had more branches than she knew.

Because it turned out that she and Matteo had another brother.

A half brother, Dominik, that their mother had given away when she was a teenager, long before she'd become an icon.

A scandalous little fact about her mother—her family—that Pia discovered by reading a tabloid.

"Did you know about this?" Pia asked Matteo in

disbelief, reaching him on some business trip some-where. When she knew he did, as the papers seemed to suggest that the new brother was dating Matteo's personal assistant—who had always returned Pia's calls before, yet was failing to do so at present. "How long have you known *we have another relative* and not told me?"

"It's not as if you've been available, Pia," Matteo said, and she would have said it was impossible for him to sound any colder than he already did. But he proved her wrong.

"I think by 'available' you mean, 'sitting in a room you might accidentally enter,'" Pia said, with a little more asperity than she normally showed her brother. Or anyone. "When the common definition also in-cludes this device I'm calling you on right now. It's very handy for the sharing of important news, like brand-new family members appearing full grown. Or even to say hello."

"If you wish to be kept up-to-date on everyday con-cerns, you would have to actually make that known," Matteo retorted. "Instead of running away from your own father's funeral and hiding out somewhere."

Pia had never thought of herself as a particular heir to the famous Combe temper. But she was so angry then, and possibly something else that she didn't know how to name, that the rest of the conversation stayed something of a blur to her.

And when she hung up, all she could think about was her mother.

Vain, beautiful, magnetic, impossible, deliriously compelling Alexandrina, who Pia had always wanted so desperately to please. And who Pia had always failed to please.

And who Pia had always thought had locked her away in that convent out of shame. Spite, perhaps. Or simple disinterest in a daughter who was so much less.

It had never occurred to her that when her mother told her that wrapping her up in cotton wool was a gift, Alexandrina had meant it. Just as it had never crossed Pia's mind that her mother's life could ever have been anything less than perfect. Or if not perfect, exactly as she'd wanted it.

Pia hardly knew how to think about a different Alexandrina. A woman who was…a person. A woman who had carried a child, just as Pia was doing now, and had given it away. An act of grace or shame, sorrow or hope, that Pia literally could not imagine living through herself.

Thinking of Alexandrina so young, and faced with such a tough decision…knocked Pia's world off balance. The Alexandrina she'd known was so smooth and polished. Even when she fought with Eddie. And had certainly not been harboring any deep hurts.

And maybe that was the hardest part of grief. It was always changing. Growing, expanding, shifting to fit whatever little pockets it found.

She had to assume it would always be that way.

And she was still sorting through what it meant to have a brother she didn't know—who, for all she knew, might want nothing to do with the family that had abandoned him long ago—when she looked up to find her very own Prince Not Quite Charming standing there in the doorway. The way he liked to do.

"How long have you been standing there?" she asked, her hands on her belly, still caught up in those confronting thoughts about her mother.

"What does it matter?" he asked, brooding and dark.

Pia forced a smile she didn't feel. "I've resigned myself to the cyber spying. It's your laptop and I have nothing to hide. Look through it at will if you feel you must. But I don't understand why it's necessary for you to lurk about your own palace like this."

"I do not lurk." His voice was even darker then, and there was a considering sort of gleam in his green gaze. "It is not my fault you are unobservant when it comes to your surroundings."

"Well, Ares—" she began, hotly.

But he held up a hand before she could continue down one of their familiar little paths that always led to the same place. Parry, retreat, regroup—and parry again. Back and forth they would go, until it was difficult to tell who struck whom. And who left the most marks.

"Come dine with me," he said, to her shock.

That did not usually happen. Ares was usually out for dinner, at this or that ball that Pia could follow on social media or in the papers the next day—not that she did such a thing. As that might be interpreted as too much interest in the man.

And maybe it was the novelty that had her biting her own tongue. She shifted, standing up—which took leveraging herself off the arm of the chaise these days—and then crossing to him.

He held out his hand as she approached. And Pia took it.

And it was as if the balance shifted. Or her world, still off its axis, tilted even more sharply. It felt as if the floors beneath her feet suddenly slanted terrifically, leaving her head spinning.

It wasn't just his touch. Or it wasn't only that. It was that solemn look, grave and intent, in those green eyes of his. Pia was sure she hadn't seen him look at her like that since...

But she didn't dare say it. She didn't dare think it.

And as Ares took her hand, then led her down the halls of the palace, she was buffeted by the memories of what happened between them that night in New York. When he had taken her hand like this and led her out of that party, and then all these restless things inside her had shifted into heat. Fire.

All that longing and need, greed and revelation.

It all kept washing over her, memory after memory.

He led her to the wing of the palace she knew was set aside for his exclusive use, and into a private dining room. It could have comfortably fit a crowd, but the table was set up to feel intimate, with a view over the ocean as the last of the sunset spread pink and orange over the horizon. Pia couldn't help thinking about the fact that they had skipped this part in New York. The sit down, have a meal, and learn about each other part.

This felt...remedial and precious, at once.

She found she was afraid to break the silence.

"I'm surprised you're here," she made herself say because it was best to rip the bandage off and dive straight in—another one of her father's favorite sayings. "Your social calendar is always so full."

"I canceled it."

"You mean, tonight's engagement?"

"All of it," Ares said.

And then did not expand on that statement at all.

The staff swept in, laying out the first course, but Pia hardly noticed it. And the babies must have sensed her agitation—or maybe it was anticipation, or something far more insidious, like longing—and as she rubbed her hand over her belly, she received a volley of kicks.

She must have sighed a little, because when she looked up, Ares was frowning at her. Not from down the length of a banquet table, but from much, much closer. Within reach.

"Is something happening?" he asked.

Aside from the hand he'd offered her tonight, Ares hadn't touched her since her first night here. And even then, it seemed to her that he had gone out of his way to avoid touching her belly. Yet when she looked at him now, he had the oddest expression on his face.

There was no doubt that he was focusing all his attention on her. On her belly, to be more precise, where her hand rubbed at the tiny little foot inside.

"One of them is kicking," she told him. "Which means the other one will likely join in any second now and make it a football match."

Ares looked as astonished as he did uncertain then. "Now? As you sit there?"

"Do you...? Do you want to feel it yourself?" Pia offered, surprised by the vulnerability she heard in her own voice.

And worse, the hope.

Ares rose from his chair, rounding the corner of the table that separated them. Then, without skipping a beat, he slid down before her. And there was a look on his face that she had never seen before. His green eyes were dark.

Pia smiled. "Give me your hands."

She didn't wait for him to offer them. She reached over, took his hands in hers, and brought them firmly against her belly.

And, sure enough, the moment his hands slid into place over her bump, two different sets of feet reacted.

Pia watched Ares's face. The jolt of surprise. The understanding of what he was feeling beneath his palms.

And then, like a dose of pure sunshine, the wonder.

"Does it hurt?" he asked, his voice hushed.

"Sometimes it's uncomfortable," she said softly. "Or surprising. Or if one of them stretches out and presses their feet up against my ribs, that aches."

He shifted, coming down on his knees before her chair, and his hands were suddenly everywhere. Moving all over her bump, as if testing it. Learning its shape.

And the more he ran his hands over her, the more Pia liked it. And in a way that had nothing at all to do with their babies or any kicking. She felt the shift in her like a flame leaping into life, from coals she'd imagined were cold.

It turned out they were only smoldering.

When Ares looked up at her again, there was a gleaming heat in his gaze that she recognized. Oh, how she recognized it. How she *felt* it.

"Pia," he said, his voice low. Hot.

And an unmistakable invitation.

Pia couldn't take this. Not for another moment. Ares

was so close, his hands on her, that look of marvel and need on his beautiful face.

How could she do anything but melt? And as she melted and ran hot, that liquid greed bloomed inside her, low in her belly and deep between her legs.

Where only Ares had ever touched her.

His gaze searched hers.

Did she whisper his name? Or did it live in her already? Always?

Whichever it was, it made Pia lose her head completely. She leaned forward, slid her hands to hold his face, and then settled her mouth to his as if she might die then and there if she couldn't taste him again.

She felt him groan, low and deep, as if it came from the depths of him. She felt his big, athletic body shake slightly, as if from the force of the same wild sensation that swept through her, too.

And then his mouth opened beneath hers and he took control.

And when he kissed her, Pia forgot that she wasn't beautiful.

When Ares kissed her, Pia felt as if she was made entirely of glory. Light and lovely, sweet and right, strung out on the heaven in his every touch. All that hot perfection.

Ares moved closer, one hand curling around her neck as if to guide her where he wanted her. The other stayed put on her belly.

She felt untethered by her own need, and anchored at the same time.

He made her feel like she could fly. Like this was flying.

Ares kissed her and he kissed her, and Pia didn't know which one of them was trying harder to move closer. To take the kiss deeper. She was frustrated that he wasn't closer. She wanted his skin on hers, his hands on her bare flesh.

She *wanted*.

Ares groaned again, then shifted back. His mouth curved at the sound of protest she made, and he pulled her up from her chair. He set her briefly on her feet, but only briefly, because he moved then to lift her into his arms.

And here she was absurdly pregnant, yet he was still making her feel as if she weighed nothing at all.

"Ares, you can't—"

"So help me God, Pia," Ares growled down at her. "If you're about to tell me that I cannot lift you when I have very clearly already done so, I will be tempted to drop you over the side of the balcony."

And she didn't think he was likely to do that.

But she didn't finish her sentence, either.

He bore her outside, onto the balcony he had just mentioned, wide and open. He lay her down on a wide, low chaise, and followed her. Then stretched out beside her so they were finally—*finally*—touching, head to toe.

And that was almost too much.

But Ares took her mouth again, and they both groaned at the heat. The mad, glorious kick of hunger.

He kissed her and he kissed her, and she kissed him back with all the longing and need she'd kept inside her all this time. All that delirious fire that he stoked in her.

Only him.

Ares was dressed for one of his royal engagements, but he pulled back to shrug out of his jacket and his shirt, giving Pia access to those wide shoulders of his and better yet, his mouthwatering chest.

She took instant advantage, moving her hands over him and letting herself exult in his strength. His heat.

Each and every perfect ridge and tempting hollow.

And everything was too hot. Too good.

He found her breasts, so plump and big now. And he made such a deep, male sound of approval as he filled his hands with them that Pia forgot to be self-conscious. He pushed up the loose blouse she wore and freed her breasts from the front clasp of her bra.

Then he bent his head to take a nipple into his mouth.

And the sensation was so intense, so wild and over-whelming. It shot through her, a molten hot line from her nipple to her hungry sex, that Pia felt herself pull too tight—

Then she simply shattered, there and then.

Ares let out a laugh of dark delight that shivered its way through Pia like a new, bright flame. Then he moved to her other nipple, taking it into his mouth in the same greedy, demanding way. She tried to breathe. She tried to fight it off, but he only sucked a little harder—

And that was it. She went tumbling from one peak to the next, and broke apart all over again.

"I can't believe how sensitive you are now," he murmured, his mouth on her belly. "Let's test it, shall we?"

Then—slowly, carefully, ruthlessly—he stripped her of the loose, easy clothes she wore.

And Pia was too busy falling to pieces, and gasping

for breath, and crying out his name, to think about the things that would have torn her apart at any other time. Her size, for example. How fat she must look. How different than before.

But she was too busy losing herself in Ares's mouth. Beneath his clever, wicked hands.

She didn't notice when he stripped out of the rest of his clothes, too, because his hands found their way between her legs, teasing her slick flesh until she broke apart again.

And again.

And then, finally, Ares went and knelt before the chaise, pulling her to the edge and opening her legs wide. He held himself there, moving between her thighs. Only then did he find her soft, wet heat with the hardest part of him.

His gaze lifted to hers. Pia held her breath. And Ares pushed his way inside.

Slowly. Carefully.

Almost as if this was sacred. Beautiful.

As if she was.

"Pia," he murmured, as if her name was a prayer.

And then he set about his devotions, one perfect thrust after the next.

And she was already coming apart. She was already in pieces. Over and over again, as if the pleasure was a wave and she was caught in the undertow, tossed and tumbling and wild with it.

She lost count of how many times he brought her to that glorious cliff and tossed her over, only to catch her on the way down and do it all again.

It was too much, and it was beautiful and perfect,

and Pia never wanted to go without it—without him, without *this*—again.

She heard a distant sound and realized that she was saying those things out loud, but she didn't have it in her to mind that, either. Not when she was captured in that undertow, lost in the whirl of it.

Pia shook and she shook, she came down a little only to feel him surge deep inside her again, and she shook even more.

Until she thought she might become the shaking.

And finally, when he hit his own cliff, Ares gathered her to him. He dropped his head into the crook of her neck and called out her name as he shattered at last.

And she understood, now, Pia thought in a kind of wonder when she surfaced to find herself tucked up on that chaise, Ares having crawled up next to her like a kind of warm, gloriously male blanket.

It had been so hard, after New York, to understand why she'd behaved the way she had there. Why she'd done those things, and so easily and carelessly when that wasn't her. That wasn't how she behaved.

But she got it now. It was this. It was Ares.

It was extraordinary.

He was remarkable.

And it was no wonder that she had never been the same since.

She found herself running her fingers up and down her belly, in the absent way she often did, and she smiled when Ares did it, too, from beside her. Tracing patterns this way and that.

Introducing himself, she thought when one baby kicked.

Letting them know who he was, she thought when the other followed suit.

"Pia," Ares said, in that low, marvelous voice of his that she loved to feel roll over her like the sweet, thick breeze from the sea before them. "You are the mother of my sons."

"That's me," she said softly, and her smile trembled a bit on her mouth. "Like it or not."

He looked up from her belly, leveling all that green intensity on her. His expression was grave. "I want you to marry me."

It was an order. A royal command.

And what surprised Pia was how deeply, how passionately she wanted to obey him.

But what did she know about marriage? Nothing but what she'd seen growing up. And certainly nothing that let her imagine two people so unevenly matched could make it work. She'd watched her parents' marriage explode time and time again, sometimes in the same evening. She'd watched it fall apart a thousand times, though they'd stayed together. She'd watched the games they played with and at each other, and the pieces they'd carved from each other that she didn't think they'd ever gotten back.

And Eddie and Alexandrina had been a love story for the ages.

Pia didn't see any reason why she should subject her babies to a far grimmer, far less exalted version of her parents' marriage. All the struggle and pain and yet none of the love.

How could she subject herself to that? And worse

still, how could she make her babies grow up like that? Hadn't it been hard enough for her?

She lay there on the balcony with the sea as their witness, naked and replete, still spinning in all that sensation and sweet hunger. She reached over and slid her hand over Ares's, holding him to her.

And she said no.

"No." She said it distinctly. "I won't marry you. But you are the father to my sons, Ares. That won't change. We don't have to be married. We can just…be parents."

He was quiet for a long, taut moment.

"And how do you think that will work when I take the throne?" he asked mildly, though Pia wasn't fooled by his almost offhand tone. "Will the two princes have alternate weekends with their father, the King of Atilia, and then spend the rest of the time in some godforsaken Yorkshire village?"

"We'll figure it out, one way or another." Pia made herself smile at him, though it felt like a risk when his green eyes were so dark. "With or without my beloved, godforsaken Yorkshire."

Ares rolled to his feet. Then he reached down and pulled her up from the chaise, letting her stand there before him as the night air danced over them.

And as Pia longed for more.

"I mean to have you as my wife," he told her, starkly.

"No," she said again, and felt something hitch in her as she said it, as if the longing was tangled up on itself. "No, you don't. You want to marry me for the babies, but it has nothing to do with *me*. You don't want *me* for a wife. You want your babies' mother."

"Why can't I want both?"

"No," she said again. Calmly and firmly, despite that tumult inside her that she feared was something even more embarrassing.

Like stark, desperate yearning, despite everything.

And Pia expected him to argue. To rage, perhaps, the way her father would have. Or go dark and broody, the way she'd seen him do before.

But Ares only smiled.

CHAPTER TEN

PIA DIDN'T KNOW what she'd expected. Perhaps she thought that having been rejected, Ares would go off somewhere. Lick his wounds with his favorite whiskey. Pretend the conversation had never happened.

Instead, he helped her dress, pulling the softly elegant knits into place. Then he ushered her back into the dining room and took his time helping her into her seat. He sat—too close to her—at the entirely too intimate table, and they…had a perfectly civilized dinner.

Complete with finger bowls at the end.

"And if I drink mine?" she dared ask him. "Will you do the appropriate thing as host? All to make me feel comfortable?"

But this was why Pia wrote columns about seemingly insignificant things like whether or not to send thank-you notes—yes, always—and whether one should flout convention in matters such as the wearing of white in the off-season—of course, if you can pull it off.

Because it was never about the finger bowls. It was about taking care of other people.

It was about whether or not she felt safe with him when Pia didn't know if she'd ever been safe in her life.

Or how she could possibly know the difference when she didn't know what such a thing felt like.

"Marry me," Ares replied, his green gaze tight on hers. Because he was relentless and he clearly didn't mind her knowing it. "And you will see exactly what kind of host I am."

Pia did not drink from her finger bowl. And she was shaken all over again, if in a markedly different fashion, by the fact Ares hadn't let it go. If he was chastened or upset by her refusal, he didn't seem to show it.

After dinner, he escorted her out into the hallway, but when she turned to make her way back toward her wing of the palace, he held fast to her arm.

"I think not," he said quietly. "We have only just begun to take the edge off, have we not?"

"The edge?" Pia repeated because she didn't dare imagine that he meant what she thought he did. What her body certainly hoped he did, as it shivered everywhere, inside and out, when she was sure she shouldn't have been able to feel a thing. Not when she'd felt too much already.

"*Cara mia*, it has been much too long since New York. My hunger for you has yet to be quenched."

Maybe she should have argued. Held fast to some or other standard…but Pia wanted him more than she wanted to fight him.

All she did was nod. Once.

Ares did not do a good job of hiding his sharp, hot grin then. He led her to his vast suite of rooms, instead. And he laid her out on his massive bed, clearly made for kings, and crawled up over her to learn every inch of her body all over again.

And when she was writhing, and out of her head once more, he turned her over. He settled her on her hands and knees, so he could slide into her from behind.

That time, she screamed his name when she burst apart.

Every time she burst apart.

And that was only the beginning of his campaign.

He had all her things moved into his rooms and when she objected, merely lifted an arrogant brow.

"I do not wish to traipse down a mile of palace corridors when I could more easily turn over and find you in my bed, Pia," he told her. Loftily.

And maybe Pia was weak. But she liked sleeping in his bed. And she liked it even more when he turned over and woke her up.

He still maintained his schedule of events. Royal necessities that meant he was always trotting off to this or that.

But he came home more than he had before.

And Pia laughed at herself when she realized that was the word she used now. *Home.* To describe this mad, fairy-tale palace where she was locked away from the world.

Or maybe, something inside her suggested, *this is where you get to retreat from the world.*

When had her prison begun to feel like a *retreat*?

She found she stopped looking at the tabloids, particularly as they now starred both of her brothers and their various romantic entanglements. It wasn't only that she didn't want the nasty, gossipy version of her family in her head. It was more that she liked focusing on her own life.

Because she had a life, for once. She was growing brand-new humans inside her. She was carrying on with her writing. And she had Ares, after a fashion.

He taught her things it was impossible to learn in a single night.

And if her giant, pregnant body was any kind of hindrance, he never showed it. He seemed perfectly capable of coming up with new, improved ways to make sure they were both comfortable while they explored each other.

Sometimes he talked. He made dark, delicious promises, then followed through on each and every one of them.

Other times, he was dark, silent, and impossibly beautiful as he moved over her, in her.

One afternoon, after he had made her sob, scream, and then beg a bit for good measure, Ares sprawled beside her. The bed was big, wide, and rumpled beneath them. Up above, the ceiling fan turned lazily, keeping the air moving. Pia could hear the ever-present sound of the ocean outside, crashing over the rocks and surging against the shore.

And Ares was hot and beautiful, all leashed power and male grace as he lay there beside her, his fingers laced with hers.

No matter what happened, Pia knew she would always remember this moment. When she'd almost forgot her body entirely, or could only seem to remember what he could do to it.

Beautiful, something in her whispered. *He makes you feel beautiful.*

"Marry me," he said, the way he always did. He had

asked her to marry him so many times now that she thought it had lost its power. Almost. Now it was just a thing he said.

Pass the salt, please. Marry me.

Pia laughed. "You know I can't."

"I know no such thing."

She sighed, shifting in an attempt to get comfortable. "You were very clear that you wanted no wife. No children. And the children were a surprise to us both, but I think we will do very well now that we've adjusted to it all. But why add marriage to the mix?"

"I remember seeing your parents at a ball," Ares said into the quiet of the room, with only the ocean outside as accompaniment. "It was perhaps ten years ago now. It was a ghastly sort of state affair, bristling with diplomats and career socialites."

As he always did, now, Ares moved his hand over her belly. Finding one baby's head, and the other's pair of feet. Saying hello to his sons. Pia had grown used to the patterns he drew there. The way she sometimes drifted off to sleep and woke to find Ares crooning nonsense to her belly.

She hardly dared admit how that made her feel. Riddled with hope. Laced through with sweetness. So full of impossible, unwieldy emotion, she felt it was one more part of her set to burst. At any moment.

"I never knew my parents to subject themselves to anything grim or ghastly," Pia said, trying to rally when everything felt too emotional these days. She was in her eighth month, and twins were usually early. Her time with them as part of her was almost over. And so, too, was her time with Ares nearing its natural conclusion.

She could feel it with every breath. "They much preferred to be the life of the liveliest parties they could find."

"I imagine it was a business affair for your father," Ares said. "There were stultifying speeches, as there always are. Much self-congratulation. Then the dancing began. There were the usual awkward couplings of diplomats, their wives, and so on. These things are typically excruciating. But then your parents took the floor."

Pia thought she knew where this was going. She smiled, settling more fully on her side. "My parents loved to dance."

"That was instantly apparent. I don't know anything about their marriage, or not anything that wasn't twisted to sell papers, but I did see them dance. I saw the way they looked at each other."

"Not only as if there was no one else in the room," Pia said softly, remembering. "But as if no one else existed at all."

"My own parents did not dance unless it was strictly necessary for reasons of highest protocol," Ares told her, propping himself up on one elbow and regarding her, an odd sort of gleam in his green eyes that made them seem burnished with gold. "And when they did, they did their best never to gaze at each other at all. I watched them dance at the same ball ten years ago and I imagine it was perfectly clear to everyone in the room how little esteem they held for each other."

"Did they not...?" Pia didn't quite know how to phrase the question.

Ares let out a laugh, but it was tinged with bitterness. "My father liked to indulge his temper. When it was aimed at me, he liked to throw things against walls. I am only grateful that he contained that rage to me alone and never aimed it at my mother." He shook his head. "They say he is a decent enough ruler, but he was a cold, unfeeling husband and is a terrible father."

"You don't have to talk about this," Pia said quietly, when she thought he wouldn't go on.

Ares's eyes glittered. "My mother provided him with the requisite heir, thus securing the bloodline and the kingdom, which was all he cared about. Once that was accomplished, he felt perfectly justified in pursuing his extracurricular interests. Without caring overmuch if that might hurt her feelings. In fact, I think I can say with perfect honesty that I have never known my father to care about anyone's feelings. Ever."

Pia tried to pull up pictures of the king of Atilia and his late queen in her head. And more, tried to think of them as people instead of pictures anyone could look at.

"Your father cheated on your mother?" she asked.

"Constantly." Ares smiled, but it was little more than the sharp edge of his teeth. "And enthusiastically. Quantity over quality, if my sources are correct."

Pia let out a breath, and directed her attention to the place where their hands were still linked.

"I think my parents cheated on each other as well," she told him, though she'd never admitted that out loud before. No matter what the papers said. "I know they loved each other, madly and wildly. Everyone knows that. But part of that kind of love is all about hurting each other. I think the glory was in the coming back together, so they always seemed to look for new ways to break apart."

Ares lifted her hand and brought it to his mouth. He pressed his lips against her knuckles and Pia's heart instantly careened around inside of her chest. Fizzy and mad, as if they weren't already naked. As if they hadn't already spent hours making each other moan.

His gaze was intent on hers. "I never wanted to marry because I watched a royal Atilian marriage play out right in front of me. My father was a brute, always. And my mother was always so sad. I never wanted that for any woman bound to me, whether by duty or desire."

He reached over and brushed her hair back from her face, and Pia didn't want to see the look on his then. It was...too open. Too complicated.

It made her heart pick up its pace.

"But I am willing to take the chance that you and I can make something different, between us. Something better, Pia."

She shook her head at him, afraid that if she investigated any further she would discover that the lump in her throat and the glassiness in her eyes could tip over too quickly into tears. And would.

Because she kept telling herself that he was joking. Or if not *joking*, precisely, saying these things she'd always wanted to hear because he thought he could convince her that way. Not because he actually believed them.

But the trouble was, she *wanted* to believe him. And the more of these sorts of things he said, the more she wanted to believe.

When she knew better.

"Ares," she began.

"We are magic in bed, Pia," he said, in a voice as

intense as the way he looked at her. "That is how we came to be here in the first place. Is the worst thing in the world to think we might as well make it official?"

"You're the one who gave me a lesson in the lines of Atilian succession." She wanted to roll out of the bed and storm away. But it took her too long to do such things—or anything—these days. So she settled for rolling away from him, and pushing herself up into sitting position.

And as she did, she was suddenly too aware of how naked she was. How huge her breasts had become. How misshapen her belly was, sticking so far out, with her belly button protruding.

"Yes," Ares was saying, watching her. "I'm concerned about the lines of succession. Should I not be? I told you the day of your father's funeral that it was no small thing to claim you carry my child. That hasn't changed. If anything, the closer we get to your due date, the more serious the matter becomes."

"Because all of a sudden now you care deeply about these things?"

"I may not have set out to make myself heirs." And there was something granite in his voice. In the gaze he leveled on her. It made something deep inside her start to tremble. "But they exist. They will be here sooner rather than later. And I would prefer it if they had access to all the rights and privileges their position as my heirs allows them."

"Why?" She was rubbing her belly, and made herself stop. "You felt one way about all of this, then you interacted with your father and everything changed. It's hard not to think you simply want to defy him."

His expression changed, and she wondered if he'd thought she didn't know. That she hadn't seen the pictures of the two of them—*King Damascus Takes Errant Heir to Task!* the papers had cackled—and seen the dark look on Ares's face.

"What do you think will happen?" he asked her, and she thought she hated it most when he sounded so *patient*. So *reasonable*.

"Do you need me to explain to you where babies come from, Ares?" she asked him, proud that she kept her voice calm.

"The world already believes you are pregnant with at least one of my children," he replied, only that cool gleam in his eyes indicating that he was even aware of the question she'd asked. "Let us say, for the sake of argument, that I let you go right now. And you set out into the world, footloose and fancy-free as you claim to want. You're lucky enough not to be impoverished, which means you will no doubt be capable of raising these babies just fine on your own."

"I've been making this argument for months."

"But the world will continue to think they are mine, no matter what lies we tell or lengths we take to conceal that truth. And what then?"

"What do you mean, 'what then?' Rumors are just rumors—"

"Rumors are rumors, yes. But thrones are thrones, *cara mia.*" And she didn't know what that note in his voice was then. Or that look in his eyes. Only that it made her tremble—again. "And we may have grown progressive in these latter days. We prefer to have our fights in ballot boxes rather than in the streets or on poppy fields. But that does not change the fact that you will be raising two boys with a direct claim to the throne of Atilia. I understand that means nothing to you, but I assure you—it will not only mean something to my people, it will mean even more to whoever succeeds me."

"Succeeds you?" She didn't understand.

"I will take the throne, and then I will die," Ares said, with certain matter-of-factness that made her want to scream. Or do *something* to protest the ruthless inevitability in his voice. "And whoever comes next, whether it be a cousin or whatever issue my father manages to rustle up in his waning years, your boys will be out there. Some will inevitably claim that one of them is the rightful king. And do you know what will happen then?"

"Let me guess," Pia said, more sharply than she intended, surely. But she couldn't seem to pull herself back. "Another war."

"The blood of Atilia runs in my veins," Ares told her, his voice low and insistent. "It is poison. It is war and it is pain. And I am sorry to be the bearer of this news, but it is in you, too, now. It is in those boys. It is who we are."

"I don't know what any of that means." But she had moved herself back as she spoke, so she was sitting up against the headboard. And she was watching him as if he might snap at any moment, and then God only knew what might happen. Or what she might do. "Of course there's nothing in your blood. Royalty is not a virus."

"I beg to differ," Ares said, with a short sort of laugh, bitter and dark. "Royalty is power, nothing more and nothing less. And power infects. It could be that some successor seeks you out, and tries to neutralize any threat that your boys present. That is horrifying enough to contemplate."

That he had already contemplated that stung Pia. When she hadn't. She hadn't thought much beyond her pregnancy. She had been too busy settling here in this palace of his. She had been too focused on her hopeless little heart.

She was already a bad mother and her children weren't born yet.

"But there is also another possibility," Ares said in that same powerfully mild way that was wreaking havoc on her. "Who knows who our sons will grow up to become? Either one of them might decide that they deserve their birthright. What do you plan to do then?"

Pia's heart clattered around in her chest. And all she could seem to do was beat herself up for the possibilities she hadn't considered.

She tried to shake it off—because she could beat herself up on her own time. She didn't have to do it when Ares was watching her like this, close and very nearly *ferocious*. "So your position is that we should marry, and that will somehow…prevent your sons from taking the throne? Or prevent someone else from taking it? Or prevent…something else? I'm not following you."

"Pia—"

"And I've already told you that I won't restrict your access from them. I mean that. But a marriage between you and me isn't about them. It's about me."

She hated the fact that her voice cracked on that last word. That it gave her away so completely. That it showed him things she didn't want him to know.

"Pia," he said again, even more calmly than before.

And this time, she didn't care how hard it was. She got herself to the edge of the bed, and shoved herself off. She had to stand still for a moment, her hand on the small of her back, and she almost burst into tears because she wanted to storm away. But there was no *storming* in her current state. There was only waddling. And she already felt bad enough. She certainly didn't need to *waddle* in front of him. Naked.

She grabbed at the coverlet that had been kicked to the foot of the bed. It was something spun from gold and unicorn dust, or so it appeared, like everything else in this place. Pia wrapped it around herself like a makeshift dress.

And she didn't understand how she had let all this happen.

It was as if she hadn't quite been paying attention. There had been all that mind-altering sex to distract her. And the exquisite sweetness of their nights together made her forget herself during the day. He'd moved her into his rooms and she'd just…let it happen. She hadn't put up so much as a token protest. In fact, it hadn't oc-curred to her to protest.

She'd been enjoying herself too much.

And now she was in her eighth month of this preg-nancy. She was enormous. And she couldn't tell if she was finding it hard to breathe because she was emo-tional, or because she had two babies pressed up hard against…everything.

But she knew that she'd miscalculated. Greatly. She had more than miscalculated.

Because what she couldn't tell him was that while he

had been indulging himself, and playing whatever game this was with her, she had been doing something far more dangerous. He had been playing a long game, trying to get her to marry him for his own suspect reasons.

But Pia had been falling in love.

And she had to bite back a little sob as that word poured through her, so bright and hot she was shocked he couldn't *see* it.

She couldn't think of anything more stupid. Or embarrassing. But it was true. She had fallen in love with Ares. If she was honest, she suspected that it had happened at first sight at that party in New York. Because she had never been affected by any other man.

But one look at Ares and she'd wandered off with him, happily. Then she'd gotten herself wildly, irrevocably knocked up. And to add insult to injury, as was apparently her specialty, she'd gone off with him again at her own father's funeral.

She'd let him lock her up here. And sure, she had a thousand excuses for herself. There were guards. There was only one road out and it was closely watched. But the truth was, she hadn't tried very hard to get away from him after that first night.

Pia had told herself she was nesting. That was what pregnant women did—every article she found online said so. She wrote columns about trusting one's gut and how best to handle awkward social interactions, while all the while she was handling her relationship with this man just about as badly as it was possible to do.

Because Ares might have decided he wanted something other than what he'd told her he wanted at the start, but it didn't matter. Because any way she looked at it, what he really wanted was his sons without the trouble of custody agreements. Which was fair enough.

But it felt even more brutal now that he didn't want *her*.

He would have sex with her. Extremely good sex, if what he said was true about this wild, greedy thing they shared. But he didn't love her. He couldn't love her. He hadn't been looking for *her* when he'd found her at Combe Manor that day. He'd been on one of his royal engagements, doing his duty to the family.

When Pia knew, thanks to her father, that when a man loved a woman he could not rest. He would seek her out, no matter what damage it did. *No matter what.*

It was long past time Pia faced the facts here, no matter how little she liked them.

"I don't understand why everything changed," she said to him, trying to keep her panic tamped down. And worse, that bright beacon of a word she couldn't say and a thing she shouldn't feel. "You were very certain about the things you didn't want."

"It's not a question about what I want," Ares said, his green gaze hooded. "It's a question of what is right."

He was still on the bed, lounging there in that seemingly careless way of his. And it made her heart kick at her. *He* did, even now.

She tightened her grip on the coverlet. "Because somehow, what is right involves war in the blood and something about poison. Oh, yes, and infectious power."

"I want to make you my queen," Ares said, and he no longer sounded quite so mild. "Do you not understand that part of it?"

"I understand it," Pia heard herself say, though she hardly recognized her own voice. "That's the problem."

She turned her head away, not sure what might be written all over her face then. What he might see. She wrapped the coverlet even tighter around her, bitterly aware that the only thing she could wrap around herself at all these days was a piece of fabric that had been made to stretch across a bed. A very large bed.

Her throat ached, but she made herself speak anyway. "I'm the size of the barn. But even if I were not, you and I both know what I look like on any normal day."

There was only silence, and Pia was forced to turn back and look at him.

Ares only gazed back at her, a baffled sort of look on his gorgeous face.

Pia made a frustrated sound. "I'm not a queen!"

"You are a queen if you marry a king. It is really that simple."

"The very idea is laughable, Ares. Do you understand me?" Her voice sounded like a sob. But she couldn't seem to stop herself. She couldn't do a single thing to avert this horror as it happened. "People would *laugh*."

CHAPTER ELEVEN

FOR A MOMENT there was nothing but the echo of Pia's raw words hanging there between them.

She wanted to snatch them back with her own two hands. Her fingers twitched as if they might try, all on their own.

"Now I am the one not following you." Ares looked bemused and haughty at once, every inch of him royal as he lay there on the bed as if he was entirely at his ease. Perhaps he was. "People would laugh why, exactly?"

Pia was shaking. Everywhere. She wrapped her hand around the nearest bedpost, hoping it would steady her. Hoping something would, when the floor seemed so treacherous beneath her. She couldn't believe he was going to make her say it out loud. And worse, she couldn't tell if he was taunting her.

"A man like you is on a certain level," she said, pulling herself up as straight as she could, despite the weight of her belly. And the far greater weight of her shame. "You must be aware of this."

"You mean that I am the Crown Prince? Yes, Pia. I am aware of it. It is the sort of thing they tend to tell you from a very young age."

"I don't mean the fact that you're a prince, although that's part of it. I mean... You." She waved her hand in his direction. Trying to take in all of it, all of *him*, as he lounged there. Golden, rangy and athletic, as if someone had come in and carved a god from marble and breathed life into the stone. "You are a beautiful man. You are meant to find a beautiful wife. No one would accept a queen like me for a man like you."

Ares stared at her for a long while. As the panic and worry inside her intensified, she focused on strange things. Like the muscle in his jaw that clenched, seemingly of its own volition. Or the way his green eyes seemed darker. More dangerous.

"I will take it that what you are telling me is that you do not believe you are beautiful," he said. Eventually.

Pia made herself smile, though she was terribly afraid that the humiliation of this might take her out at the knees. Or maybe she only hoped it would.

"My mother was widely held to be the most beautiful woman in the world. Yes, she had her issues. She was not always kind, or good. Or even polite. And judging by the pills and the alcohol she took at the end, she was also not very happy." She blew out a breath, and hoped he couldn't hear how it shook. "My brother thinks it was deliberate, but I don't. For a while I thought maybe I pushed her to it, and my father, too, having fallen pregnant the way I did. But now I think it was an accident, because the one thing I know about Alexandrina San Giacomo is that she had no intention of going out with a whimper."

Alexandrina had been an opera heroine, always. Any death scene she'd planned would have been long-winded, theatrical, and would have required a vast audience. Most important, she would have needed to make certain she stayed beautiful throughout.

Pia didn't know when her certainty that she was to blame had…shifted. She suspected it had to do with spending all this time with Ares. All she knew for certain was that somehow, it had been a long while since she'd felt personal guilt about her parents' deaths. One had been an accident. The other had been inevitable. Her pregnancy had nothing to do with either.

Which didn't make it any easier.

She remembered that Ares was watching her. Waiting, all that leashed power of his coiled and tight.

"What my mother always had, what everyone knew and agreed on, was that she was beautiful. No matter how drunk, or tired, or under the weather. Men would stop in the street to stare. Sometimes they burst into song. Does that sound ridiculous?" She shrugged. "A serenade in the street was merely an unremarkable day in my mother's life. I grew up knowing exactly what *beautiful* meant. And seeing exactly what it looked like."

"I see." Ares's voice sounded almost…strangled.

"Do you?" she demanded.

Pia didn't understand what was sloshing around inside of her then. It was too much sensation. It was too much emotion. It was *too much*.

And maybe Alexandrina had it right. Maybe it was better to make everything an opera. Because at least then you could be in control of when the curtain went up, when it went down, and everything in between. How funny that she'd never understood that until now.

She took the coverlet from around her, and tossed it aside, the way her mother would have. With flourish.

"Do you really see?" she demanded. "Look at this body, Ares. It was never much to begin with, and after this? It will be a different body altogether. Forever. It will never snap back. There will be stretch marks, everywhere. And that's the least of it. I've seen pictures of my mother when she was pregnant. She looked like at any moment, someone might happen by and write a sonnet to her beauty."

"Is this an argument you truly wish to win?" he asked.

"It's not an argument. It's reality. I'm not my mother, and I'm certainly not beautiful like she was."

"I don't know how to say this," Ares said, as if he was choosing his words carefully. "But I cannot think of much I care less about than your mother's supposed beauty."

"It wasn't 'supposed.' It wasn't an opinion, it was a fact."

"Your mother was a lovely woman," Ares agreed, shrugging one shoulder. "But what of it? The world is filled with beautiful women."

"You're making my point for me," Pia said, wishing she hadn't tossed the coverlet aside. She could hardly go scrabbling after it now she'd made such a show of casting it off. She was forced to stand there instead, tall and proud, when she wanted nothing more than to curl up in a ball and cringe away into oblivion somewhere. "The world is filled with beautiful women, and you ought to go out and find yourself one of them."

"Pia. *Cara mia.*" And Ares looked as if he was biting back a smile, which Pia couldn't understand at all.

"Perhaps you do not understand to whom you are speaking. I am Crown Prince Ares of Atilia. I have dukedoms and earldoms to spare. I am, by definition and royal decree, possessed of the finest taste. Any woman who graces my arm is beautiful by virtue of her presence there. Obviously."

Pia opened her mouth to argue, but stopped when he rolled himself up to sitting position, never shifting his gaze from her face.

"But you? The mother of my children? The only woman alive I have ever asked to be my queen? *Of course* you are beautiful." He shrugged again, so arrogant and assured that it should have hurt him. Yet clearly did not. "It never occurred to me that you could imagine otherwise."

"You can't throw compliments at me and think that it will change the fact that I am not, in any way, the kind of woman a man like you goes for."

"I suggest you look down at your very pregnant belly," Ares said, his voice slightly less patient and mild. "I have already gone for you. Repeatedly."

"Stop saying these things!" She threw the words at him, unable to control her voice—or anything else— any longer. "I know what I look like. I know what I am. Pretending that I'm something else isn't going to get me to marry you."

"Then what will?"

And Pia kept trying to suck in more air. She couldn't seem to form another word.

And that was when Ares moved again. He rolled to his feet, then came to her, wrapping his hands around her shoulders and holding her up.

"You are the only woman I have ever asked to marry me," he told her, his voice serious and his gaze darkly intense. "But if that is not enough for you, think back to the party where we met. Why do you think I was drawn to you? At first, before we spoke a word to each other? If you are so misshapen, such a hideous troll—do you imagine it was curiosity that drew me to your side?"

This was ridiculous. Tears were spilling over, tracking their way down her cheeks, and Pia wanted to die. She wanted to sink to the floor of the palace, and be swept out to sea.

"I don't know," she said, her voice cracked and much too thick. "I looked up and you were...there."

"I was there because I saw you smile," Ares said. "I heard you laugh. I was there because I followed that smile across the room, simply because I wanted to get close to it. And then, when we met, I wanted to get even closer. None of that has changed."

"Ares..."

"Marry me because every time I have asked you to follow me so far, you have," he said, words in his eyes that she was afraid to believe in. "Follow me because I have yet to lead you anywhere you didn't like. You call this palace a prison, yet here we are, together—and it feels more to me like an escape. Marry me, Pia, and we will make our marriage another kind of refuge. The sort we can take with us wherever we go."

"You only want—"

"Our sons," he finished for her. "Yes, of course I want them. Let's raise them together."

And maybe she had always been this weak. Maybe

it was the way he made her feel, and she couldn't help herself. She liked it too much.

She knew better, but Ares looked at her as if she was beautiful. And when he did, she was tempted to believe it. Here, now, she did believe it.

And that belief trickled down into her, making her feel warm. Safe.

And there were worse things, surely. There were men who didn't want their own babies and who went to great lengths to avoid their responsibilities. There were men who didn't make her heart kick at her the way it did whenever Ares was near.

A whole world full of them, in fact.

There were marriages, especially amongst the sort of people she knew, that were little more than business transactions. There were cold, brittle unions, husbands and wives who were faithless, others who exulted in causing each other pain.

There were a thousand ways to have a terrible marriage.

But maybe what that meant was that Pia could decide how to make hers a good one. Or a decent one, anyway. Better than most. And maybe there wasn't only one fairy-tale way to get there.

Maybe there were twin boys. A palace fit for Rapunzel. And months spent doing nothing but circling around and around the inevitable. Maybe there were wild, hot nights of sex and longing with the only man she'd ever wanted to touch.

Already that sounded better than half the marriages she'd ever heard of.

And Pia loved him, though she knew better than

that, too. She loved him even though she was sure that the years would pass and whatever protestations he'd made here tonight about her supposed beauty would fade. He would regret this. He might take his own father's path.

Pia knew that she would still love him then. That she would always love him. So what would be worse? Never having any part of this? Or losing what little she had?

In front of her, Ares shifted. He dropped onto his knees, his gaze locked to hers as the afternoon sun poured in and highlighted every last perfect, glorious inch of him.

Both of them were naked. Pia's belly was so big it could take over the whole of the room on its own, and maybe the world. Ares didn't put his hands there. Instead, he reached up and took hers in his.

"Pia," he said, very gravely. "Marry me. Be my queen and mother to my sons. And promise me that from time to time, you will smile at me the way you did in a stranger's party in Manhattan."

And her heart kicked at her, but she couldn't tell if it was signaling danger or excitement. Hope or anxiety. All of the above.

And she knew better. *She knew better.*

The worst thing she could possibly do was believe.

But her hands were in his much bigger ones. And his gaze was so serious that it made her flush a little.

And she had two baby boys inside her who deserved their father.

What do you deserve, dear girl? that voice inside asked her, the way Alexandrina would have. *Do you really think* you *deserve a prince?*

But Pia shoved that aside.

Right here, right now, he believed she was beautiful.

She didn't have to believe him to hold on to that for as long as she could.

For as long as he'd let her.

"Very well, then," she said, surrendering. Or, if she was honest, taking a leap into faith, despite everything. And having no idea where she might land. "I will do it, Ares. I will marry you."

Ares didn't realize until Pia finally agreed to marry him that a part of him had worried that she would not. That she would actually refuse him.

And it was one thing to make pronouncements about how he wished to live his life wifeless and childless and alone. It was another to be rendered such things because the woman he wanted would not have him.

But she had agreed at last. And he was ready—had been ready, in fact, since the day he'd met with his father and had decided on a different future.

And two days after Pia finally acquiesced, he found her on an achingly perfect morning by the sea, having her breakfast out on one of the palace's many terraces. For a moment he stood away from her, taking her in as she gazed out toward Kefalonia. This woman who had made him into a man he didn't recognize. A crown prince who wanted to claim his throne. A man who was no longer content to step aside for the father he had always hated.

Pia sat in the loose, flowing dress he had chosen for her, her dark hair back in a loose braid. The breeze from the ocean picked up strands and made them dance, this way and that, and he thought the sea itself paled beside her.

He could not believe she had ever imagined she was anything less than beautiful. Stunning, even.

He had met her mother. And he had found Alexandrina San Giacomo beautiful, yes, but brittle with it. Expectant. Her beauty was her currency, and she had been well aware of it. There was nothing wrong with that, to Ares's mind. He admired it, as he certainly knew when his own looks worked in his favor.

But Pia was beautiful in a different way altogether. Her beauty was unstudied. Artless. Her gray eyes were dreamy, her sweet mouth soft. Right now she was gloriously pregnant, ripe and lush, and it only added to her many charms.

Alexandrina had been a weapon. But Pia was a precious gem. As perfect as she was pretty.

And soon to be his princess. And one day, his queen.

He must have made a noise, because she glanced over then. And Ares had the pleasure of watching the way her eyes glowed with pleasure before she blinked it away to something far more guarded.

But the smile that curved her mouth was as bright and engaging as that first one back in New York.

It made something in him seem to turn over, then hum.

This one, a voice in him said, like some kind of gong. *This one*.

Mine, Ares thought.

He moved over to her, sliding a hand over her cheek and loving the way she leaned into his touch. The way she always did. She had no walls. She held nothing back.

She was heedless, hedonistic in bed, and he found that she made him insatiable.

There were no ways he didn't want her.

"I don't know what you have planned for today," he said.

Her gray eyes were soft and bright as she looked up at him. "I'm very busy, actually. I plan to lounge about, pretending to work, for several hours. After which I will very officiously go seat myself somewhere, open up the laptop, and type very studiously. I won't be working, of course. I'll be checking email and scrolling through things I don't care about on the internet, which is a very important part of my process. After several hours of that, I will write a single sentence, which will be so exhausting that I will instantly need to send for snacks. I plan to repeat this several times throughout the day, until I can break for an early dinner, and pretend none of it ever happened. And you?"

And that was the part Ares couldn't understand. He found her…entertaining.

He didn't understand it, but he liked it. True, he'd never seen anything like her before, anywhere in the royal family, or, for that matter, in any of the dreary noble houses of Europe. Everything was duty and history. Ancestral obligation and debts paid in to the future. Marriages were solemn contracts for the production of heirs, and everyone in those marriages worked hard to appear studiously joyless—if his own parents were any guide.

But the woman he would reign with was entertaining. She smiled, laughed. She even dared tease him. Ares chose to see it as a gift.

He went down before her, on the traditional single knee. Then he reached into his pocket, pulling out a small box with great flourish. He cracked it open, looking up to find Pia with her hands over her mouth and her gray eyes wide.

"I do not know if you recognize this ring," he said. "It has a legend attached to it. It was handed down through my family for generations, and each woman who wears it is said to be the queen the country deserves. Good, kind. It was my grandmother's. She left it for me when she died, that I might put it on the hand of my own queen one day. Will you take it?"

And he found that something in him was tense and tight until she let out a breath, nodded once, jerkily, and extended her hand that he might slide the ring into place.

Together, they stared down at the collection of three perfect sapphires, ringed with diamonds. Taken together the stones created the sense of something bigger than the sum of its parts. The ring itself was history. But on Pia, it looked like art.

"Thank you," she whispered, her voice catching. "It's so beautiful."

"I was hoping you would think so."

He helped her to her feet, aware that it was harder for her to rise these days. He swept his eye over the dress she wore, white and flowing, and making her look very nearly ethereal. He reached down to the table and picked up one of the flowers that sat there in a small vase, then tucked it into the top of her braid.

She was breathing loud enough that he could hear it. And her eyes were glassy when he was done with the flower. He wanted to lean down and kiss her, claim her—

But kissing Pia was no quick affair. It required time because Ares never stopped at one kiss. How could he?

"Come with me," he said.

And Pia held out her hand, because Pia always held out her hand. She trusted him enough to follow him into the unknown, and that was a responsibility Ares took seriously. More than seriously. He felt the weight of it move through him, and he vowed as he led her through the palace that he would honor it. Care for it.

And her.

Always her.

He hadn't planned for any of this. And he hadn't known, until that day in his father's study, how best to handle his impending fatherhood.

But now it was all so beautifully clear.

"What are we doing?" Pia asked, as he led her through the great salons and out to the wide terrace overlooking the steepest part of the rocky cliffs below. The ocean stretched itself in the sun, rambling out to the horizon. And there, beneath the makeshift canopy he'd had his staff prepare from sweet-smelling vines and bright flowers, a priest waited.

He felt her hand shake in his.

"Is this...?"

"This is our wedding, Pia," he said, looking down at her. Another tension gripping him because she could still balk. She could demand the cathedral on the Northern Island. She could refuse him. *She could still refuse him.* "Here, now."

"But..."

Ares took her hands in his. And he thought that he could lose himself forever in all that gleaming gray. He intended to. "Do you trust me?"

"I... I don't..."

"It's a simple question. You either trust me, or you do not."

"I trust you," she whispered.

"Then why wait?" he asked. "You know as well as I do what a royal wedding will be like. The pomp and circumstance, all in aid of a future throne. We can do this here. You and me, no one else. And our babies."

Her eyes glistened. Her smile seemed to tremble on her lips. Even her hands in his shook a little.

"Just you and me," she whispered.

There was a faint breeze from the sea spread out below them. The priest spoke his words, and when it was time for their vows, Pia had stopped shaking.

"I vow to honor you, keep you safe, and pledge my life to yours," Ares said, intoning the traditional vows of the kingdom.

"And I you," Pia replied.

He reached into his pocket and pulled out another box. Inside sat two rings. Two bands of gold. He slid the smaller one onto Pia's finger, so it sat flush against his grandmother's. And something dark and primitive roared through him at the sight.

He handed her the bigger ring and she took it, shifting her hand to slide it onto his finger.

And that was it, Ares thought. It was done.

"And now, Your Highness, you may kiss your bride," the priest declared.

And Pia was smiling again as he angled his face to hers, then took her mouth with his.

For a moment there was nothing but that kiss, sweet and perfect. Then another.

There was only the two of them, and the vows they'd made. Ares moved closer, pulling Pia further into his arms, because she was his. And he couldn't get enough of her.

And he doubted he ever would.

He kissed her again, deeper and wilder—

And that was when the helicopter rose up from below. It bristled with reporters, cameras in hand and pointing straight toward them.

Pia started to pull away, stiff with horror.

"Kiss me again," Ares commanded her.

"But the paparazzi—" she began.

"Kiss me, Pia," he told her, and he could hear the satisfaction in his own voice. He could feel it thrumming in his veins. He could very nearly picture the king's apoplectic rage when he saw these pictures—and understood what they meant. "I want them to see. I'm the one who called them here."

CHAPTER TWELVE

PIA DID AS Ares asked—as he commanded—because she could see no alternative.

And because she couldn't think. She kissed him, and the helicopter was right there, and everything was whipping around while she knew there were pictures being taken—

She was sure she could hear them laughing already.

Before she could object, or scream, or do any of the things that clambered inside of her and threatened to come out of her, violently—Ares pulled away. He shouted something to the priest over the noise of the helicopter's rotors.

He even waved.

Then he was leading her back inside the palace, leaving the helicopter and its paparazzi cargo behind. For a moment she let him lead her on, because she was too busy reeling to do anything else. She was blind and her heart *hurt* and it was a lie.

It was all a lie.

What had happened—what had just happened—hit her, hard.

I called them, he had said.

She dug her heels in, yanking her hand from his, and moving her hands around to the small of her back as she panted a little at the exertion and the low, dull pain that bloomed there. And she didn't know whether to look at him directly, or do her best to look away, maybe up and down the gallery where they'd stopped.

"What did you do?" she demanded. "What do you mean, you called them?"

"I called them," he said again, much too calmly for her peace of mind, and even looked a bit quizzical. As if she was the one who had stopped making sense in a dizzying rush.

And he was the man she loved. The man she had married in what she'd foolishly imagined was a quiet, sweet, personal ceremony.

She'd believed his *just the two of us*, and all the while he'd had a helicopter full of reporters waiting.

Which meant none of this had been romantic.

You knew better, she reminded herself bitterly. *And you did it anyway.*

Something in her turned over, spinning around in a nauseating loop. For a moment, she thought she might be sick. A kind of cramp ran through her, centering low in her belly, and she moved a hand to curl beneath the heaviest part of it. And she held it there, wishing she could hold herself together as easily.

"Tell me why," she managed to say. "Tell me why you would do this. We ran away from my father's funeral to avoid these people and you called them here... You must know that they took pictures that will be everywhere within the hour."

He raised a brow. "That was my clear intent."

Pia looked around, wildly, because she thought her legs might cease to hold her. There was a bench to the side, beneath a huge painting that she had studied in finishing school, the better to make sparkling cocktail conversation. She waddled over to the bench and sank down on to it. Gratefully.

Though she looked at Ares—her *husband*—and that awful feeling in her belly got worse.

"I do not understand why you are looking at me as if I killed a man," Ares said.

And what struck her most was how truly, effortlessly beautiful he was. He was dressed in one of his usual royal uniforms, complete with the sash that proclaimed him the crown prince of these islands. Even here, in a controlled environment with less intrusive lighting, he looked as if the sun beamed down upon him.

Pia should have known when Marbella had laid this particular dress out this morning. It was pure white. And while the hilarity of wearing all white while this astonishingly pregnant did not escape her, she couldn't quite bring herself to laugh.

Because she had believed him, and he had been putting on a show.

And all the things she'd told herself about the heartache she'd experience had been *one day*. Far off the future. Far away from here, now, *today*.

Yet here she was anyway, with a fantasy ring on her finger and a fantasy man, and a fantasy new marriage, too. The reality was a girl the size of a whale in a white dress that seemed pointed, a staged kiss, and all the sniggering she was sure she could already hear out there— or maybe her ears were ringing. She couldn't quite tell.

"I've spent my whole life in my father's shadow," Ares was telling her, standing over her with all that *light* he made on his own, and Pia should never have let herself do this. She should never have been so weak, risking not only her own humiliation—but her sons'. "I've never been good enough for the man. He ranted at me about our bloodline until I wished I could reach my hand inside my own body, and exsanguinate myself to escape it. The only thing that worked was keeping myself away from him. Excusing myself from the damned bloodline. But then you came along and changed everything."

"And you felt the best way to celebrate this change was with the paparazzi?"

Pia felt raw inside. Torn wide-open.

And worst of all, like such a fool.

Because she'd believed him. She'd believed that not only did he care for her, not only did he want her, but that deep down—whether he knew it or not—he might even love her.

She had believed what she wanted to believe, clearly.

And Ares had been setting up a photo opportunity to get at his father.

"I realized the last time I saw my father that I have abdicated my responsibilities entirely where he is concerned," Ares told her, still standing where she'd left him in the middle of the wide hall. "And the closer we get to the birth of our own two sons, the more I realize what I owe not only them, but this kingdom. I think our subjects deserve better."

"Power infects," she said, sounding hollow to her own ears. "You told me that."

"Better to claim it, then," Ares replied, something flashing in his green eyes. He crossed to her, then crouched down to put himself at eye level. "Better that than to let it sit about, festering. I want to be the kind of king these princes—" he put his hand out to touch her belly, and for the first time she wanted to slap it away "—can look up to. No temper tantrums like winter storms, brutal and unpredictable. No shards of crystal littering the floors while they stand there, hoping not to be hit. I want to be a better man, Pia."

There was a roaring thing in her, grief and shame, and she wasn't sure she could keep it inside her skin. She wasn't sure she could survive this. Or that she wanted to.

"You're not talking about being a better man, Ares," she threw back at him. "You're talking about being a king. You begged me to marry you, and I surrendered. You didn't tell me that it would be a business arrangement. You didn't convince me by promising me a convenient union we could both use to our own ends. You made love to me. You made it *romantic*."

And she would hate herself forever for the way her voice cracked on that.

But she pushed on anyway. "How could you make it romantic?"

Ares looked floored. Astounded, as if it had never occurred to him that she could possibly have a problem with what had happened here today.

"I do not understand the issue," he said stiffly.

"You could have asked me. You could have appealed to my practical side. You didn't have to *sleep* your way into it." And there were tears then, and those were worse. They felt too salty against her cheeks. They felt like a betrayal, or one more betrayal, and her heart felt tattered. Broken beyond repair. "You could have asked, Ares, and I would have come around."

"Pia—"

"But you pretended it was something else," she said, and the cramping was getting worse with every word she spoke. She rubbed at her belly, sucking in a breath as she tried to make herself comfortable. Or just make it through this conversation. "You pretended that you cared."

"I do care."

"You even told me I was beautiful." And her voice dropped on that, into something so painful it hurt her to hear herself. "Why did you have to lie to me? Has this whole thing been a game to you from the start?"

"This is not a game." He rocked back on his heels, and even now, the moment he stopped touching her she wanted only for him to start again. "How can you think it?"

"How could I think anything else?"

"I don't know what this is, Pia. Of course I care for you. You are the mother to my—"

"You told me I was beautiful," she said again, and her eyes were too blurry to see him now, which she took as a kind of blessing. There was a strange fire low in her belly, and that cramping that wouldn't stop. "And the worst thing is, I wanted to believe you. I did believe you. Why would you do this to me?"

"What did I do to you?" he roared at her, as if even now, he didn't understand.

"You made me think that you could love me," she

told him, though she thought it might kill her. There was a sob in her voice, and something heavy, like a stone, over her heart. And yet she kept going, though her face twisted. "Because only a man who loved me could find me beautiful."

Ares's face changed then, into something like alarm, and that was even worse. "Pia."

But she'd started down this road. She'd humiliated herself. Why not throw all her cards on the table? After all, what was there left to protect?

"I love you," she told him, sealing her doom. "And I never would have told you that. I would have kept it to myself because I know better. I still know better. But you told me I was beautiful, and I hoped, and you gave me your grandmother's ring. And I wanted so badly to believe it could all be real."

He moved closer to her, a harsh look she'd never seen before on his face. "Pia, you need to—"

She lifted up her hand to keep him back, because she couldn't trust herself. And she tried to struggle to her feet, but her legs refused to help her. And she reminded herself that no one actually died of heartache, no matter how terrible they felt. No matter how awful *she* felt right now.

"It's not the first time I've been made a fool of, and I doubt it will be the last," she told him. "You have what really matters to you. Legitimacy for your heirs. But I need you to promise me something, Ares. No matter what, you must never lie to me again. I need you to promise me that whatever games you need to play, it will never be this one. Never again."

"I will promise you anything you want, woman,"

Ares all but shouted at her. "But right now, you are bleeding."

It seemed to take Pia a lifetime or two to look down at the white dress she wore. The way it pooled around her feet.

And at the way what she'd taken for anxious cramps and heartache was instead bright red, and spreading out across her lap.

"Promise me," she said, though she didn't mean the same thing any longer. Or she didn't think she did.

But then it didn't matter what she meant, because the darkness came rushing at her, and sucked her in deep.

There was too much blood.

Ares caught Pia as she began to slump over, and he was already shouting for his staff. For someone to call back that damned helicopter. For help.

But there was blood. Everywhere.

He swung Pia up and into his arms, and he barely felt the weight she carried in that marvelous belly of hers. He strode toward the staff who yelled at him, or for him, he didn't care which.

Her face was so pale. And the blood kept coming.

It was the longest helicopter ride of his life. And when they landed on the Northern Island, on the top of the Royal Hospital, Ares was still holding her. And found he wanted to start knocking heads together, or start tearing people apart—*something*—when the medical personnel that met them on the roof took her from him to strap her on a gurney.

"She is my wife," he told them, aware he must sound mad with terror, with grief. Fierce with the fear that burned in him. "She will one day be your queen. She is carrying the heirs to this kingdom and you must save her. *You must.*"

And then, despite all his arrogance, all his consequence and power, he could do nothing but watch them rush her away.

Someone led him to a private room, eventually. They offered him a change of clothes, but he refused it. He sat in a chair with his head in his hands, and he waited.

While inside, his heart threatened to burst.

He could not lose Pia. He could not lose his sons.

He had spent his whole life doing everything he could to avoid having a family, and he was about to lose his before he got the chance to enjoy them.

Pia couldn't believe he had called her beautiful.

But Ares couldn't believe she loved him.

His first reaction was denial. Rage, that she would take this there, when it had worked fine as it was.

Because he knew what no one dared say to his face.

That there was nothing about him anyone could love, except his mother. And she had died a long time ago now.

But there was no one else on this earth, not even his father, who shared that sentiment. Ares was a monument to a throne, that was all. He was not a person. He existed in the first place only because his father needed an heir. Any child his mother had could have taken on that role. But no one *loved* him.

Except Pia.

And Ares could argue with himself all he liked. He could tell himself that she was mistaken. Or that she didn't know enough about men and had fallen for the first man who had ever touched her—

But he knew that wasn't true. There had been any number of men at that party, but Pia had smiled at him.

Him.

Ares knew now that she had never done anything like what she had that night in New York, but she'd done it for him. She'd given him her innocence. She had suffered his reaction to the news that she was pregnant. She'd come with him to the islands, and allowed him to lock her away for his own peace of mind, not hers.

She had done all these things, and he knew that there could only be one reason. The one reason he never would have come up with on his own, because the word wasn't in his vocabulary.

She loved him.

Once he understood that, Ares couldn't understand how he had ever managed to convince himself that it was anything else. That it could be anything else.

And now she had blood all over her. Blood, again. Blood always.

And if that blood was poisoned, the way he'd always believed, he had done that, too.

And Ares found that while he had no trouble thinking of the ways he could pay for the sins of that bloodline, he couldn't bring himself to imagine that Pia might also pay that price. Or either one of the babies she carried.

He could not lose her.

God help him, he could not lose her, not now. Not when he had only begun to grasp how very much she meant to him.

She was the only woman he had ever been this intimate with. There was the astonishingly good sex, yes, but they'd spent all this *time* together. Time enough to get to know her. Time enough to understand how much more it was he wanted to know her.

Time to understand that he wanted, badly, to meet his own sons.

Ares needed more time.

He thought he could spend a lifetime trying to imagine what Pia might say next. He thought he could spend another one learning the different shades of meaning in her smiles.

She was the only woman he had given his grandmother's ring. The only woman he had asked to marry him, not once, but time and time again.

She was the only woman, period.

She needed to live, so he could tell her so. So he could tell her a thousand things. So he could apologize for treating her like a pawn—

She just needed to *live.*

"Your Highness," came a voice from a doctor at the door, and Ares's head shot up, but he couldn't read anything on the man's face. "Your wife is stable, but the babies are in some distress. We will be performing a cesarean section immediately."

"Early," Ares managed to say, his head spinning. "It's too early."

"Twins are always early," the doctor replied. "But we must make haste."

And Ares followed, unable to do anything else.

Because he could not lose Pia. And he could not lose these babies he had yet to meet. And he had not realized until now, until he found himself in these antiseptic halls, how very thoroughly lost he had been since the first moment he'd set eyes on this woman.

His wife.

His future queen, and mother to the future king of Atilia.

Ares, by God, would make sure she lived long enough to assume each and every one of those roles.

And tell him she loved him once more.

CHAPTER THIRTEEN

PIA WOKE UP in a panic. A desperate, confused rush—

"Pia. *Cara mia.*"

Her head snapped around, and she found him there. *Ares.*

With those grave green eyes, and a stern set to his beautiful mouth. Ares, her prince, though he appeared to be wearing hospital scrubs. Of all things.

She felt herself calm, just a little. Because Ares was there, and that meant—

"My babies—" she blurted out, her heart exploding inside her. She tried to sit up, but her abdomen protested sharply, and she had the terrible notion that she'd had surgery. And that meant... "What happened to my babies—"

"We have all been waiting for you," Ares said, very solemnly, and the calm sound of his voice made her stop. Made her breathe. "Allow me to make the introductions."

And then he reached into the double bassinet she hadn't seen beside the bed, and carefully lifted up a tiny little bundle. It sported a wrinkled pink face and a shock of dark hair peeking out from beneath a little white beanie.

"I present to you our first born," Ares said, something rich and awed in his voice. "He is perfect in every way. I inspected him myself."

Pia accepted her baby, a rush of something so intense and primitive slamming into her as she took him that she was happy—fiercely so—she was already in a bed. Because she feared it would have knocked her over. She gazed down at the tiny bundle in her arms, making sounds she hadn't heard herself make before. She saw him scrunch up his nose, and his perfect little mouth, and she understood that she would never be the same again.

"And his brother," Ares said, and placed the other baby in her other arm. As if he knew that she needed to touch them both. "He is equally perfect in every way. I can verify this personally."

And that same wave took her over again. Harder, deeper.

She bent her head to one, then the other. She checked to make sure each one was breathing. And as she did, each tiny boy began to make tiny little noises, as if they understood exactly who she was and were offering their own form of greeting.

She could already tell they were that smart. That beautiful. That absolutely perfect.

"You were there?" she asked.

"They came out of you, directly into my hands," Ares said, and it sounded like another vow. Like an impossible intimacy.

And when she met his gaze, her chest ached.

"I want to feed them," she whispered.

Or, having missed their birth, maybe she needed to.

And Ares was there beside her, so she didn't have to worry over all the various things she'd read about how best to get each one of them where they needed to go. He helped her. He set a pillow over her abdomen, which stuck out significantly less than it had when she'd last seen it.

He opened up her gown, and he helped her guide one greedy mouth to her swollen, aching breast. Then the next, placing each little body beneath one of her arms, snug against her sides, so she could hold them in place like American footballs.

And she had read a thousand articles about how difficult breastfeeding was, and had read endless forums about how to manage it with hungry twins. She'd expected a battle. But there was no battle to mount, because it was happening. She felt one twin latch on, then the other. And they both began to pull at her.

Pia looked up at Ares while each of the perfect creatures they'd made together fed from her breasts, and she understood what family was on a primitive level she'd never imagined existed before.

She had known love. She had loved. She was still in love with the maddening man who stood beside her.

This was something else, this communion between the four of them. This needed a new word. This was like a new sun, bright and hot inside of her, taking her over, burning her up, terrifying and magical—and it was theirs.

They had done this. They had made this happen.

Nothing would ever be the same. But at the same time, everything was finally…beautiful.

And when the babies were fed and she and Ares had

held each of them against their bare skin a while, a nurse
came in to check them again, then whisked them off
for more tests. Pia tried to move in her bed, winced at
the pain from her abdomen, and realized that she still
didn't know what had happened to her.

"I can tell you this story using all kinds of medical
terminology," Ares said. "But what really matters is
that I nearly lost you. And Pia. No matter how I let you
down today, trust me when I tell you that losing you is
unacceptable to me. It is unthinkable."

She stared back at him, and he told her quickly and
matter-of-factly about the rush to get her to the hospital. Her hemorrhage, the emergency cesarean section.
How close she'd come to dying, and how terrified he
had been.

"You told me you loved me," he said, as he stood
there next to her bed, stiff and tense, as if that was an
insult.

And Pia didn't want to remember this part. Not when
she was still filled with that perfect sense of overwhelming, impossible, helpless love. She didn't want to remember their wedding ceremony. That helicopter. All
the cameras.

"It doesn't matter," she said now. "We're parents,
Ares, to two perfect little boys in desperate need of
names. Let's just concentrate on—"

"You told me you loved me, Pia," Ares thundered
at her. "And no one has told me that before, not unless
they'd given birth to me themselves. That isn't the kind
of thing you can just *say* to a man."

She wanted to cry again. "I'm sorry if I insulted you."

"I have spent the last five hours begging gods I've

never believed in to save you," he told her then, tall and still golden. And he had held their babies in his hands when she couldn't. He had been there. "Our wedding photos are all over every paper in the land, just as I wished, and it is like ash to me. Because there is no point in any of this, Pia, unless you are here. With me."

"Ares…"

"I have no idea how to love anyone," he told her, his green eyes blazing. "But for you, I will learn. I have no idea what a father does except crush his own son, but for the ones we made, I will learn how to do it right."

He moved closer, taking her hands in his, and then going down on one knee beside her hospital bed.

"You don't have to do this, Ares," she said.

"When I thought I would lose you, every moment we spent together went through my head in a rush," he said urgently. "And I could see it so clearly then, how much you loved me. How much you have always loved me. And how much I have failed you, time and again."

"No," she said fiercely. She winced as she sat up, but she reached out and took his beautiful, beloved face in her hands. "You are not a failure, Ares. I love you. That's not conditional on how you behave. That doesn't come with a list of duties or expectations. I just love you. It's as simple and as complicated as that, and I don't know how it works, either."

"I used you like a pawn. I will never forgive myself."

"I already have," she said, and as the words came out of her, she realized they were true. "I've spent my whole life hating how I looked because I wasn't my mother. Hating my body because it never looked like hers. But look what it did today."

"You were magnificent," Ares told her, his voice thick. "You are always magnificent, Pia."

"Let them laugh if they like," Pia said, her eyes on Ares. "They don't matter. They never did. The only thing I have to be embarrassed about is that I ever let them get to me in the first place. Even in my own head."

His mouth formed her name, but he turned his head so he could kiss her palm.

"I spent my whole life watching my parents tear themselves apart and call it love," Pia told him, a new conviction growing inside her. As if it had always been there. As if her babies' arrival had jogged it loose. "I used to think that was romantic. Now I suspect it was deeply unhealthy. What I want with you is the chance to explore the difference."

"I love you," Ares told her. "And I will spend the rest of this life proving to you that it's not only because I thought I would lose you today. But because in thinking you were lost to me forever, I understood that forever was meaningless to me without you."

"We made them," she whispered. "And Ares. They're perfect."

"They're beautiful," he whispered back. "And so are you."

And for a moment they grinned at each other, wide and bright and brimming with hope and possibility. There were two new, shiny little lives, and both of them would do their best to protect each one of them. To honor them and raise them.

Together.

"Pia," Ares said, a quiet command. "Be my wife."

"It will be my greatest honor," she said, tears streaming down her face, but this time, they were not tears of pain. This was joy, this unwieldy, unsteady thing that held her in so tight a grip. *Pure joy.* "And you must be my husband."

"It will be my privilege," he said solemnly. "You will be my queen one day. But know this, Pia. You are already, and always will be, queen of my heart."

And when he leaned over and pressed his mouth to hers, Pia tasted salt and sweetness. The great tangle that led to forever, and all the knots they'd tied in each other already that would keep them steady and connected as they headed there.

He kissed her, and it was like a fairy tale.

He kissed her, and she kissed him, and they woke each other up from that deep, dark enchantment that was the lives they'd led without each other.

Without love.

There and then, in a hospital room with the paparazzi calling their names outside, they started their new life. Together.

Full of love, light, and laughter to hold it all together, like glue.

Twenty years later, six weeks after his father's death and his formal acceptance of his new role, King Ares of Atilia was crowned in the Great Cathedral.

He took the long walk up the cathedral's august aisle that he had believed, once, he would never take.

The crowd cheered for him outside. The Atilian nobles and European aristocrats filled the pews. The famous Atilian choir sang ancient songs of power and glory.

But Ares's gaze was on his family.

His fine, strong twins, Crown Prince Pollux and Prince Castor, who stared back at him with pride and love—something Ares had done his best to earn every day for two decades. Beside them, the rest of his children stood tall. His middle children, seventeen-year-old Leto and thirteen-year-old Nyx. And his second set of twins, his mischievous ten-year-old daughters, Helen and Clytemnestra, who looked like the young women they would become someday.

Someday, Ares thought as they beamed at him, but not today. No need to rush into it.

He had never built any significant bridges with his father, who had divorced and married twice more, but had never produced another child. The old king had died in a fury, and had been found with crystal shards all around him like a halo. Ares figured that was as close as Damascus was likely to get to the good place.

The older he got, the more Ares wished he could have worked things out with the man, but he understood the ache of it had more to do with his relationship with his own children. And the man he hoped he was in their eyes, the father he was first and always, before he was a king.

And when he talked to them about bloodlines, what he talked about was love.

Ares kept walking, taking in Pia's brothers as they stood in the row behind his children. Because they were important to Pia, Ares had made them important to him, too. And as the years passed, he found Matteo Combe and Dominik James were more to him than a duty. They became more like…brothers.

And as all their families grew, with sets of twins to

go around, it was hard to remember that Matteo was the one who had punched Ares at that funeral. Or that there was ever a time that Pia didn't refer to her sisters-in-law, the impressive Dr. Sarina Fellows Combe and high-level Combe Industries executive Lauren Clarke James, as not only her sisters, but her friends.

With every step he took, Ares counted the ways he was a lucky man.

He had been born a prince, but it had taken Pia to make him a man. And it was only with Pia by his side that he could take his throne and become a king.

Ares reached the front of the cathedral and climbed the short stairs, then bent his head to accept the priests' invocations.

He thought about his kingdom. About the Southern Palace that rarely stood empty these days, and more often rang with life and laughter, as it was meant to do. He thought about his people, who had accepted it when he'd told them that he'd kept his relationship with Pia secret because the two of them had needed a time that was only theirs.

And most of all, he thought of the woman who was there at his side when the priests placed the crown on his head, then handed him the ceremonial scepter.

He watched as they fit her with a crown of her own, but her gray eyes shined brighter than any crown. Especially when she looked at him and smiled.

Ares held out his hand to her, breaking ancient custom.

And Pia took it, because she always did.

Because she trusted him. She loved him.

And the way he loved her in return would have scared him, if she didn't meet it so fiercely, so fully.

The only war he'd ever fought had been against himself, and Pia had taught him how to put down his arms.

He lifted her hand to his mouth.

"You have accepted the crown of the kingdom, and I have made you my queen," he said.

"You have."

"But there is a greater role for you to play," he told her, knowing his voice carried not only to the furthest corners of the Great Cathedral, but was being heard on television sets and radios around the world. "You are the most beautiful thing I have ever beheld. I count myself lucky every day I get to spend with you. You have made me a better man, and in so doing, will help me be the fair and just ruler my people deserve."

Her eyes gleamed with unshed tears. She whispered his name.

"I promised you a long time ago that this day would come," he said, and let himself grin, there before his children, his extended family, his subjects, and the planet. "Pia, love of my life, will you wield your crown not only as the queen of Atilia, but as the queen of My Heart?"

She stepped back, smiling, and then executed a perfect, deep curtsy.

"Your Majesty," she said, distinct and sweet, while the gleam in her gaze promised him a long, hot night ahead, "it will be my pleasure."

Ares kissed her when she rose, as if this coronation were the wedding day he and Pia had kept to themselves, and were now, finally sharing with the world. And she kissed him back as if they were alone.

The priests finished their blessings. And the roar of the crowd outside made the stained glass shake.

And then, when it was done and the bells began to toll, King Ares of Atilia took his beautiful queen by the hand, and led her into their sweet, bright, happy future. Just like those fairy tales Pia had mentioned all those years ago, when they were new.

Ares was the king. He would make it so. He would make it beautiful, like her.

For her.

And day by day, year by year, that was exactly what he did.

* * * * *

THE QUEEN'S
NEW YEAR SECRET

MAISEY YATES

To my husband.

This has been the best ten years of my life,
and I know the next ten will be even better.

CHAPTER ONE

KAIROS LOOKED ACROSS the bar at the redheaded woman sitting there, her delicate fingertips stroking the stem of her glass, her eyes fixed on him. Her crimson lips were turned up into a smile, the invitation, silent but clear, ringing in the space between them.

She was beautiful. All lush curves and heat. She exuded desire, sexuality. It shimmered over her skin. There was nothing subtle or refined about her. Nothing coy or demure.

He could have her if he wanted. This was the most exclusive and private New Year's Eve party in Petras, and all of the guests would have been vetted carefully. There was no press in attendance. No secret gold diggers looking for a payout. He could have her, with no consequences.

She wouldn't care about the wedding ring on his finger.

He wasn't entirely certain why *he* cared about it anymore. He had no real relationship with his wife. She hadn't even touched him in weeks. Had barely spoken to him in months. Since Christmas she had been particularly cold. It was partly his fault, as she had overheard him saying unflattering things about the state of their union to his younger brother. But it hadn't been anything that wasn't true. Hadn't been anything she didn't already know.

Life would be simpler if he could have the redhead for a night, and just forget about reality. But he didn't want her. The simple, stark truth was as clear as it was inconvenient.

His body wanted nothing to do with voluptuous redheads sitting in bars. It wanted nothing but the cool, blond beauty of his wife, Tabitha. She was the only thing that stoked his fantasies, the one who ignited his imagination.

Too bad the feeling wasn't mutual.

The redhead stood, abandoning her drink, crossing the room and sauntering over to where he sat. The corner of her mouth quirked upward. "You're alone tonight, King Kairos?"

Every night. "The queen wasn't in the mood to go out."

Those lips pursed into a pout. "Is that right?"

"Yes." A lie. He hadn't told Tabitha where he was going tonight. In part, he supposed, to needle her. There was a time when they would have been sure to put in a public appearance during every holiday. When they would have put on a show for the press, and possibly for each other.

Tonight, he hadn't bothered to pretend.

The redhead leaned in, the cloud of perfume breaking through his thoughts and drawing him back to the moment, her lips brushing against his ear, his shirt collar. "I happen to know that our host has a room reserved for guests who would like a bit more...*privacy.*"

There was no ambiguity in that statement.

"You are very bold," he said. "You know I'm married."

"True. But there are rumors about that. As I'm sure you know."

Her words stuck deep into his gut. If the cracks were evident to the public now...

"I have better things to do than read tabloid reports about my life." He *lived* his tragic marriage. He didn't want to read about it.

She laughed, a husky sound. "I don't. If you want a break from reality, I'm available for a few hours. We can bring in the New Year right."

A break from reality. He was tempted. Not physically. But in a strange, dark way that made his stomach twist, made him feel sick. It was down deep in the part of him that wanted to shake Tabitha's foundation. To make her see him differently. Not as a fixture in her life she could ignore if she wished. But as a man. A man who did not always behave. Who did not always keep his promises. Who would, perhaps, not always be there.

To see if she would react at all. If she cared.

Or if their relationship had well and truly died.

But he did nothing. Nothing but stand, moving away from the woman, and the temptation she represented. "Not tonight, I'm afraid."

She lifted her shoulder. "It could've been fun."

Fun. He wasn't sure he had any idea what that was. There was certainly nothing fun about his line of thinking. "I don't have fun. I have duty."

It wasn't even midnight, and he was ready to leave. Normally, his brother, Andres, would be here, more than willing to swoop in and collect the dejected woman, or any other women who might be hanging around eagerly searching for a *royally* good time.

But now, Andres was married. More than that, Andres

was in love. Something Kairos had never thought he'd see. His younger brother completely and totally bound to *one* woman.

Kairos's stomach burned as though there was acid resting in it. He walked out of the club, down the stairs and onto the street where his car was waiting. He got inside and ordered the driver to take him back to the palace. The car wound through the narrow streets, heading out of the city and back toward his home.

Another year come and gone. Another year with no heir. That was why he had commanded Andres to get married in the first place. He was facing the very real possibility that he and Tabitha would not be the ones producing the successor to the throne of Petras.

The duty might well fall to Andres and his wife, Zara.

Five years and he still had no child. Five years and all he had was a wife who might as well be standing on the other side of a chasm, even when they were in the same room.

The car pulled through the massive gates that stood before the palace, then slowly toward the main entrance. Kairos got out without waiting for the driver to assist him, storming inside and up the stairs. He could go to Tabitha's room. Could tell her it was time they tried again for a child. But he wasn't certain he could take her icy reception one more time.

When he was inside her body, pressed against her, skin to skin, it still felt as if she was a thousand miles away from him.

No, he had no desire to engage in that farce, even if it would end in an orgasm. For him.

He didn't want to go to bed yet either.

He made his way up the curved staircase and headed

down the hall toward his office. He would have a drink. Alone.

He pushed open the door and paused. The lights were off, and there was a fire going, casting an orange glow on the surroundings. Sitting in the wingback chair opposite his desk was his wife, her long, slender legs bared by her rather demure dress, her hands folded neatly in her lap. Her expression was neutral, unchanging even as he walked deeper into the room. She didn't smile. She gave almost no indication that she noticed his presence at all. Nothing beyond a slight flicker in her blue eyes, the vague arch of her brow.

The feeling that had been missing when the other woman had approached him tonight licked along his veins like a flame in the hearth. As though it had escaped, wrapping fiery tendrils around him.

He gritted his teeth against the sensation. Against the desire that burned out of his control.

"Were you out?" she asked, her tone as brittle as glass. Cold. Chilling the ardor that had momentarily overtaken him.

He moved toward the bar that was on the far wall. "Was I here, Tabitha?"

"I hardly scoured the castle for you. You may well have been holed up in one of the many stony nooks."

"If I was not here, or in my room, then it is safe to say that I was out." He picked up the bottle of scotch—already used this evening by his lovely intruder, clearly—and tipped it to the side, measuring a generous amount of liquid into his glass.

"Is that dry tone really necessary? If you were out, just say that you were out, Kairos." She paused then, her keen eyes landing at his neck. "What exactly were you

12   THE QUEEN'S NEW YEAR SECRET

doing?" Her tone had morphed from glass to iron in a matter of syllables.

"I was at a party. It is New Year's Eve. That is what people customarily do on the holiday."

"Since when do you go to parties?"

"All too frequently, and you typically accompany me."

"I meant, when do you go to parties for recreational reasons?" She looked down, her jaw clenched tight. "You didn't invite me."

"This wasn't official palace business."

"That is apparent," she said, standing suddenly, reaching out toward his desk and taking hold of the stack of papers that had been resting there, unnoticed by him until that moment.

"Are you angry because you wanted to come?" He had well and truly given up trying to figure his wife out.

"No," she said, "but I am slightly perturbed by the red smudge on your collar."

Were it not for years of practice controlling his responses to things, he might have cursed. He had not thought about the crimson lipstick being left behind after that brief contact. Instead, he stood, keeping his expression blank. "It's nothing."

"I'm sure it is," she said, her words steady, even. "Even if it *isn't* nothing it makes no difference to me."

He was surprised by the impact of that statement. By how hard it hit. He had known she felt that way, he had. It was evident in her every interaction with him. In the way she turned away when he tried to kiss her. In the way she shrank back when he approached her. She was indifferent to him at best, disgusted by him at worst. Of course she wouldn't care if he found solace in the arms of another woman. So long as he wasn't finding it with her. He imagined the only reason she had put up with his touch for so long was out of the hope for children. A hope that faded with each and every day.

She must have given up completely now. A fact he should have realized when she hadn't come to his bed at all in months.

He decided against defending himself. If she didn't care, there was no point discussing it.

"What exactly are you doing here?" he asked. "Drinking my scotch?"

"I have had a bit," she said, wobbling slightly. A break in her composure. Witnessing such a thing was a rarity. Tabitha was a study in control. She always had been. Even back all those years ago when she'd been nothing more than his PA.

"All you have to do is ask the servants and you can have alcohol sent to your own room."

"My own room." She laughed, an unsteady sound. "Sure. Next time I'll do that. But I was actually waiting for you."

"You could have called me."

"Would you have answered the phone?"

The only honest answer to that question wasn't a good one. The truth was, he often ignored phone calls from her when he was busy. They didn't have personal conversations. She never called just to hear his voice, or anything like that. As a result, ignoring her didn't seem all that personal. "I don't know."

She forced a small smile. "You probably wouldn't have."

"Well, I'm here now. What was so important that we had to deal with it near midnight?"

She thrust the papers out, in his direction. For the first

time in months, he saw emotion burning from his wife's eyes. "Legal documents."

He looked down at the stack of papers she was holding out, then back at her, unable to process why the hell she would be handing him paper at midnight on New Year's Eve. "Why?"

"Because. I want a divorce."

CHAPTER TWO

TABITHA FELT AS if she was speaking to Kairos from somewhere deep underwater. She imagined the alcohol had helped dull the sensation of the entire evening. From the moment she'd first walked into his empty office with papers in hand, everything had felt slightly surreal. After an hour of waiting for her husband to appear, she had opened a bottle of his favorite scotch and decided to help herself. That had continued as the hours passed.

Then, he had finally shown up, near midnight, an obvious lipstick stain on his collar.

In that moment, the alcohol had been necessary. Without it the impact of that particular blow might have been fatal. She wasn't a fool. She was, after all, in her husband's office, demanding a divorce. She knew their marriage was broken. Irrevocably. He had wanted one thing from her, one thing only, and she had failed to accomplish that task.

The farce was over. There was no point in continuing on.

But she had not expected this. Evidence that her ice block of a husband—dutiful, solicitous and never passionate—had been with someone else. *Recreationally.* For pleasure.

Do you honestly think he waits around when you re-fuse to admit him into your bed?

Her running inner monologue had teeth tonight. It was also right. She *had* thought that. She had imagined that he was as cold to everyone as he was to her. She had thought that he was—at the very least—a man of honor. She had been prepared to liberate him from her, to liberate them *both*. She hadn't truly believed that he was off playing the part of a single man while still bonded to her by matrimony.

As if your marriage is anything like a real one. As if those vows apply.

"You want a divorce?" The sharpness in his tone penetrated the softness surrounding her and brought her sharply into the moment.

"You heard me the first time."

"I do not understand," he said, his jaw clenched tight, his dark eyes blazing with the kind of emotion she had never seen before.

"You're not a stupid man, Kairos," she said, alcohol making her bold. "I think you know exactly what the words *I want a divorce* mean."

"I do not understand what they mean coming from your lips, Tabitha," he said, his tone uncompromising. "You are my wife. You made promises to me. We have an agreement."

"Yes," she said, "we do. It is not to love, honor and cherish, but rather to present a united front for the country and to produce children. I have been unable to conceive a child, as you are well aware. Why continue on? We aren't happy."

"Since when does happiness come into it?"

Her heart squeezed tight, as though he had grabbed

it in his large palm and wrapped his fingers around it. "Some people would say happiness has quite a bit to do with life."

"Those people are not the king and queen of a country. You have no right to leave me," he said, his teeth locked together, his dark eyes burning.

In that moment, it was as though the flame in his eyes met the alcohol in her system. And she exploded.

She reached down, grabbed the tumbler of scotch she'd been drinking from, picked it up and threw it as hard as she could. It missed Kairos neatly, smashing against the wall behind him and leaving a splatter of alcohol and glass behind.

He moved to the side, his expression fierce. "What the hell are you doing?"

She didn't know. She had never done anything like this in her life. She despised this kind of behavior. This emotional, passionate, *ridiculous* behavior. She prized control. That was one of the many reasons she had agreed to marry Kairos. To avoid things like this. She respected him, and—once upon a time—had even enjoyed his company. Their connection had been based on mutual respect, and yes, on his need to find a wife quickly. This kind of thing, shouting and throwing things, had never come into play.

But it was out of her control now. *She* was out of control.

"Oh," she said, feigning surprise, "you noticed me."

Before she could react, he closed the distance between them, wrapping his hand around her wrists and propelling them both backward until her butt connected with the edge of his desk. Rage radiated from him, his face, normally schooled into stone, telegraphing more emotion than she'd seen from him in the past five years.

"You have my attention. So, if that is the aim of this temper tantrum, consider it accomplished."

"This is not a tantrum," she said, her voice vibrating with anger. "This is the result of preparation, careful planning and no small amount of subterfuge. I went to a lawyer. These papers are real. These are not empty threats. This is my decision and it is made."

He reached up, grabbing hold of her chin, holding her face steady and forcing her to meet his gaze. "I was not aware that you had the authority to make decisions concerning both of us."

"That's the beauty of divorce, Kairos. It is an uncoupling. That means I'm free to make independent decisions now."

He reached behind her, gripping her hair, drawing her head back. "Forgive me, my queen, I was not aware that your position in this country superseded my own."

He had never spoken to her this way, had never before touched her like this. She should be angry. Enraged. What she experienced was a different kind of heat altogether. In the very beginning, the promise of this kind of flame had shimmered between them, but over the years it had cooled. To the point that she had been convinced that it had died out. Whatever potential there was had been doused entirely by years of indifference and distance. She had been wrong.

"I was not aware that you had become a dictator."

"Is it not my home? Are you not my wife?"

"Am I? In any meaningful way?" She reached up, grabbing hold of his shirt collar, her thumb resting against the red smudge that marred the white fabric. "This says differently." She pulled hard, the action popping the top button on the shirt, loosening the knot on his gray tie.

His lip curled, his hold on her tightening. "Is that what you think of me? You think that I was with another woman?"

"The evidence suggests her lips touched your shirt. I would assume they touched other places on your body."

"You think I am a man who would break his vows?" he asked, his voice a growl.

"How would I know? I don't even know you."

"You don't *know* me?" His voice was soft, and all the deadlier for it. "I am your husband."

"Are you? Forgive me. I thought you were simply my stud horse."

He released his hold on her hair, wrapping his arm around her waist and drawing her tightly against his body. He was hot. Hard. Everywhere. The realization caused her heart rate to go into overdrive, her eyes flying wide as she searched his gaze. He was aroused by this. By her. Her circumspect husband who barely made a ripple in the bedspread when he made love to her was aroused by *this*.

"And how can that be, *agape*? When you have not let me near you in almost three months?"

"Was it I who didn't let you near me, or was it you who didn't bother to come to me?"

"A man gets tired of bedding a martyr."

"A woman begins to feel the same," she said, clinging to her anger, trying to ensure that it outstripped the desire that was wrapping itself around her throat, choking her, taking control of her.

He rolled his hips forward, pressing his hardened length against her hip. "Do I feel like a martyr to you?"

"I've always imagined it's the bright future of Petras

glowing in your mind's eye that allows you to get it up when you're with me."

He curled the hand pressed onto her back into a fist, taking a handful of material into his grasp and tugging hard. She heard the fabric tear as cool air blew across her now bare back. "Yes," he said, the word dripping with poison. "I am so put upon. Clearly, the sight of your naked body does nothing for me." He pulled her dress down, baring her breasts, covered only by the thin, transparent lace of her bra. "Such a hardship."

He leaned in, tilting his head, pressing a hot, open-mouthed kiss to her neck, the contact so shocking, so unlike anything that had ever passed between them before, she couldn't hold back the sharp cry of shock and pleasure.

She planted her hands on his shoulders, pushing him away. "Who else have you done this with tonight? The woman with the red lipstick? Did you have her like this too? Am I benefiting from the education that she gave you?" He said nothing, he only looked at her, his dark eyes glittering. Her stomach twisted, pain, anger overtaking her. She grabbed hold of the knot on his tie, pulling hard until it came free. She tossed the scrap of silk onto the ground before grabbing hold of his shirt, wrenching it open, buttons scattering over the marble floor.

She stopped, looking at him, her breath coming in short, hard bursts. He was beautiful. He always had been. She'd been struck by his sheer masculine perfection from the moment she'd first seen him. So young, so foolish. Nineteen years old, away from home for the first time, and utterly taken with her new boss.

Of course, she had never imagined that a young American girl who had come to Petras on a study-abroad program would have a chance with the king of the nation.

Oddly, he was almost more compelling now, in this moment, than he'd been at the first. She had slept with this man for five years. Had seen him naked countless times. The mystery should have been gone. She knew they didn't light the sheets on fire, they never had. It was her, at least she imagined it was. He was her only lover, so she had no one else to compare it with.

Apparently, *he* went out and found women with red lipstick, and things were different. *He* was different.

Rage mingled with the sexual heat rioting through her.

She ran her hands over his chest, the heat of his muscle and skin burning her palms. She should be disgusted by him. She shouldn't want to touch him. Instead, she was insatiable for him. If he had been with another woman, then she would wipe her from his mind. Would erase her touch from his body with her own. She would do what she had not managed to do over the course of five years of marriage. She would make him crave her. Make him desire her.

And then she would leave him.

She leaned forward, parting her lips, scraping her teeth over his chin. He growled, pressing her up against the desk again, pushing her dress the rest of the way down her hips, allowing it to pool on the floor. She didn't recognize him in this moment, didn't recognize herself.

"Did you have someone else?" She asked the question through clenched teeth, as she worked the buckle on his belt, then set about to opening the closure on his dress pants.

He leaned in, claiming her mouth with his, the kiss violent, hard. Bruising. He forced her lips apart, his tongue sliding against hers as he claimed her, deep and uncompromising. She let the rage of the unanswered question simmer between them, stoking the flame of her desire.

He took hold of the front of her bra, pulling it down, revealing her breasts. He bent his head, taking one tightened bud into his mouth and sucking hard. She gasped, threading her fingers through his hair, holding him tightly against her. She wanted to punish him, for tonight, for the past five years. She didn't know what else to do but to punish him with her desire. Desire she had kept long hidden. Until tonight, they had never so much as yelled at one another. This was more passion than either of them had ever shown.

Perhaps it was the same for him. An outlet for his anger. A punishment. But it was one she would gladly allow herself to be subjected to. Because for all that she knew she would walk away from this damaged, destroyed, she knew that he would not walk away from it unscathed either.

He shifted, blazing a path between her breasts with the flat of his tongue, his teeth grazing her neck, her jaw, before he finally claimed her mouth again. He reached between them, freeing his erection, so hot and hard against her skin.

She planted her hands on his shoulders, pushing them beneath the fabric of his shirt, scraping her fingernails along his flesh, relishing the harsh sound that he made in response. He tightened his hold on her, setting her up on the surface of his desk, moving to stand between her spread thighs. He pressed his arousal against her slick, sensitive skin, still covered by her flimsy panties, rolling his hips, sending a shock wave of pleasure through her body.

"Answer me," she said, digging her fingernails more deeply into his shoulders.

He shifted, sliding his hands down beneath the fabric of her underwear, his fingertips grazing the sensitized bundle of nerves there. "You want to know if I did this to another woman?" His words were rough, jagged. He hooked his finger around the edge of her panties, drawing them to the side, pressing the head of his shaft to the entrance of her body. "You want to know if I did *this* with another woman?"

"Just answer the question," she hissed.

"I think you would have me either way."

Her face heated, humiliation pouring through her. He was right. In this moment, she would be hard-pressed to deny him or her body anything. "Is that why you won't tell me? For fear I'll turn you away?"

"I'm used to you turning me away, Tabitha. Why should I waste a moment of regret over it now?"

She slid her hands down his well-muscled back, cupping his ass. "You would regret this." She rolled her hips forward, taking him deeper inside her body, just another inch. "You would regret not finishing this."

"No," he said, and for a moment, her heart sank. For a moment, she thought he meant he would not regret losing out on this moment between them. For a moment, she thought that yet again, she was alone in what she was experiencing. "I was not with anyone else. I did not touch another woman. She propositioned me. She whispered in my ear. I said no."

Then he kissed her before driving deep into her body. She gasped, and he took advantage, tasting her deeply as he flexed his hips again, withdrawing slightly before seating himself fully inside her again.

A rough groan escaped her lips, white-hot pleasure streaking through her. She clung more tightly to him, wrapping her legs around his back, urging him on. Urging him to take it harder, faster. She had no patience. Had no more desire in her to cultivate an effort to take things slow, to practice restraint. There was nothing but him, nothing but this. Nothing but years of anger, frustration, being uncovered as their inhibitions were stripped away layer by layer, with each thrust of his body into hers.

A shudder wracked his large frame, pleasure stealing his control. She relished that. Took pride in it. But it wasn't enough. She wanted to give him pleasure, she absolutely did. Wanted him to think of this later, to regret all of the years when they didn't have this. To look back on this one moment and ache forever. For the rest of his days, no matter whom he married down the road. Whoever came after her, whether she bore children for him or not, Tabitha wanted him to always think of her.

But pleasure wasn't enough. She wanted to punish him too. She dug her fingernails deep into his skin and he growled, angling his head and biting her neck, the action not gentle at all, painful. He flexed his hips, his body making contact with that sensitive bundle of nerves, and she knew that he was trying to do the same to her that she was doing to him. As if she deserved his wrath. As if she deserved his belated, angry gift of pleasure. *He* was the one who had done this to them. This was his fault.

She tightened her grip on him, met his every thrust with a push from her own body, met his each and every growl with one of her own. She had been passive for too long. The perfect wife who could never be perfect enough. So why bother? Why not just break it all?

She closed her eyes tightly, fusing her lips to his, kissing him with all of the rage, desire and regret that she had inside of her, the action pushing them both over the edge. It had been so long. So very long. Not just since she had been with him, but since she had found pleasure in his arms. So many months of coming together when she was at the optimum place in her cycle, perfunctory couplings that meant nothing and felt like less than nothing.

This was different than anything that had come before it. He'd given her orgasms before, but nothing like this. Nothing this all-consuming. Nothing this altering. This devastating. This was like a completely different experience. She was falling in the dark with no way of knowing when she would hit the bottom. All she knew was that she would. And when she did, it would be painful beyond anything she had ever known before. But for now, she was simply falling, with him.

The last time. The last moment they would ever be together.

She wanted to weep. With the devastation of it. With the triumph of it. This was it for them. The final nail in the coffin of their marriage. How she desperately needed it. How she resented it. She wanted to transport herself somewhere in the future. Years from now, maybe. To a time when she'd already healed from the wounds that would be left behind after they separated. A moment in time when she would have already learned to be Just Tabitha again, and not Tabitha, Queen of Petras, wife of Kairos. But Tabitha, on her own.

At the same time, she wanted to stay in this moment. Forever. She wanted to hold on to him forever and never let go.

Which was why she needed to let go. She so badly needed to let go.

The pleasure stretched on, an onslaught of waves that never ceased and she couldn't catch her breath. Couldn't think beyond what he made her feel. It wasn't fair. It just wasn't fair. Why was this happening now? She had always believed this was there between them, that it could be unlocked, somehow, but they had never found it. Not until this moment. This very last moment.

Finally the storm subsided, leaving her spent, exhausted. Smashed against the rock. She was wrung out. She had nothing left in her to give. No more rage. No more desire. Nothing but an endless sadness for what her life had become. She looked at the man still holding her tightly. The man still inside her body. The man she had made vows to.

A man who was a stranger, half a decade after she'd first made love to him.

"I hate you," she said, the words a hoarse whisper that shocked even herself. A tear slid down her cheek and she didn't bother to wipe it away. "For every one of the past five years you have wasted, I hate you. For being my husband but never really being my husband. I hate you for that too. For not giving me a baby. For making me want you even when I hate you."

He pushed away from her, his gaze dark. "Let me guess, you hate me for that too."

"I do. But the good thing is, that after today, we won't have to see each other."

"Oh, I think not, *agape*. I think we will have to see each other a great many times after today. A royal divorce is going to be complicated. There will be press. There will be many days in court—"

"We signed a prenuptial agreement. I remember the

terms well. I don't get anything. That's fine. I've had quite enough from you."

He made no move to dress, made no move to collect her clothes. And he didn't look away as she bent to gather them, pulling them on as quickly as possible, internally shrinking away from his gaze. Finally, she was dressed. It was done. It was over.

She made her way toward the door on unsteady legs, everything inside her unsteady, rolling like the sea.

"Tabitha," he said, his voice rough, "I want you to know that I don't hate you."

"You don't?" She turned to face him, her eyes meeting with his unreadable face. As immovable as stone.

He shook his head slowly, his eyes never leaving hers. "No. I feel…" He paused for a moment. "I feel nothing."

She felt as though he had stabbed her directly in the heart. Anguish replaced any of the pleasure, any of the satisfaction that had been there before. He felt *nothing*. Even in this moment he felt nothing.

The rage was back then, spurring her on, keeping her from falling over. "You just screwed me on your desk," she said, "I would have thought that might have made you feel something."

She was all false bravado. It was either that or burst into tears.

His expression remained bland. "You're hardly the first woman I've had on a desk."

She swallowed hard, blinking back more tears. She had made the right choice. She knew she had. Had he yelled at her, had he screamed, had he said that he hated her too, she might have wondered. But those black, flat, soulless eyes didn't lie. He felt nothing. He was indifferent, even in this moment.

Tabitha had heard it said that hate was like murder. But she knew differently. It was indifference that killed. And with his, Kairos had left her mortally wounded.

"I wish you luck in your search for a more suitable wife, Your Highness," she said.

Then she walked out of the door, out of his life.

CHAPTER THREE

"WHERE IS YOUR WIFE, Kairos?"

Prince Andres, Kairos's younger reformed rake of a brother, walked into Kairos's office. There was still glass on the floor from where Tabitha had shattered it two days ago. Still a dark stain where the scotch had splashed itself over the wallpaper.

All of it shouted the story of what had happened the night Tabitha had left. At least, it shouted at Kairos. Every time he walked in.

It was nearly as loud as his damned conscience.

I feel nothing.

A lie. Of course it was a lie. She had stripped him down. Reduced him to nothing more than need, desperate, clawing need.

Another woman walking away from him. Threatening to leave him there alone. Empty. While his pride bled out of him, leaving him with nothing.

He couldn't allow that, not again. So he'd said he felt nothing. And now she was gone.

"Why? What have you heard?" Kairos asked, not bothering to explain the glass, even when Andres's eyes connected with the mess.

"Nothing much. Zara tells me Tabitha called to see if

I could find out if you were using your penthouse any-time soon. I wondered why on earth my brother's wife would be stooping to subterfuge to find out the actions of her own husband."

Kairos ground his teeth together, his eyes on the shards of glass.

I feel nothing for you.

If only that were true. He was...he didn't even know what to call the emotions rioting through him. Emotions were...weak and soft in his estimation, and that was not what he felt.

He was beyond rage. Beyond betrayal. She was his wife. He had brought her up from the lowest of positions, made her a queen, and she had the audacity to betray him.

"No explanation, Kairos?"

Kairos looked up at his brother. "She probably wants to go shopping without fear of retribution."

"Right. Are the coffers of Petras so empty she has to worry about your wrath? Or is her shoe closet merely so full."

Kairos had no idea what her closet looked like. He never looked farther than her bed when he was in her room. "She left me," he said, his tone hard, the words like acid on his tongue.

Andres had the decency to look shocked. Surprising, because Andres was rarely shocked and he was never decent. "Tabitha *left* you?"

"Yes," he ground out.

"Tabitha, who barely frowns in public for fear it might ignite a scandal?"

Kairos dragged his hand over his face. "That is the only Tabitha I know of."

"I don't believe it."

"Neither do I," Kairos said, his voice a growl.

He paced across the office, to the place where the remains of that glass of scotch rested. It reminded him of the remnants left behind after an accident on the highway. One of the many similarities the past few days bore to a car crash.

I hate you.

He closed his eyes against the pain that lashed at him. What had he done to make his wife hate him? Had he not given her everything?

A baby. She wanted a baby.

Yes, he had failed her there. But dammit all, he'd given her a *palace*. Some women couldn't be pleased.

"What the hell did you do?"

"I was perhaps too generous," Kairos said, his tone hard. "I gave her too much freedom. Perhaps the weight of her diamond-encrusted crown was a bit heavy."

"You don't know," Andres said, his tone incredulous.

"Of course I bloody don't. I had no idea she was unhappy." The lie was heavy on his chest.

You knew. You didn't know how to fix it.

"I know I haven't been married very long…"

"A week, Andres. If you begin handing out marital advice before the ink is dry on your license, I will reopen the dungeons just for you."

"Perhaps if you'd opened the dungeons for Tabitha she wouldn't have left you."

"I am not going to keep my own wife prisoner." But dear God, it was tempting.

Andres arched a brow. "That isn't what I meant."

Heat streaked along Kairos's veins, and he thought again of that last night here in his office. Of the way she'd felt in his arms. His cool ice queen suddenly transformed into a living flame…

I hate you.

"We do not have that sort of relationship," Kairos said, his voice stiff.

Andres chuckled, the sound grating against Kairos's nerves. "Maybe that's your problem."

"Everything is not about sex."

Andres shrugged. "It absolutely is. But you may cling to your illusions if you must."

"What do you want, Andres?"

"To see if you're okay."

He spread his arms wide. "Am I dead and buried?"

His brother arched a brow. "No. But your wife is gone."

Kairos gritted his teeth. "And?"

"Do you intend to get a new one?"

He would have to. There was no other alternative. Though the prospect filled him with nothing but dread. Still, even now, he wanted no one else. No one but Tabitha.

And now that he'd tasted the heat that had always shimmered between them as a tantalizing promise, never before fulfilled…

Forgetting her would not be so easy.

"I do not want a new one," he said.

"Then you have to go and claim the old one, I suppose."

Kairos offered his brother a glare. "Worry about your life, I'll worry about mine." He paused for a moment, staring again at that pile of broken glass. The only thing that remained of his marriage. "I will not hold her prisoner. If Tabitha wants a divorce, she can have her damn divorce."

* * *

Tabitha hadn't seen Kairos in four weeks. Four weeks of staring at blank spaces, eyes dry, unable to find any tears. She hadn't cried. Not since that single tear had fallen in his office. Not since she'd told him how much she hated him—and meant it—with every piece of herself. She had not cried.

Why would you cry for a husband that you hated? Why would you cry for a husband who felt nothing for you?

It made no sense. And so, she hadn't cried. Tabitha was nothing if not sensible. Even when she came to divorce, it seemed.

She was slightly less sensible when it came to other things. Which was why it had taken her a full week of being late for her to make her way to the doctor. She had no choice but to use the doctor she had always used. She didn't want to, didn't want to be at risk by going to a doctor who was employed by the royal family. But her only other alternative was going to one she had no relationship with. One she had no trust in at all. News of her and Kairos's divorce had already hit the papers, and it was headline news. If she went to an ob-gyn now, everything would explode. She couldn't risk it. So she was risking this. She swallowed hard, her hands shaking as she sat on the exam table. Her blood had already been drawn, and now she was just waiting for the results.

She had waited so long to come to the doctor because she was often late. Her period never started on time. For years upon years every time she had been late she'd held out hope. Hope that this time it wasn't just her cycle being fickle. Hope that it might actually be a baby.

It was never a baby. *Never.*

But it had been a full week, and still nothing. And she

couldn't overlook the fact that she and Kairos had had unprotected sex.

Nothing unusual there, though. They always had. For five years they'd had unprotected sex, and there had been no baby. The universe was not that cruel. How could God ignore her prayers for five long years, and answer them at the worst possible moment?

It couldn't be. It *couldn't* be.

For the first time, when the doctor walked back into the room, her expression unreadable, Tabitha hoped for the *no*. She needed it. Needed to hear that the test was negative.

She knew now that she couldn't live with Kairos. It was confirmed. She couldn't make it work with him. He didn't care for her. And she…she felt far too much for him. She could not live like that. She simply couldn't.

"Queen Tabitha," Dr. Anderson said, her words slow. "I had hoped that King Kairos might have accompanied you today."

"If you read the paper at all, then you know that he and I are going through a divorce. I saw no reason to include him in this visit." The doctor looked down and Tabitha's stomach sank. A *no* was an easy answer to give. A *no* certainly didn't require Kairos's presence.

"Yes, I do know about the divorce," the doctor said. "All members of royal staff had been briefed, of course."

"Then you know why he isn't here."

"Forgive me for asking, my queen," the doctor said. "But if you are in fact carrying a child, is it his?"

"If I am? You've seen the test results. Don't play this game with me. Do not play games with me. I've had enough."

"It's just that…"

"This is *my* test. It has nothing to do with him. My entire life does not revolve around *him*." Tabitha knew she was beginning to get a bit hysterical. "I left him. I left him so that he wasn't at the center of everything I did. We don't need to bring him into this."

"The test is positive, my queen. I feel that under other circumstances congratulations would be in order," Dr. Anderson said, her tone void of expression.

Before this, before the divorce proceedings, Dr. Anderson had always been friendly, warm. She was decidedly cool now.

A King Kairos loyalist, clearly. But Dr. Anderson didn't have to live with him.

"Oh." Tabitha felt light-headed. She felt like she was going to collapse. She was thankful for the table she was seated on. Had she been standing, she would have slipped from consciousness immediately.

"Based on the dates you have given me I would estimate that you are…"

"I know exactly how far along I am," Tabitha said.

Flashes of that night burst into her mind's eye. Kairos putting her up on the desk, thrusting into her hard and fast. Spilling himself inside of her as they both lost themselves to their pleasure. Yes, there was no doubt in her mind as to when she had conceived. January 1.

The beginning of the New Year. What was supposed to be the start of her new beginning.

And all she had was a chain shackling her to Kairos now that she had finally decided to walk out the door and take her freedom.

Of course this was happening now. When she'd released hold of her control. Her inhibitions. There were reasons she'd kept herself on a short leash for so many years. She'd always suspected she couldn't be trusted. That she would break things if she was ever allowed to act without careful thought and consideration.

She'd been right to distrust herself.

She balled her hands into fists and pressed them against her eyes.

"Are you all right?" Dr. Anderson asked.

"Does it look like I'm all right?" Tabitha asked.

"It's only that...*is* it the king's baby?"

Rage fired through Tabitha then. "It is *my* baby. That's about all I can process at the moment."

Dr. Anderson hesitated. "It's only that I want to be certain that I didn't overstep."

As those words left the doctor's mouth, the door to the exam room burst open. Tabitha looked up, her heart slamming hard against her sternum. There was Kairos. Standing in the doorway, looking like a fallen angel, rage emanating from him.

"Leave us," he said to the doctor.

"Of course, Your Highness."

The doctor scurried out of the room, eagerly doing Kairos's bidding. Tabitha could only sit there, dazed. She supposed that there was no such thing as doctor-patient confidentiality when the king was involved.

She turned to face her nearly ex-husband—who was looking at her as though she were the lowest and vilest of creatures. As if he had any right. As if he had the right to judge her. After what he had said. After what he had done.

"What's the matter, Kairos?" she asked, schooling her expression into one of absolute calm and stillness. It was her specialty. After years of hiding her true feelings behind a mask for public consumption, she went about it with as much ease as breathing.

"It seems I'm about to be a father." He moved nearer to her, his dark eyes blazing. Any blankness, any calm he had presented the night she had left him standing in his office was gone now. He was all emotion now. He was vibrating with it.

"You're making an awfully big assumption."

He slammed his hands down on the counter by the exam table. "Do not toy with me, Tabitha. We both know it's my child."

"Except that *you* don't. Because you can't know that. You haven't seen me in weeks. I didn't go to your bed for months before our last time together." Heartbreak made her cruel. She'd had no idea. She'd never been heartbroken before him.

"I am the only man you have ever been with. You and I both know that. You were a virgin when I had you the first time. I sincerely doubt you went out and found the first lover available to you just after leaving my arms."

She swallowed hard, her hands trembling. "You say that as though you know me. We both know that you don't. We both know that you feel nothing for me."

"In this moment, I find I feel quite a lot."

"I've only just found out. It isn't as though I was keeping a secret from you. Where exactly do you get off coming in here, playing the part of caveman?"

"You were going to keep it from me. The doctor called me. If you knew you were coming to the doctor to get a pregnancy test, why didn't you include me?"

"Because," she said, looking at the wall beyond him, "that's the beauty of divorce. I don't have to include you in my life. I get to go on as an individual. Not as one half of the world's most dysfunctional couple. I would have told you. I was hardly going to keep this from you. If for no other reason than that the press would never let me."

"How very honorable of you. You would let me in on my impending fatherhood based on what the media would allow you to keep secret. Tell me, would you allow them to announce it to me via headline?"

"That sounds about right considering the level of communication we've always had. Honestly, I haven't much noticed the absence of you in the past four weeks. It was pretty much standard to our entire marriage. Sex once a month with no talking in between."

"Still your poisonous tongue for a moment, my queen. We have a serious issue to deal with here."

"There is no *issue*," she said, her hand going protectively to her stomach. "And there is no *dealing* with it. What's done is done."

"What exactly did you think I was suggesting?" His dark features contorted with horror. With anger. "You cannot seriously think I would suggest you get rid of our child. Just because you and I are experiencing difficult circumstances at the moment—"

"No. That isn't what I thought you meant. And what do you mean difficult circumstances? We are not undergoing difficult circumstances. If anything, we're experiencing some of the best circumstances we've had in years. We aren't together anymore, Kairos. That's what we both need."

"Not now. There will be no discussion of it."

She stood up, feeling dizzy. "The hell there won't be. I am not your property. I can divorce you if I choose, discussion or not."

"Can you? I am king of Petras."

"And I am an American citizen."

"In addition to being a citizen of Petras."

"I will happily chuck my Petran passport into the river. As long as it will get you off my back."

"We are not having this discussion here," he said through clenched teeth. "Get dressed. We're leaving."

"I have a car."

"Oh, yes, my driver that you're still using. From the house that I own that you are currently living in."

"I will sort things out later," she said, stinging heat lashing her cheekbones. It was humiliating to have him bring up the fact she was dependent on him to not be homeless at the moment. Particularly since she had made such a big deal out of knowing she would get nothing from him after the divorce. But still, he wasn't using his apartment in town, nor was he using the car and driver that were headquartered there. So he could hardly deny her the use of them. Well, he *could*. But he wasn't, so she was taking advantage.

"Oh, I sent your driver home. The only driver currently here is mine. You are leaving with me. Now."

He stood there, his arms folded across his broad chest, his dark eyes glued to her.

"Don't look at me. I have to get dressed."

"It is nothing I haven't seen, *agape*."

She treated him to her iciest glare. "Rarely."

The biting word hung between them and she felt some guilt over it. Truly, the state of their sex life was partly her fault. If not mostly her fault. But having him touch her out of duty... It had certainly started to wear on her.

Eventually, it was just easier to lie back and think of Petras. To close her eyes and think of other things. Hope that it would be over quickly. To not allow herself to feel a connection with him. To shut walls around her heart, and around her body. The less she felt during sex, the less pain she felt when it was over. The less disappointment each time he got up and left immediately after, each time the pregnancy test was negative. The less distress she felt over the fact that any intimacy between them was all for the purpose of producing a child. That it was completely void of any kind of emotion between the two of them.

Yes, the fast, disappointing sex in the dark was mainly her fault.

"As you wish, my queen." He turned away from her, his broad back filling her vision. And, damn him, she felt bad. Guilty. He did *not* deserve her guilt.

She kept her eyes on him as she stripped off the hospital gown she was wearing. On the way the perfectly cut lines of his suit molded to his physique. He was a handsome man. There was no denying it. He was also a bastard.

She finished dressing, then cleared her throat.

Kairos turned, the fierceness in his expression wavering for a moment. An emotion there that she couldn't quite put a name to.

"Let's go," he said.

"Where are you taking me?"

"To the palace." He hesitated. "We have some things to discuss."

"I don't want to discuss this right now. I've only just found out I'm pregnant. I believe you had to know before I did."

"You at least had a suspicion."

"You think that makes it easier? Do you think that makes any of this…?" Her voice broke, her entire body shaking. "I should not be devastated in this moment. I hate you for this too. I was supposed to be happy when I finally conceived. You've stolen that for me."

"Who stole it, Tabitha? I was not the one who asked for a divorce."

"Maybe not. But you made your feelings for me perfectly clear. It's poison now, already working its way through my system. You can't fix it."

He said nothing as they walked out of the exam room and continued down the long vacant hallway toward a back entrance. His car was waiting there, not one driven by a chauffeur. One of his sports cars that he got great enjoyment out of driving.

He was a low-key man, her husband. Responsible, levelheaded. Serious.

But he liked cars. And he very much enjoyed driving them. Much too fast for her taste. But he never asked her opinion.

"I'm not especially in the mood to deal with your Formula 1 fantasies," she said, crossing her arms and tapping her foot, giving him her best withering expression.

"Funny. I'm not particularly in the mood to put up with your attitude, and yet, here we are."

"You have earned every bit of my attitude, Your Highness."

"So angry with me, Tabitha, when you spent so many years with so little to say."

"What *have* I said, my lord?"

He made a scoffing sound in the back of his throat. "My lord. As if you are ever so deferential."

She arched her brow. "As if you ever deserved it." She breezed past him and got inside the car, slamming the door shut behind her and setting about to buckling her seat belt while he got in and started the engine.

"What happened, Tabitha? *What happened?*"

"There was nothing. Like you said. Nothing. And I can't live that way anymore."

"You're having my baby. I don't see you have an option now. Clearly the divorce is off."

He revved the engine, pressing the gas and pulling the car away from the curb.

"The divorce is no such thing," she said, panic clawing at her insides. "The divorce is absolutely on. You might be royalty, but you can't pull endless weight with me. I am not simply another subject in your country. I have rights."

"Oh, really? And with what money will you hire a lawyer to defend those rights? Everything you have is mine, Tabitha, and we both know it."

"I will find a way." She didn't know if she would. He wasn't wrong. She was nothing. Nothing from nowhere. She had climbed her way up from the bottom. From a poor household on the wrong side of the tracks with parents who would spend every night screaming at each other, throwing things. Her mother hurling heavy objects at her stepfather's head whenever the mood struck her.

And that was before everything had gone horribly wrong.

There had been no money in her household. Not enough food. All there had been was anger. And that was an endless well. One that her parents drew from at every possible opportunity. That was her legacy. It was all she had. It was why she had vowed to find something different for herself. Something better.

What she had found was that sometimes everything that filled the quiet spaces, everything that went unsaid, was more cutting, more painful than a dinner plate being hurled at your head.

Kairos said nothing but simply kept driving. It took a while for her to realize they weren't heading back to the palace, but when she did, a cold sense of dread filled her. She realized then that she honestly couldn't predict what he might be doing. Because she didn't know him. Five years she had been married to this man and she knew even less about him today than she had on the day they had married. Impossible, seemingly.

She'd spent three years as his PA prior to them getting engaged and married. Three years where she had cultivated a silly, childish crush on him. He had smiled easier then, laughed with her sometimes.

But that was before his father had died. Before the weight of the nation had fallen on his shoulders. Before his arranged engagement was destroyed by his impetuous younger brother. Before he had been forced to take on a replacement wife that he had never wanted, much less loved.

Those years spent as his PA had been like standing on the outside of a forest. She had looked on him and thought, *I recognize him. He's a forest.* Being his wife was like walking through it. Discovering new dangers, discovering that it was so dark, she could barely see in front of her. Discovering she had no idea where the trees might end, and where she might find her freedom. Yes, the deeper she walked, the less she knew.

"You aren't planning on driving your car into a river or something dramatic, are you?" she asked, only half joking.

"Don't be silly. We spent years trying for an heir, I'm not going to compromise anything now that we have one on the way."

"Oh, but otherwise you would be aiming for a cliff. Good to know."

"And leave Andres to rule? Don't be ridiculous."

It occurred to her suddenly, exactly where they were heading. Unease stole over her, her scalp prickling. "What are you planning?"

"Me? Perhaps I'm not planning anything. Perhaps I'm being spontaneous."

"I don't believe that."

"You're so convinced that I don't know you, and yet, you think you know me, *agape*? How fair is that?"

She didn't think she knew him. But she wasn't about to admit that now. "You're a man, Kairos. Moreover, you're a distinctly predictable one."

"If I cared about your opinion at all I would be tempted to feel wounded. Alas, I don't."

He turned onto the private airfield used by the royal family and her heart sank. Her suspicions were very much confirmed. "What is it you think you're doing?"

"Oh, I don't think I'm doing anything. This is the situation, my darling bride, either you come with me now or we do this here in Petras."

"Do what, exactly?"

"Come to an agreement on exactly what we will do now that we are to be parents. And by come to an agreement, I mean what I will decide. Do not forget that I am the king. Whatever laws might govern the rest of the people do not apply to me."

Rage filled her, flooded her. "Since when? You've never been the most flexible of men, but you've never been a dictator."

"I've never been a father before either. Neither have

I ever been in the position of having my wife threaten to leave me."

"I didn't threaten to leave you, Kairos. I left you. There is a difference."

"Regardless. Come with me, and we will have a discussion. If you refuse, then I will ensure that I get full custody of our child, and you will never see him. I give you my word on that. And unlike you, when I make a vow, I keep it."

CHAPTER FOUR

KAIROS LOOKED AT his wife, who was seated across the cabin from him on his private plane. He had a feeling she was plotting his death. Fortunately, Tabitha was quite petite or he might harbor some concern over her having access to any cutlery. At this point, he doubted she would hesitate to attempt to take him out with her fork. In many ways, he couldn't blame her. But he had to guard his own self-interest, and guard it he would.

There was no room to be soft in this.

She was having his baby. An heir. *Finally*.

At any other time this would have been a cause for celebration. The completion of his duty in many ways. A fulfillment of deathbed promises made to a father he'd never quite pleased during his life.

The moment he'd found out, the only thought he had was how he could capture her. Keep her with him. He had no idea what he was going to do beyond that. But he had managed to get her on the plane, even though it had taken threats. Now, they were en route to his private island off the coast of Greece. The villa there had always been used by the royal family of Petras for vacations. Kairos had never taken Tabitha there. He had not been on a vacation since he had taken her as his wife.

Of course, this was no vacation. Some might call it a kidnapping. But he was king. So he imagined he could classify it as some kind of political detention. She was, after all, carrying the heir to the throne of Petras. If she were to leave, it would be kidnapping on her end.

At least, that's how he was justifying things. And he was king. The amount of people he had to justify his actions to was limited to one. Himself.

She didn't look angry. She looked as smooth and unruffled as ever. Her hands were folded in her lap, her legs crossed at the ankles, her lovely neck craned as she looked out the window. She managed to appear both neutral and haughty, a feat he had only ever seen managed by Tabitha.

Years of routine. A marriage so mundane he could go days without looking at her. Even if they were in the same room. He would look in her direction, but, he realized, never truly look at her. It was easy sometimes to go a full week without words passing directly between them. Communication with a phone or servant as the go-between.

And in the space of the past four weeks everything had changed. She had asked for a divorce. Then he'd torn her clothes off and taken her like a rutting animal. Now there was a baby.

The past four weeks contained more than the past half decade they'd spent as husband and wife. He was having a difficult time wrapping his head around it. Around who he had become in her arms in those moments in his office. He was angry. Enraged that she would walk away from him after all he had done for her. Enraged that half-formed fantasies he had barely let himself dream would never come to be.

He had imagined they would be married all of their lives. He had never imagined she would end it.

"Are you quite comfortable?" he asked, because he could think of nothing else to say and he had grown quite uncomfortable with his role as uncivilized beast and the little play they were currently acting out.

He was the responsible one. He'd never acted out, not once in his life. His father had impressed the weight of the crown upon him at an early age, and Kairos had always taken it seriously. He had seen the consequences of what happened when one did not. Had had it ingrained in him.

Control was everything. Duty. Honor. Sacrifice.

He was surprised how easily he had cast it off the moment his wife had handed him divorce papers.

And so, he was attempting to reclaim it.

As you kidnap her. Brilliant.

"Yes," she said, her tone brittle. "Very. But then, I don't have to tell you your private plane is luxurious. You already know."

"Indeed."

"How long had I been working for you the first time we flew on this plane?"

"A couple of months, surely," he said, as though he didn't remember it clearly. He did. There was something so charming and guileless about her reaction to the private aircraft. It had stood in stark contrast to the response of his fiancée at the time, Francesca.

He had noticed it then, as he compared the two women unfavorably. Francesca was, of course, eminently suitable to be a royal bride. That was why he had selected her. Love had never come into play. She had been raised in an aristocratic family, trained to be the wife of a political leader from an early age.

Of course, it had all blown up in his face when she had slept with his brother. That might not have bothered him so much, had she not done it quite so publicly. Not that she had intended for it to go public. Ruining her chances of becoming the queen of Petras had not been the plan. That much he knew. Still, a video had surfaced of the two of them together, and that did it for their wedding.

He needed to find a wife to fill in for the royal wedding that was already planned, and quickly. And so, he had selected Tabitha to be his bride. A logical decision. An acceptable flesh-and-blood woman.

Perhaps all women were destined to go crazy at some point in their lives. His mother certainly had. Walking out on her husband and children in the dead of night, never resurfacing again. Francesca most certainly had when she'd compromised her position as queen simply so she could experience some pleasure with Andres. Obviously, Tabitha was the newest victim of the craze.

Or maybe it's you.

He gritted his teeth.

"I was impressed with it then," she said. "I remain impressed. I am less impressed with the fact that you hijacked my person."

"It was a hard-line negotiation, not a hijacking. Surely you see the difference."

"The end result is the same to me, so why should I care about semantics?"

"You were quite impressed with the plane," he said, his voice hard, "as I recall."

"Don't tell me you remember."

"Of course I remember. You were very young. Wide-eyed about everything you encountered here in Petras. Especially everything concerning the royal family and the palace. I had a fair idea about your background, because of course I screened you before hiring you. I knew you came from a modest upbringing."

"That's a generous way of putting it."

"Impoverished, then. Yes, I knew. But you were bright, and you were certainly the best person for the job. You were motivated, in part because of your past. I thought, possibly more driven than any of the other candidates to succeed."

"Are these the same thoughts you had when you selected me to be your wife?"

He could sense the layers hidden beneath the question, but couldn't guess what they were. "I also knew you," he said.

She made a scoffing sound, uncrossed her legs, then recrossed them the opposite direction, annoyance emanating from her in a wave. "Oh. You *knew* me. As in, were acquainted with me. How very romantic."

"Did I ever promise you romance, Tabitha?" She said nothing, her glare glacial now. "No. I did not. I told you that I would stay faithful to you, and I have. I told you that I would be loyal to you, which I have also done. That I would do my duty to God, country and to you. I have done all of that, to a satisfactory degree, many would say. You were the one who decided it wasn't enough."

Righteous anger burned through him. He had not lied to her. He had not told her he would give hearts, flowers or any frilly symbol of weak emotion. He had pledged commitment.

She seemed to have no concept of that at all. He would never have taken her for being so faithless. He had thought she was like him. Had thought she was logical. Had thought that she understood sacrifice. That duty and honor superseded emotion.

"A theoretical marriage is a lot different than actual marriage. I can hardly be held to assumptions I made before I had ever had a…a relationship."

"Certainly you can. Everyone makes vows before they marry. For the most part, they have never made such vows before."

"And sometimes marriages end. Because in spite of the best intentions of everyone involved, things don't work out the way you thought they would."

"As I am also not a fortune-teller, I fail to see how I can be held accountable for not fulfilling needs you did not voice to me. In addition to not being able to see the future, I cannot read your mind."

"Even if you could, I can only imagine that you would find it unworthy of listening to."

"When exactly did you become such a pain?" he asked, not bothering to temper his anger. "You were not like this before we were married."

"That's because before we were married, you paid me to be your assistant. An assistant is not a wife."

"I was very clear when I proposed to you that this would not be a typical marriage. That it would in fact reflect some of the duties that you took on as an assistant."

"Well, maybe nothing changed, then. Nothing but me." She crossed her arms, closing herself off from conversation, and turned away from him.

He gritted his teeth, and determined that he would not speak to her again until they landed. Once they were on the island… He didn't know. But she wouldn't be able to escape him. Not until he allowed it.

If that was kidnapping, then so be it.

But he was not going to take the end of his marriage lying down. The sooner she realized that, the better.

CHAPTER FIVE

IT WAS STRANGE, landing on what you knew was your husband's private island, an island you had never been to before. He'd never brought her here, to this place, to this villa. It was incredible, like every property the Demetriou family owned. Just like the penthouse downtown that she was staying in while she avoided the reality of her life, just like the palace.

This was different. White walls, a red roof, placed on white sand in the middle of the blue, glittering bright sea. Like a beautiful piece of jewelry, perhaps part of the crown jewels. It was isolated, nothing like the palace, so filled with staff, tour groups and political leaders. Nothing like the penthouse, enveloped in the busy motion of the city.

She blinked against the sun, pale light washing over everything around them.

"Why don't you come in?"

She looked at Kairos, suddenly overcome by a sense of déjà vu. Of being in a new place with him, for the first time. That day she'd first walked into his office as his assistant.

"Come in. Sit down."

Tabitha shifted where she was standing, unable to de-

cide what exactly she should be staring at. At the most beautiful, opulent surroundings she had ever seen, or at the most blindingly handsome man she had ever laid eyes on.

She crossed the room, taking a seat across from him at his desk.

Tabitha was suddenly brought straight back into the present as she imagined that desk. The one they had conceived their baby on. Walking into his office that day, she never could have imagined that eight years later she would end up screwing him on it after asking him for a divorce.

She blinked against the stinging sensation in her eyes. They weren't tears. She was not going to cry any tears for him. For the man who didn't feel anything for her.

She followed him into the villa, unable to remain entirely unimpressed with her surroundings. She was used to opulence. She had spent years working with him in the palace prior to their marriage, and had had a good dose of exposure to it even before she herself was royalty. After nearly a decade in these kinds of settings she should be used to them.

But a small part of her was still very much that girl from the single-wide trailer, utterly unable to believe that she now rated entry into these sorts of places.

This—this small weakness for luxury—was the flaw in her armor. At least, the entry point by which to reach many of the others.

Everything in the room was white, large windows looking out over a lush garden, an infinity pool and beyond that the sea provided the only color. That was one of the first things she had noticed when she came to live in the palace. Even when she was simply in the apartments provided for her as an employee, the decor had been simple, but the quality unsurpassed.

It made her feel small and gauche to think of her observations now. The linens had been pure white, no pattern, or ornate embroidery to draw the eye. It was all in the feel of it. So soft it was like touching a cloud. Everything was like that. The tissues and the toilet paper even. Tiny pieces of luxury that added up to the kind of comfort she had never even imagined existed.

"My room is upstairs, at the end of the hall, feel free to choose whichever quarters suit you best."

She looked over at him, reminded yet again of that first meeting.

She had never seen an office quite like this. And she had never seen a man quite like him. When she entered the prestigious university that was currently facilitating this study-abroad program she'd been exposed to a higher class of people, a higher class of living than ever before. But this was somewhere far beyond that.

For one thing, he was a prince. No matter how blue the blood, that placed him several rungs higher on the social ladder than any of the old-money Americans she'd encountered. For another, he was unlike any of the other men she interacted with at university. He was a man, a real man, for a start, not a boy barely edging into his twenties.

In his perfectly cut custom suit he was daunting to say the least. Add the fact that his face was objectively the most beautiful masculine work of art she'd ever seen, and she found herself unable to speak. That never happened. She'd learned early on that if she wanted to im-

prove her position in life she would have to attack her goals with single-mindedness. She could never afford to look like she didn't belong, because people would be all too willing to believe her. So she had cultivated confidence from the beginning.

It deserted her then. All her words drying up completely.

"It's nice to meet you," he said, not offering her his hand, but rather a simple incline of his head. "I have read your file, and taken the recommendation of my advisor into consideration. However, I did not follow the advice. I merely took it under consideration."

She frowned, not entirely sure what to make of the comment. "Really?"

"Yes. A fact you should be grateful for, as he felt you were a bit too pretty to serve my needs."

Her face burned. But it wasn't with anger, as it should have been. Well, there was a bit of anger, but also a wave of excitement that had no business being there. "I was not aware my looks had anything to do with whether or not I would be a qualified assistant."

"They don't. Not to me. Though, I imagine his concerns center squarely around my younger brother, Andres, not me."

She was well educated on the royal family. Applying for a job at the palace without proper knowledge would be foolish. She was well familiar with Prince Andres and his reputation with women. She was also immune to such things. She was focused. She'd been accused of having tunnel vision by people who were nice, and of being frigid by people who weren't. None of it bothered her. She had goals. And once she reached those goals she could ex-

*pand her horizons. Until then, she would move on with
a single-minded focus and make apologies to no one.*

No, Prince Andres didn't concern her.

*The fact that some of her focus had splintered the
moment she'd seen Prince Kairos concerned her a little
bit. But that was an anomaly. Nothing to be concerned
about. She would be back to normal as soon as she became accustomed to him, to the surroundings. Assuming
she had a chance to do so.*

"There's no need to be concerned," she said.

"You haven't met him yet."

*"I don't need to meet him. I have not gotten as far
as I have in my life by being silly, or easily seduced by
princes. I'm here because this is not the kind of work experience that can be matched. I'm here because of what
this will do for my résumé in the future. I'm not here to
become the subject of tabloid gossip."*

*He smiled and the expression echoed in her stomach.
"Then congratulations. I would like to hire you." And
there he stood, extending his hand.*

*She stood as well, wrapping her fingers firmly around
his, ignoring the zip of heat that passed between them.
She had just told him that she had no desire to become
tabloid fodder, and she would not be undermined by betraying the fact that his touch affected her.*

She buried it. Buried it down as deep as it would go.

"Excellent."

"Very. If you're ready, I can show you to your quarters."

"Do you need me to escort you?"

Tabitha blinked, coming back to the present sharply.
"No. You can send my things up later. I'm assuming you
had my things packed."

"No," he said. "However, your room should be stocked with all the amenities you might require."

"Translated into direct English, please, rather than your particular brand of doublespeak."

"I called ahead. Clothing, makeup and other toiletries should be delivered shortly. To the room of your choosing. There are no servants in residence at this house, that's part of the attraction to it."

"I wouldn't know, as this is the first time I've ever been here."

"I haven't been here since we were married, as you well know. I've been busy running the country."

"You're right. I am well aware."

She turned away from him then and walked up the stairs, acutely aware of his dark gaze following her every move. She didn't know why he should watch her with such attention now, when he had certainly never done so before.

She stiffened her posture and continued on, as though she were completely unaware of his attentions. She'd spent a very long time pretending she didn't notice how little he saw her. This should be no different.

She scoffed when she reached the landing and looked down the expansive corridor. There were a dozen rooms on this floor, at least. He had made it sound different somehow. Talking about his room being at the end of the hall, saying there were no servants in residence. Still, she should have known that his family owned nothing modest.

She selected the first door, if only because it would be the farthest away from him.

It was white like the rest of the rooms in the house. A four-poster bed was at the center, with gauzy, pale fabric draped over the carved wooden spires. The floor was marble with a plush rug at the center. The only color was provided by a jade vase positioned on a table set against the far wall, with bright cheery crimson flowers bursting from it. She wanted to take the vase, and the flowers, and hurl it to the ground.

Its very existence made her angry. As though it were trying to tell her she should be happy to be here. As though it were trying to prove that this was a wonderful, beautiful place.

Most of all, it made her furious because she had to wonder if this was the only room that contained flowers. If her husband had known she would choose this one because of its proximity, or lack thereof, to his room.

If he knew her so well, while not knowing her at all.

Suddenly, a wave of exhaustion washed over her. She was pregnant. Kairos had all but kidnapped her and brought her to an island. He wanted to negotiate, or terminate her parental rights.

She stumbled over to the plush bed, sinking down onto the covers. She felt weighted down by despair, as though her clothing were woven together with thread fashioned from lead. She closed her eyes, letting the bed pull her in as her clothing pushed her down. Her head was swimming with thoughts, confused, present and distant. Mainly, though, as she drifted off, she thought of Kairos. Of the day he asked her to be more than his assistant.

"Two weeks, Tabitha. The wedding was to be in two weeks' time. Now there is a video all over the internet of Francesca and Andres having my wedding night without me." Kairos's hands shook as he relayed the story, a

glass of scotch in his hand, his normally completely cool demeanor fractured.

His dark hair was disheveled as though he had been running his hands through it, his tie loosened. She had so rarely seen her enigmatic boss appearing to be anything beyond perfectly composed that Tabitha's resolve, built over the past three years of working for him, was tested. And was failing.

She had become accustomed to the taciturn man who walked into his office in the morning, barking orders, setting about the workday with efficiency that was swift, brutal and beautiful to behold.

This man, this man who seemed tested beyond his limits, was a stranger to her. Brought her right back to square one.

"What are you going to do?" she asked.

"You're my personal assistant, I thought you might assist me."

She laughed, her stomach tightening. "Well, cheating fiancées and doomed royal weddings aren't really my forte."

"I thought everything was your forte," he said, treating her to a look that burned her down to her toes.

"After the wedding I'm leaving. You're going to have another assistant. You're going to have to get a little bit more self-sufficient." It was probably the wrong time to bring that up, but she felt somewhat desolate about it. But she was done with university now, she had a business degree and had achieved most of it remotely while acting as Kairos's assistant, a special privilege given to her since she'd been selected for the job.

She should be excited. Looking forward to the change this would bring. To the advantage she would have with a degree from a prestigious school and three years of work experience for the royal family of Petras.

Instead, she felt as though she was being ripped away from her home. Felt as though she would be leaving a part of herself behind.

"I don't want another assistant," he said, his voice rough.

"That's just the alcohol and the emotional distress talking," she said.

"Perhaps. But nothing says that alcohol and emotional distress aren't honest."

"Probably more honest than the general state of things."

"Probably." He studied her hard. "I like you," he said, "I want you to know that."

Her stomach tightened further, her breath rushing from her lungs in a gust. "Well, that's flattering."

"You have been the perfect assistant, Tabitha. You have more poise than many women who were raised by kings. You are smart, diplomatic, and most importantly, you have not slept with my brother. Or, if you have, it wasn't captured on video."

She thought of the devastatingly handsome Prince Andres, and felt nothing. Kairos was the only man who had ever tested her resolve. And he never even tried. "I can honestly tell you that Andres has never so much as tempted me."

"Is there anything you do not excel at? Any skeletons in your closet?"

"I... You read my résumé."

"Yes. If you recall, I read yours and that of several hundred other hopefuls. You were indeed the most suitable. Beyond that which I could have ever anticipated."

He set his glass of scotch down on his desk. "I don't know why I didn't see it before."

She couldn't breathe. God help her, she couldn't breathe. "See what?"

"Tabitha. I think you should marry me."

"Tabitha, are you well?"

Tabitha started at the sound of Kairos's voice. It was rare for her to be woken up by him. In fact, she couldn't recall if she ever had been. He didn't spend the night with her. He never had.

She opened her eyes, bright afternoon light filtering into her vision. She suddenly remembered where she was. Remembered that it was not that day when he first proposed, or any of the days in between that she'd spent as his wife. No, it was now. She was carrying his baby. They were divorcing.

The hopeful little ember that burned in her stomach, thanks to that dream, that memory, cooled.

"Not especially," she said, pushing into a sitting position and scrubbing her hands over her eyes.

Suddenly, she felt self-conscious, childish because of the gesture. She was not in the habit of waking up in front of him. For all that they had a physical relationship, they had very little intimacy.

She dropped her hands to her sides, balling them into fists.

"I brought your clothing up. And everything else."

"Did you…" She looked around the room. "Did you put it all away?"

"Yes. I was hardly going to ask you to do it. And as I said before, there are no servants in residence here."

"You don't have any service at all?"

"I occasionally employ the services of a chef. But for the purposes of this trip, some preprepared meals were brought along with your things."

"It's just you and me, then?"

He nodded, his dark gaze unreadable. "Yes."

"On the whole island?"

"On the whole island," he confirmed.

"Oh."

"What?"

"I don't think we've ever...really been alone before."

"We are very often alone," he said, frowning.

"In a palace filled with hundreds, in a building other people live in."

"I have never kidnapped you before either. You've also never been pregnant with my baby. Oh, yes, and we have never been on the brink of divorce. So, a season of firsts. How nice to add this to the list."

She stood up, stretching out her stiff muscles. "Where exactly do you get off being angry at me? We are here because of you."

"I'm angry with you because this divorce is happening at your demand."

"Had I not demanded we divorce, I wouldn't be pregnant."

"Had you not frozen me out of your bed perhaps you would have been pregnant a couple of months sooner."

She gritted her teeth, reckless heat pouring through her veins. "How dare you?" She advanced on him, and he wrapped his arm around her waist, pulling her close. "Don't."

Her protest was cut off by the press of his mouth against hers, hot and uncompromising, his tongue staking a claim as he took her deep, hard. She had no idea where these kinds of kisses had come from. Who this man was. This man who would spirit her away to a private island. Who kissed her like he was dying and her lips held his salvation.

It stood out in such sharp contrast to that kiss on their wedding night. The first time they had been alone in a bedroom like this. His kiss had been gentle then. Cool. She had waited for this moment. For heat to explode between them. Because she felt it. She had always felt it. It had been there from the moment she first walked into his office, no matter how hard she might try to deny it.

But everything he'd done had been so maddeningly measured, so unreasonably controlled. She had been shaking, from the inside out. With nerves, with desire. He had been gentle. Circumspect.

He left the lights off. That surprised her, because she had imagined that he would prefer to see her. At least, she had imagined that men preferred such things. She had no experience with them, and suddenly she regretted it. She hadn't. Never. Until now. Now, she was married to Kairos. She was his princess. She was his wife. And she had no idea how to please him.

They had two weeks to adjust to the idea of marrying each other, and during that two weeks he hadn't touched her. He had waited, because he'd said there was no point in doing anything differently. Not when it was so close. Not when he had the chance to do right by her.

She had told him, of course, that she was a virgin. In case he found the idea appalling in some way. In case he disliked the idea of being with a woman who had no practical experience. He had not been appalled. But it was then he'd insisted they wait.

So here she was, a bride dressed in white, and all that it symbolized, married to a man she didn't love. A man who did not love her, about to find out what all the fuss was about.

She might not love Kairos, but she was attracted to him. In her mind, this was ideal in many ways. She didn't love him. But she respected him. She cared for him. She was attracted to him. They had everything pleasant going for them, and nothing outrageous or unpleasant. Nothing that would turn them into the kinds of screaming monsters her parents had become under the influence of love and passion.

And so she waited. Waited for him to close the distance between them. But he was in no hurry. Finally, he crossed the room, a dark silhouette. She could see him working his tie, removing his jacket, his shirt. She could see nothing of his body, but she could tell that he was naked by the time he reached her. It was then that he kissed her. Cool, slow. Different to how she had imagined.

His skin was hot, but his movements were chilled and deliberate. He divested her of her gown quickly, making no ceremony of it. His touch was skilled, easily calling out a response in her as he teased her between her thighs, stroked his thumb over her nipples. But it was happening quickly, and she didn't know what she was supposed to do. Didn't understand her part in it. And he gave her no hints. He had her on her back quickly, testing her readiness with his fingers. Sliding one inside her first, then another, stretching her. He did this for a while, as though he were counting the time. As though he had read a textbook on how to make a woman's first time hurt as little as possible.

Then he settled between her thighs and pushed into

her quickly. She gritted her teeth against the pain, biting her lip to keep from digging her fingernails into his skin. She didn't have an orgasm.

He did. Of course he did.

He withdrew quickly after that, moving into the bathroom and starting a bath for her. Then he returned, ushering her in, waiting until she was submerged in the water before meeting her gaze. "I imagine you want some time alone."

No. She absolutely did not want time alone. She wanted him to hold her because she was pretty sure she was going to break apart. He had changed something deep inside of her. And he hadn't finished. She was shattered, but she wasn't remade.

"Yes," she heard herself saying, not sure where the response had come from.

"I'll see you in the morning."

She snapped back to the present, to this moment. To this kiss that bore no resemblance to anything that had occurred on that night. He had accused her of changing, but he wasn't the same either.

He kissed her neck, down to her collarbone, retracing that same path with the tip of his tongue. She found herself tearing at his shirt, her heart thundering hard, every fiber of her being desperate to have him. Desperate to have him inside her again. Like that night in his office. That night when the promise that had been broken on their wedding night was finally fulfilled.

I feel nothing.

His words from that night reached between them, hit her with the impact of a slap.

She pushed away from him, breathing hard. "Don't."

"You want to," he said, his words cutting and far too true.

"So? We don't have to do everything we want." She, of all people, truly shouldn't. "Anyway, I know from experience that sex with you produces a host of regrets."

"Do you regret being pregnant?"

"How can you not regret it? You're going to find a new wife." She disentangled herself from his hold, moving away from him, over to the window, turning her focus out to the view. Out to the sea below. "Having your heir belong to the wrong woman must be an upsetting prospect."

"Not especially. Because I do not intend to divorce you."

"Why?"

"You are having my child. There is no reason for me to marry another. None at all."

"So, you're suggesting we simply...*ignore* our marriage?"

"If you prefer. I should like to reach some kind of agreement with you, but you have been very unreasonable lately."

"And you have been a cold fish for the last five years."

She found herself being tugged back up against him, his lips crashing down on hers. He gripped her chin with his thumb and forefinger, his dark eyes blazing into hers. "Did that feel cold to you?" he ground out after they separated.

"You contrary man. Why do you only want something once it's been taken from you?"

He drew back as though she had slapped him. "I..."

"You can't deny it. And you don't have an answer."

His expression went blank. "If you regret the pregnancy, perhaps you should simply turn custody of the child over to me."

Everything inside of her screamed at the thought. "You misunderstand me," she bit out. "I don't regret having a child. I regret having *your* child. It would have been better for me to wait to get pregnant until I could find a man that I actually wanted to spend my life with."

He took a step back, his eyes filled with rage. His face, normally so controlled, normally schooled into such a careful, neutral expression, telegraphed every bit of his anger. "Such a pity then that it is my child you carry. Dinner is served in an hour. If you do not join me you can starve."

"Are you going to lock the kitchen?"

"I may yet. Do not test me, Tabitha, for you will not like the result." He turned, walking out of the room, slamming the door hard behind him.

He had commanded that she not test him. And so that was exactly what she intended to do.

CHAPTER SIX

KAIROS COULD NOT fathom his own behavior. But then, he could not understand Tabitha's either. He had given her more credit than this. Had chosen her to be his wife because she was smart, faithful, levelheaded. Because she had served him as his assistant for years and never given him reason to distrust him. During his engagement to Francesca he had thought he might forge something of an emotional connection with her. His trust had been misplaced. Francesca had betrayed him with Andres.

He owed Andres a fair amount of anger for that. Both of them, really. And yet, he had never been able to muster much of it up. He was only grateful he had discovered Francesca's duplicity prior to making vows to her. And it had given him a chance to find someone better. To re-evaluate what he expected out of marriage.

Women, it turned out, betrayed you eventually.

Well, you, specifically.

He took in a sharp breath, looking out through the living room at the terrace, at the table that was set with dinner for both of them. If she didn't come down…

He was seized with an image of himself storming back upstairs, flinging the door open, throwing her over his shoulder and carrying her down to the dinner table. Failing that, perhaps he would just throw her on the bed and finish what they had started earlier.

He gritted his teeth, battling against the erotic images that were battering against his mind's eye. Threatening to shatter his control. He had already behaved appallingly where she was concerned, and he would not compound his sins.

Why not? She left you. The one thing she promised she would not do.

He hated this. This feeling of helplessness. She inspired it in him more often than any other human being on the planet. From the first day they had married. He had never felt any hint of awkwardness around her when she was his PA. And he'd been determined to hang on to that relationship. That meeting of the minds, the mutual understanding, that felt so right. It had made her the best assistant he'd ever had. By all rights, a nineteen-year-old from Middle America should never have been able to serve him the way that she had. And yet, for three years, she had been by far the most efficient and hard-working PA he'd ever had.

She'd transcended her circumstances and risen to the occasion. He imagined she would do that as a wife as well.

Though, it was disingenuous to pretend that all of the unforeseen issues fell on her shoulders. Their disastrous wedding night had been his fault.

He hadn't satisfied her. He had hurt her. And with his actions, it felt as though he had built a wall between them. Yes, a certain amount of distance was desirable. He didn't want to become emotionally entangled with her. Not with feelings that went beyond cordial affection.

But when they had entered her suite, and his lips had touched hers for the first time without an audience, something had shifted inside of him. The rock wall he had built up around his control was cracking, crumbling. He had felt...a deep ache that had transcended anything he could remember feeling in recent years. A desire for something that he couldn't put a name to. Like seeing something familiar, shrouded in fog. Something that called to him, echoed inside of him, but that he couldn't identify.

Frustrating. Terrifying.

He went into the bathroom, running some hot water. She would probably be sore. He had done his best to make it as painless as possible, since he had known it was her first time, but he knew he had failed, on more than one level.

She didn't seem happy with him, when he ushered her into the bathroom.

He stood there, watching her as she submerged herself. It was a strange thing, seeing her naked now after so many years of looking at her as nothing more than an employee. Now she was exposed. Uncovered. He had been inside of her body...

He felt his own body stir in response to that memory. He had to go. Until he could get a handle on his response to her, he had to leave.

Unless she asked him to stay.

But he would not force that issue. Not after he had handled their first time so badly.

"I suppose you want some time alone?" he asked.

She shifted beneath the water, drawing her knees up to her chest and looking down. "Yes."

Her words rebuilt some of the wall inside of him. It

was good. It reminded him of why distance was impera-
tive. Why control mattered.

"I'll see you in the morning."

He walked out of the bathroom and dressed quickly in
her room, before leaving and heading to his own quar-
ters. Once he was inside, he stripped his clothing off
again, heading straight for the shower. He turned the
cold knob as far as it would go, stepping beneath the icy
spray, gritting his teeth.

He would not repeat the same mistakes again.

He would not.

"I'm here." Tabitha's voice drew his attention to the top
of the stairs. She was there, looking more beautiful than
he could ever remember. Was this change happening inside of her beginning to affect her appearance? Her blond
hair was loose, bouncing around her shoulders. So different to the usual restrained bun she often chose to wear.

Her dress was also completely unlike anything she
would've worn back at the palace. But then, the instructions he'd left for the personal shopper tasked with amass-
ing a small wardrobe for her here in the island hadn't
been any more explicit than her size.

The dress had skinny straps and a deep V that made
the whole gown appear to be resting precariously over
her full breasts. It looked as if the slightest tug would
snap those straps and see the dress falling down around
her waist, settling on her voluptuous hips. She had applied a bare minimum of makeup, a light pink gloss to
her lips, a bit of gold on her eyes. It was a more relaxed
look than he was accustomed to seeing.

His body responded with a hunger that was becoming predictable.

"I'm glad you decided to join me."

"Well, now you won't need to put a lock on the pantry."

She began her descent, her delicate hand resting on the banister. His eyes were drawn to her fingers, to her long, elegant fingernails, painted a delicate coral that matched her dress.

"I'm pleased to hear that, *agape*."

"Don't call me that," she said, her tone sharp.

"What?"

"*Love*. It's always been a little bit of a farcical endearment, but it just stings all the more at the moment."

She breezed past him, heading outside to where the table was set for them. He followed after her, trying not to allow that helpless sensation to overtake him again. How did she do this to him? He ruled an entire nation. He was the master of his, and every domain, within its borders. Somehow she made him feel as inept as a schoolboy who didn't even have dominion over his own bedtime.

"I am sorry, I shall try to endeavor not to call you nice things," he said through clenched teeth.

She paused, looking over her shoulder, one pale eyebrow raised. "Just don't call me things you don't mean."

It was hard to think of a political response to that. Of course he didn't love her.

He cared for her, certainly. There was nothing duplicitous about his lack of emotion. He had made that clear when he proposed to her that afternoon in his office after his engagement to Francesca had blown all to hell. He had outlined exactly what the relationship between Tabitha and himself would be. Had told her he intended to base it upon the mutual respect they had for each other.

That thought, of just how honest he'd been, of how she had known fully, and agreed to this, reignited his anger.

And he forgot to search for the political response.

"Actually, my queen," he said, "I could instead call you exactly what you are. Not a queen. Simply a woman that I elevated far beyond her station. Far beyond what she was equipped to handle."

"Are you going to malign my blood now you've mixed your royal lineage with it? Perhaps you should have thought of that before you used my body as the vessel for your sacred heir."

She continued to walk ahead of him, her shoulders stiff. She took her place at the table, without waiting for him to come and hold her chair out for her. For some reason, the lack of ceremony annoyed him. Perhaps because it was yet more evidence of this transformation from his perfect, biddable wife, into this *creature*.

It wasn't perfect. And you know it.

He didn't like that thought. It only damaged the narrative he was constructing in his mind about the truth of his marriage. The one that absolved him from any wrongdoing.

The one that said he had told her how their marriage would work, and now she had an issue with it. That, the fact she had been warned, meant that now the fault rested on her alone.

It allowed him to open up all sorts of boxes inside of him, boxes he normally kept closed, locked tight, and pull out all the hurt and anger kept there, examining it, turning it over, holding it close to his chest.

He took his seat across from her, lifting his water to his lips. For a moment, he regretted not serving alcohol out of deference to her condition. She didn't deserve his deference.

"How is it you expected we might discuss things with more success cut off from civilization?"

"For a start," he said, leaning back in his chair, "I very much appreciate having you somewhat captive."

"I'm not sure how I'm supposed to feel about that."

"Oh, don't concern yourself. I'm not worried about how you feel."

"No, of course you aren't. Why start now?"

He set his water glass down hard enough that some of the clear liquid sloshed over the side. "I'm sorry, have I done something recently that conflicted with our initial marriage agreement?"

"You are…" She looked up, as though the clear Mediterranean sky might have some answers. "You're distant. You're cold."

"A great many people might say that about you, *agape*."

"Don't call me that," she said, blue eyes flashing.

"I don't recall agreeing to your edict, Tabitha."

"You want a list? I'm working on a list," she said, ignoring his words. "The only time in five years you ever bothered to get angry with me was when I told you I was going to leave you."

"You *want* me to get angry with you?"

"I want you to feel *something*. Anger would be a start."

"You have your wish. I am exceedingly angry with you."

"You barely speak to me. You only touch me when attempting to conceive. I am essentially part of the furniture to you. If you could have had an heir with a bureau in possession of childbearing hips, I've no doubt you would have done so."

"The same can be said of the way you treat me. Moreover, I never promised you anything different. What vow have I broken?"

A slash of color bled out over her pale cheekbones. "A woman expects her husband to treat her a certain way."

"Does she? Even when the husband told her exactly how things would be? If your expectations differ from the reality I lined out for you early on, I fail to see how that's my fault."

"Nobody imagines their marriage is going to be a frozen wasteland."

"A frozen wasteland is exactly what I promised you," he said, his tone biting. "If I had promised to love and cherish you, then I suppose you would have every right to feel cheated. To feel lied to. But I promised you respect, and I promised you fidelity, I promised that I would treat you as an equal. If I have failed on that score then it has only been in the days since you violated the promises *you* made to *me*."

"I know what you said. What *we* said, but... Five years on things feel different. Or they feel like they *should* be."

"I see. Were you ever going to tell me that? Or were you simply going to freeze me out until I was the one who asked for an end to the marriage?"

She curled her fingers into fists, and looked away from him. "That isn't..."

"Do you not enjoy being held accountable for the breakdown of our union, Tabitha? Because if I recall, you spent the past five years doing much the same thing you accuse me of. If an honest word has ever passed between us, I would be surprised. Did you think I didn't notice that you have grown increasingly distant? Did you think it didn't bother me?"

"Yes, Kairos, I imagined that it didn't bother you. Why

would I ever assume that you cared about there being any closeness between us?"

"Because there was a time when I at least called you a friend."

Her golden brows shot upward. "Did you? Do you consider me a friend?"

"You know that I did. I assume you remember the day that I proposed to you."

"Oh, you mean the day that you watched a video of the woman you had chosen to marry having dirtier sex with your brother than I imagine you ever had with her? The day that you—drunkenly—told me you thought I would be a better choice to be your queen? I find it difficult to put much stock into anything you said that day."

"Then that's your mistake. Because I was sincere. I told you that we could build a stronger foundation than Francesca and I ever could. I told you that I had been having doubts about her even before her betrayal."

"Yes, that's right, you did. And why were you having doubts, exactly?"

"The way you behaved…it was such a stark contrast to Francesca, even on her best of days. I found myself wishing that it was you. When we traveled together, when I went to you to discuss affairs of the state…I found myself wishing that you were the one I was going to marry. I respected your opinion. And I felt like I could ask you questions, when with everyone else I had to simply know the answers."

He felt stripped bare saying these things now, without the buffer of alcohol, five years older and a lot more jaded than he had been then. But she needed to hear them. She needed to hear them again, clearly.

"And while it is a very nice sentiment, it isn't exactly

the proposal every girl dreams of," she said, her tone brittle.

"It seems very much that you are angry with yourself for accepting a proposal you now deem beneath you. How high you have risen. That the proposal of a king is no longer good enough for you."

"Maybe I am the one who changed. But people do change."

"Only because they forget. You forget that you are going to have to leave my palace, leave Petras, search for a job. Struggle financially. Perhaps even face the life that you were so eager to leave behind. Marriage to me offered you instant elevation. The kind of status that you craved."

"Don't," she said, "you make me sound like I was nothing more than a gold digger."

"Oh, you would have done all right finding gold on your own. But validation? Status? For a piece of white trash from Nowhere, USA, that is a great deal more difficult to come by."

She stood, shoving her plate toward the center of the table. "I don't have to listen to you insulting me."

"You want me to call you something honest. Though, I hasten to remind you that I learned these words from you. This is what you think of yourself. You told me."

"Because I trusted you. Clearly, my own fault."

"No, I think I was the one who was foolish to trust you."

"We could go back and forth for days. But it doesn't solve anything. It doesn't erase the fact that I think we're better off apart. We should never have been a couple, Kairos, and you know it. As you said, I'm little more than a piece of white trash from a tiny town. You're the king of an entire nation. You wanted to marry someone else."

"You might be right. But it's too late for regrets. We are married to each other. And more than that, you're carrying my child."

"Plenty of people work out custody arrangements."

He stood, knocking his chair backward and not caring when it hit the ground with a very loud thump. "And do those people still want each other? Do they exist constantly on the verge of tearing each other's clothes off and having each other on the nearest surface?"

The pink in her cheeks intensified. "You can only speak for yourself on that score."

"Really? I don't think that's true." He was suddenly gripped by lust, lust that mingled with the ever-present anger in his chest. He wasn't sure whether he wanted to yell at her, or press her against the wall and claim her body again. Both. He wanted both. Even though neither made sense. "You want me."

"Go to hell." They were the harshest words he'd ever heard on her lips. So much sweeter than the sophisticated chill had ever been.

"There. There at least, some honesty. Perhaps you should try it more often."

"I gave you honesty."

"Your version of honesty was a list of complaints that you could have, and should have voiced years ago. Ideally, before you accepted my proposal. What changed? What changed that you can no longer stand what you agreed would be enough to make a marriage?"

His words hit her with the force of the slap. And she just stood there, reeling. Tears prickled her eyes, her tongue was frozen. He was making too much sense. Making too good a case for how aggrieved he was by her request for divorce. He was right. She had not spoken an honest word to him. She hadn't asked him for what she wanted. Hadn't told him she was unhappy.

But she didn't know how to do it without opening herself up, and reviewing bits and pieces of pain that were best left hidden. Didn't know how to do it without confronting her fears. And anyway, she hadn't imagined that he would care.

She hadn't trusted herself enough to voice them. To deal with them.

She wasn't sure she trusted herself now.

"It isn't what I wanted," she said, her voice hollow.

"You just said what you wanted changed."

"Yes. No. It isn't that simple," she said, panic gripping her neck, making it impossible for her to breathe.

"It seems fairly straightforward to me, *agape*, but then, I do not know much about the inner workings of the female mind. Throughout my life I have seen women act in ways that are inexplicable to me. My mother walking away from her position at the palace, Francesca compromising our union for a bit of stolen pleasure. You divorcing me. So, it comes as no surprise to me that I do not understand what you're trying to tell me now."

"You don't know everything about my past," she said.

It was for the best that he didn't. Best that he never did. She looked back on the Tabitha she'd been, before university, before she'd put distance between herself and her family, and saw a stranger.

But he didn't seem to know the Tabitha she was now. And she didn't know how to make him. Didn't know how to make him understand who she was. *Why* she was.

She didn't even know if it would change anything.

If nothing else, it would show him. Why he should let her go. Why she wasn't suitable. And it would remind her too.

"Do I not know you?"

"No. I know you did some cursory searching, as far as I was concerned. My name. But you don't know everything. In part because I don't have the same last name as my mother, nor is her name the same as the one listed on my birth certificate, not anymore. I don't share a name with my stepfather either. Not having those names excludes quite a lot from a cursory search. Of course, you found nothing objectionable about me. Nothing but good marks in school, no criminal record, no scandal."

"Because that's all that mattered," he said, something odd glittering in his black eyes.

"Yes. It is all that mattered. You were only looking for what might cause problems with my reputation, for you, as far as the public eye was concerned. You weren't actually looking for anything real or meaningful about me."

"Come off your high horse, Tabitha. Obviously you didn't care whether or not I found anything meaningful out about you, because you deliberately concealed it from me."

She lifted her shoulder, her stomach sinking. "I can't argue with that. I can't argue with a great many of the accusations leveled at me today. I wasn't honest with you. I didn't tell you. I preferred to run away, rather than telling you what I wanted. But a lot of it is because… I don't actually know what I want. I started feeling dissatisfied with our relationship, and wanting more. And that confused me."

"Well, hell, if you're confused, what chance do I have?"

"I can't answer that question," she said, sounding defeated. Feeling defeated. "I don't know the answer. All I know is that I never thought I would marry. Then I met you, and I can't deny that I felt...attraction. It confused me. I had spent years getting through college, school of every kind, really, with a single-minded focus. I wanted to be better than my birth. I knew that education was the only way to accomplish that. I set about to get good grades, high test scores, so that I could earn scholarships. And I did that. I knew that if I split my focus, I wouldn't be able to. Then the internship at the palace came up, and I knew I had to seize it. I didn't have connections, I didn't have a pedigree. I knew that I needed a leg up in order to get the kind of job that I wanted."

"I imagine, ultimately, the chance to become queen of the nation was too great a temptation to pass up?"

She laughed, hardly able to process the surreal quality of it all even now. "I guess so. It was a lot of things. A chance to have you, physically, which I wanted. A chance to achieve a status that I'd never even imagined in my wildest dreams. I'm from nothing. Nothing and nowhere, and I wanted something more. And that... How could I refuse? Especially because your criteria suited mine so well. You see, Kairos, I didn't want love either. I didn't want passion."

"You said you were attracted to me."

"I was. I am. I suppose that's something I can't deny now. But I thought perhaps I could just touch the flames without being consumed by them. Then I realized that holding your fingertips over a blaze for five years is nothing more than a maddening exercise in torture. You're better off plunging yourself in or disengaging."

"And you chose to disengage?"

"Yes. I know that I can't afford to throw myself in."

"Why is that?"

"Reasons I haven't told you. Things you don't know."

"I'm not playing twenty questions with you, Tabitha, either tell me your secrets, or put them away. Pretend they don't matter as you did all those years. Jump into the fire, or back away."

Her throat tightened, her palms sweating. She hadn't thought about that day in years. She had turned it into a lesson, an object, a cautionary tale. But the images of the day, the way that it had smelled, the weather. The sounds her stepfather had made as he bled out on the floor, the screams of her mother when she realized what had been done... Those things she had blocked out. The entire incident had been carefully formed into a morality tale. Something that served to teach, but something she couldn't feel.

Not anymore.

Use what you need, discard the rest.

"I never wanted passion. Or love. Because...I shouldn't. I'm afraid of what I might be. What I might become. I think I've proven I have the capacity to act recklessly when I'm overtaken by strong emotion," she said, realizing that to him, the admission must seem ridiculous. For years all he had ever seen was the carefully cultivated cool reserve she had spent the better part of her teenage years crafting from blood and other people's consequences.

"Tell me," he said.

She was going to. Her heart was thundering in her ears, a sickening beat that echoed through her body, made her feel weak.

But maybe if she said it, he would understand. Maybe if she said it he would get why what he'd offered had seemed amazing. Why it had felt insufficient. Why she'd chosen to end it instead of asking for more.

"I was walking home from school. I was seventeen at the time. It was a beautiful day. And when I approached the trailer I could already hear them fighting. Not unusual. They fought all the time. My mother was screaming, which she always did. My stepfather was ignoring her. He was drunk, which he very often was."

She didn't let herself go back to that house. Not even in her mind. It was gritty and dirty and full of mold. But more than that. The air was heavy. The ghost of faded love lingering and oppressive, a malevolent spirit that choked the life out of everything it touched.

"I didn't know," Kairos said.

"I know," she said. "I didn't want you to." It stung her pride, to admit how low she'd started. To admit that she had no idea who her biological father was to a man for whom genetics was everything.

She was a bastard, having a royal baby. It seemed wrong somehow.

You always knew it would be this way. Why are you panicking now that it's too late?

Because the idea of it was one thing, the reality of it— all of it—her marriage, her past, her life, was different.

She'd spent the past year growing increasingly unhappy. And then Andres had married Zara. Watching the two of them physically hurt. It twisted her stomach to see the way they smiled at each other. Put a bitter, horrible taste in her mouth.

Made her feel a kind of heaviness she hadn't felt since she'd stood in that grimy little trailer.

"Tell me," he said, an order, because Kairos didn't know how to ask for things any other way.

"She kept screaming at him to listen. But he never did. She was so angry. She left the room. I thought she was going to pack, she did that a lot, even though she never left. Or that maybe she'd given up. Gone to take a nap. She did that sometimes too depending on how much she'd had to drink. But she came back. And she had a gun."

CHAPTER SEVEN

A COCKTAIL OF cold dread slithered down into Kairos's stomach. He could hardly credit the words that were coming out of his wife's mouth. Could hardly picture the gentle, sophisticated creature in front of him witnessing anything like this, much less being so tightly connected to it. Tabitha was strong. She possessed a backbone of steel, one he had witnessed on more than one occasion. When it came to handling foreign dignitaries, or members of the government and Petras, she was cool, calm and poised. When it came to organizing his schedule, and defending her position on hot-button issues, she never backed down.

But for all that she possessed that strength, there was something so smooth and fragile about her too. As though she were a porcelain doll, one that he was afraid to play with too roughly. For fear he might break her.

If she were that breakable, you would have shattered her on your desk.

Yes, that was true. He had not thought about her fertility then. Had not taken care with her, as he had always done in the past.

But still, he hadn't thought in that moment. He simply

acted. This revelation challenged perceptions that he had never examined. Not deeply.

"What happened?" he asked, trying to keep his voice level.

"She shot him," Tabitha said, the words distant and matter-of-fact. Her expression stayed placid, as though she were discussing the contents of the menu for a dinner at the palace. "She was very sorry that she did it. Because he didn't get back up. He died. And she was sent to jail. I don't visit her."

She spoke the last item on the list as though it were the gravest sin of all. As though the worst thing of all was that she had distanced herself from her mother, not that her mother was a murderer.

"You *saw* all this," he said, that same shell he had accused her of having wrapping itself around his own veins now, hardening them completely.

"Yes. It was a long time ago," she said, her voice sounding as if it was coming straight out of that distant past. "Eleven…twelve years ago now? I'm not sure."

"It doesn't matter how long ago it was, you still saw it."

"I don't like to think about it," she said, her blue eyes locking with his, looking at him for the first time since she had started telling her gruesome story. "I don't think you can blame me for that."

"No, not at all," he said.

"It wasn't relevant to our union. Not relevant to whether or not I would be good for the position."

"Except it clearly was, as I think it is probably related to the action you have taken now."

She looked down. "I can't argue with that. I was growing frustrated in our relationship, and I don't like to give those feelings any foothold on my life. I don't like to allow them free rein."

"Surely you don't think you're going to find a gun and shoot me?"

"I'm sure my mother didn't think she would do that either," Tabitha said, starting to pace, her hands clasped in front of her. She was picking at the polish on her fingernails, something he had never seen her do before. It was then he noticed that she wasn't wearing her ring. How had he missed it before?

Perhaps you were too wrapped up in imagining those fingers wrapped around your member to notice.

He gritted his teeth. Yes, that was the problem. Whatever had exploded between them was stealing his ability to think clearly.

"Where is your ring?"

She stopped thinking and looked at her fingernails. "I took it off."

"It was very expensive," he said, though that was not his concern at all, and he wasn't sure why he was pretending that it was.

"I know. But it is also mine. That was part of our prenuptial agreement if you recall."

"I don't need the money, I was just concerned something might have happened to it."

"It's in a safe. In a bank. It's fine. But there is no point in me wearing it when I'm not your wife. I would hate to start gossip in the press."

"We already have."

"Imagine the gossip if they knew my past as well."

"Enough. No one is going to find out. Because I will not tell. Anyway, it is not a reflection on you."

"Isn't it? My genetics. Our child's genetics."

"If blood determined everything I would be a tyrant or absent." He didn't like to speak of his parents. Talking about his father, and his rages, was much simpler than talking about his mother, who was not there at all. But either way, it was a topic he preferred not to broach.

"Well, you're neither of those things," she said, "but Andres isn't exactly well-adjusted."

Kairos laughed, thinking of his brother and the large swath of destruction Andres had spent the first thirty years of his life cutting through the kingdom, through Kairos's own life. "He has settled, don't you think?"

Tabitha laughed. "I suppose he has. I'm not quite sure how they managed. A real marriage. Especially out of their circumstances. If any marriage came about in a stranger way than ours, it's theirs."

"Zara is not exactly conventional. Or suitable," Kairos said.

Tabitha looked up at him, deep, fathomless emotion radiating from her blue eyes. "Perhaps I should have been more unsuitable?"

Her words made his heart twist, made his stomach tighten. "Tabitha, I cannot imagine the things you have seen," he said. He wasn't sure why he said it. But then, he didn't know what else to say.

"I'm the same person."

The same person from before she had told him about her experience, he knew that was what she meant. But for him it only highlighted the fact that he didn't truly know her at all. She was right. The Tabitha who had witnessed the murder of her stepfather was the same woman he had been married to for the past five years. The same woman he had known for nearly a decade.

But he didn't *know* her. Not really. How could he? She

was all things soft, beautiful and contained, and he had imagined she had grown that way, like a plant that had only ever experienced life in a hothouse.

It turned out she had been forged in the elements. An orchid put to the test in a blizzard. And she had come out of it alive. Beautiful. Seemingly untouched.

It humbled him in a strange way.

"We do not know each other," he said.

"I've been saying that," she said.

"Yes, you have been. But I didn't realize how true it was until now. You know *my* life, so I did not imagine there were such secrets between us."

"We don't talk about your life," she said, "not beyond what you had for dinner last night."

He couldn't argue with the truth of that statement. "There is nothing to tell. The evidence of my life is before you. You have seen who I am by my actions. I don't see the point in rehashing how I felt when my mother left."

"You felt something," she said, her voice muted.

"Of course I did," he said. The very thought opened up a pit of despair inside of him. Helplessness. And a dark, black rage he would rather not acknowledge lived within him. "We are strangers."

"Strangers who have sex," Tabitha added.

"Yes," he said, "certainly. And yet, I'm not even entirely certain I know your body."

Her cheeks turned pink. "You did all right with it last month."

"And the times before that?" This line of questioning was not pleasant for him. What man liked calling his own prowess into question? But it wasn't so simple as prowess. He had the ability, but he'd always held back with her. Always.

That was the very beginning of where he had gone wrong. He had imagined that he needed to go slowly, that he needed to mitigate the passion between them.

The truth of it was he had been attracted to her from the moment she walked into his office. Even during his engagement to Francesca. And while he had never acted on it, it had been there, shimmering beneath the surface like waves of heat over the sand. He wanted her. He had always wanted her.

He had kept a part of himself closed off because it was so strong. Because, like her, he rejected strong emotion, strong desire.

But perhaps it would be possible to open up the physical, to have that, while keeping the rest of it safe. Perhaps it might give her what she craved. Or at the very least thaw some of the chill that was between them.

"Yes, I did then. Or, maybe my clumsiness was simply covered by the explosion between us," he said.

"There was nothing clumsy about it," she said, the color in her cheeks intensifying.

"I have held back every time we've been together," he said. "Except then."

"Why have you held back?"

"Why have you?"

"I think I explained that." She swallowed visibly. "Anyway, it doesn't matter. We don't work. We've established that."

"Have we?" Desperation clawed at him like a wild beast. "I'm not sure that's true. We've both admitted to holding back. And I think it's safe to say that we're both liars."

"I never lied to you."

"There is one very specific word I can think of in response to that. It has to do with the excrement of a bull."

"Crassness does not suit you, Kairos."

"Or, perhaps it does," he said. "How would you know?"

"I wouldn't. And it isn't my job to know. The function of ex-wives is just to walk off into the distance and spend all of your money. It isn't to know you."

"All right," he said, an idea pushing its way into the forefront of his mind even as the words exited his mouth. "You will be free to do so. But I have conditions."

She frowned. "What are you talking about? We both know I don't actually get any of your money."

"It doesn't have to be that way. The prenuptial agreement is very rigid. And I am a man of means. It is unreasonable of me to withhold a portion of that from you after all you have…suffered at my hands. Moreover, you are the mother of my child and therefore a consistent lifestyle will need to be kept whichever household he is staying in at a given time, don't you agree?"

"I don't…I don't understand."

"As I said, there will be conditions to this agreement."

"What do you want?"

What he wanted was for everything to go back as it had been. What he wanted was the wife she had been all those years ago. The wife he had imagined she would be forever. The perfect complement to the man he presented to her, the man he presented to the world. Yes, they were liars, but they had told such compatible lies. Such quiet lies.

This explosion of truth wasn't compatible, and it wasn't quiet. It had left rubble and shrapnel everywhere, the shattered pieces of the life they once had littering the ground in front of them. There was no ignoring it. There would be no putting it back together as it was. But he wouldn't leave it. Wouldn't give up.

They were having a child together. He would not be an absentee father. He would not allow her to be a distant mother. There would be no echoes of his childhood. Not if he had anything to do about it.

And he *did*. He was king, after all.

"Two weeks. I want fourteen days of honesty. I want your body, I want your secrets. I want everything. And if, at the end of that time, you feel like you still don't know me, if then, you feel like you cannot make a life with me, then I will give you your divorce. And with it, much more favorable terms than we originally agreed upon. Money. Housing. Shared custody."

"Why?" She looked stricken, as though he had told her she had to spend two weeks in the dungeon, rather than two weeks with her husband.

"It doesn't matter why. I am your king, and I have commanded it. Now," he took a deep breath, trying to cool the flame that was roaring through his veins. One of triumph. One of arousal. "Either take off your dress, or tell me another secret."

CHAPTER EIGHT

TABITHA'S HEART WAS pounding so hard, she thought she might pass out. She wasn't entirely certain whether she was living in a nightmare, or a fantasy. Kairos did not ask her to take her clothes off. He just didn't. He didn't make demands of her like this at all. And yet, there was no denying that now, her normally cool and controlled husband was looking at her with molten fire in his dark eyes, his gaze intense, uncompromising.

"I'm certain that you did not command me to take my dress off here on the balcony." Retreating into her icy facade was the most comfortable response she could find. After all, the cold didn't bother her. It was this heat, this searing, uncompromising heat that arched between them.

"I am certain that I did." The sun had lowered in the sky some since they had first come outside, and now the rays cut through the palm trees, illuminating his face, throwing his high cheekbones and strong jaw into sharp relief. He looked like a stranger. Not at all like the man she had married. A man who would never have made such a command of her. She was shaking. Shaking from the inside out. Because she had no choice. Had no choice but to accept his devil's bargain. She would be a fool not to. He was offering her a chance to raise her child without struggle, without fighting for custody, without fighting for the bare necessities.

But deeper than that, more shamefully than that, she simply wanted to obey. Even though she could hardly imagine it. Slipping her dress off her body, out here, in the open air, the breeze blowing over her skin. To just let go of everything. Of her control. Of her fear.

"We're the only ones here." His words jolted her out of her fantasy.

He was right, of course, there was no one else here. There was no one to see. But that wasn't what concerned her. The fact that there was no one around only frightened her more. There would be no consequences here. No one to stop them. No perfectly planned and well-ordered events on their calendar to interrupt. No rules, no society, no sense of propriety. There was nothing to stop her from stripping off her clothes, from closing the space between them and wrapping herself around his body, giving herself over to this desperate, gnawing ache that had taken her over completely.

She turned away from him, heading toward the entrance to the villa. She felt the firm hand on her shoulder, and found herself being turned around, pressed against the wall. Her eyes clashed with his, electricity skittering along her veins, collecting in her stomach. "Where do you think you're going?"

"Away from you. Away from here. Because you're crazy."

"Your king gave you an order," he said, his tone shot through with steel. It should make her angry. It should not make her feel restless. Shouldn't make her breasts ache. Shouldn't make her feel slick and ready between her thighs. But he did. *He* did.

His anger, his arrogance—never directed at her before, not like this—was a fresh and heady drug she'd never tried before.

"I see." She swallowed hard. "And will he punish me if I don't comply?"

"I would have to set an example," he said, his tone soft, steady and no less strong.

"For who? As you have already stated, there is no one here."

"For you. For the future. I cannot have you thinking you can simply defy me. Not if this is to work."

"I haven't agreed to—"

He reached up, gripped her chin and held her tight. "You may not have agreed to stay with me forever, *agape*. But you have no choice other than to agree to this two weeks. I do not wish to spend any of that time arguing with you. Not when I could find other uses for your mouth."

She gasped, pressing herself more firmly against the wall, away from him. Erotic images assaulted her mind's eye. Of herself, kneeling before him. Tasting him, taking him into her mouth. She had never done that before. Not with him, not with anyone.

Strange, now she thought about it. Other people traded that particular sex act so casually, and she had never even shared it with her husband.

It didn't disgust her. To the contrary, it intrigued her. Aroused her. And yet, she was shrinking away from him as though she were afraid. She would not be so easily cowed. Would not allow him to claim total control in this way. She was strong. She had not got to where she was in life by folding in on herself. He might be the king, but she was a queen, for God's sake.

"Could you? That would be a first, then." She lifted her hand, curved it around his neck, losing her fingers through his hair. "Shall I get on my knees and bow down before Your Majesty?"

It was his turn to draw back, dark colors slashing his high, well-defined cheekbones. "I did not mean…"

Of course he didn't. He never meant such salacious things. Ever. He had likely only been thinking of a kiss. He probably hadn't even intended for her to take her dress off.

On the heels of that thought, her hand moved to her shoulder and flicked the strap of her dress down. "Words are powerful," she said, pushing at the other strap so they both hung down. "Once they're spoken you can't erase them. Even if you didn't intend for them to be taken in a certain way. Once you speak them, they belong to whoever hears them." She reached behind her back, grabbing a hold of the zipper tab and drawing it down to the middle of her back. The top of her dress fell, exposing her bare breasts to him.

"Tabitha," he growled, his tone a warning.

"What is it? Is my obedience not to your liking? Is this yet another one of our miscommunications?" She pushed the dress down her hips, taking her panties with it, standing before him, naked, and, somehow, not embarrassed.

"You seemed so confident this was what you wanted only a moment ago."

He said nothing as she lowered herself to the patio in front of him. She was shaking. And she wasn't entirely certain if it was the desire or rage. Or if it was some twisted, unholy offspring of the two, taking her over completely. She wasn't entirely certain it mattered. Just as she was sure inexperience wouldn't matter here either.

She didn't know what sorts of things Kairos had done with women before her. They barely talked about their own sex life, so they'd had no reason at all to discuss experiences either of them had had prior to their marriage. Of course, for her, there hadn't been so much as a kiss. As far as he went? He was a mystery to her.

But one thing she knew for certain, if he was as faithful to her as he claimed to be, no one had done this for him in at least five years. Time healed all wounds, and likely erased memories of oral pleasure. At least, she could hope.

She reached up and grabbed hold of his belt buckle, working the leather through the metal clasp. Her hands were shaking, as much from nerves and determination as from desire. It was impossible for her to tell if this was really her defining move in a power play, or if she was simply acting out of need. Out of lust. She supposed that didn't matter either.

He reached down, grabbing a fistful of her hair, stopping her short. "Tabitha. I would not ask this of you."

She looked up at him, at the desperation in his dark eyes, and something twisted, low and painful inside of her. "Why do you think it's a sacrifice?"

"It offers nothing to you."

"Isn't that what this two weeks is about? My service to you?" She immediately regretted the words the moment they left her mouth. That it was too late to call them back. As she had only just said to him, once words were spoken they could not be erased.

"No," he said, his voice rough, "I do not require you to lower yourself in this way."

Her eyes stung, a deep, painful ache that started behind them and worked its way forward. She said nothing. Instead, she tugged his pants and underwear down slightly, exposing his rampant masculinity to her. She didn't often examine his body. More often than not, they made love in the dark. If she ever saw him naked, it was most likely an accident.

Her breath hissed through her teeth as she ran her palm over his hardened length. He was beautiful. Five years, and she had never had the chance to truly appreciate that. Five years and she had never knelt before him in this way, had never even contemplated doing what she was about to do. She had been so determined to keep control, so absolutely hell-bent on maintaining the facade of the perfect ice queen that she'd even allowed her fantasies to become frozen.

She regretted it now, bitterly. Wasted time freezing in the cold when she could have been warm. Like sleeping out in a snowbank only to discover that the front door had been unlocked the whole time, the lit hearth in a warm bed available to her if she had only tried.

Why had she never tried?

She curled her fingers around him, leaning forward and flicking the tip of her tongue out across his heated flesh. His hips flexed forward, a harsh groan escaping his lips. His fist tightened on her hair, so tight it hurt. Yet, she didn't want him to release her. Didn't want him to pull away.

He didn't. And so she kept on. Exploring the entire length of him slowly, relishing the flavor of him. She raised her eyes and met his as she shifted, taking him completely into her mouth.

"Tabitha," he said, his tone warning even as he tugged her head back sharply.

She resisted him, not allowing his hold to interrupt

her exploration, tears pricking her eyes as he pulled hard on her hair. It occurred to her then how debauched the whole scene must look. How very unlike her and Kairos it was. Her naked, at his feet, with him mostly dressed, standing out there on the terrace of his fine, well-ordered home, the gentle beauty of the ocean acting as a backdrop to their licentious activities.

That thought only aroused her further. She had no confusion about what she felt now. None at all.

She was starving. Starving for a banquet that had been laid out before her for five long years while she wasted away in an abstinent state. And she was going to have her fill.

She rested her hands on his thighs, could feel his muscle shaking beneath her palms. Could feel just how rigorously she tested his control. She was drunk on the power of it, drunk on him. On a desire that she had kept buried so deep, so well hidden, even she might have been convinced that it wasn't there.

But now that she had brought it out, opened the lid, set it free, she was consumed by it.

She didn't know this creature. This creature down on her knees, uncaring that the cement bit into her skin, unconcerned with the fact that she was naked, outside, with the sun shining on her bare skin. She was not, in this moment, the sophisticated woman she had fashioned herself into in order to walk freely in Kairos's world. But she wasn't the girl from the trailer park either. She was something new, something wholly and completely different. And in that was a freedom she had not anticipated.

She had not moved from one cage into another, as she had imagined she might. Rather, she had slipped through the bars completely.

Suddenly, she found herself being hauled to her feet. "Not like this," he said, his tone dark and rough. "I need to have you properly."

She expected him to release his hold on her, to allow her to go back into the house and walk up the stairs, so that they might find a bed or some other civilized surface to complete their exceedingly uncivilized activities.

But as much as she had surprised herself in the past few minutes, Kairos surprised her even further. He turned toward the table, sweeping his hand across the high-gloss surface and sweeping their plates onto the ground, the porcelain shattering, the silver clattering on the hard surface.

Then she found herself being laid down on the pristine white tablecloth, his large body covering hers as he tested her readiness with the blunt head of his erection. He bent his head, kissing her neck, blazing a trail down to her breasts, sucking one nipple deep into his mouth as he sank into her body.

He filled her so completely, so utterly. She shuddered with the pleasure of it. This act had become so painful in the past couple of years. So intimate, the act of two bodies becoming one, and yet a brick wall might as well have existed between them even while they lay as close as two people possibly could.

But that wasn't happening now. Now, she felt him go so deep she was certain he touched her heart. There was no darkness to shield her body from his gaze, none to protect her from the look in his eyes. So she met them, boldly, even though she knew she was taking a chance on finding no connection there. On seeing nothing but emptiness.

They weren't empty. They were full. Full of heat, fire and a ragged emotion she could think of no name for.

It didn't matter, because soon she couldn't think at all. She was carried away on a tide of pleasure, molten waves wrapping themselves around her body until she was certain she would be consumed completely, dragged to the bottom never to resurface.

Just when she thought she would burst, when she was certain she couldn't endure another moment, pleasure exploded deep inside of her, rippling outward. She held on to him tightly, counting on him to anchor her to earth. Then he began to shake, his movements becoming erratic as he gave himself up to his own release.

She turned her head to the side, looking down at the ground, puzzled by the spray of glass she saw. And then it all slowly came back to her, piece by piece. They were on the table. He had broken the plates. The glasses. Had left the food strewn all over the ground for the birds.

He had been...he had been consumed by desire for her.

It was only then she realized that the table surface was uncomfortable. And even with that realization she didn't want to move. Because he was still inside of her, his chest pressed against hers. And she could feel his heart beating. Could feel just how affected he had been by what had passed between them. Could see the evidence all over the ground.

"What happens if we get hungry later?" The question fell from her lips without her permission. But she hadn't eaten very much of her dinner, and it seemed an important thing to know.

"There is plenty in the pantry. There are biscuits."

"American or European?"

"European," he said.

It seemed a little bit absurd to be discussing cookies in such a position.

She was about to say as much when she found herself being swept up into his arms again. She expected to be set on the ground, but he kept her scooped up, held tightly against his chest. "You don't have shoes," he said. She looked down, and saw that he was still wearing his. He stepped confidently over the remains of their plates, shards of glass cracking beneath each of his steps. He brought them both into the house, continuing through the living room and up the stairs. "There will be no question of you sleeping alone."

"We never share a room," she said.

Never. Not from the first moment. The first heartbreaking night of their marriage when he had left her sitting alone, having just lost her virginity with nothing more than a warm bath for comfort.

"We only have two weeks, *agape*," he said, not heeding her request that he refrain from endearments, "and if two weeks is all there is, then I will take every moment."

For the second time in the space of less than twenty-four hours, Kairos watched Tabitha sleep. He found it fascinating. Yet another facet to his wife he hadn't seen over the course of the past few years. Surely she must've dozed off on flights, long car rides. She *must* have.

But he couldn't picture it. The only image he had in his head was that of Tabitha sitting with rigid posture, her hands folded in her lap. Did he truly take so little notice of her? Or was she simply so uncomfortable in his presence that she couldn't do anything but sit as though her life depended on her balancing a book on her head.

She was thoroughly exhausted now. From what had transpired downstairs during dinner.

Erotic images flashed before his mind's eye. Of her kneeling before him. Of him begging her not to.

It was an act he simply wasn't comfortable with. He didn't want someone serving him in that way. Giving him pleasure while he reciprocated nothing. And yet, the moment her tongue had touched him he had been lost. He had not been holding her hair to move her away from him, but rather to anchor himself to the ground.

He was lying next to her now, still naked, but not touching her. She was sleeping on her side, her elbow beneath her cheek, her knees drawn up slightly. She looked young. Vulnerable. Everything she was. Though she wore the facade of a stone wall, he knew she was soft beneath it. He just chose to ignore it when it suited him.

She stirred, rolling onto her back, stretching her arms up over her head, her breasts rising with the motion.

Kairos had never been one to gaze at art. He found it a pointless exercise. The world had enough to offer in terms of beauty without adding needless glitter to it. But she was art, there was no other word for it. She looked as though she was perfectly formed from marble, warm life breathed into her making her human, but still almost impossible in her loveliness. And he was turning into a fool, thinking in poetry, which was something he held in even lower esteem than art.

Her blue eyes opened slowly, confusion drifting through her expression. "Kairos?"

"Yes. Two weeks. The table."

She blinked. "Oh. Yes. That happened."

"Yes."

"I'm hungry," she said, pushing herself into a sitting position, causing her breasts to move in yet more interesting ways.

"I think I can help with that."

CHAPTER NINE

TABITHA WAS BAREFOOT, wearing nothing but Kairos's white dress shirt, the crisp fabric skimming the tops of her thighs. She was certain that her makeup had come off sometime between dinner, being ravished on the table and sleeping for at least three hours afterward.

She didn't make it a habit of being so uncovered in front of him. He never saw her with messy hair, or mascara streaked down her cheeks. And she never saw him as he was now. Shirtless, wearing nothing but a pair of black dress pants. His feet were bare too, and she found something strangely erotic about it.

This was the sort of thing she imagined most couples would take for granted after five years. Rummaging around for food late at night, barely dressed after an evening of sex on the dinner table.

Well, she imagined that sex on the dinner table wasn't all that typical regardless of the type of relationship you had.

The memories made her face heat, made her body feel restless.

She didn't know who she was. Not anymore. The thought should scare her, because she'd left normalcy and control, the things she had prized for so many years, shattered on the floor of the balcony.

But she was going to eat cookies with Kairos, after just getting a taste of the man she'd always suspected lurked somewhere beneath the starched shirts and perfectly straight ties.

It was hard to care about anything else.

"You promised cookies," she said, backing against the kitchen counter, folding her hands in front of her reflexively. It was the position she often assumed around Kairos. It kept her posture straight, kept her from reaching out and touching him, or anything silly like that. It was more of a concern right now than it usually was.

It seemed silly. She should be satisfied, at least marginally. That was hands down the best sex they'd ever had. And what had happened between them a month ago had been pretty amazing. Still, this had nearly obliterated the memory of that.

Forget all the years that had come before it.

"I did," he said, turning toward one of the cabinets and opening it.

She watched much closer than necessary as he reached up to grab a tin that was placed on the top shelf. The muscles in his back bunched and shifted as he moved. She felt a strange, reckless sensation wind its way through her body. Like a shot of adrenaline straight to the system.

"The cookies," he said, turning to face her, the Americanized term sounding strange on his lips. "As promised. Because *I* keep my promises."

"Do you intend to badger me constantly?" she asked, reaching out and taking the tin from his hands. "Make sure I keenly feel the depths of the wound left in you by my betrayal?"

"If badgering is what it takes," he said, "then certainly."

"I promised you two weeks. I don't see the point in you haranguing me constantly." She pried the lid off the tin and reached inside, pulling out a piece of shortbread and lifting it to her lips. She nibbled on it slowly, watching his expression to see if she might find any clues to what he was thinking. As usual, there were none.

"I'm not haranguing you," he said. "I'm simply a man who knows what he wants."

"Yes, you want me to keep on being your wife. For your continued convenience."

"Yes, for my continued convenience. For the welfare of our child as well, if you have forgotten."

Her stomach sank. The truth was, for a moment, she *had* forgotten. It was so easy to forget about the tiny life she carried inside her womb. After all, she had found out less than twenty-four hours ago. And in the time since then she had been extradited to a private island by her estranged husband, made love to enthusiastically on a table and had eaten cookies barefoot in a kitchen. All of it was a bit out of the ordinary.

It was difficult for her brain to decide which particular extraordinary detail to hold on to. She had a feeling it was protecting her from reality a bit, too. Preserving her from the stark truth that she was going to bring a child into a very unsettled situation.

"Of course I haven't forgotten," she said, because the alternative would most certainly break the spell that was momentarily cast over him. He would take a dim view to her forgetting that she was carrying his baby. The baby was the only reason he was attempting reconciliation with her, after all.

"Honesty, Tabitha," he said, his tone chastising, "we have an agreement that we will strive for honesty over this two weeks."

"Sex is easier," she returned, ignoring the heat that assaulted her cheeks. "And more fun."

A strange expression passed over his face. "You have no argument from me on that score."

"Cars," she said, looking at his handsome face, trying to do something to get a handle on the heat that was still thrumming through her veins.

"What about them?" he asked.

"Why do you like them? It's strange. You're a very practical man. Cars don't seem especially practical."

"I don't suppose they are," he said, leaning back against the counter, curling his fingers over the edge and gripping it tight. "But I…I never had hobbies. While my peers were out going to parties and…whatever else they did, I was studying. Not just to get through school, and then university, but studying everything my father did so that I could emulate him. I didn't deviate from his lesson plan for my life. One of the very few normal things I learned was how to drive. It was a practical skill, after all, so he allowed one of his men to teach me. I learned quickly and…for me, that was my only bit of freedom. I would take drives across the country. Alone. Otherwise I was never alone. There was always security detail, or my father or one of his advisors. So that's why I like cars. Freedom and solitude."

She swallowed hard, an unexpected lump of emotion lodging itself in the center of her chest. She hadn't expected anything so complete. So honest. "Your father didn't teach you himself?"

"No," he said. "He was very busy."

She nodded. "Of course."

She hadn't known the king well. By the time they'd married, the old man's health was declining and he hadn't had the energy to take many visitors, much less a commoner daughter-in-law put into place because of his disappointing younger son's scandalous behavior.

"I didn't want him to teach me anyway," he said.

"Why not?" she asked.

"Because I loved it. My father had a way of taking things I loved and turning them into something forbidden. Something I couldn't have." A muscle in his jaw ticked. "I didn't want him to do that with the cars."

"What did he do?"

"He was so very concerned about forming me into the kind of leader Petras needed. A man of principles. A man of control. Levelheaded. When I...when I showed too much enthusiasm, he was eager to snuff it out."

"Why?" she asked, her heart twisting for him.

"Because. He knew that distractions could become weaknesses. Easily."

He pushed away from the counter, closing the space between them, close enough she could feel the heat from his body. Far enough that she couldn't quite touch him. But oh, how she wanted to. How she craved this man.

It wasn't a new hunger, but it was reinvigorated. The tastes of him she'd had made her crave him all the more. Where before, she could control it...now it felt somewhere beyond her.

"Was it there the whole time?" he asked, his voice rough.

Her heart slammed into her chest and she looked down at her hands, frowning deeply when she noticed a large chip in her polish. Strange. She'd just painted them. "Was *what* there?"

"This. This insanity. Was it in you? In me? Was it between us from the very start, needing only a bit of anger to act as an accelerant?"

She lifted her shoulder. "I don't know."

Except she had a feeling she did. It was in her. She knew it. Perhaps it was in both of them. Which made them a deadly combination if ever there was one.

All it took was a little bit of anger. All it took was a little bit of anger to ignite a spark and start a blaze. But whether or not that blaze would be contained to last, or whether he would turn to violence, she didn't know.

She pressed the edge of her thumbnail against the polish on her ring finger and stripped a large flake of coral away.

She blinked, quickly realizing she'd been responsible for the other chip as well. Something she'd always done to her manicures when she was younger. Something she'd trained away.

She was regressing.

"It has never been like this for me. Not with any other woman. I have never…" A crease appeared between his dark brows. "I have never allowed a woman to do for me what you did out on the terrace."

"Oral sex?" she asked, her brows raised. She was a little bit embarrassed by her own frankness, but she hadn't been able to hold it back. Anyway, what was the point of being embarrassed to say something when you had already done it? It didn't make much sense.

"Yes," he said through clenched teeth. "It is not something I ever saw much use in."

"The way I hear tell of it, most men find it extremely useful."

"Have you done that before? For other men?" There was an edge to his voice now. Jealousy. That Kairos could be jealous over who had received her favors made her feel reluctantly satisfied.

She looked up at him, her heart thundering. "If I had?"

"I would call him a lucky bastard. And I would *probably* not put a price on his head."

"That's quite proprietary of you, Kairos," she said. "Very out of character."

"Have I been *in* character for any moment in the past month, Tabitha? Answer me that."

"Not in your character as I know it," she answered carefully.

"Not as I know it either. Staying in control is usually so much easier."

"I test your control?"

"Do you not see?"

"I haven't—" she took another bite of her cookie "—not for five years."

"I suppose I became much more desperate when I thought I might lose you. I could feel this," he said, the admission raw, "this thing between us. I realize now that I could always sense it there."

His words echoed with truth, reflecting everything she knew down deep inside.

"But I never wanted… It is not what I wanted for my marriage," he continued. "My parents were never happy. My father was distant, a man who put his country before all else, because what is a king but a servant to his people? He was not a loving father. He was not warm. He could be very hard. Especially on Andres. But I considered what he gave to me to be guidance. Necessary. He knew that I would someday be as he. A king. But he was not married to you. He was married to a temperamental, flighty woman who let every bump in the road upset her. Who felt things too deeply. I vowed that I would find a woman who was different. You were perfect. Such perfect reserve. And then, the first time I ever touched you, the first time we made love, there was something else there. The very thing I didn't want. That kind of uncontrollable desire that leads to poor decisions made in anger and desperation."

"I didn't want that either," she said, her voice soft.

"I know you didn't want it. Now you resent me for making sure that I did what we both claimed we needed in a marriage? For keeping you at a distance when you asked for that distance?"

"I told you," she said, studying her wrecked manicure, "it doesn't make sense. It's too tangled up in all of my issues to approach sense."

"I suppose it makes as much sense as me being angry at myself. I had you on that desk when you presented me with the divorce papers and most of my anger was directed at me. For having a chance to have you, five long years to make love to you in any way I chose. Squandered. In the interest of control. Control I felt a deep conviction over, but that in the end I despised. You tell me how that makes sense."

"I can't tell you how. Only that it does. Because it mirrors much of what I feel."

"I think that's enough honesty for one evening, don't you?" he asked, his tone growing hard suddenly, his dark eyes shuttered.

"I'm not done with the cookies," she said, taking another one out, this one dipped in chocolate.

"Then, I will wait. Because I find I'm not done with you."

"Oh," she said, putting the cookie back in the tin. Suddenly, she didn't care much about the cookie.

"Come on, *agape*. Let's go to bed."

Kairos had never spent the night with a woman. Not even his own wife. He questioned why he hadn't now. Because it was a thing of brilliant luxury. Luxury and satisfaction he had never known, to wake up with a soft, beautiful woman twined around his body. During their nap the evening before, they had not touched while they'd slept, but sometime during the night she had moved nearer to him, or he nearer to her. Her soft legs were laced through his.

Last night he'd had her more times than he could count. Every time he thought he was satisfied, desire would reach up again and grab him by the throat, compel him to have her. Another side effect of not sleeping with your wife was that intimacy was confined to a single moment. Something planned, something carefully orchestrated. There was always a definite start time. Then an end when he returned to his own bed.

The lines blurred when you didn't leave the room.

He found he quite liked the lines blurred.

He drew the covers back slightly, the pale morning light washing over her curves, revealing bruises on her skin. One on her back, four at her hips. His fingerprints.

He gritted his teeth, regret warring with arousal inside of him. There was something primal and masculine in him that celebrated the fact his mark remained. The fact that he had declared her his with these outward signs.

She no longer wore his wedding ring, but she wore his touch like a brand.

What kind of monster was he?

"Tabitha," he asked, "are you awake?"

"No," she mumbled, rolling over onto her stomach, her blond hair falling over her face like a golden curtain. "If I were awake my eyes would be open."

His chest tightened, his stomach twisting. There was something charming about her like this. Not bound by her typical control, not conscious of the fact that she thought of him as little more than a stranger.

"You answered my question," he said.

"It would be rude not to," she muttered.

"I suppose that's true."

She turned over again, baring her breasts to his gaze, and he felt himself growing hard again.

She must be sore. He needed to practice restraint. He found he did not want to. For the first time in his life he was starting to think restraint was overrated. At least, where sex with one's wife was concerned.

"Why are you looking at me like that?" she asked, opening her eyes to a squint.

"Like what?"

"Like you want to...eat me. Or perhaps ask me deep questions."

"It is a bit early for either, I'm afraid. I require caffeine."

"I don't suppose I'm allowed to have very much caffeine," she said, her tone regretful.

"One cup of coffee will hurt nothing. Let's go downstairs."

"I have to get dressed."

"Why?"

She blinked. "I don't know. Because it seems like the thing to do?"

"Certainly don't dress on my account."

She shot him a deadly glare and got out of bed, crossing the room completely naked and making her way to the wardrobe. There was a white, silk robe in there, and she retrieved it, wrapping it over her curves much to his dismay. "This will do," she said.

"I suppose." He got out of bed, retrieving his pants from the night before and dragging them on, not bothering with underwear or his belt.

He had the strangest urge to pick her up and carry her downstairs, just as he had done when they'd gone upstairs last night. That made no sense. And if Kairos was anything, it was sensible. At least, he had been before the past few weeks. Impending fatherhood and divorce did that to a man, he supposed.

They made their way down the stairs in silence, setting about to prepare cereal and coffee, keeping it simple as both of them preferred to do. He was not accustomed to lingering over large breakfasts. Typically, he was eager to dive into his day. He realized now that he had abandoned the palace with only Andres in his stead, and very little explanation for why.

He dismissed the thought, for the first time in his life dismissing the weight of his responsibility.

That's what a spare was for, after all. To be used in cases of death, dismemberment or divorce. Divorce that needed to be stopped.

It was time Andres took his position a little bit more seriously anyway.

"And what plans have you made for us on this fine day," Tabitha asked, seated across from him at the table inside the dining area. He would have preferred to eat outside, but he had not yet cleaned up the mess of glass and food they had created last night. A drawback to not having staff in residence. The consequences of his actions were very much his own. Fine when he was engaging in normal activities. Less so when he was throwing his wife atop the most convenient surface and consigning anything in his way to the category of collateral damage.

"What makes you think I have some kind of grand plan?"

"Well, I would have thought my captor might be running the show."

"Your captor," he said. "I thought that we had moved beyond that."

"You are still holding me here, are you not?"

"You have agreed."

She sniffed. "Under sufferance."

"Oh, yes, your suffering is great. I believe I made you suffer a minimum of five times last night."

He was gratified to see her cheeks turn a deep shade of rose. A strange sense of satisfaction overtook him. He enjoyed her like this.

He did not think she was goading him because she was angry, not seriously. Rather, he had the feeling that she liked the sparks that crackled between them when they sparred. It was new. Like the unleashed sexual energy between them, this unveiled annoyance was new. Typically, they both buried their barbs much deeper.

"I didn't think a gentleman spoke to a lady in such a way," she said, her tone arch.

"I have found that being a gentleman is boring. Surely you must find being a lady similarly dull."

"In certain environments, yes."

"The bedroom being one of them."

"You may have a point." She lifted her coffee mug to her lips and took a sip. She turned her head, gazing out toward the ocean, the sun bathing her face in a warm glow. The corners of her lips turned up slightly, the breeze rippling through her blond hair.

It was a foreign moment, unlike any he'd had in recent memory. Where they were both relaxed. Companionable, even if only for a few moments.

"Perhaps we should go for a walk?"

"Not while I'm in my robe," she said.

"No. Of course not. But perhaps, you can look and see if my staff were so kind as to provide you with a swimsuit, and we could go down to the ocean."

"We never do things like this."

"I know. But this is the time for us to explore things we've never done. That is the purpose."

"Yes, so you said. I just didn't think it extended to long walks on the beach."

"Why not? Perhaps you will discover we enjoy it. Perhaps it is something we will want to do with our child."

Her smile turned sad. "You do play dirty."

"I will play however I must. If I can make myself seem indispensable to your vision of a happy family, then I'll win. I'm not above using any means necessary."

"I did not take you for being cutthroat, Kairos."

"I hide it well. I rarely need to use it. My title insulates me from much pushback. From much criticism at all. Even if it exists, the teeth aren't sharp enough to do me any harm."

"Will *you* be wearing a swimsuit? I'm wondering if I can look forward to a show."

"I suppose it would be impractical of me to attempt to swim without one."

"Okay, now I'm starting to fear that you've been body snatched. My husband is talking about spending leisure time on the beach. And also, participating in recreational activity."

"No, sadly for you, I remain Kairos. I have not been snatched and replicated by a more biddable man. But if nothing else, I hope this proves to you that even if it is not in my nature to behave a certain way, I can try to change. I can try to accommodate your needs, even if I don't understand them perfectly."

She nodded slowly, and he had a feeling that she found something in his speech unsatisfactory. But then, that was not terribly unusual.

"All right, I'm going to go change. I'll meet you back down here," he said. Because if he joined her in her room, they would never leave.

Not that he minded. But he supposed it ran counter to appealing to her emotions.

"All right. Let's see if either of us can rise to the challenge of being leisurely."

Whoever had done the shopping for Tabitha's wardrobe deserved a raise. That was all Kairos could think as he walked behind her on the beach, taking in the sight of all the bare skin that was on display for his enjoyment. It was a white bikini, one that scarcely contained her perfect figure. The sort of thing she would never have worn on a regular basis.

But this was not a regular basis. This was outside the status quo. And he meant to take advantage of that.

For the moment, that meant admiring Tabitha in her bikini.

"You're staring at me," she said, not looking back at him.

"How do you know?" he asked, feeling a stirring of humor in his chest.

Such a rare feeling. He felt light, happy almost. Yes, things were unsettled between them, but the chemistry they were exploring was off the charts. And right now, he was on a pristine, private beach and she was barely clothed. There was nothing to dislike about the moment.

"I can feel you looking," she said.

"I was not aware you had a sixth sense, *agape*. I learn more secrets about you every moment."

"I don't have all that many."

He caught up to her, keeping pace with her strides. "But you do have some?"

"I told you the biggest one," she said, the humor leaching from her tone as she said those words.

"Are there more? Surely there must be. You are not defined by one traumatic event. Tell me. I want to know more about you."

"I was born in Iowa."

"I don't know anything about Iowa."

She laughed. "No one does. Join the club."

"Did you like it there?"

She laughed. "Do I still live there, Kairos?"

"No. But one cannot be the queen of Iowa. So I suppose in your case, you did not have to *dislike* it to leave."

"The queen of Iowa does have a nice ring to it, though."

"Perhaps not as elegant as the queen of Petras."

"Perhaps not."

He leaned closer to her, taking her hand in his, pausing for a moment when she went stiff beside him. "Tell me more."

"My mother was single until I was eight. Then she married my stepfather. You know how that ended. It was… It was not all bad. She wasn't. He wasn't. He was… the only father figure I ever had. He was kind to me." She closed her eyes. "I remember once he bought me a present for…no reason. My mother never did things like that." Her eyes fluttered open again. "But they were very wrapped up in each other, and I was an only child. Mostly, it was lonely."

"What about friends? Didn't you have friends?"

"Some. People studying advanced subjects in school. Other students who actually enjoyed getting good grades." She paused, a fine line creasing her brow. "Someone came to speak at the school when I was young. A doctor. She had grown up in the area, with no money, nothing. It was a very poor town, and seeing someone come out of it and do what she did was inspiring. She told us that if we worked hard enough we can all achieve it. She talked to us about scholarships. About the kinds of things we could hope to find if we needed to succeed on merit rather than on status or money. I felt like she was speaking to me. I was smart, but we had nothing. My resources were all inside of me. And I was determined to use them. It was all I was given on this earth. I didn't want to waste them."

"From where I'm standing, I would say you didn't." How had he ever seen this woman as soft? She was pure steel. Brave as hell. She was braver than he was, truth be told. All he'd done was fall into line with what was expected of him. She had defied expectation at every turn. Had been brought into this world with no opportunity and from it had fashioned herself into royalty. He imagined there were very few people who could say the same.

"But you don't get into good universities without hard work," she said.

"I would imagine not. I got in with a pedigree."

"People do, but I got in by being exceptional. I had to be. There's so much competition for scholarships. Especially the type I needed. Full rides. Living expenses paid. I needed every bit of help I could scrounge up for myself. My mother went to prison for killing my stepfather during my last year of school. But I just...kept working. I was so close to being eighteen, social services sort of let me be. And I...stayed in the house by myself."

"Tabitha..." His heart ached for her. For this woman who had been so lonely for so long.

"It was all right. I mean, it wasn't in some ways, but in others... I could study in peace. I just kept going to school. And when I got to university, keeping what I had was dependent on maintaining a near-perfect grade point average. I could never afford to have boyfriends. Couldn't waste any time or energy on parties. I had to be single-minded. And I was."

"And a year into school you decided to move to Petras to take a job as my assistant," he said. "Why exactly?"

"As I said, I wasn't after a university experience. I wasn't about making friends. I wanted to secure my future. The internship allowed me to complete my classes, and to gain the kind of work experience that most people would give a body part away to acquire. To work for the royal family? For someone with my background that's more valuable than money. That's a connection. The kind of connection someone like me can't typically hope to ever obtain."

"And then you married me instead."

"You made me an offer I couldn't refuse."

His heart expanded, a sense of fullness pervading his chest. He could hardly breathe. "You're very brave, Tabitha. I never fully appreciated that."

She looked down, tucking a strand of hair behind her ear. "I don't know if I'm especially brave. I was just more afraid of repeating the same life I'd already had as a child than I was of striking out on my own and failing."

"I've heard it said that courage isn't the absence of fear."

"No. Without fear we would not move very fast."

"Is that why you were running from me?"

She frowned, turning away from him and continuing on down the beach. For some reason that action pushed a long-ignored memory to the front of his mind.

"Don't go." He was twelve years old. He might as well be a man. He never cried. And yet, he could feel emotion closing down hard on his throat, strange prickling feeling pushing at the backs of his eyes.

The hall was empty except for him and his mother. He knew that she wasn't simply going out for a walk. She didn't have anything in her hand beyond her purse. But still, he knew. As certain as if she had announced it, he knew that this was the last time he would ever see her.

"Stay here, Kairos," she said, her voice steady. If there was any regret inside of her, she certainly wasn't showing it.

"You can't go," he said, calling on his most commanding tone. Of course, his voice chose that exact moment to crack in two, as it had been doing with increasing fre-

quency lately. "I am the prince," he continued, drawing strength from deep within him. "I forbid you."

She paused, turning to face him, the expression in her eyes unfathomably sad. "It will end eventually, whether I leave now or not. Do you think I have anything your father wanted? No. But he wanted you. He wanted Andres. In that way, I didn't fail. Remind him of that when he's raging about this tomorrow."

She turned away from him again, continuing down the long hallway. And he forgot to be brave. Forgot that he was supposed to be a man.

A cry escaped his lips and he ran after her, wrapping his arms around her, pressing his head against her back and inhaling the familiar scent of her. Honey and tuberose, mixed with the powder she applied to her face.

His cheeks were wet, tears falling easily now. "Don't go. I won't give you orders again. I'm begging you, please don't leave. Mom, please."

She rested her hands against his forearms, then curled her fingers around his wrist. She pushed down hard, extricating herself from his hold. "I have to."

And then she walked away from him. At the palace door.

And he never saw her again.

He was breathing hard, his chest burning, his brain swimming with memories he usually kept locked down deep.

And then he looked at Tabitha.

He was treading on dangerous ground with her. He wasn't neutral. And this wasn't strictly sexual. It never had been.

Dammit. He had to get it together. He needed this time to convince her to stay with him. But he would never,

ever be…that again. Never again would he allow himself to feel so much for someone that the loss of them would break him.

Never again would he be reduced to shameful begging in his own home to keep a woman with him.

He was different now. Harder. He was the man his father had commanded him to be. Not the boy who'd clung to a woman who felt nothing for him and wept as though his heart were breaking.

"I didn't work years to improve my position in life only to settle for an existence that makes me unhappy."

"What does happiness have to do with anything?" Kairos asked. "Happiness is just a socially acceptable word for selfishness. We all talk about how we need to be happy. About how our happiness must come first. In which case, leaving her husband and children isn't abominable. It's brave. Because you were only preserving your own happiness, am I right?"

"That isn't true."

Anger fired through his blood, the memory of his mother walking away still at the forefront of his mind, superimposing itself over this moment. Over this woman. "Of course it is. You can wander off into the far reaches of the world and eat, pray, love to your heart's content regardless of who you leave behind because you're on a journey to your essential truth and damn anyone else's."

"That isn't what I'm doing. We were both drowning in that marriage, don't pretend we weren't."

"I have a feeling we might have drowned either way," he said.

"I'm trying. I said I would try. Must you make this unpleasant?"

He had a feeling that he must. Fighting with her did

something to ease the swollen feeling in his chest. And he found he was much more comfortable with anger than he was with anything tender or painful.

There was nothing wrong with attempting to forge a stronger physical connection between the two of them. But he needed to remember who he was. What his responsibilities were. And what they wanted. He could not afford to be preoccupied with her in any emotional sense.

He had to maintain control while making her lose it.

Had to find a way to convince her to stay with him while maintaining the distance he required.

He had imagined that global distance would be beneficial. That it would prevent his wife from leaving him. He had been wrong. He needed distance. She had to need him.

"My apologies, *agape*," he said. "I'm much more useful when it comes to interacting with heads of state than I am with making pleasant conversation."

"I'm not sure I have very much practice with casual conversation myself."

"That could be a problem. I'm given to understand that children like to make conversation about very small things. Such as insects and the shapes of clouds."

A strange, soft expression passed over her face and had made his heart clench tight. "Well, I have very little to say on the subject of insects. But I do think that cloud looks like a unicorn."

He moved so that he was standing beside her, oriented so that he was facing the same direction she was. "I don't see it."

"What do you see?"

"A war horse. With a lance growing out of his forehead."

"That's a unicorn."

"Clearly, we have different perspectives on things."

Then she smiled, and he thought that he must be doing something right. As long as he continued on, insulating himself against any sort of attachment beyond the practical, he would be able to bind her to him.

He had been blinded by the sex. By the unexpected connection it had provided. But now, in the bright light of day, when she was not on her knees before him, offering up the most tempting image and indulgence he had ever experienced, he had a bit more clarity.

His path was clear. And he would allow nothing to make them deviate from it.

CHAPTER TEN

KAIROS HAD ANOTHER romantic dinner prepared for them out on the terrace. It was dark, the stars in the sky shining brightly as warm air mingled and cooled with mist from the sea, and washed over her skin as she closed her eyes, taking a moment to enjoy the beauty of it. Of what it felt like to be here.

There were only nine days left. Nine days until she had to make a decision about whether or not she was going to leave him. But then, she wasn't entirely sure there was a decision to be made.

Yes, she could have his money if she left after fulfilling the terms of his bargain. But she was starting to think that would be nowhere near enough. Neither would shared custody. Because in that scenario she wouldn't get to be with him. She would never see what kind of father he was to their child. Her child would have a life divided in half. She would never be able to watch the way he interacted with Kairos. Would never be able to fully understand what his life at the palace was like.

Right now, tiny as it was, her baby lived inside of her. She couldn't imagine relinquishing so much time with him once he was born.

She realized that yet again, she was worrying about

the future. Existing in the present, but only by half. She had spent her entire life that way. Living for a moment she wasn't yet in. It struck her, suddenly and sharply.

"I don't know if I've ever really been happy before," she said, looking up from her plate and meeting his gaze.

He looked at her, his expression guarded. He had been a bit more cautious with her since their walk on the beach the other day. Had not been quite so relaxed. Initially, she had attributed it to some kind of leisure fatigue on his part. She had rarely seen Kairos being anything but the stately ruler with posture so stiff he would make a military general envious. Now she wondered. It was something else.

But unless he told her, she wouldn't know. That, right there, was the summation of their entire relationship.

"Another bit of commentary on my skills as a husband?" he asked, his tone dry.

"No. Commentary on myself. I'm always thinking ahead. No matter where I was, it was never enough. It's never been enough. I arrive at a goalpost and I'm immediately looking ahead to the next. I spent all of high school anticipating how I would get into a university. Then I spent all that time calculating my next move. Spent every moment of my internship with you figuring out how I would parlay that into a fabulous gold star on my résumé, what job I would get when it was finished. And then, by the strangest twist of fate I could ever have imagined, I ended up being queen of the nation. I have no goal beyond that, Kairos. You can't go up from there. I was—and am—at the very top. Secure for life, in a position where I can make a difference in the world. And I've still never been happy."

"I was born a prince, I'm not certain I've ever been

particularly happy about it," he said, his tone hard. "But we are in a position to do much good. Isn't that more important than happiness?"

"I suppose. As is security. Or at least, in my experience it's difficult to be happy without security. But... Don't you think it's possible to have happiness as well?"

"I don't give it much thought."

"I think for me I've never allowed myself to rest because of the fear."

He froze then, his dark eyes flat. "Is that so?"

"Yes. I don't...I don't think I've ever honestly feared that I would turn into my mother. You're right, Kairos. I never feared that I would actually pick up a gun and shoot you in a jealous rage. But I... Attachments frighten me. How do you know who you can trust? She was my mother. She raised me from the cradle. I never imagined she would do something like that. I never saw it coming. How do you... I have always struggled to figure out how you trust someone after that. I knew her longer than I had known anyone, and still, she did something so far outside of what I imagined she might be capable of."

"I do understand something of that. It might have escaped your notice but my trust has been betrayed a time or two in my life."

Guilt twisted her stomach, because she knew that she was part of that now. A part of the betrayals that he had experienced.

"I've been thinking a lot about it. A lot about happiness. About trust. I've been waiting to feel a magical sense of both for a very long time. For my position in life to hand me happiness, for time to grant me trust of the situation I'm in. Neither has come. And so, I'm left with only one conclusion."

"That is?"

"I have to choose it. I'm going to have to make a decision to be content. I mean, for the love of God, I'm a queen with a handsome husband, a private island, a palace and a baby on the way. Choosing happiness should not be that difficult. But I think in order to achieve that I'm going to have to choose trust as well. I've been so reluctant to do that. Because the idea of having my trust misused scares me. The idea of trusting *myself* scares me. But...I can't predict the future. Neither can I control you. I can't control any of the circumstances around us, all I can do is make choices for myself. If I want to trust you, then I have to decide to trust you." She looked down, then back up again. "Trust is just like happiness. You can't wait for the evidence. Then it isn't trust. You have to choose it. And be ready to be damned along with that choice if it comes to it. But I trust you."

"So simple, *agape*?"

"Why not? So many things in life are hard. We have no control over them. I know you're well familiar with that too. Who can dictate the things that live inside of us if not us? Why do we look around, trying to claim dominion over things we cannot, while we let the things we could dominate us?"

"I didn't realize I was going to get psychology with my meal."

"I thought it paired nicely with the fish, as we can't have wine."

"And here I thought anthropology went better with fish."

"Not my field of expertise."

"A disappointment," he said. "You always seem expert in everything you try."

"Everything?" she asked, arching a brow.

His gaze turned hot. "Yes," he said, his voice rough now. "Everything."

"Hmm. Well, but then, you haven't got much experience with some of what we've been doing." She had a feeling she was edging into forbidden territory, but she wanted to ask him about this.

"This is true," he said.

"You were not a virgin when we married."

He paused, his fork halfway between the plate and his mouth. "No," he said.

"So it isn't inexperience that caused you to go without a woman...without...what I gave you recently."

"True. Are you really in the mood to examine my past relationships?"

"No," she said. "Not especially. I only want to know why. I mean, you had sex with other women but not... not that. Is it control?"

He set his fork down. "I...I'm not certain how to answer that."

"With the truth. Not your carefully reasoned version, or what you think I might want to hear. Or even what you think makes sense. The real reason. The truth."

He looked as though she'd hit him, and for a second, she felt sorry for him. But not much beyond a second. "I never felt like I deserved such a thing." The words fell from his lips reluctantly, and she could tell that even he was mystified by them.

"Why?" she asked.

"I've never liked the idea of sitting back and taking something like that as my due. You can't... You have to earn things. And serve. You can never just...take."

"I mean, I agree. Reciprocation and being generous is

certainly appreciated, but what does that have to do with letting your partner show you she wants you?"

"I've never felt I could afford such a thing. To give in to such selfish desire," he said, uncomfortable now. Clearly.

"Don't you think now after so many years...don't you think you might deserve something for you, Kairos?"

He curled his hand into a fist and she watched the tendons there shift. Everything about him was so strong. So beautiful. "Are you through eating?" he asked.

"Yes."

"I find that I am ready for bed."

Her heart fluttered, excitement firing through her body. She never tired of this new, more physically attentive Kairos. He didn't bother to hold back the attraction that burned between them. This was sex for the sole purpose of forging a deeper connection between them, finding pleasure with each other, rather than timing their unions around her cycle. It was an entirely different experience, and she loved it.

"Then, I am too," she said, without hesitation.

It occurred to her, as he swept her into his arms and carried her away from the terrace, that he might have been redirecting the conversation. That he was replacing the promise of honest talk with sex.

But she wouldn't allow those thoughts to poison the moment. She had chosen happiness. She had chosen trust. And so, she would cling to those things, as she clung to him.

In his arms, it wasn't difficult to feel perfectly content in the present. To feel secure.

And to trust that everything would work out in the end.

* * *

In spite of her resolution to trust more, she found herself overtaken with a sense of disquiet over the next couple of days. Kairos was definitely distancing himself again. She had lived under the carefully constructed frost blanket he preferred to lay out over everything for too many years not to recognize when he was gearing up to roll it out again. He made love with her every night, yes, but she didn't wake up held securely in his arms as she had done initially here on the island.

Instead, she awoke with a yawning stretch of space between them. He slept on the side of the bed nearest the door, and she couldn't help but think that one morning she would wake up and he would have gone completely. As though he were inching ever closer to the exit with each passing night.

Trust, she reasoned, was not blind stupidity. Trust was going to have to extend to herself as well, not just to him. She had to trust her own instincts where he was concerned. Something had changed, and it wasn't anything good. It was reverting back.

She couldn't help but wonder if he had gotten too close to that fire she talked about earlier, and was running from it now. If all of the intimacy, not just the sex, was getting to him. For the first time, they had really begun to talk. To peel back the layers beneath their clothes and look at who they were, not who they pretended to be.

This thing between them was uncomfortable. That much she knew. It always had been. That was why they had both turned away from it so resolutely.

She was done with that. Sadly for him, she wasn't going to allow him to run.

They had less than a week. Less than a week to fix

this thing between them. She wanted to stay with him. She had made that decision. But she wanted their marriage to be something more. She was not going to determine to remain his wife only to have things revert back to their icy state.

No, she was going to effect change. Permanent change.

Conversation didn't seem to work with him. The only way through to Kairos seemed to be using her body. When he decided to transform her from personal assistant to wife, it had been because of her mind. Because they connected on a logical level.

She was done appealing to logic. She was going to make the appeal with her body. She was going to come at all of this from a different direction. She wondered now if she had tried to seduce him sooner if things would have changed before she walked out.

There was no denying the heat that shimmered between them.

But intimacy had been missing from their sexual encounters in the past. Honesty had been missing.

She intended to reach for both tonight. To strip him bare completely, not just of his clothes, but everything else.

She had dug into the back of that wardrobe, every piece of clothing provided her by a stranger, and found a bright red dress that she would normally never have chosen. She felt as though it was painted over her curves, clinging so tightly to everything, she was certain that each and every flaw her body claimed as its own was on very loud display.

She had never worried terribly much about her figure. Why, when her husband spent so little time looking at it? But now, she intended to use it as a weapon. To be sufficient ammunition to blast that mountain of a man down to his knees.

She took a breath and looked at herself in the mirror. She hardly recognized the woman she saw there. Her blond hair was spilling over her shoulders, unrestrained. She had not styled it within an inch of its life, had not tamed it into submission. Rather, it looked a little bit wild. She was wearing lipstick that matched the dress, also much bolder and brighter than she tended to be.

But a seduction of this importance required bold and bright.

She walked down the sweeping staircase, her fingertips skimming the rail. She had repainted her nails to match the dress and to get rid of the chipped polish she had been wearing for the past few days. She wasn't going to nervously pick at this manicure. In part, because she wasn't going to be nervous.

She gritted her teeth, repeating that mantra over and over again. As though, if she thought it enough times it would make it true.

Then she saw Kairos, standing at the foot of the stairs, wearing a white shirt that was unbuttoned at his throat, revealing a tempting wedge of bronzed skin, just a hint of his dark chest hair. She loved his chest. Could spend hours exploring it with her hands, her lips and her tongue. She found that she had very few inhibitions where he was concerned. That, at least, had made the past week fun.

She smiled as her foot hit the floor and she stood, waiting to see if she could discern his reaction to her appearance.

He was stoic, as ever, his expression schooled into hard granite. But it was that grim set of his mouth, that determination in his eyes that let her know that he was in fact affected. His jaw was so tight, the veins in his neck were standing out, his hands clenched into fists, the enticing muscles of his forearms flexed with the strength that it took for him to restrain himself.

Yes, she was certainly having an effect.

"Are you dressed for dinner?" he asked.

"Actually, I'm dressed for dessert."

Kairos was not entirely certain when he lost control of the situation. Whether it was the moment he caught sight of Tabitha descending the stairs in that dress that clung to her body like a lover, outlining her full breasts, slim waist and perfectly rounded hips. Whether it was when his eyes zeroed in on her lips, painted a bold red, and he immediately imagined her leaving that color all over his skin.

Or whether it was sometime much earlier. Whether it had been slowly sifting through his fingers like sand through an hourglass from the moment they first arrived on this island. He had brought her here to force her to come around to his way of thinking. But standing here, his world seemingly turned on end, he was beginning to wonder who was in charge.

She closed the distance between them, pressing her breasts against his chest, curling her fingers around the back of his neck and drawing his head down for a kiss. It was slow, achingly so. He wanted to wrap her in his embrace, crush her up against him and claim her completely. To show her that she was not the one in control here. But he didn't want this to end. He was so desperate to see what she had planned.

Even while everything in him denied it.

Distancing himself from Tabitha over the past few days had not been a simple task. He had tasted paradise.

unrestrained, unmitigated bliss at her hands, and then he had put up a wall. Had drawn a veil between them, blunting their every interaction since. Not allowing himself to get lost in it, not completely, not again. He knew his reasoning was sound, but it was a torture that he had not counted on.

She flicked her tongue out, tracing the edge of his upper lip slowly. Heat fired along his veins, molten fire pooling in his stomach. And he almost lost his control completely in that moment. She pressed her palm against his chest, against where his heart raged, almost out of control, then slid her fingertips down over his stomach, to his belt buckle. She looked up, her eyes meeting his, and his breath caught in his throat.

She meant to do this slow, that he could see clearly. It also might kill him, that he could see clearly too.

She worked his belt through the loop slowly, an echo to that first time she had gone down on him out on the terrace. She finished undoing the clasp on his pants, slipped her hands beneath the fabric and curled her delicate fingers around his aching flesh. His breath hissed through his teeth, his entire body going rigid beneath her touch.

She deepened her kiss as she stroked him, mirroring the rhythm of her hand with her tongue. An involuntary shudder wracked his entire body and she squeezed him tightly as she bit his lower lip.

"Tabitha," he growled. Begging. Cursing. Warning.

"What?" she asked, her tone a model of innocence.

"Do not test me," he said, not even knowing entirely what he meant. Only that he was desperate to push her away, but he wasn't strong enough. Physically, of course he was strong enough. She was a soft, petite woman, and physically he could overpower her if he chose. It was his spirit that wasn't strong enough. He was powerless beneath her touch. And if one of them was going to make the choice to walk away from this moment, it would have to be her. Because he could not. He had tried over the past few days to practice restraint and he was all out of it.

Not just the past few days, the past five years. Five long years of being married to a woman such as her and holding his desire for her in check. He could not. He could not endure the restraint any longer.

"Oh, *agape*, I have come here to test you. And I hope very much you fail," she said, angling her head and kissing his neck, her teeth scraping the sensitive skin there. "I came here to give myself to you. As a gift. One without strings. One you can use as selfishly as you wish. You can enjoy this, enjoy me, to your heart's content."

A feral sound escaped his lips, and he tightened his hold on her, sliding his hands down her thighs and lifting her up, her dress riding up past her hips, her legs wrapped around his waist as he carried her from the base of the stairs into the living area.

He moved over to the couch, lowering himself down onto it, keeping a hold of her hips. He sat, with her straddling his lap, her arms wrapped around his neck, his grip on her tight. She arched against him, pressing the heat of her against his heart and arousal, a short, luxurious sound of pleasure resonating through her as she did.

"I like this view," he said, sliding his hand up her waist and moving it to cup her breast, teasing her nipple with his thumb. "It is a beautiful dress. But I think I would prefer it on the floor."

He reached around, taking hold of the zipper tab and drawing it downward, letting the dress fall around her waist, revealing pale, perfect breasts. He leaned in, lowering his head and drawing one tightened bud into his mouth before circling it slowly with the tip of his tongue. She shivered beneath his touch and a surge of satisfaction claimed him. Stole every thought from his mind. He could think of nothing else but having her, consuming her, giving her mindless pleasure as she had done for him.

He tightened his hold on her, reversing their positions so that she was sitting down on the couch and he was overhead. He lowered himself onto the floor, grabbing hold of her dress and pulling it from her body, finding her completely bare beneath it. He swore, lowering himself further so that he was down on his knees, a supplicant worshipping at the temple of her beauty.

She was so beautiful, so perfectly aroused and uninhibited for him. He was so hard it was a physical pain. He wanted nothing more than to free himself completely from his clothes and bury himself deep inside of her.

But then it would be over. Far too quickly. And she was not half so mindless as he needed her to be.

He realized then that this was the definition of being thoroughly seduced. To the degree that Tabitha was no longer even the aggressor. His body was convinced that this was absolutely his idea and that there was no other course of action. He was not going to fight against it.

He moved his hands slowly along her inner thighs, avoiding the most feminine part of her. Relishing it when she shifted beneath his touch, a needy, disappointed sound escaping from her as he avoided the place he knew she was desperate for him to touch.

"Kairos," she said, her tone holding a hint of steel. A hint of demand.

"Patience, *agape*," he said.

"Why?" she asked, "I've waited five years for you to look at me like this. Why should I wait another moment?"

She was not wrong. He had never done this for her before. Had never tasted her.

He regretted it bitterly.

But he would not allow the regret to linger for much longer. Because he would satisfy that desire soon. Would satiate his appetite for her. But only after he had made her beg for it.

He moved his hand between her thighs, his finger gliding through her slick flesh, over the bundle of nerves there. She arched her back, letting her head fall back, thrusting her breasts forward, her chest rising and falling quickly with her sharp, uncontrolled breaths.

He teased the entrance to her body with his fingertips, spurred on by every restless shift of her hips as she sought out deeper penetration. "You want me," he said, his voice so rocky he barely recognized it. "You really want me."

"Yes," she gasped. "Kairos, stop teasing me."

"So wet for me, my sweet wife. I know you didn't marry me because of any passion between us. But you *do* want me." He didn't know why he felt compelled to hear her say it. To hear her confirm it yet again. Perhaps because she had left him. Perhaps because he knew she had been unhappy for so long. Because he knew he had not satisfied her physical needs as well as he could have.

Because he needed to know, beyond a shadow of a doubt that he was not alone in this deep, howling need that overtook him completely. That made him feel restless and needy. That made him feel as though he would die if he was denied her. Forget oxygen, Tabitha was the most essential element for his survival.

And he needed to know that he wasn't alone.

"I want you," she said.

"More than you have ever wanted another man?"

"I have *never* wanted another man. You're the only one. The only man I've ever kissed. The only one I've ever touched."

On a feral growl, he moved his hands, gripping her hips hard and tugging her toward the edge of the couch as he lowered his head, tasting her deeply, all semblance of restrained seduction gone completely. He was starving for her. And she was the sweetest dessert he had ever conceived of. He had been a fool to have her all these years and never have her in this way. He had been a fool to have her in his life, in his bed, and to hold himself back from her.

He was lost in her, lost in this. Lost in the needy sounds she made, in the sweet, soft surrender of her entire body. She shuddered beneath him as release overtook her. And still, he didn't stop. Didn't stop until she was sobbing, until she was begging, until another climax overtook her and she was trembling.

"I can't," she said, her tone spent.

"You can," he said, not sure where his confidence came from, not certain how he could make such a proclamation about her body. Only that in this moment, he felt as though he owned a part of it. A part of her. "You will." He kissed her inner thigh before rising up and wrapping his arm around her waist, lowering her down onto her back and positioning himself over her. "I need you," he said, kissing her lips deeply as he thrust into her.

She cried out, arching up against him, pressing her breasts against his chest, pushing her hips up against his as he buried himself inside of her. She met his every movement with one of her own, met each kiss, each sound of pleasure.

He tried to go slow, tried to keep things measured, controlled. But he was beyond any of that now. Beyond anything but his intense need for her. Arousal roared through his veins like a beast, overtaking him, consuming him. And he gave up on control. Gave up on slow. On gentle or restrained. He slipped his hands beneath her bottom, drawing her up hard against him as he thrust in deep. As he increased the intensity, as he let the world fade away, he lost himself completely in the tight, wet heat of her body.

Her internal muscles clenched tightly around him, and he felt another orgasm radiating through her. It called irresistibly to the beast inside of him. As though it was just the thing he had been waiting for. It grabbed him by the throat and he could do nothing but submit to it. To the wild, unquenchable pleasure that gripped him tightly and shook him until he was left there, bleeding out on the ground, completely and utterly defeated by the strength of the desire that had claimed him.

When it was over, he realized where he was. Naked, utterly vulnerable, utterly claimed by the woman beneath him.

He had no walls up, no defenses.

And it was unacceptable.

He pushed away from her, forcing his fingers through his hair, resting his elbows on his thighs as he leaned forward, trying to catch his breath.

"Kairos?" Her voice was soft, questioning, and he hated himself for the bastard that he was. Hated that she was now asking for things that he could never give.

And it was his fault. Because he had given in to her.

Because he had sought to bind her to him while knowing he would never be able to give all of himself. Still, even feeling like the lowest form of life on the planet, he knew he could do nothing else. He knew there was no other course of action to be taken. He needed her. Needed her in his life forever, and at the same time he knew his own weaknesses. Knew that he had to keep his defenses strong.

This could not be endured.

"Thank you for a lovely dessert, Tabitha," he said, rising to his feet. "I find I am in need of a bit of solitude."

He rose to his feet.

"Kairos," she said, her voice shaky. "Stay."

It was all so familiar. So blindingly, painfully familiar. In this scenario, she was the boy he'd been, abandoned, shunned.

And he had become the one leaving.

No. He was doing this for her. To spare her any more pain. To spare himself, the country, from what might happen if he were to ever surrender to his own base needs.

He was not the villain here. Even if she couldn't see it now.

He turned away from her, walking from the room. And no matter how much he burned to take one last look at her, he refused. Denied himself now as he should have done from the first.

He had been weak tonight. He would not be so again.

CHAPTER ELEVEN

"KAIROS?"

The sound of Tabitha's voice pierced Kairos's sleep. He had gone back to his room after their encounter in the living room, and he had stayed there for the rest of the evening. At some point, in spite of his discomfort, he must have fallen asleep.

"What?" he asked, not quite awake enough to sort through whether or not it was strange she was waking him up in the middle of the night.

"Kairos," she said, again. There was something in her voice that jolted him completely into wakefulness. Something tremulous, something terrified.

"What is it?"

"I'm bleeding." The word ended on a sob. "Kairos, I'm bleeding."

He shot out of bed, giving no thought to clothes, giving no thought to anything but figuring out what was happening. "What do you mean you're…?" It hit him then, exactly what it meant. "The baby."

He flipped the light on, and got a look at her face, her eyes large, her skin waxen. He had never seen Tabitha look quite like this. It occurred to him then that *she* might also be in danger. "How much blood?"

"Enough."

"How do you feel?"

"Terrified."

"I meant do you feel like you've lost too much blood?"

Her eyes grew rounder still. "Too much blood for someone who's having a baby."

"I need to call someone," he said. In that moment, his brain was blank, and he had no idea who to call. Why could he think of nothing? He was renowned for being cool under pressure. He was king of an entire nation, after all. But everything he knew, everything he thought, everything he felt was wrapped up in utter terror.

A helicopter. They needed a helicopter.

That jolted him out of his frozen state, and he reached for the phone that was sitting on his nightstand, dialing his right-hand man of the palace with one touch. "The queen is having an emergency," he said, his voice frayed. "We need a helicopter. Now. Medical personnel onboard would be ideal, but if that isn't possible, speed is more important."

"Of course, Your Highness," his man said. "We should be able to send one from the closest island and have you back in Petras in less than an hour. Further instructions will be texted to you, as far as where you should wait to be picked up."

Kairos hung up the phone, looking toward Tabitha. "Help will be here soon," he said.

She only looked at him with very large eyes, and he realized how empty and useless his words were. "Will it be too late?"

Suddenly, all of his power, his title, his status, meant nothing. Everything he had worked his entire life to become was reduced to useless ash. He didn't know the

answer to the only question that mattered. He had no
control over the outcome of the only thing Tabitha cared
about in this moment. He could be a king, or he could be
a homeless man, standing on a street corner begging for
change. It wouldn't make a difference in this moment.
Never before had he been so aware of his own failings.
Of his own limitations.

"I don't know," he said, hating himself for not having
a better answer.

She closed the distance between them, collapsing
against him. He wrapped his arms around her, holding
her against him, feeling unworthy that she was seeking
comfort in his arms. He had nothing concrete to give her.
He was of no use.

The minutes stretched on, a concrete bit of evidence of
the relativity of time. It felt like hours since he had made
that phone call. He found a pair of pants for himself, but
bothered with nothing else. He would need to be decent
when the helicopter arrived, but he could not take the
time to cover more than society demanded.

Tabitha said nothing. Periodically, she would make a
small, distressed sound that would pierce his heart and
send a wave of pain through his body. The silence, the
endless minutes, gave him plenty of opportunity to reflect on the evening. On his actions.

He had lost his control. He had been rough with her,
little more than an animal. And now this. Surely it could
not be a coincidence. It was a direct result of him losing himself. Losing sight of what he must be. Of what
was important. In pursuit of his own emotions, he had
compromised her. Their future. The future of the entire
kingdom. Five years, and this was the only time they

had ever successfully conceived a child, and now they were losing it.

Because of him.

Because he had become everything he despised.

At that moment his phone vibrated, and he looked down and saw a message giving instructions on where they were to meet the helicopter. "Hold on," he said, scooping Tabitha up into his arms and carrying her down the stairs, outside into the windy night. The approaching helicopter whipped the trees brutally, the sound thundering through his body. "Hold on," he said again, unsure whether she could hear him over the noise.

The giant machine touched down, and Kairos crossed the space, Tabitha held securely in his arms. Too little too late. Everything he was doing now was too little too late.

He got inside the helicopter, never releasing his hold on Tabitha. "Is anyone in here a medical professional?" The pilot and the only other men inside the cockpit shook their heads. "Then just fly as quickly as you can."

Tabitha felt weak, dazed. But then, she imagined an emergency, early-morning helicopter flight and all of the emotional trauma that had gone with it was bound to leave anyone feeling weak and dazed.

She had been in the hospital for a couple of hours now, waiting on results. She'd gotten an ultrasound, but of course the tech hadn't been able to tell her much of anything. She had to wait for the doctor. And they were also waiting for results of her blood work.

She had dozed off and on. Kairos, as far she could tell, had not even sat down since they'd arrived. She wanted to believe it was concern for her, but after the way he had distanced himself from her last night, she had serious doubts about that. A sinking feeling settled over her, dragging her down. As if she had much farther down to go.

Just then, the door to the hospital room opened and the doctor came in.

"Queen Tabitha," she said, her voice soft. "King Kairos. I'm very sorry to see you at such a stressful time."

A distressed sound filled the room, and Tabitha realized it had come from her. Hearing apology on the doctor's lips had sent a sharp, piercing pain through her. If the doctor was sorry, there was no good news for her. No good news for her baby.

"Your Majesty," the doctor said, "don't lose faith. I don't love the results that I have in front of me, but they could be worse. We were not able to see a heartbeat on the sonogram. But you have not miscarried. There is definitely something. It could very well be that it is just too early to see anything yet. Your hCG levels are quite low. I'm hoping that in a week's time we will be able to see the heartbeat, and that these levels will have doubled, which will give us an indication for how viable the pregnancy is."

Tabitha's ears were ringing. The words the doctor had just spoken were rattling around in her head, as she made an attempt to translate them.

"So she hasn't lost the baby," Kairos said, moving to stand nearer to her hospital bed.

"No," the doctor said, "at least, she hasn't miscarried. It's impossible for us to determine whether or not the fetus is viable at this point."

A tear rolled down Tabitha's cheek. She wanted the doctor to be angry, to be upset, and she knew that was counter to anything helpful. Still, she felt as if the world was falling apart. The least everyone around her could do was look as if they could see that. Like they could feel it too. Instead of throwing around all these technical terms with a calm, clinical tone that set her teeth on edge.

"Well, that's good," Kairos said, his tone as modified as the doctor's.

"The bleeding could have easily been the result of a blood vessel rupture, and might not indicate any serious issue at all."

"Until then…" Kairos spoke. "Should she be on bed rest? Should she be doing anything special?"

"If she's going to miscarry, at this stage bed rest won't help. Whatever activity she feels up to should be okay." The doctor finally turned her attention to Tabitha. "Get rest when you feel you need it. Sleep as much as you need to. Just listen to your body."

"I'm sort of angry at my body at the moment," Tabitha said. "It isn't doing what it's supposed to."

"It's hanging on as best it can," the doctor said. "Don't be too hard on it. Or yourself. If you're comfortable with it, I would like to discharge you tonight, so you can spend the week resting at the palace."

"And if she needs anything?"

"I can be there as quickly as possible, or she can be brought here. But I really do think that since we're in for a bit of a wait, it's best if you just go home and make yourself comfortable."

"A week?" Tabitha asked.

"Yes. Unless… If you miscarry between now and then, we will have our answer. But hopefully, things will stay stable. And when you come back we'll have good results."

Tabitha blinked hard, trying to hold back any more tears. "Okay." She took a deep breath. "Okay."

"Do you have any more questions for me?"

"That will be all," Kairos said.

Tabitha didn't have the energy to protest him making proclamations on behalf of the both of them. She closed her eyes, waiting until she heard the doctor's footsteps recede from the room.

"Are you ready?" he asked.

She swallowed hard. "I suppose so."

She stayed silent on the ride home and when he helped her walk into the palace, leading her back to her bedroom. She had not been here in over a month. It felt foreign, strange. She wished very much that she could go back to the island. Go back to earlier yesterday evening. She had felt happy. She had felt as though pieces were finally falling into place. Yes, she knew that she was still going to have to fight to claim him, but she'd been ready to do it. They'd had their fourteen days. And now it was shortened, taken from them. Now they were back here, in the palace, in the middle of reality. Facing an uncertain future. The possibility of a grief that she didn't feel prepared to handle.

It wasn't fair. She had finally gotten up the nerve to leave him, only to fall pregnant with his child. And now, after working so hard to forge a connection with him, to try and repair their marriage, she might be losing the baby.

What was the point of any of it?

She extricated herself from Kairos's firm hold, and crawled onto her soft bed, turning away from him, drawing her knees up to her chest.

"Are you all right?"

"No," she said, surprised at the strength in her response. "No, I'm not all right. This is wrong. All of it is wrong."

"I know."

"Not like I know it," she said, being petulant. Being unfair. Because it was her body that was enduring all of this uncertainty and pain. Because she was the one who cared so much that she had to walk away rather than spend a lifetime in pain, loving a man who didn't love her back.

The realization made her stomach clench tight. She loved him. Of course she did. She was such a fool, she never even let herself think the words for fear of the deeper implications. For fear of how much pain it would cause her in the future. But it didn't make it less true.

She wanted to be sick. Realizing that she loved him now, even as the beautiful future she had begun to imagine for them slipped away. If she lost this baby, what would be left for them? More years of trying? Or would he finally be done with her?

She knew the answer. He would stay with her. He had already made that clear. It was one reason he had pushed Andres to marry Zara, because then they could provide the country with an heir.

Misery stole over her. They were going to be right back where they started. Unless he felt differently now.

"I'm very sorry that you're having to go through this," he said.

"Aren't you going through it too?" Now she was just being spiteful. He'd said that he knew. That he understood. And she had attempted to lay a bigger claim to it than he had. Now he was giving her that claim, and she was angry because he didn't seem as affected as she was.

"Of course I am," he said. "You have no idea how important this child is to me. As the ruler of the country, it has been instilled in me from birth what my responsibilities are in this role. Producing an heir is at the forefront of those responsibilities at this stage of my life."

She sat up, anger overtaking some of the weariness. "Is that the only reason it matters to you?"

"Of course not. How can you even ask me that? I have my doubts of what manner of father I'll be. My own father had an iron fist and he certainly put me on the path to being a good ruler. But in terms of being a father, and not just a drill instructor? I'm not certain he was successful on that score. I want more for our child. I want to be different. And I don't know how to give it. I'm already worried about it. I've already thought about what it would be like to hold this baby. To walk on the beach with him or her, as we did together this week. Do not insult me by asking if the throne is the only reason I care."

"It's all you talk about."

"It's the easiest thing to talk about."

Silence settled between them. She wasn't sure what to say to that. He was right. Talking about the kingdom, the throne, was much easier than discussing feelings. Fears. Much simpler than talking about the feelings that were crowding her chest, making her feel as though she couldn't breathe. Love. Stupid, terrible love that she didn't want to feel.

"This has to work," he said, his tone desperate.

Yes, it did. Because if they didn't have the baby, what did they have? Nothing more than a cold union, and no reason to try and hold it together. She felt as though she was going to have a panic attack. She couldn't breathe.

"Tabitha," he said, his tone suddenly harsh. "Are you okay? You look like you're going to pass out."

"I need to lie down."

"Yes."

She rested her head on her pillow, pulling the covers up to her chin. "Today was terrible."

"Tomorrow will be better," he said, his tone firm and distant.

"Stay with me?" She knew that she shouldn't ask. She knew that it betrayed too much. But she just wasn't in a place to protect her pride at the moment.

There was nothing but silence in place of where his answer should be. She waited. And he said nothing.

"Please," she said.

"I had better not. You need to get some rest. You do not need me taking up any of your mattress. I'll be in my room if you need me. Keep your phone by your bed, call me if necessary."

She gritted her teeth, pain, anger lashing at her. "And will you deign to answer these texts? We both know you ignore me very often."

"I promise I won't," he said, his tone like iron.

She said nothing else to him. Instead, she waited for him to leave. She closed her eyes, turning away from him, listening to his footsteps, to the sound of the door closing. Her head was swirling with too many possibilities. Too many thoughts. It was a good thing the media didn't know about the baby yet. There was no way she could handle any of this publicly, when she had no idea how to deal with it privately.

And why are you thinking about the media at a time like this?

Because that was easier than thinking about her husband.

He was already distancing himself. Truth be told, he had been even before the medical scare.

It was then she realized that for all the talking she had done about her past, he still hadn't done any talking about his own. Yes, on paper, she knew exactly what had happened during Kairos's childhood. She knew his mother had left when he was only twelve. But she didn't know how he felt about it. Didn't know how it had impacted him at the time. Or how it impacted him now. She had told him everything—about the way her stepfather had died. About why she had worked so hard to change her life.

And all the time he had listened, but he had never given her anything in return. He had quieted any thoughts and concerns with kisses, and she had let him.

Suddenly, she sat up, rolling out of bed and walking toward her bedroom door before she could fully process what she was doing. She was tired. She was distraught. She needed to speak to Kairos.

She padded down the hall to his bedroom, which was situated right next to hers. She didn't bother to knock, rather she just opened the door. He was standing by his bed, his back facing her, his bare skin filling her vision. No, she couldn't afford to get distracted by such a thing. Anyway, right now, she was too physically tender to allow sex to cloud what was happening between them.

He turned sharply, his brows locked together. "Are you okay? You don't need to come to get me. I'll come to you. You should be lying down."

"Nothing new happened. But I was thinking. We...we need to talk, Kairos."

"Do we? I think we both need to rest."

"Of course you do. Because you don't want to talk to me. You're more than happy to allow me to talk to you.

In fact, you encourage it. You don't give me anything in return."

"Do I not give you anything? You could have fooled me. I thought I gave you quite a bit on the couch last night."

"Sex is not intimacy," she said, her voice vibrating with emotion. "It certainly can be. It has been for me. But I don't think it is for you. I think you use it to distract me. To distract yourself. I have given you so much of myself this past week. I told you about my past. I told you why I left you. What I wanted. For us, for our future. I feel like you've given me none of that in return."

"What is it you want from me, Tabitha?"

"Honesty. It's time for you to talk to me. I made the choice to trust you, Kairos, and I need you to trust me too. I need to know that we're going to have more than this distance between us."

"I can't promise that."

"Why not? You're going to have to do what I did. You're going to have to make a decision. You should be able to promise too."

"Well, I'm not going to do that. I can't."

"Why not?"

"It is not possible for me. Tabitha, I have to be strong. I have to be the king. I cannot afford to look back and examine my past. And I will not. I cannot afford to be vulnerable. Not to you, not to anything. We will have our child, and everything will make sense. I have to confess to you now that we may never have the marriage that you want. But it is still no less than I ever promised you. I have to serve Petras first. It requires me to maintain a certain amount of distance."

"Kairos," she said, her throat closing uptight, sorrow filling her chest.

"You will not be unhappy. I think we understand each other better now. I understand you. And this… This is my honesty. It is all I can give. I am sorry if it hurts you. I truly am. But there is nothing to be done."

She nodded, swallowing hard as she turned away from him. She had tried. She had failed. She didn't know if there was anything else she could do.

"Good night," she said, walking out of the room and heading back toward hers. She closed the door firmly behind her, feeling that there was something definitive about it. About this separation. It felt very final.

No matter what, he was never going to drop his guard. He had said it now, admitted to it. He thought everything would be fine because they would have their child, and it would give her purpose. The connection she craved. But if they didn't, then she would be left with nothing. And even if they did, there was not enough between her and Kairos to want to stay in the union. She loved him. She needed him to love her too, and nothing less.

That, she realized, was the happiness she had been searching for.

She had moved through life looking for status, looking for money, for security. But she had forged no connections. Until her marriage to Kairos. And even then, in a palace, with beautiful clothes, she had been unhappy. There was more to life than that. There was love. That was what she truly craved. No money could buy it, no title could bestow it. And she could not force Kairos to feel it for her.

She lay down on the bed, the cool sheets doing little to ease the hot thrum of anxiety rioting through her veins.

She was going to have to make a decision about where to go from here. But not tonight.

Tonight she was just going to sleep. She was going to cling tightly to better thoughts of the future. She wrapped her arms around her midsection and closed her eyes tight. She was going to cling to her baby too. Pray that she made it through the night without more bleeding. Pray that she made it through with this at least.

For the first time it was easy for her to wish that she could just stay in the present. Here in the palace, married to Kairos, such as that marriage was. Pregnant with his baby. With her baby. But no matter how much she knew these things for certain, who knew what would happen tomorrow? Who knew where she would be? She didn't have a clue.

Tears started to fall from her eyes, and she didn't bother to wipe them away. Didn't bother to keep control, or pretend it didn't hurt.

This was all because of love. And even now, she couldn't regret it. She had been afraid of this. Of hurt, of heartbreak. And still, even having the worst fear confirmed, even knowing that opening herself up would only cause her pain, she regretted nothing.

At least this was honest. At least this was real. At least she wasn't hiding.

She would rather be wounded in the light than slowly fade away in the darkness. No matter how much it hurt.

CHAPTER TWELVE

KAIROS FOUND THAT he couldn't sleep. He spent the rest of the early morning hours doing paperwork in his office, then went to the dining room for coffee and breakfast. He was shocked when he saw Tabitha sitting at the table, a mug of tea in front of her, along with a piece of toast. She was dressed impeccably, in her usual style. A pristine black dress, a single strand of pearls, her blond hair pulled back into a bun. The only indication that she had not slept well was the dark circles under her eyes.

"Are you well?" he asked, moving to the head of the table to sit down.

"I'm still pregnant, if that's what you're asking."

"Yes, that is what I was asking." Except it wasn't. He wanted to ask her how she had slept. He wanted to ask if he had wounded her terribly last night. But he could not.

"All right, then, now that that's out of the way. There is something else we need to discuss."

"I would like to have some coffee first."

"And I don't want to wait. In this instance, I feel I should get my way. As I'm the one who is pregnant and in distress."

"I'm in a decent amount of distress, having not had any sleep or caffeine."

She shot him a pointed, deadly glare. "Why didn't you stay with me last night?"

"Because you needed rest."

"And you were going to keep me up all night, telling me ghost stories?"

"No, not ghost stories. But I may not have respected the fact that you needed rest, and not my lecherous advances."

"I have a bit more respect for your control than that, Kairos. I hardly think you're going to accost your recently hospitalized wife."

He gritted his teeth. "You don't know that. Neither do I, frankly. The way that I treated you before the bleeding started was appalling."

"On that score we can agree."

He thought back to how roughly he handled her, how desperate he'd been. He would never forgive himself if anything happened to their baby. Because of him. It would all be because of him.

"I am sorry," he said, his voice rough. "Do forgive me for how rough I was. I lost myself in a way I did not believe possible."

"What are you talking about?"

"I was too rough with you."

"That isn't what I thought you were talking about. I thought you meant after. When you left me. I was upset about that. I needed you to stay. I needed you to hold me. You had... Kairos, you had never done that to me before. It had never been like that. I needed to stay with you, to rest in that experience with you. Otherwise, it's just sex. It isn't intimacy at all."

Relief washed over him, but along with it came anger. Frustration. "I told you, intimacy is not something we can share. Not in the way you want it. You wanted honesty, and I am willing to offer. I'm just sorry it isn't the grand revelation you were hoping for."

"I don't understand why. I still don't understand."

"I cannot make you understand," he said, his temper fraying now. "There is nothing I can say beyond what I have already said."

"Tell me something. Tell me something real about you. Tell me… Tell me what happened when your mother left. Tell me what it is like to have your father raise you."

"I have told you about my father already. He was cold, he was distant. He was trying to make me strong. And I understand why. I cannot resent him for it, even if I cannot claim to have felt happiness in my childhood. It made me the man that I am, the man that I must be."

"Stop it. You're not a robot. You're a human being. Stop pretending that you don't have any feelings. Stop pretending that a childhood being raised by a drill sergeant was fine just because it turned you into what you consider to be an ideal ruler. It's false, Kairos. It all rings so incredibly false. And I can't live a life that way anymore. I simply can't. I spent too many years hiding. Too many years pursuing empty things, looking for happiness that I was never going to find hiding behind a wall. I was so deeply concealed I couldn't even see the sun. Yes, I didn't feel very many bad things, but I didn't feel good things either. Right now? I have never been more terrified than I am right now. I have never prayed so hard for something to work out. I want this baby more than you can imagine. And the very idea of losing it fills me with so much pain… I can barely even think of it at all. But I wouldn't trade it. Not for anything. I wouldn't go back and protect myself by never becoming pregnant.

Because it's touched deeper parts of myself that I never even knew existed. It makes me hope. With a kind of intensity I didn't know I could feel. And it's the same…it's the same with you."

The back of his neck prickled, cold dread living in his chest and radiating outward. "What do you mean?"

"This can't last," she said, her tone filled with sadness, with regret.

"What can't?" he bit out.

"This. Us. I can't go back to the way things were. And if this scare with the baby has taught me anything, it's that what we tried to build on the island still isn't strong enough."

"No. That isn't true," he said, terror clawing at him now.

"It is. Because I can't fight against a brick wall. Not forever. And yes, for a while, I thought maybe it could be different. I thought maybe I could make it work for the sake of the baby. But if that's the only reason we're doing this, then we're not building a strong enough foundation. We only make each other miserable. We'll make our child miserable."

"Or, do you secretly believe you're going to lose it? Are you hoping that you will?"

He regretted his words when he saw her reaction to them. She drew back, as though he had slapped her. "Of course I don't. I want more than anything for our child to be born healthy. But, Kairos, we might lose the baby. And then why are we together? If there isn't an answer to that question, we shouldn't be together no matter what happens."

"You don't think that the heat between us is a reason to stay together?"

"No. Because it isn't enough. Because I can't get so

close to what I want and then have you pull away. It's cruel. I can't exist this way, not anymore."

"Why are you changing things?" he roared, standing up from his seat, rage propelling him forward. "We had a bargain from the beginning. Are you such a liar, such a manipulative bitch?" He hated himself. Hated the words that were coming out of his mouth, but he couldn't stop them. He felt as though the floor was dropping out from beneath him. He had given her everything he was able to give her, and still it wasn't enough. Still she was leaving him. How dare she? He was the king. She was carrying his child. She was his wife.

"Because I changed. I'm sorry. I love you, Kairos. If you can't love me back—I don't mean just *saying* that you love me to make me stay—I mean showing me. I mean giving me parts of yourself. Giving me your soul, not just your body, then I can't stay. Because it hurts too badly."

He felt as though she had reached inside his chest and grabbed hold of his heart, squeezing it tight. She stood up, taking a step away from him, and he felt as if she was going to pull his heart straight from his chest now. That if she took another step away she would take it with her.

Perhaps you should be grateful if she did.

He couldn't breathe.

"Do not leave me," he said.

"What would you give me? And I don't mean clothing, or money, or even pleasure. What will you give me of yourself? Kairos, I've witnessed terrible things. Things that no child should ever have to see. I spent my life hiding because it fractured my view of people. Because for a long time I believed that everyone was hiding something dark and frightening beneath the surface. I had to choose to trust you, and it was the hardest thing I have ever done. So when you tell me that you can't give more to me, I believe you. And I'm not going to sign up for blind faith. For going on for another five years, living in hope that someday you might fall for me. That someday you might break down the wall you've put up around yourself."

"I am a king. I have to put a wall around myself."

"Why?"

He didn't like these questions. Didn't like that her words tested the logic of his argument. "Because I must," he answered. He refused to dig deeper. Refused to uncover that dark well, the lid to the center of his chest, the one that housed the truth of all this. The outcome would be the same, so there was no point. No point at all.

"And I must do this. I have to go, Kairos. I have to."

She turned away from him and he found himself staring down his worst fear. As the woman who rooted him to the earth, who kept his heart beating, began to walk away from him. He had lowered himself completely and begged for his mother to stay, and it had made no difference. And here he was again, facing down his fear. He had to wonder if that moment on the beach wasn't a cautionary tale so much as it was a premonition.

She kept walking away, and he said nothing.

Tell her to stay.

His entire body seized up, his throat closing. And still, he said nothing.

He watched her walk out, her shoulders straight and still. Proud in that way Tabitha always was. And so silent, even when she was hurting. Five years he'd been married to her and most of the time she'd been in pain.

Because of him.

At least this way, she's free of you.

He was free of her too. He should be grateful. He did not need a wife. Everything would be fine with the child, there was no other option. The child would be fine. He would have his heir, and the country would be secured.

That was all that mattered. There was no honor in being a divorced king, but his father had been. This country had been absent a queen for a very long time.

And so it would be again.

He laughed into the empty space, a bitter, hollow sound. He had always aspired to be the king his father was. And now, he had become so.

A king without a queen, who had surrounded his heart in a wall of stone as cold as the castle that he lived in.

Without her, it would be all the colder. But he would welcome it, embrace it. It would make him the leader he had always needed to be. It was a small sacrifice to make for the good of the nation.

A good ruler led with his head and not his heart. A good thing too. Because when Tabitha walked out, she took his heart with her.

And still, he let her leave. In the end, he counted it a blessing.

Finer feelings were for men who had not been born with a kingdom to protect.

He clenched his jaw tightly, and curled his fingers into fists, tightening his hold until his tendons ached. He welcomed the dull pain because it distracted him from the sharp, bitter anguish in his chest. An ache he had a feeling he would have to become accustomed to.

But it was nothing he had not dealt with before. He would make room for this pain next to the one left by his mother. And he would go on as he always had.

There was no other option.

CHAPTER THIRTEEN

FOR THREE NIGHTS, Kairos was plagued with nightmares. Images of a woman walking away from him, of his voice not working, his feet being stuck to the spot. He hated this. This feeling of powerlessness. And in his sleep, it refused to abate. During the day, he did what was required of him. He even issued an official statement regarding the separation of himself and the queen.

Part of him had imagined that if he took official steps to deal with the divorce, it would set things right inside of him. That it would make things feel final. But nothing took away the dreams.

He threw the covers back on his bed and stood, walking out the double doors that led to a balcony that overlooked the mountains and the forest back behind the palace. There was still snow on the ground here in Petras at the higher elevations, and it blanketed everything in glittering frost, making the time spent on the island seem even more surreal. Even more removed from time.

He was continually waiting for a sense of relief to hit. With Tabitha gone, he would not have to contend with the more conflicting elements of their relationship. He would be free to focus again with a kind of single-mindedness he hadn't fully managed since they married.

The icy air bit into his bare skin and he did nothing to shield himself from the cold as he walked farther out onto the balcony, resting his hands on the balustrade and looking out over all of the land that he bore responsibility for. This was his birthright. This was what he would leave to his child, should he ever truly have one.

Usually, he felt some sense of pride looking down at Petras. Tonight, the bare landscape seemed as empty as he was. It did not seem full of promise, at least, not for any future he cared about. He should be angry. Angry that Tabitha had proven to be as false as every other woman in his life.

But he was not. Because for whatever reason, he could not make comparisons between Tabitha and his mother, not now. Yes, that moment had reminded him of the day his mother had walked away, but she was not his mother.

And he'd never truly been afraid of that. He'd told himself he was. That he needed a cold, loveless union to prevent himself from falling prey to a fickle, passionate woman. But that had never been his real fear. *He* was his real fear.

When he had fallen to his knees and wept after his mother had left, when he had refused to leave his room, to get out of bed for days after she had gone, his father had told him that he showed the same signs of weakness that had caused his mother to abandon her duty.

And Kairos had known it to be so. After their mother had left, many people looked at Andres and thought that he was a reflection of the queen. Flighty, free-spirited, and given to reckless, spontaneous action. But Kairos had known the truth.

Andres—while giving the impression of being the feckless spare—did everything with a measure of cold calculation. He did it for the response of the people around him, did it to test their loyalty. And he did it to great effect. But it was Kairos who had that deep well of emotion down in his soul. The one that he could not control. The one that would cause him to act recklessly, to abandon his duty if emotion dictated.

He had wanted to be his father. Desperately. To be the kind of leader that the country needed. But he had known that he wasn't. He was his mother, through and through. Weak, emotional. And so, he had sought to destroy it. To go out of his way to erect barriers between those deadly emotions and his decisions. So he had trapped both himself and Tabitha in a union that could have been, and should have been so much more than he was willing to allow it to be.

Because he was afraid. Afraid of what he might do. Afraid of how weak he might truly be.

You just have to choose. You have to choose to trust.

No. He could not make that choice. Couldn't choose to trust himself or Tabitha.

He gritted his teeth against the anguish that assaulted him. He wanted her. Just thinking about her sent a wave of longing over him. A wave of longing that was destined to go unmet for the rest of his life.

He thought back again to the night his mother had left. To the look in her eyes. Sadness. Fear. She had been afraid. He had never fully realized that before this moment. How could he? When she had left, he had been little more than a boy, concerned entirely with his own emotions and not at all with hers. She was the enemy of that tale, and nothing more. That had been reinforced by his father, and also by his increased understanding of the way she had treated Andres when he was a boy.

But, for some reason, now all he could see was the fear. It twisted the memory, changed it. Made the moment into something different altogether. She wasn't walking away from him. She was running. Running from the palace. From that life. Likely, from the weight of responsibility.

Oh, how he knew that fear. That very same fear. He was running, even now.

He turned away from the balustrade, walking back into the bedroom, and pulled on his pants. Then he took a sharp breath and walked out the door, stalking down the hall, headed for his office. He badly needed a drink. Something, anything to quiet the demons that were rioting through his mind.

He pushed open the door, making his way to the bar at the far end of the room, shutting out all of the memories currently assaulting him of what it had been like to take Tabitha in here. To put her up on that desk and release five years of desperate sexual tension in one heady moment.

He ignored the images that were assuming control of his consciousness and poured a measure of liquor into a glass. Behind him, he heard the door open. He turned, part of him expecting to see Tabitha there for some strange reason.

But no. Tabitha was gone. And it was only Andres.

"What are you doing up?" Kairos asked.

"I got up to ask you that question. It isn't every day I see you wandering around the palace without a shirt. Actually, it isn't any day." Andres walked into the room, over toward the bar. He took the whiskey bottle out of Kairos's hand and set about to pouring himself a generous portion. "Do you want to talk about it?"

"I would rather be publicly flogged, then tarred in honey and rolled over an anthill."

"Excellent. Pretend that I didn't ask, but that I'm commanding we talk about it instead."

"Excuse me, Andres. If you have forgotten you are the spare? I am your king."

Andres waved a hand. "All hail." He took a sip of his drink. "Does this have something to do with your wife?"

He looked down at his glass. "She left."

"Right. This is after your last-ditch reconciliation attempt of the past week and a half or so."

"Yes."

"I hate to be the one to tell you this, Kairos, but that is not how a reconciliation is supposed to work."

"I'm not in an exceptionally good mood, Andres. So unless you want to find yourself in the…stocks or something, you might want to watch the way you speak to me."

"I don't know what century you're living in, but there are no stocks in the town square anymore."

"I might be tempted to build some."

"Tell me what's happening," Andres said, all teasing gone from his tone now. "It can't end like this between the two of you."

"Why not?"

"Because you love her. And I know she sure as hell loves you, though I can't quite figure out why."

Kairos lifted the glass to his lips, trying not to betray just how frightening he found Andres's words. "She said she loved me."

"I see," Andres said. "As one who nearly destroyed his own chance at happiness, take my advice. If a woman like that loves you, then you would be a fool to refuse her." Andres paused for a moment. "Actually, it's very close to advice you gave me. You told me that if Tabitha looked at you the way that Zara looked at me, you would never let her go. But she does, Kairos. She always has. I know you don't find emotion easy. I certainly don't, or haven't, in the past. But that doesn't mean it isn't worth it."

"What did you think of our father, Andres?"

Andres frowned. "I don't know. He didn't have very much time for me. I wasn't of any great value to him."

"And our mother?"

"You know she had no patience for me," Andres said, speaking of how she used to leave him at home during royal events. Afraid that he would cause a scene, that he would somehow find a way to sabotage things.

"Did you ever...? Did you ever wonder why?"

Andres laughed, a short, bitter sound. "Well, as it's the source of all of my emotional issues, I have wondered a time or two."

"They have much to answer for, our parents," Kairos said.

"As do I," Andres said. "Have I ever told you, with all sincerity, how sorry I am about what happened with Francesca? Because I am. Very sorry."

"I know," Kairos said. "And to be honest with you...I was only ever relieved. It was never her for me. Never."

"That doesn't excuse me. Neither does our mother's exit. I know it wasn't only me. But I did blame myself. Now, I understand that there must have been other things happening. I just don't know what."

Kairos nodded slowly. "Yes. I was there. The night that she left. I tried to—I tried to stop her. Looking back, I feel like she seemed afraid."

"It's strange you should say that. What I think of her

now, that's what I think. She didn't seem so much angry at me, as afraid of…something."

"Did you ever want to find her?"

"No one knows what happened to her."

"No," Kairos said, his voice broken. "That isn't true."

"Kairos?"

"I know where she is," Kairos said. "I have known. I went searching for her after our father died. Or rather, I had someone do a bit of searching. I haven't made contact. But I do know that she's living in Greece, using a different name."

"I don't think I want to speak to her," Andres said.

"And I don't blame you. Not with the way she treated you. But I…I might need to."

"You do what you have to. But I may not be able to support you with this."

"Tabitha's pregnant," he said. He had been determined not to tell his brother, particularly as everything was in a precarious position at the moment, but he found he couldn't hold back any longer. He needed Andres to understand why he was going to pursue contact with their mother. Especially after all she had put his brother through. "It isn't going well. The doctor's concerned that she will miscarry. But she is pregnant, for now."

Andres cursed. "I…I'm not entirely certain what to say to that. Whether or not to congratulate you."

"It's difficult. That's why…that's why I tried to save our marriage."

"Is that the only reason?"

"No. Of course not."

"Did you tell her that?"

"I don't know what to tell her. I don't…I don't know how to do this. I spent too many years training myself not to feel things. I don't recognize any of it now. I don't know how to move forward now."

Andres nodded slowly. "I think you're lying to yourself. I think you know full well how to proceed. I think you know full well how you feel. I just think that you also happen to be terrified."

Kairos couldn't argue with that. "That's why I need to talk to our mother. I have to find something out."

"And you don't think you'll give the poor woman a stroke? Calling her after twenty years of no contact?"

"Well, I think she nearly gave me one when she left me crying on the palace floor as a twelve-year-old boy. We can consider ourselves even."

"I thought I was a little bit more well-adjusted since my marriage, but all of this emotion still makes me slightly uncomfortable."

"Extremely."

"Do whatever you have to do, Kairos, but do not let Tabitha get away." Andres turned and walked out of the office, leaving Kairos alone.

Now, all he had to do was wait until it was late enough for him to call a woman he hadn't seen in more than two decades.

He was afraid. He didn't know if he could trust her, or himself.

But if he had learned one thing from Tabitha it was that you had to make choices. And he was making them now.

"Hello. Is this Maria?" Kairos could scarcely breathe around the lump in his throat as he waited for the response to come down the telephone line.

"Yes," the response came, questioning, uncertain.

"Then I am hoping I've reached the right person. It

is entirely possible I have not. But I am King Kairos of Petras. And if that means anything to you, then you are the person I'm looking for."

There was nothing in response to that but silence, and for a moment, Kairos was certain she had hung up the phone.

"Hello?" he asked.

"I'm here," she said. "I'm here."

"You are my mother."

"Yes," she said, her voice a whisper.

"I am very sorry to call you suddenly like this. Especially because I do not have time to make light conversation. There are some things I need to know. And it may be difficult."

"You don't have to apologize to me. I'm the one who should be apologizing."

"Perhaps," he said, ignoring the knot that tightened in his chest. "But there will be plenty of time for that. Later."

"I hope so. What is it you need to know, Kairos?" she asked, her voice wrapping itself around his name like an embrace.

"I need to understand why you left. And I need to know why... I need to know why you treated Andres as you did. He will not ask."

"He grew up to be quite a lot of trouble, didn't he?" The question wasn't full of judgment, but rather a soft, sad sort of affection.

"You have read the tabloids, I take it?"

"Some. I could never resist the chance to look upon you again. Even if only for a moment."

"He has settled. He has a wife. He is a good husband to her. Where I fear...I am not so accomplished as a spouse." He took a deep breath. "This is why I need to know. I need to know why you left."

"It took me a very long time to answer that question for myself," she said, her voice sounding thin. "A lot of therapy. A lot of regrets. Please, know that I regretted it. Even as I was leaving. But there was no going back."

"My father's doing?"

"Yes. He could not... He said he could not forgive me. And that the damage was already done. It wasn't only that he refused to take me back...he refused to let me see you."

It didn't surprise him to hear that about his father. And perhaps, because it was so unsurprising, he couldn't find it in him to be angry. He only felt a strange sense of relief over the fact that she had thought of them again. She had wanted to come back. Selfish, perhaps. But he found comfort in it.

"I knew it would come to that point with him," she continued, her voice sad. "I always had. My family raised me to be the queen. To marry the king. I was trained. But I always feared that I would not be equal to the task. Your father would get so angry when Andres would act up. That's why I stopped having him come to events. I was afraid he would start taking it out on him. As it was, he simply took it out on me."

"He didn't hurt you?"

"Not physically. But...it was very trying. I was afraid of where it might lead eventually. I was just so afraid of doing something wrong. And you boys were a reflection on me. In your father's eyes, if you did something wrong, it was directly related to a weakness of mine. And I...I wasn't strong enough to fight against that. I was so low. And I just left you with him. That was the hardest thing later. Once I was gone. Realizing that I had abandoned you to stay with that cold man who... But I didn't feel I was helping you. Not by being there. I certainly wasn't helping Andres. I couldn't be the mother that he needed. I did more harm to him than I ever did good. Once I realized that...I just...I didn't feel I did a good enough job as queen. And I didn't feel I did a good enough job as a mother. At that point, I had convinced myself that you were better off without me. I was just so afraid that if I didn't leave, he would make me go. And for some reason, that seemed worse. And if I waited for that...well, I might have done more damage to you both by then and I was so afraid of that."

Kairos nodded, before realizing that she couldn't see him. "Yes," he said, his voice rough, "I can understand that."

"You can?" she asked, her voice so filled with hope it broke his heart.

"Yes. I have been afraid too. But someone very wise once told me that sometimes we just have to make a choice. A choice to trust. The choice to let go."

He realized, right then, that he had a choice to make. To release his hold on the past, to refuse to allow any more power over the present. Tabitha was right. You couldn't wait for these things to go away. Couldn't wait until a magical moment of certainty, couldn't wait for a guarantee. It didn't exist.

There was no magic. Sometimes, you had to get up and move the mountains all on your own.

"That is very wise. But I'm not certain I deserve for anyone to choose to let my sins go."

"I'm not certain that matters either," he said. There were so many years between this moment, and that moment in the hall in the palace when his mother had left. So much bitterness. So much pain. Part of him railed against the idea of releasing it, because shortly, it couldn't be so simple.

In truth, he knew it wouldn't be simple. But it was the only way forward.

"Come and visit us," he said. "When you can. The palace will facilitate your travels."

"Oh," she said. "Are you... You're certain you want to see me?"

"You left because of fear. I pushed my wife away because I was afraid. There is nothing more to fear now. Anger, hurt, it doesn't have to stand in the way. At least, not if we make the choice to put it away."

"You would do that for me?"

"For me. For me, first. Don't get the idea that I turned into anything too selfless. I realized that I had to speak to you, to put all of this to rest first before I could move on with my life. I want very much for us to get on with life. All of us."

"I would very much like that too, though I don't deserve it."

"Heaven forbid we only got what we deserved. If that were the case, then there would be no point in me going and trying to fix things with Tabitha," he said.

"Go. You should always go. I didn't. And I will never stop regretting it."

"No more regrets. For any of us."

CHAPTER FOURTEEN

TABITHA FELT WRUNG OUT. She hadn't had the energy to try and secure herself a place other than Kairos's penthouse, and to his credit, he hadn't come after her. Also, to his discredit, he hadn't come after her. She didn't know what she wanted. She didn't know what she had expected. Something. To hear from him.

You expected him to stop you.

Yes, two days ago when she had walked out of the palace, she had expected him to prevent her from leaving. But he hadn't. He had simply let her go. Damned contrary man.

The bright spot was that she had no more bleeding. She was feeling well, and not terribly drained. At least, not physically. Emotionally, she felt exhausted. She was sad. As though there was a weight in each of her limbs, pulling her down, trying to bury her beneath the earth. She was beginning to think it might succeed. That the weight would win. That the overwhelming heaviness would become too great a burden, that she would simply lay her head down and not get up and spend the rest of her days in bed, watching life go by.

Why did she have to love him so much? It was more convenient when she believed herself simply unhappy because of distance. Not unhappy because she was the victim of unrequited love.

She walked out of the bedroom, into the kitchen, feeling extremely contrary, because she wanted to lie down desperately, but she also needed to get something to eat. She stopped as soon as she walked into the main part of the room. She pressed her hand to her chest, as if it would keep her heart from beating right out of it.

"Kairos," she said, stopping cold when she saw her husband standing there.

He looked as if he hadn't slept in the past two days. His black hair was disheveled and there were dark circles under his eyes. His white dress shirt was undone at the collar, the sleeves pushed up to his elbows. He looked devilish and devastating. Like every good dream she could hope to have for the rest of her life. So close, so real, but untouchable.

"Are you all right?"

"Is that going to be the first question you ask me every time we see each other from now on?" And she realized just then that they would see each other again. At least, if all went right with the pregnancy, which she desperately wanted.

They would be forced to see each other at sonograms. At the hospital when she went into labor. Every time they passed their child back and forth. She would have to watch him walk away, taking a piece of her heart with him. Not just because he was holding their child, but because he was leaving too.

There would be no clean break, no getting over it. And if he remarried... If he had more children with another woman... She would be forced to see that too. And photographs of it in the papers, and clips of it on TV. A woman standing in her position.

She pressed her hand to her stomach, and doubled over, a harsh cry escaping her lips.

"Tabitha!" Suddenly, his strong arms were around her, holding her close. "Tabitha, what is it?"

"I can't do this," she said, her voice nearly a sob. "How can I see you and not have you? How can I watch you with another woman? How can I watch her take my place, and hold my child and bear more of yours? Kairos, this can't be endured. I can't."

"You're the one who left," he said.

"Yes, I left. Because I can't live with you when you don't love me either. Why do you have to make everything impossible?" She straightened, and he took a step back, but she followed the motion, pressing herself against his chest, hitting him with her closed fist, even while she rested her head there, listening to the sound of his beating heart. "Why do I still love you?"

"I never quite understood why you loved me in the first place," he said, his deep voice making his chest vibrate against her cheek.

"I don't either. I was very careful. I was supposed to marry a man so cold he could never melt the walls I built up. You didn't hide it well enough."

"What?"

"How wonderful you are. Even when I couldn't see it, I could feel that it was there. And I just wanted...I want everything you hide from me."

"I want to stop hiding," he said, his voice rough.

She lifted her head, looked into his dark eyes. "You what?"

"I called my mother. And I...I have to tell you something. I never wanted to tell you about the night my mother left. It was a defining moment for me. A mark of my great failure, a warning against what I might become. My greatest weakness."

"You aren't weak. If there's one thing I know about you, Kairos, it's that."

"But I have been. Just not…in the way that I recognized weakness. I have been afraid. Like you, I've been afraid of being hurt again. Afraid of undoing everything I have learned. And that if it happens, I will no longer be able to do what I need to do as king of this country. It isn't that I feel nothing, Tabitha. I feel things, so deeply, and I spent a great many years trying to train that away."

"What happened when your mother left?"

"I saw her. I saw her walking out and I knew. I knew because I always felt I was more like her than I was like my father. She felt things so deeply. At first, it was one of the very beautiful things about her. But I… Talking to her, I understand. My father took that softness and twisted it. He made her feel like there was something wrong with her. Like her feelings were going to bring down the kingdom. I understand, because he did the same with me. He saw me crying after she left. I started the moment I fell to my knees and begged her to stay, and she walked out anyway. And I didn't stop. He saw me, twelve years old and weeping like a baby for my mama, and he told me that I could not afford such emotion. Such weakness. But you see, it is this false strength that has become my greatest enemy. It has kept me safe from heartbreak, but it has destroyed any chance I might have had at a normal life. At love. And when you told me you loved me…I didn't know how to respond. Or, rather, I didn't know how to be brave enough to respond."

"Kairos, of course you're brave. You're the strongest man I've ever known."

"Who was reduced to trembling by your declaration."

"Love is terrifying. It's certainly the most terrifying thing I've ever confronted."

"But everything of value comes at a price, does it not? Otherwise it would have no value. And so, I think the price for love is that you must lay down your fear. Your anger. Your resentment. Because you cannot carry them and carry love along with them. But no one can put them down for you. And very often, time is not enough to reduce the burden. So you must set them down. As you said, for you, trust had to be a choice. You chose to trust me, and I used it badly. For that, I am sorry."

"I was going to say that's okay. But it really isn't. You hurt me. So badly."

"I know." He reached up, cupping her cheek. "I know. Tabitha, my arms are empty now. I set everything down. Everything that will get in the way of you. Of the love that I want to give you." He wrapped his arms around her, pulling her into his embrace. "I put it all away so that I could carry my love for you. It's all I want. It's all I need."

Her heart was thundering hard, her throat tight, aching. She could hardly believe the words she was hearing. She was afraid for a moment that she might be dreaming. "You love me?"

"I have. From the beginning. But there was too much in the way. Too many things I didn't need. All I need, all I have ever needed, is you. You make me a stronger man. My love for you is what makes me think that I should be."

"We don't even know... Kairos, if I lose this baby, I don't know if there will ever be another one." She swallowed hard. "Five years, it took five years for us to conceive this one and now…"

"It doesn't matter. It…it matters, because of course I want to have children with you. But as far as whether or not I stay with you, there is no condition placed upon your ability to bear children. The country will do just fine with Andres's children if need be. Or with the children of the distant cousin if we must. The country will survive, that much I know. But I will not survive without you."

She tilted her head up, pressed a kiss to his lips. "I love you," she said, her heart so full it could burst.

"I love you too. Whatever lies ahead, we will face it together." He took hold of her hand, curled his fingers around it and pulled it against his chest, placing it right over his beating heart. "I am stronger because of you," he repeated. "Never forget that. You're the one who showed me that we always have a choice. That you can choose to let go of the painful things in the past, so that you can have a future."

"I'm so busy being happy, I realized that for myself," she said. "Because I'm so glad that now, no matter what our pasts, we're going to have a future together."

"Yes, my love, we will."

"I'm so glad, *agape*," she said, smiling up at him.

"I imagine I'm allowed to call you that again."

"Yes, because now I know you mean it."

"Do you see it?"

"What?" Tabitha asked, holding on to Kairos's hand so tightly it hurt.

"That little flicker there." Kairos pointed that out on the sonogram monitor, and they both looked at the doctor.

"You have a heartbeat," she said, smiling at Tabitha. She

moved the wanderer over Tabitha's stomach, and a slight frown creased her brow. "Actually, I see another one."

All of the breath left Tabitha's lungs in a gust. "Two?"

"Yes." The doctor paused, highlighting two different places on the screen. "There," she said, pointing, "and there."

"What does that mean?" Tabitha asked, knowing that she was feeling sick. But for the past week she had been certain they would find a living baby inside of her. She could hardly process what they were seeing now.

"Twins," the doctor said.

Tabitha looked up at Kairos, who was looking a bit pale and shell-shocked. "It looks like you'll be getting your heir and spare all in one shot," Tabitha said.

"Neither of them will be a spare," Kairos said, his tone fierce.

"Of course not. But that is what they call it. And it's what you call your brother."

"I'm going to outlaw the term," he said, his eyes glued to the screen. "Twins. You're absolutely certain?"

"Completely," the doctor said. "It's very likely the bleeding was nothing, and she was simply too early in her pregnancy last week to see a heartbeat."

"Well," Kairos said, bending down and kissing her cheek. "You are certainly full of surprises, my queen."

"Quite literally, at the moment."

Kairos laughed. "Yes. Very much."

Tabitha sighed happily, her eyes on the screen, on the evidence of life in front of her. "I'm glad you put all your burdens down, Kairos."

"Is that so?"

"Yes. Because for the next eighteen years we're definitely going to have our hands full."

EPILOGUE

NEW YEAR'S EVE was officially Kairos's favorite holiday. It had been for the past five years. Ever since that New Year's Eve when his wife had been waiting in his office at midnight, ready to demand a divorce.

Because since then, everything had changed. Most importantly, he had changed.

He looked around the large family area in the palace. Everything was still decorated for Christmas, the massive tree in the corner glittering. This was the last night they would have it. The last night before all of the holiday magic was removed and everything returned back to normal.

The children were already protesting. The twins, along with Zara and Andres's brood—which was in Kairos's estimation a bit much at three, with one on the way—were not ready for the holidays to be over.

"I don't want to go to bed," Christiana said, pouting in that way of hers that was both aggravating and irresistibly charming. At four, she had discovered that she could use her cuteness against her parents to great effect.

"I don't either," said Cyrena, turning an identical pout his direction.

"It is nearly midnight," he said.

"It is not," Christiana said.

"Well," Tabitha responded, "it is somewhere in the world."

Andres laughed. "That isn't good enough," he said, "not for my niece. She's far too clever for that."

"Worry about your own children, Andres," Kairos said.

"Mine do not know their numbers yet. I live in fear of that day."

"And when they learn to spell," Zara said, placing her hand over her rounded stomach.

"The horror," Kairos said. "Okay, girls. It is truly bedtime. But I am certain if you ask her very nicely, Grandma Maria would love to come and read to you."

His mother smiled at all of them from her position on the couch. Reconciliation was never easy. It had been particularly difficult for Andres. And as far as Kairos went, it came and went like the tide for the first year or so, as he dealt with anger, sadness at all the missed years and then determination not to miss any more because of mistakes that were long past the point of correcting.

All they could do was move forward now. And now, when he saw his mother with his children, with Andres and Zara's children, he knew that none of them regretted their decision to release their hold on the past.

"Of course I will," she said. "I never tire of reading to them."

She ushered the children out of the room, and then Andres looked at Zara. "Are you exhausted yet, princess?"

"Very," she said, "and my feet hurt."

"Well, we can go back up to my bedroom, and I will rub your feet. And possibly some other things."

Zara smacked him on the shoulder, then followed

him out of the room anyway, leaving Kairos and Tabitha alone.

It was then that Tabitha turned to him, smiling at him, unreserved, unrestrained. Perfection. "Do you think we'll make it until midnight tonight?"

"I do always try to stay awake until midnight on New Year's Eve. Just in case you decide to ask for a divorce. I would hate to sleep through it."

She laughed. "Not a chance." She looked around the room. "Can you imagine if we had given up then? Can you imagine what we would have missed?"

"I don't like to. I'm so grateful that you gave me a second chance."

"So am I." She leaned against him, wrapping her arm around his waist. "Do you remember when I told you how hard it was for me to be happy in the present? How difficult it is for me to simply be in the moment?"

"Yes," he said.

"It isn't now. I have lived in a million perfect moments since you said you loved me. And this is one of them."

Kairos looked around at the Christmas decorations, the evergreen twisted around the pillars, the large tree and the clear lights that glittered in the midst of the dark branches. And he had to agree. The perfect moment, the perfect woman.

The perfect life.

* * * * *

MILLS & BOON

THE HEART OF ROMANCE

A ROMANCE FOR EVERY READER

MODERN

Prepare to be swept off your feet by sophisticated, sexy and seductive heroes, in some of the world's most glamourous and romantic locations, where power and passion collide.

HISTORICAL

Escape with historical heroes from time gone by. Whether your passion is for wicked Regency Rakes, muscled Vikings or rugged Highlanders, awaken the romance of the past.

MEDICAL

Set your pulse racing with dedicated, delectable doctors in the high-pressure world of medicine, where emotions run high and passion, comfort and love are the best medicine.

True Love

Celebrate true love with tender stories of heartfelt romance, from the rush of falling in love to the joy a new baby can bring, and a focus on the emotional heart of a relationship.

Desire

Indulge in secrets and scandal, intense drama and plenty of sizzling hot action with powerful and passionate heroes who have it all: wealth, status, good looks…everything but the right woman.

HEROES

Experience all the excitement of a gripping thriller, with an intense romance at its heart. Resourceful, true-to-life women and strong, fearless men face danger and desire - a killer combination!

To see which titles are coming soon, please visit

millsandboon.co.uk/nextmonth

LET'S TALK
Romance

For exclusive extracts, competitions
and special offers, find us online:

JOIN US ON SOCIAL MEDIA!

Stay up to date with our latest releases, author news and gossip, special offers and discounts, and all the behind-the-scenes action from Mills & Boon...

 @millsandboon

 @millsandboonuk

 facebook.com/millsandboon

 @millsandboonuk

It might just be true love...

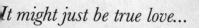

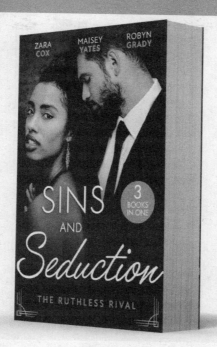

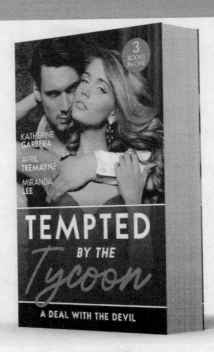

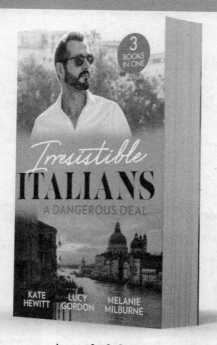

MILLS & BOON
A ROMANCE FOR EVERY READER

- **FREE** delivery direct to your door

- **EXCLUSIVE** offers every month

- **SAVE** up to 25% on pre-paid subscriptions

SUBSCRIBE AND SAVE

millsandboon.co.uk/Subscribe